Necropolis PD

by Nathan R. Sumsion

Parvus Press, LLC
PO Box 224
Yardley, PA 19067-8224
ParvusPress.com

Necropolis PD
Copyright © 2019 by Nathan Sumsion

ISBN 13 978-0-9997842-3-5
Ebook ISBN 978-0-9997842-2-8
Cover art by Ronan LE FUR
Cover design by R J Theodore
Designed and typeset by Catspaw DTP Services

For Becky

Necropolis PD *would have never come to be without your inspiration, love and support. I'm looking forward to all the mysteries we'll solve and challenges we'll overcome together, both in this life and whatever comes after.*

Chapter 1

I STARE INTO THE VACANT, SUNKEN *eyes of a cadaver's face, inches from my own. The viscous eyes, fogged over and yellow, reflect my own gaze blurrily back at me. The corpse pins me down, the full weight of it crushing me into the cold ground. The face looms closer as I struggle to push the body away from me. Its eyes, they grow nearer still. And then they blink.*

The recent memory replays incessantly in my brain, looping endlessly in my thoughts. It's a nightmare that plagues me whether I'm awake or asleep. Looking back, it's odd how clear some events seem now that it's too late to do anything about them.

If only I hadn't hit the snooze button one morning three months ago and hadn't rolled over those extra ten minutes, I may not have run into unexpected traffic in the pre-dawn hours on the usually sleepy streets. If only I took that left instead of the right at the long red light, trying to shave some time off my drive. If I hadn't stopped at the scene of the accident. If I hadn't stepped out of my car to help. If I hadn't chased that . . . thing.

Or the door . . . if only I hadn't opened that damned door,

the hinges screeching, with its rusted patina of orange covered with peeling once-blue paint raining down like snowflakes. That forgotten door, the lock forced and the handle bent. One door out of all those I've entered throughout my life. Walking through this one door stranded me far from home with little hope of ever returning. Changing any of those decisions could have prevented me from coming here. Right? Or did it go back further than that?

I keep turning these choices over and over in my mind, trying to drive away the thoughts of the blinking corpse, whenever sleep threatens to overtake me.

Wrong decisions. Wrong decisions and their consequences.

Sliding further into my seat, I sink into the shadows around me and further into the gloom, bury myself away from the gaze of everyone around me. I've been sitting here at my booth in the corner for hours, alone. Empty, stained glasses that once held flat, warm beer sit on the table in front of me. The buzz from the alcohol isn't enough to keep my thoughts from bothering me.

The shadows are thicker here, literally deeper, denser than they should be. The light from the room's few oil lamps fails to penetrate the shadows like it should, the glow falling short of reaching all the way to my seat. There is a small lamp on my table, but the glass is cracked, the metal base dented, and the whole thing is cold without oil to fuel a flame. They will fill it again soon I'm sure, but not until after I leave. No one wants to call attention to me.

I finger the hunk of metal hanging from around my neck by a piece of twine. A talisman, they call it. They claim it is something to protect me, to deter those who would do me harm. It is supposed to be enough to keep all but the most determined away, so I assume it's a warning sign of some kind. Or actual magic, something that would have been laughable to me before all of this.

The metal looks and feels like lead, but I can't tell for sure. It's about the size of a playing card, with a crude symbol I don't recognize carved in it. I am given a new one each morning with the promise that if I keep it on me, and keep it visible, I may live another day. Seriously, it sounds so ridiculous, something I wouldn't have believed in pre-school, much less now. I can't tell if it is a joke, a prank at my expense, but I don't dare put it to the test. I nervously take my hand off of it. The tingling sensation in my fingers is surely just my imagination.

The dead eyes blink at me, the mouth below smiling with split lips. A foul stench wafts out from the blackness behind jagged yellow teeth inching closer to me. A fluid thicker than drool drips from the mouth onto my face.

Closing my eyes, I try to dredge up some other memory, but I can only recall that dead face leaning towards me. My current surroundings do little to distract me, but they're the best I can manage. I'm listening to the drone of conversation floating around me without paying attention to the words. The bar is crowded with despairing patrons, tables full of morose souls with hardly any room to turn much less move, except for a small bubble of space around my table. My hand grips tightly to a shot glass—the one glass before me not empty, the liquor in it untouched.

Typically, I have a pint of what passes for beer in this place. But tonight, I need something stronger. Judging from the thickness, the color—hell the weight of the glass—I'm sure I'll regret my decision later.

I sneak a glance at the bodies around me. Most ignore me. But some of them gaze back at me with all-too-familiar dead eyes. Do their eyes flicker to the hunk of metal hanging from my neck? Or is it just my neck that gets their attention? What about the blood pumping through my arteries, the breath coming out my mouth?

"You gonna drink that or stare it to death?" The voice coming at me sounds like gravel scraping across glass. It reminds me of another voice: the one that won't leave my thoughts.

You're a long way from home, aren't you, child? it said, a whisper slipping from a dead face. *Such a long way to come to die.*

I glance up into cold eyes and an uncaring stare, the hard frown of the bar's friendliest waitress. She stands over me at my table, her disinterest radiating in waves. Her hair has the color and brittleness of straw, pulled back into a ponytail, the bald patches beneath mostly hidden. She is dressed in a faded blouse and short skirt full of holes and smeared with dirt and grime, the colors looking brown in the gloom. Her clothes do little to hide her skeleton-thin frame underneath. She has an empty tray tucked under her arm, which could easily carry away the glasses on my table. She conveniently ignores them.

My gaze returns to the glass in my hand. "Don't worry, Annabelle, I'll drink it. Thanks," I say, feigning cheer I don't feel.

She turns before I'm finished answering, and mutters as she shuffles away, her putrid scent lingering in the air. I bring the glass to my mouth but stop and slowly lower it again as I get re-lost in thought. Some dead man's white shirt itches across my shoulders, and I tug absently at the dark tie knotted loosely around my neck. My clothes are hand-me-downs from who-knows-where. The stink doesn't completely wash out of them, no matter how much I try. I won't even hazard a guess as to how it got these stains. A coffin got raided at a funeral home somewhere to get this cheap suit on me, no doubt. The suit coat sits beside me on my bench; it's too hot for me to consider actually wearing it. I can feel the trickle of sweat running down my back. My belt is cinched to keep too-big pants from slipping down. They are not the clothes I wore when I arrived in this town, but they are all I have to my name, now. My old clothes were too bloodstained, too saturated with pus and shit and gore to salvage.

A loud sigh escapes me in the hopes it will push back the despair waiting to take hold. I lived in sheer terror for the first several weeks I was here, my brain exhausted by the constant fear, but, now, I've settled into a state of numbness, the acceptance of inevitability. Running away never worked; they caught me easily. And punished me. Hiding didn't work either. They could always track me down. And then punished me. I've lived here longer than I expected to, though I think I hear the final ticks of the clock.

Somewhere in the crowd, at least one of my captors waits patiently, observing. I don't know them all; I can't recognize every one of them, but I've been told at all times, no matter where I go, someone is watching me. And if I stray too far, if I ask too many questions, if I do anything they don't want me to, I go back into the cell where I spent my first two months here. The dark hole filled with pain and questions and cold. My hand spasms at the memory, nearly tipping over my glass.

I've taken to coming here, to Warner's, what passes for a bar down the street from where I'm living now. To call it a dive would be an insult to scuzzy bars everywhere else. No matter how run-down or trashed a bar gets, they can take solace that this place exists in the world to make their wreck of a watering hole better by comparison.

The hours slip past as I wait here, while they examine me, weigh me on their scales of justice and decide my fate. This is one of the few places they'll let me go, so it's become my new home when I can take no more of the isolation of my apartment, when being surrounded by a horde of strangers is preferable to spending another minute alone. It's not the kind of place I would normally hang out since it lacks TV screens and Wi-Fi signals and other modern amenities. I have yet to see electricity or modern conveniences anywhere. The kerosene lamp on my table probably passes for cutting-edge tech. Warner's is dreary, depressing and lonely, but it has become my favorite place in this town. It's one of the few places where I can stay any length of time. Where I can have the façade of company, but where I'm left alone.

None of the patrons here attempt to speak to me. I make them uncomfortable. I remind them of what it was like to be alive, perhaps. As long as I stay out of their way, as long as they don't have to actually acknowledge I'm here, they tolerate my presence. They cast curious glances at me out of the corners of their eyes. Some of these glances are frankly hungrier than others. The observers mill in the shadows, staying out of the dim light as much as possible. Conversation quiets if they notice I'm paying attention. Annabelle has to interact with me since her job requires it, but she's usually the only one.

Warner, this place's namesake, is behind the bar slinging drinks. It looks like he measures his lifespan in geologic ages. He grudgingly allows me to come here. As far as I know, he never leaves except to go in back the kitchen or down into the cellar. I think it's where he brews the rotgut liquor he passes for drinks. Behind him, rows of liquor bottles extend into the shadows, their labels all unfamiliar and all hand-made. A lazy curl of smoke burns off the ever-present cigar hanging from his pinched lips. His cragged face is lit by a fire that crackles in a massive fireplace on the far side of the room, his bare scalp reflecting the light wherever he turns. He growls and snaps anytime someone actually orders a drink, but then pours it and slams the glass down, handing it over with curses and glares. I hope he doesn't live off his tips.

The room consists of a long wooden bar, booths lining the walls on all sides, and mismatched tables haphazardly arranged with chairs jammed between. The chairs tend to be crooked, unsteady, so I avoid them when possible. Plus, using one would put me in the middle of the throng, and no one wants that. No matter how crowded the place is, when I show up, this booth frees up pretty quickly. Warner's has a quaint charm to it if you can get past the needs-to-be-condemned décor.

There are two smaller spaces off the main room. One holds a large table set aside for private meetings. The doors are usually closed, so I rarely see who uses it. The other room holds four booths, but they are all taken up by some historian with papers and photos sprawled over every possible surface. Since that, at least, looked interesting, I once tried starting a conversation with him, but he proved as unfriendly as the rest of the stiffs around here. I'm not sure what hold he has over Warner to rate him an entire room, but he's evidently been here as long the bar.

Up in an alcove overlooking the floor, some guy sits at a battered piano, plunking out meaningless melodies. The keys have lost their finish and one leg's been replaced by cinderblocks. This guy is better than most who come through; his plunking is more-or-less in tune. Lacking a jukebox, this is the best I can hope for.

I feel cold, rubbery skin brush my cheek; it reeks of blood and death. His nose presses up against mine, horribly intimate. I struggle frantically to keep him away, pushing him with one arm while the other searches blindly in the refuse beneath me for something, anything to use against him.

I focus on the present, look through slits in the blinds to my side, and stare into the dim, wet streets outside. There's no way to determine what time it is. It's impossible to guess whether it's day or night. The sky is overcast, the gray ever-present. It's always so hot. And it is forever cloudy here, raining or not. It's gloomy even in the middle of the day. The sun hasn't shone since I came here.

Sighing, I look down at the glass in front of me. Tonight. I find out what they've decided, tonight. They won't let me go home. Of that much, I'm certain. So they either kill me, or, hell, I have no idea what a different alternative might be. One way or another, my months of terror and captivity are over tonight. And I'm powerless to affect the outcome.

I curse myself. Before I came here, I had so many months, years of doing nothing, wasting the hours and days away, carelessly spending what little I had. And now, at the end, I can only see all the things I have yet to do.

My hand finds something—a chunk of wood from a broken pallet. I feel slivers bite painfully into my palm as I grab it and shove it at the thing on top of me.

The guy at the piano starts a new tune that grates on my nerves. No way I want to suffer through it sober.

I down my drink in one swallow. Then I grimace and use every muscle I have to keep that swallow down while I hold onto the table for dear life, my world tilting crazily around me. Holy Hell, that is strong. How do the locals stand it? My nasal cavity feels like it's been fire-bombed. I'm not their typical clientele, I understand, but I have serious concerns about what damage it might be doing to my insides. Note to self: steer clear of the varnish Warner calls hard liquor and stick to beer. I'm starting to suspect the bottles on the shelves behind Warner are different brands of embalming fluid rather than alcohol.

I feel a lurch. I can't figure out if it's me or something nearby until someone's knees bang against my own under the table. My vision swims back into focus and through my tears I see a dark shape looming from the other side of the booth. Someone is sitting across from me. Now that I think about it, some of those shudders and lurches could have been made by this giant of a man striding across the room.

Even in the gloom, I recognize the smile that forms in the darkness.

"I've been looking for you, Jacob Green," the hulking shadow says.

"Marsh," the words burn in my throat. And like every other time I've seen him, I wait for the pain to begin.

Three months ago . . .

A late night out with friends drags on. We've all had too many beers, and the night descends into complaints about the homework and assignments we all should have been doing. I'm in my last year of school, and I'm anxious for it to be over. I think we all are. Finally, I say goodnight and walk home with Amber. The wind cuts right through our layers of clothing, ignoring our coats like they aren't even there.

Laughing, we lean on each other until we arrive at my ratty one-bedroom apartment on the third floor of a building near campus. Despite the chill, we start peeling off each other's clothes outside the door while I'm trying to get the keys into the lock. We stumble over each other and eventually make it into the bedroom where we collapse exhausted into my bed. I fall asleep an hour later, further exhausted.

I sleep in too late, hitting the snooze instead of getting ready. That puts me ten minutes behind. I always have a hard time getting going in the mornings, but I can usually pull it together when I need to. This morning though, I'm dumb. Careless. Late.

I don't even say goodbye to her. Every morning I say goodbye, but this one time, I forget.

It is the last time I ever see her.

Driving in my car, I'm sure that if I can hit the lights just right and win the parking space lottery, I'll make it to my first class on time. Traffic usually isn't a concern in Lincoln, at least not on the route I typically take.

I'm late enough that there is a line in the left turn lane near campus, so I decide to roll the dice and go right, hoping to shave off some time.

But there's an accident. It happened maybe seconds ago. If my radio hadn't been so loud, I probably would have heard it. I might have avoided it.

I am on the verge of being late, and with this professor, I can't afford that. There will be repercussions. But the accident is bad. I see blood. I could drive around, maybe still manage to get to class on time.

No. I have no choice here. I would regret the decision for the rest of my life if I were to drive on. I stop. I get out of my car. After everything that's happened to me, all the wrong decisions I have made, this one I have no qualms about. I just wish things could have worked out differently.

There is so much blood. A car has slammed into something and the hood is crumpled—like it wrapped around a telephone pole that isn't there. What did it hit?

The passenger has come through the windshield, slumped over the hood of the car, his body below the waist still inside the vehicle. His neck is at an odd angle, and I can see brain through part of his missing skull. This is the first dead body I've ever seen up close. It's not what I expected.

There is movement on the other side of the car. The driver's door is open. I hear something. It is still dark, and we are too far from a street lamp for me to see more. I walk around the back of the car to the other side.

I don't understand what I am seeing. The door is open. The driver, she has her seatbelt on. She is dazed, and blood covers her face. Someone is helping her, leaning in close to check her out.

No, that isn't what's happening. As I draw close, the driver is reaching out to me.

"Help . . ." she whispers. "Monster . . ." as her eyes roll up into her head.

It doesn't make sense, but it is the last thing she says. The man crouching over her has his back to me, but I can tell that whatever he's up to, he isn't concerned with helping her. Is he groping her body? Rifling through her pockets? What is he doing?

"Hey!" I shout in confusion and anger. I just watched a woman die in front of me, and this guy can't be bothered to stop sniffing her or pawing at her or whatever he is doing. The driver looked to me for help while I stood there and did nothing.

The man freezes at the sound of my voice. I can't see him clearly, but he doesn't turn to face me. He is wearing a suit that is old, tattered and worn. It is a dark shade, but in the dim light, I can't tell the color.

"What the hell are you doing?" I yell at him, my voice an octave higher than normal. Pieces of the shattered windshield cover his left side, some embedded in his skin. The glitter of broken glass twinkles from his left sleeve. He doesn't look hurt; he doesn't look like he notices it at all. I don't understand. It just adds to the surreal quality of the scene.

He stands up slowly, and for the first time it hits me that I might be in danger. He's tall, taller than I am. And he knows I've seen him doing something to the driver of the car. What will he do to keep me quiet?

I take a hesitant step backward, expecting him to turn and face me. He cocks his head and looks slightly to the side. He turns enough that I can see blood on one side of his face, but I can't see anything else.

I raise my hands to defend myself, but instead of attacking, he squats, grabs the driver's purse, and takes off. I just stand there stupidly, my mouth hanging open. Seriously, did he just steal from a dead person?

He doesn't just jog away; he runs full-tilt, like his life

depends on it.

I glance over my shoulder, but I don't see anything. I realize I've been holding my breath, and I gasp in a lungful of air, dizziness poised to overwhelm me. The street is empty. The street lights are still on, and dawn is threatening, the sun nearly at the horizon.

"Are you serious?" I yell after him.

I watch him run away. I'm still stunned, in absolute shock. There are two dead bodies in front of me, but my eyes keep going to the driver slumped to the side, her arm still reaching out to me. And the blood. So much blood. She has a ragged wound at her neck, the edges exposing muscle and spine, the blood still oozing out on to her shirt. All this has probably taken at most a minute or two, but it seems like ages since I got out of my car.

I'm shaking, and I roughly wipe away the tears I hadn't noticed in my eyes. I could stop right here. Just stay at the scene, wait for the police. I could report what I have witnessed. Have a story to tell my professor, my friends. Silently mourn the life of the woman I couldn't help. But that story would end with this sick, crazy psycho running away.

I can't stand that. He ignored her dying breaths, and then, instead of helping her, he stole her purse. Given how dark it is here, I didn't even see his face. If I talk to the police now, I wouldn't even be able to give them a description.

He'll get away with it.

I don't know what I plan to do, but I can't let him just walk away from this. I have to catch him. He has to pay for what he has done.

It seems like such a naïve decision now, but at the time it was the only choice my conscience would allow me to make. So I ran after him. Chased him. And eventually found him. Right before I met Marsh.

Chapter 2

Why do you keep coming back to this dump?" Marsh asks me, holding up a hand to call for some beer. "Warner is an asshole."

I'm still trying to get my head right after the liquor that's now burning its way through the lining of my stomach. His features haven't completely come into focus, but focusing isn't necessary; no one else can be that huge. I'm not small myself, I'm just over six feet. He dwarfs me, a solid mass of muscle, gristle, and rage. I'm nothing to Marsh, a splash against a wall of stone. I've been in a fight or two, but this guy has been killing for lifetimes.

Annabelle places two pints of beer on our table. He downs his entire glass in one swallow, grimaces, and before I can reach for mine, he grabs that too. He signals for another while guzzling, then brings his attention back to me. The waitress grumbles under her breath and wanders away.

Unfortunately, my vision finally clears, and I can see Marsh despite the gloom. His face is wrinkled, creases so deep they nearly divide his skull. Unlike most people here, his skin is intact, leathery, not rotting or exposing tendons and muscle underneath. His flat nose, broken dozens of times, overshadows a mouth that somehow smiles and scowls at the same time. He squints at me, not to get a better look, but because one eye is permanently pinched together. The over-hanging brow throws his eyes in shadow, though I can detect a menacing gleam when he turns. I'm glad he's sitting in the corner's shadow. I don't know if I want to see clearly the ugliest face in all creation right now. His thick brown sideburns are more than a few decades out of style: thick, curly, straight down to the bottom of his jaw. The liquor isn't sitting well in my stomach, and his presence isn't going to settle it much. His gray-green skin and his few remaining teeth aren't visible, but I know this man's face better than almost anyone else's I've met, especially when its ominous gaze falls my way.

"Kid, it's time to talk," he says. I've been considered an adult for a few years now, but compared to him, I might as well be in diapers. I have no idea how many decades or, hell, centuries older than me he is. His body looks near its prime, but the gaze from behind his eyes seems like he has seen centuries pass.

"Jacob Green. Jake. We've made our decision," Marsh says solemnly. His smile is gone, and his default scowl is in its place. He uses my actual name this time, formal. It does not reassure me.

We, he says. He's speaking as a representative, then. He's not just here to torment me in his spare time but in the official role of Captor, capital C. The other noises in the room fade away, and he has my undivided attention. His deep voice sounds like an engine rumbling to life. Even in the best of times, it sends shivers down my spine. But what he says clarifies things for me real quick. This is it. I've been expecting someone to come to me today and inform me of my fate. And if they sent Marsh to talk to me, killing me is definitely on the table. No matter how fast I am, I'm within his reach.

No struggle. No problem.

During my short, unending stay here, Marsh has been tasked with keeping me alive long enough to answer their questions. And I fear I've reached the end. I have no answers left. So, now, what does that mean for me?

Anywhere else in the world, being in a crowded room would offer me some protection from harm, but I doubt this crowd would mind much if Marsh ended me. I try to remain calm, but I can't read anything from his expression. He's not lying; I'm reasonably sure of that. I usually read people fairly well. The people here are much harder to read. I've always had a knack for sensing what people are thinking, but I'm too nervous tonight. I can't tell if it's going to be good news or bad. Bad seems to be the most likely outcome. I stare at his good eye as he leans forward slightly, part of his face emerging into the light. His eye is a watery dull blue that looks back at me without interest or concern.

Waiting him out is pointless. He'll just sit there staring at me until the cold death of the universe, not blinking. The bastard never blinks. He barely moves, sitting deadly still in his cheap, dark suit that struggles to keep his muscles in check. His outfit is similar to my own, dark gray, and about four times as large. His shirt is stretched so tight, a sneeze will send it exploding into streamers. It may have been white once, but that day is long past. His tie hangs loose at the collar, but only extends down to about mid-chest. No tie in existence could wrap around his neck and reach his belt at the same time. He's got a trench coat on over the top that looks like it could double as a cover for my car.

He doesn't react when Annabelle places two more glasses of beer on the table. She stares at him for a moment, glances at me, rolls her eyes, and walks away once more.

Finally, I break. I'm pretty certain Marsh could sit for nights on end if he wanted to.

"So? What's the decision? You going to kill me? Keep me quiet about this place?" It comes out as more of a squeak than I wanted.

I'm not going to beg. I'm scared, I'm resigned, but I'm determined to maintain a minimum amount of dignity until I know for sure it's bad news. Then, once I confirm it's bad, I'll start crying like a baby, pride be damned. Marsh's expression doesn't change. He holds still, not blinking, more like a column of stone than a body of flesh. Finally, he leans farther forward, his face fully emerging out of the gloom. It's as bad as I remember. I can smell the fetid rot on his breath, see the glaze over his pinched eye. And then I shudder as his lips split into a feral grin, revealing his large, browning teeth.

"No, kid. We're not going to kill you. Not today, anyway."

He slams both his hands down on the table. I can't help it; I jump, my knees slamming into the underside of the table. I try to regain my composure as I look at the two items he has put on the table. They both gleam in the dim light. Neither makes any sense to my brain.

One is a gun, but not like any gun I've ever used before. It's like a revolver bred with a shotgun; it's huge, like a bazooka's lost little cousin. It is crafted out of dark iron, symbols carved into the metal of the barrel, with a polished wooden grip. I'm scared to touch it. I've seen one like it aimed at me before and never want to experience that again. Staring down the barrel pointed in my face, I thought it seemed to reach on forever, like I could fall into the tunnel of darkness aimed at me. I can barely tear my eyes away from it. This time, though, it's the grip extended towards me, not the barrel.

And next to the gun, a badge.

Marsh still isn't blinking, and his grin remains fixed on his waxen features. He shifts in his seat, leaning closer still. Marsh's face is inches from mine, his one good eye looking out from a cold, green face.

"We're giving you a job, kid. Congratulations!" The chuckle that accompanies his words doesn't reassure me at all, nor does the cruel gleam in his eye. "You're the newest member of the Necropolis PD. We're going to be partners!"

Two months ago . . .

The chill from the barren floor seeps into my bones; there is no escape from it. My tattered clothes provide scant comfort, barely holding together after repeated abuse and damage over the past few weeks. I've been fighting off sleep for hours, huddled on the ground in the corner of this dark, freezing room. There is no escape from the cold. I've been trying to wrap myself into as small of a ball as possible, arms wrapped around me to trap in as much heat as I can. A heavy mist curls lazily across the floor, and the carcasses of some large animals hang nearby. Horse? Cow? Ox?

I'm in a meat locker, I'm terrified, and I don't dare close my eyes for more than a moment.

There are things in here with me. I can hear them, nearby in the dark. Chittering. Scratching. Scurrying across the floor. I thought they were rats, but rats don't get that big. When I nod off, they get close enough to bite, their teeth tearing through my clothes like paper. I'm bleeding from several bites and from the raking of tiny claws across skin. Sometimes I swear I hear their laughter. Occasionally, I'll see their little eyes reflecting red in the dim light. They stay away when I'm awake, when I'm moving, but over the hours, they've been growing bolder, inching closer.

My arms are numb, my shoulders a dull ache. I can no longer feel my hands, toes, or wrists. Breath fogs in front of me, and I shiver uncontrollably, miserable and alone.

Near the door, one of the carcasses begins to swing. Then another. Something large is approaching me in the gloom. A shadow lurches into view, followed by a low chuckle that causes my shivers to intensify. Marsh arrives and squats down, hovering over me. Behind him, I can hear the scrabbling of dozens of other naked feet on the floor, the scratching of ragged claws and nails. What horrors lurk in the dark behind him?

"What do you want?" I cry, tears escaping my eyes. I'm relieved to see him. The things in the dark won't get near while he's here.

"Answers, of course," Marsh responds with a smile, and despite everything, I hear sympathy in his words. "Answer my questions, kid, and I'll call them off."

I look past him, helplessly envisioning the things behind Marsh. He is all that stands between them and me. If he leaves and doesn't take them with him, they'll be on me. I've seen what they do to the carcasses hanging here, gnawing at the flesh, at the bone. I've seen what little remains once the creatures are gone.

"I've told you everything I know," I plead. Hell, if I know the answer to anything he wants, I will tell him. I'll do whatever it takes to get this to end. I've been here for hours. This guy Marsh, this dead man, is all that is keeping me alive. He could crush me without a thought; his strength is beyond anything I've seen before. He could kill me with one hand and dump my body before walking away and not thinking twice.

Or he could simply walk away.

Marsh loosens his tie. "I'm sure you believe you did, kid. But you know what's been my experience?"

I am too tired to answer. I can only shake my head.

"In my experience, there's always more to know. Don't keep dragging this out. Tell me what I want to know, and this will all be over."

I stare at him, without hope. I've answered all their questions, but they don't like what I have to say. I can't give him the right answers; I don't know what they are.

He's terrifying. He hit me the first time we met. It felt like a bus crashed into me, but it was clear he took no joy in it. When he saw the other things closing in, he kept them off of me. He broke bones, pummeled anyone who got too close, letting them know he was serious. Whenever I see his face, I know he's there to keep the creatures and the dead things from eating me. When Marsh shows up, I'm safe for a short while. If he doesn't lose his patience with me. If he doesn't just give up and leave me to my fate.

"OK," he says, sadly. "I'll check on you again in a few hours. Get comfortable."

The carcasses swing as he passes through them on his way out of the room. The chittering resumes and closes in as I fight to keep my eyes open for as long as I can.

Chapter 3

I JUST STARE BACK. MY BRAIN keeps misfiring, trying to process what's happening. Are the gun and the badge anything other than some kind of punishment, some kind of trick? I try to say anything. I go for something articulate. Something eloquent.

"I, uh, what?"

Nailed it.

Marsh leans back and folds the tree trunks in his sleeves in front of his chest. "You got a problem with this?" His scowl is beginning to look unfriendly. Unfriendlier. Having been on the receiving end of Marsh's unfriendliness before, I wasn't eager to repeat it. But my brain isn't working for me. For the past few months, I've lived every day in terror of Marsh, afraid of what he would inflict on me, or what would be inflicted on me because he wasn't there. Afraid of what questions he would ask that I had no hope of answering. And now, instead of my Captor, still capital C, he's going to become my what? Babysitter? Coworker? Partner?

When I first found out Marsh was a cop, I thought that meant I could appeal to his sense of justice and get some degree of protection. I quickly learned the folly of that. His job is to protect the city and, fair or not, protect it from the likes of me. Protect it from the living.

I'm the sole living person in a town full of dead things who, up until now, unanimously wanted me dead or gone. They wanted me lost or consumed or forgotten. And now I'm being told to stay. Earlier, I thought my options were death or being tossed down some dark hole for eternity. This, whatever this is, I don't understand. I'm reluctant to trust the near-crippling sense of relief that washes over me at the knowledge that I'm not going to be killed. I didn't realize how sure I was that my death was the night's only possible outcome.

My mouth opens, but nothing comes out. I close it, then try again. Considering my other option is death, I'm going to take his offer. But I definitely feel the hooks sinking in. As Amber would say, "Nothing is free, Jake. Look for the price tag on everything that comes your way." At the time, I'd accused her of being overly cynical. Maybe I was just overly optimistic. There's more to this offer than I can figure out now. There has to be.

"Why?" I finally manage. "What did you call it? Necropolis PD? A police officer? I'm no cop. I don't know the first thing about how to be one. I mean, cops, they have skills. They're tough. Me? I can't."

Marsh's hand snakes out so fast I almost don't see it. He grabs my wrist, painfully crushing it, pressing one finger on the vein there. "You got a pulse?" He asks me, looking amused at my struggle to break free.

"Yes! I said yes," I stammer, wincing in pain. I'm trying to pull back, but it's like moving a mountain.

His other fist thumps down on the table, and he lets me go. I manage not to jump this time. Barely. I scoot as far away from him as the crowded booth with allow. "Then you're one up on everyone else here," he says.

"What does that even mean? What good is that?"

"The captain asked for you specifically. We've got a problem, and we need your help."

"What kind of problem can I possibly help out with?"

My arm hurts.

He shrugs. "It's something we've never seen before. The fact that you're living will give you a unique perspective on things. For as long as you last."

"But—"

"Kid, I'm trying to help you out here. I've got a soft spot for you."

I stare in disbelief. "Are you kidding me? I've barely survived these past few weeks!"

He chuckles at this.

"Exactly. Imagine if I didn't like you."

Marsh leans over and yanks the talisman painfully against my neck, snapping the twine. "You're not going to need that any more. But if I were you, I'd put that badge on pretty quick."

He scoots out of the booth and stands up. Towering next to the table, he blocks out all the light coming from behind him. All I can see of him now is the twinkle in his good eye. I hastily grab the badge and put it in my pocket.

"C'mon. Let's go," he says.

"What? Where?"

"Enough with the questions, already! Just follow me."

He puts his hand on my shoulder and steers me out the door. Whether I want to or not, I'm going with him.

Chapter 4

MARSH GUIDES ME TO A section of the city I've never seen before. My thoughts are a swirling vortex of confusion. A police officer? For a bunch of dead people?

My thoughts are in such a state that I don't even pay attention to where we are going; I just let Marsh steer us through the crowds. We can't have walked more than a couple of blocks when Marsh stops in front of a seemingly empty storefront. Like most of the buildings here, it looks abandoned and on the verge of collapse. Bricks are missing, walls sag, grime and graffiti cover most of the façade. The windows are more-or-less intact, but newspapers are taped over the inside of the panes, blocking our view of what lies within. He mumbles a few words, inaudible to me even though I'm only a few feet from him, and I hear the door unlock. Did he just open a door by talking to it? He swings the door open, and I follow him in.

Paint cans, scaffolding, and garbage line the floor along the walls of the room. There's something in the middle of the dust-covered floor, hidden underneath a tarp. The gloom in here is too dark for me to see any details.

Marsh turns a switch on the wall like a key, and a pair of gaslights on the walls slowly illuminate the room. The tarp on the floor looks like it's covering something the size of a body.

My suspicions are confirmed when Marsh pulls the tarp aside. A dead person. I have no concept of how old they might be. It could be days, weeks, or years. To me, they're simply dead, so I don't know what I'm supposed to be looking for. Marsh just stares at me expectantly.

I lean closer to the body. Long white hair sticks out wildly from the head. If it weren't for the clothes, I wouldn't even be able to tell if the body was a male or female. Since it's wearing a suit and tie, I'm going to guess male. And up close, he smells nothing like roses.

There appear to be burn marks around the eye sockets. The eyes are missing, but given how long the body may have been laying here, I have no idea if that's significant or not. Was that how the person was killed? Something burned their eyes out? Am I supposed to know who this is?

"I don't . . . What am I looking at?"

Marsh's shoulders slump, like he'd been expecting me to utter some revelation that was going to break the case wide open.

"For crying out loud, Green. It's a corpse! Some detective you're going to be."

"Yeah, it's a corpse. So what?"

He shakes his head sadly. "Green. It's. A. Corpse. Don't you get it? We need your help to solve a murder."

Finally, it clicks. A murder in a city of the dead. Where people can't die.

As if things couldn't get any weirder.

An hour later, I still barely understand what's going on, or what Marsh expects of me. We're back at Warner's. My table's open, and I sit down, but Marsh doesn't move to join me.

"I'll come pick you up after dinner tomorrow. Night shift. Be ready. It'll be fun."

"Wait! I don't understand this. You've got to answer some more questions for me!"

He sneers, amused. "I don't gotta do nothing, kid. Just because I have a soft spot for you doesn't mean I want to be partnered with you every night. The captain wants you. I don't. You annoy the crap about of me, but you're good for a few laughs. Play your cards right, I might not end up killing you. Be patient. Be ready. Tomorrow."

"But . . ." I try. Marsh just ignores me. He lumbers away, the mass of Warner's clientele parting in front of him as he goes. He towers over everyone here, not just me. Even dead as the rest of the crowd is, they're still wary of him. Conversations quiet as he nears and tentatively pick up again after he's gone. Terrors of the night, creatures from humanity's nightmares, scattering out of the way in fear of the man who is going to be working alongside me. Great. I glance down to the gun in my hands.

A gun? What good is that? Everyone here is already dead. Every person I've met here is literally a corpse walking around, animated by who knows what magic or witchcraft or science or sheer stubbornness. I would call them zombies if Marsh hadn't knocked me senseless the first time I referred to him as one. Zombies are mindless, shambling meatsacks that shuffle around trying to eat flesh or brains. The people, he was very clear on that, here are alert, intelligent, conscious. Well, OK, maybe just conscious. They talk and sometimes carry conversations. Not what I would expect from zombies or walking corpses I've seen in movies although I'm pretty sure eating me isn't entirely off the table. I'll occasionally catch a few of them sizing me up. Marsh's constant presence is probably all that's kept them away. Or the talisman. Which

I don't have anymore.

Death could not hold them down. What good is a gun going to do? No matter how huge a gun it is. It's heavy, like a cinderblock. It looks comically large in my hand. The muzzle is about six inches in diameter. What kind of bullets does it take? I realize I'm staring down the barrel to try and see what's inside. Cautiously, I set it back down. I could blow my head off before I learn how to use it.

It could be my imagination, but the crowd now seems to be giving me even more clearance than before. A few are staring at me, dead eyes in dead faces looking at me curiously, whispering to each other. I remember having dreams like this, surrounded by zombies with no escape. Trying to dodge grasping hands before they tore me apart, before they dismembered me into a bloody stew as they choked down my body. Fortunately, it doesn't go like that. They stare. They whisper. They slug back a few drinks. Then they turn back to what they were doing and ignore me again.

I swallow nervously and pull the badge out of my pocket. It's a gold shield nestled inside a black leather wallet. Real gold? No idea. There's a star inside the shield and a faded engraving of a skull in the center, though there are no words or names. It looks ancient. The surface looks like it was hammered by hand, not machine. It tingles strangely when I touch it, like static electricity, similar to how the talisman felt, but stronger. I feel a shiver in my spine. I slide it away. Knowing my luck, it's probably radioactive.

It seems he's telling the truth. I sigh, and I'm surprised to realize a weight of some sort has been lifted from me.

They aren't going to kill me.

I really thought they would. When I saw Marsh tonight, I thought he was going to be the last thing I ever saw. Tears form in the corners of my eyes, and I try and keep them down.

I found my way to their hidden city, their warren of

forgotten streets and abandoned buildings, their refuge where they are safe from the living world. I was sure they would just kill me to protect their secret. Would killing me make me one of them? Or would I just be dumped in a ditch and forgotten? Or God forbid, would someone eat me? Apparently, they have something different in mind for me.

I wait for my hands to stop shaking. I'm a police officer now. Laughter escapes my lips, sudden and incredulous. I can't help it; the situation is just so surreal. Zombies surrounding me is one thing, ghouls, whatever. I can accept that. But there's no way I can believe I'm a police officer.

Wait a minute. I have a gun now, a possible means of escape. Maybe a shot from this hand cannon will knock a few people down, clear a path to the door, or at least through a window. I could make it out of the building, get a head start.

But I'm pretty sure Marsh wouldn't give me a way out of here. No, whatever weapon he's given me isn't going to be enough to get home on my own. If anything, he's watching me, measuring my responses, seeing what I do with my newfound options.

I want to scream. Do I try and escape? It's tempting. I want to go home. I glance at the door, thinking. Calculating. But ultimately, I know it's futile, a wish I can't fulfill.

The risk is too much. I just don't know enough yet to understand the ramifications of my decisions. What would happen? What punishment would I be facing if I failed? Would I be putting anyone else in danger? Do they know about Amber or my family?

I realize I've been standing by my table, holding the gun down at my side, staring at the door. I'm getting more glances now. Some nervous. Skittish.

I grab my suit coat and sling it over my arm, putting the gun out of sight. No one is looking directly at me, everyone carefully avoids my eyes, but I know I'm the center of attention. As I make my way to the door, the crowd parts for me as quickly as it parted for Marsh. The reasons are different though. In my case, they're probably worried I'm contagious, like they'll catch a case of breathing.

What did he mean that the captain asked for me? How could I possibly help them with anything? Solve a murder? What am I supposed to do?

I stare at the walking, shuffling corpses surrounding me. The words they speak dwindle as I get near. The wave of whispering builds at my back as I pass, pushing me to the door. I try not to run. Try not to sweat. I try in any way not to just freak the hell out and start screaming.

Three months ago . . .

He is fast, this bastard I'm chasing. My thoughts keep returning to that poor woman, dying while this guy stole her valuables, her purse worth more to him than her life.

I can't let him get away with it. I don't want to try and fight him; I just want to see where he goes so I can tell the police later, get a good look at him, so I can give a description.

He doesn't even try to lose me. He never looks back over his shoulder; he just runs. He hops over chain link fences, runs down still streets, the lights inside a house here or there turning on as people around us wake up to a new day.

I manage to keep him in sight. He plunges straight through a cedar fence, exploding into someone's backyard. I run through the hole he leaves behind just in time to see the German Shepherd running off the back porch towards me. On the far side of the yard, the man vaults over the fence. I awkwardly climb over the top, falling into the yard just as the dog slams into the wooden planks in a snarling fury.

Is he on drugs? What kind of maniac runs through a wooden fence?

I get to my feet, but I can't see the man I am chasing. I climb over the far fence and am at the end of the street. The road is a dead end, perpendicular to a creek about eight feet across. I look frantically around and notice the jogging trail running alongside the water, nearly hidden by the overgrown weeds.

It is darker here. He has to be somewhere. I stand on the trail, looking up one way and then the other. Nothing. To my left, the creek stretches straight and even, leading to a short bridge several blocks off. I look to the right and see a bridge closer, taller, but equally devoid of people.

Frogs croak off to my left, some ways off, loud and insistent. I hear nothing from my right. Desperate, I set off running to my right, hoping they were scared into silence by the passage of the man I am chasing.

The path leads up to the bridge. The bridge isn't much of anything, with a waist-high stone railing on either side. As I approach it from the side, I can see it is tall enough to stand underneath, and there is a concrete platform beneath it. On the far side of the bridge, the jogging path turns from a dirt track to a paved one.

Empty.

He had to have come this way.

That's when I hear it. The creak of rusted hinges from below the bridge.

I lean out over the edge of the overgrown grass and see a rocky bank along the creek hidden by the long weeds. It runs under the bridge, unlike the path which led me up top.

I run back down the path a bit and drop down over the side with the weeds, landing on the rocks a couple feet below. I move quickly under the bridge.

There is a door there, underneath the bridge. One of the two bulbs overhead is broken, but I can still make out some details. It is a service entrance of some kind, leading into the sewers. It looks like it hasn't been used any time in the past decade.

I hesitate as I walk up to the door. It is dented and dirty, much of the paint missing or flaking off onto the ground. I have no idea what I'll find behind it. If this is where that maniac is hiding, I don't want to stumble into him. But if it leads somewhere, I need to know where. Either way, surely it'll be locked. I reach out and grab the handle.

It opens, and I hear the same telltale squeak I heard moments before. I open it a crack and peer inside. The room beyond the door is a nightmare. A few steps lead down to a concrete room holding a massive machine of some kind hooked to ductwork going into a wall. There's a large grate on the far wall covering a sewer tunnel, and it's pulled back, leaving a gap wide enough to squeeze through. The tunnel beyond stretches into darkness, lit only by occasional dim lights. A stack of old pallets about four feet high is leaning against the machine, with other trash scattered around the base.

My feet seem to move of their own accord, pulling me into the room. I can't be seeing what my brain is telling me is in front of me.

To the side are several corpses heaped into a pile. There must be a dozen. Judging by the smell, they have been there a long time. I try not to gag. I want to find this guy, sure, but I'm not crazy. I'm out. This is as far as I'll go. I'll bring the cops back here, even without this guy's description.

I turn around to leave, and he is standing right behind me, blocking my exit. His eyes glow faintly in the gloom of the room. Blood covers his mouth, neck, and chest. His skin is old, wrinkled, his gray hair a tangled mess. Teeth too long to be contained in his mouth still have chunks of flesh clinging to them. I can smell the rot on his breath, the coppery tang of blood. His fingernails, blood-soaked and long, sit like daggers on the end of fingers already too much like knives.

This is the first moment I realize this thing I've been chasing isn't human.

My scream barely escapes before he is on me. He tries to tackle me, land on top of me, but I manage to pivot, tossing him to the side. I break for the door, making it up two stairs before he grabs the collar of my shirt, his nails digging painfully into my neck, and he yanks me back, hurling me across the room. I crash into the pallets, shattering several, feeling sharp points dig into my back as the mess cascades down over me.

I suck in a ragged breath, trying to tell which way is up.

"How did you follow me here?" he asks, his voice like nothing I have ever heard before. It's an accent I can't place. It is both loud and a whisper at the same time, full of fury, hammering my brain and tickling my ears. My skin breaks into gooseflesh.

He lands on top of me, one hand on my throat, the other pinning my left wrist painfully to the ground.

He leans in close, and I know, I just know he is some dead creature. A living thing can't look like he does: a corpse that hasn't received the message it's supposed to be dead.

I stare into the vacant, sunken eyes of a cadaver's face, inches from my own. The viscous eyes, fogged over and yellow, reflect my own gaze blurrily back at me. The corpse pins me down, the full weight of it crushing me into the cold ground. The face looms closer as I struggle to push the body away from me. The eyes, they grow nearer still. And then they blink.

The dead eyes blink at me, the mouth below smiles with split lips, a foul stench wafts out from the blackness behind jagged yellow teeth inching closer to me. A fluid thicker than drool drips from the mouth onto my face.

"You're a long way from home, aren't you, child?" it says, a whisper slipping from a dead face. "Such a long way to come to die."

I feel cold, rubbery skin brush my face, it reeks of blood and death. His nose presses up against mine, horribly intimate. I struggle frantically to keep him away, pushing him with one arm while the other searches blindly in the refuse beneath me for something, anything to use against him.

My hand finds something—a chunk of wood from a broken pallet. I feel slivers bite painfully into my palm as I grab it and shove it at the thing on top of me.

It howls, loud and long, ringing painfully in my ears. He falls against me, his teeth brushing against my throat.

Several seconds go by before I realize nothing is happening. I am not being bitten. I'm not being killed. I look at my hand, holding tight around a chunk of wood. The wood is lodged in this monster's chest, buried deep into the ribcage. My hand is bloody, both from him and from several large splinters stuck into my skin. I look at the face of my attacker but see only a rotting corpse long dead. The eyes that glowed with fury seconds ago are shriveled, sightless. Blood pours out of its open mouth onto my neck, down my shirt.

I wrestle in horror trying to get the thing off of me. I toss it to the side and scramble backward away from it. My lungs are gasping for air. My throat hurts where he grabbed me.

What just happened?

To my side, I hear the grate slowly squeal as it is peeled back further from the wall. The temperature drops several degrees, and I feel my terror grow.

A shadow looms in the tunnel entrance, blocking out all lights behind it. Small glowing red eyes peer out from the dark, and a hunched, balding figure calmly walks out.

The shadows move unnaturally, independent of this new person's movements. My throat is dry. He stands, surveying the scene. He looks at the dead man at my feet, at me, at the pile of bodies on the other side of the room. A tear falls down my cheek.

"Tsk. Et alors. This won't do at all," he says, looking at me thoughtfully. Curiously. He points at the bodies. "Et voici, you see all this?"

I nod numbly.

In a blink, the man is beside me. He grabs me by the throat, pinching my windpipe closed effortlessly. He is so much stronger than the other man! He slams me into the pile of corpses. I can feel them at my back, my shirt starting to dampen from the fluids oozing out of them.

"Celui-ci? These corpses right here?" He points at the bodies beneath me. The stench of the bodies beneath me is overpowering.

I try to speak, can't, so weakly I nod again. I try clawing at his hand, but it feels like rock.

"Ah, c'est dommage. Very unfortunate. For you, obviously. For me, that remains to be seen."

He smiles then, and I'm pretty sure I feel warm piss begin trickling down my leg. "Allons-y. Let's take you to Marsh."

The shadows somehow lunge at me, enveloping me in darkness beneath his red gaze, and I black out.

Chapter 5

THE SOUND FROM THE CROWD in Warner's cuts to merciful silence as the door closes behind me. I step to the side and lean against the stone wall, the bricks at my back giving me a small sense of security. People move past on the sidewalk, pretending to ignore me.

Warner's is on the ground floor of some featureless, five-story, nondescript building, one of any countless number churned out around the country after the Second World War. But it seems older than that, ancient, a temple from some bygone time with security bars over picture windows and red brick walls. Unlike many buildings I've seen here, this one has all its windows and doors intact on the main floor, while the upper floors look ready to collapse. Whole walls are missing, bricks crumbling and littering the ground where they have fallen over the years. Paint is flaking off. It could be any forgettable building from any run-down neighborhood in any large city.

Gaslights burn on street corners, dimly lit even during what passes for daytime. They throw a glow up on the underside of the clouds that blanket the town, and they provide beacons of light in the continuous thin fog. I'd never encountered fog in the heat before, but it appears natural here. The buildings crowd together in this downtown area, brushing up against each other, looming over their neighbors, leaning together over alleyways and courtyards. An Art Deco building stands across the street, some buildings with bamboo shingles are a block down, and there's rusted metal next to adobe, mid-century frames beside centuries-old brick. All around fences are falling down from neglect, roofs are missing from exposure, holes gape in walls, windows are broken, entire floors have collapsed, debris is scattered, and garbage piles up. It's like someone flung discarded structures from around the world at random into one big dreary dump.

I have no idea how big this place is. I can't see more than a block or two in any direction, thanks to the fog. How many of the undead live here? A couple thousand? Ten thousand? It's at least that much based on what I've seen so far. Well, the ones with bodies, anyway. I have no idea how many it is when counting the ghosts.

I've never reached the edge of town. Marsh let me try, once, while I was under his care. He just urged me on, shooing me with his hands, a smile on his face. I tried. The fog didn't let me go far. I wandered aimlessly in the dark, the temperature dropping enough during the night that I started to shiver. I don't know if I even made it close the town's edge. I was pathetically eager to see the glow from Marsh's lantern when he came to get me.

If I do ever reach the edge of this place, will I be allowed to leave?

Clopping approaches from close by, and I ensure I'm as far from the street as I can be. Horses are common here, and they are cold-hearted bastards. The occasional horse-drawn carriage moves through the streets, and they are nearly as dangerous as Marsh. They don't stop for anything. I give those things plenty of room.

A massive black apparition with glowing red eyes materializes out of the fog, trotting past me. The woman riding it ignores me completely, half her face gone but for the skull underneath, her hair a halo almost crackling with energy. She is something out of a nightmare, but it is what she is riding that concerns me most. The horse returns my glance with a hungry crimson stare. Like all the horses I've seen here, its ribs protrude starkly from under its skin, its breath blowing like steam, visible against the fog. It whinnies and lunges my way, but a flick of the rider's wrist pulls it back on track. I don't move, I've learned my lesson. I stay clear of them ever since getting nipped the one time I wandered too close. For all I know, they get fed chumps like me.

I haven't seen a car here. I haven't seen anything that runs on electricity. I still hope to hear a motor running somewhere, but every day I'm disappointed.

Necropolis, Marsh calls it. He says it like a title rather than a description. It's not the real name, though no one has bothered to tell me what the name is. It doesn't appear on any map. It's hidden from the rest of the world. How I managed to find my way here is as much a mystery to me as it is to them. It's one city, but it somehow exists in more than one place. It makes my head hurt thinking about it.

I look at the dead walking up and down the streets. They are dressed in suits and ties, dresses, overalls, and hats. Most of it is a few decades out of date. Occasionally, I see someone with bell-bottoms or corduroys, a top hat or Victorian blouse, something stylish from some bygone age. But they carry briefcases, bags, and go about business like I'd see anywhere else in the world. What are they doing? Do they still have jobs? Doesn't death mean you no longer have to work? None of them appear to be in any hurry, though. I don't sense urgency from anyone.

Do I know any of them? Somewhere out there in the mass of shuffling corpses, do I have an ancestor? A friend?

My home is only two blocks away, so I slowly make my way there, moving with the flow. It's nothing to brag about, rather it's something I actively avoid. I had no choice in it; it's where I was placed. I arrive all too quickly.

It feels darker here. The brick and dirt on the ground are wet with a slimy, persistent leak from somewhere inside the building. Gray walls lean out dangerously, with gaping holes and blocks crumbling to dust exposing support beams and disintegrating insulation. Only a few of the dark windows still contain glass or even boards covering the gaping holes. I'm on top, four stories up. I enter through an open doorway, the doors themselves long gone. There is a dark foyer with cracked checkerboard tile, a wall of unused empty mailboxes to my left. Breathing through my mouth, I struggle as the stench is enough to make me gag.

A flight of stairs winds up on my right, lit only by the dim ambient light shining through windows spaced every story. I climb the empty stairs, one hand steadying me against the wall, ready to catch myself if I stumble on something. The hairs on the back of my neck rise. There should be noises. I have neighbors. There should be the sounds of people here. But I can't hear anything inside, just the horses and people moving slowly outside. This place might as well be abandoned. Tattered strips of wallpaper hang in the hallways, and the carpets are worn through and torn on the floor, neglect piling up in corners. There are gas lights on each landing, enough to light patches of the hallways and see the cluster of eight doors on each floor.

I reach the top landing and walk down the hall, hugging the wall because I don't like the way the floor sags in the center near my apartment. There is my door at the end of the hall, #412. It looks like it would fold under a gentle breeze. I carefully enter, wincing at the loud creak as I swing it open. It protests again as I close it behind me. I haven't bothered locking it since I've been here. I'm not worried about my possessions walking away. I look at everything I own: a musty chair, an uneven card table, an ancient clay pot stove, an oil lamp, and a cot. They don't even fill the single room. The stains and mold on the walls and floors add a little extra flair to the place. I won't even talk about the bathroom.

Flopping down in the chair, I ignore the groan of protest it makes at my weight. If I try not to move too much, I should be fine. Sometimes, if I angle myself just right, I can even avoid a spring digging into my back.

Normally, back in the sane world, I would be getting home from work or late classes. I would pop some frozen meal into the microwave, something devoid of nutrition or taste that would just fill my stomach. Or if I were lucky, Amber would help me cook something.

Amber had started staying over more and more frequently. For the first time, things were starting to get serious with someone. Was there going to be something there? How long will she wait for me to get back before she moves on? Did she even try and look for me?

I dismiss that train of thought before it can depress me further and look at the empty room I'm in. I'm used to living by myself, but this is definitely different than before.

If I were back home, I would sit down at my desk to draw or paint, or at my computer and work on some project or other. Or more likely, I'd fire up whatever MMO I was playing that week. I wonder what my guild is up to these days? Do any of them even miss me? Did they even notice? None of them knew my real name, so it's not like they could go looking for me. Anyway, none of these options are possible here.

I laugh again at the thought of being forced to become

an officer of some kind, that they think my skills will some-how help them solve this problem of theirs.

My skills? I'm an artist! Put whatever modifier you want on that: aspiring, starving, struggling. None of that will help me find a killer. During the last couple of years at school, I've focused on developing skills in digital arts. I don't think the people here have ever seen a computer, so what few talents I do have are useless. Years of school and tens of thousands of dollars down the drain.

Even if I had a computer, it wouldn't work. There is no power here. No microwaves, phones, light switches, TV, ra-dio. What the hell did people do to pass the time before elec-tricity came around?

I close my eyes.

I've got another night of staring at the wall ahead of me, and I want to ration it out. That lasts about thirty seconds before I'm already bored. Some bottles of the weakest beer I could get from Warner's take up a shelf in the icebox, which is still enough to get me hammered after about half a dozen swallows.

When I open my eyes, a disembodied green, semi-trans-parent face is staring back at me from through the wall right in front of me. It blinks at me curiously. My scream would have woken the dead—if they weren't already awake.

Chapter 6

"THAT WILL BE QUITE ENOUGH of that!" the face announces primly as the rest of her floats through the wall and into my apartment. A real, physical chill radiates from her, so cold my bones ache.

I jump up and run to the other side of the chair. "Who the hell are you? What do you want?"

A transparent woman is hovering in the air above the floor of my apartment. A ghost. I've had encounters with ghosts here, and they haven't been pleasant.

She stops floating towards me, bobbing slightly in place. Her eyebrow arches and the corners of her mouth twitch into a smile. "Are you trying to put that chair between us? After you just saw me float through the wall?"

I straighten and scowl, trying to act casual. "It sounds stupid when you say it like that."

"Good, then you understood me clearly," she says. I take a closer look at her. Her hair is pulled tight in a bun, and I guess she's in her late thirties. Well, thirties if she were alive. She is dressed modestly in a long plain skirt, checkered blazer over a plain blouse buttoned at the neck, a brooch of some kind on her lapel. She has a small mole above her lip, just above the corner of her mouth. It's strange, seeing a person that doesn't have an actual body. If I reached out to her, my hand would pass through her. Everything about her, from clothes to skin to hair, is transparent green and blue, swirling from one color to the other in a mélange, like two plumes of smoke chasing each other in a windstorm. One striking difference between her and the more corporeal residents here is that her face and body look healthy, and she's got no gaping holes or rotting wounds. She looks like she must have when she was alive, except not glowing and being see-through.

She floats in the air, just shy of meeting me eye-to-eye. I have no idea how tall she is since her feet aren't visible. Her body just kind of fades out below the knees, like she forgot about completing the rest of her body. My eyes don't know where to rest; I keep glancing down where her feet should be, expecting them to fade into view. Then I glance back at her face, at her disapproving scowl. I want to avoid that, so I glance at her body again, realize it could look like I'm checking her out, and then go through the cycle again. Resigned, I settle on staring at her nose—not her mole!—so I don't quite meet her gaze.

"My name is Elizabeth Greystone. You will refer to me as Ms. Greystone. I am your liaison with the Police Department. We will—"

"Hi. I'm Jacob Green. Jake. Pleasure."

I extend my hand then realize my error. It's not like she can actually shake my hand. Her mouth is a pinched, straight line, her smile definitely long gone.

I wait.

I lower my hand.

"If you are quite through interrupting me, I am attempting to explain my expectations and outline the working parameters of our partnership."

A sigh escapes my lips. I'm failing spectacularly at this first impression so far. Since this woman is the first person here that appears to be talking to me willingly without hurting me first, I'd like to make nice. I'd like to think she's not going to inflict massive pain somehow or haunt me to death. I'm not quite sure what she can do to me, or how much authority she has over me, but it's becoming clear she doesn't like me much. And partnership? What is this about?

She floats there, staring at me. Waiting. The chill in the air is definitely something real and not just something I'm imagining based on her personality. There is a barely-audible static that seems to come from her vicinity.

"Yes? Please continue," I say uncertainly, concentrating on her and trying to ignore the noise and cold radiating from her. I shuffle from foot to foot awkwardly.

Her scowl deepens. Her eyes literally blaze more intensely. *"Ms. Greystone."*

"I'm sorry?"

"'Please continue, Ms. Greystone.' You will address me properly and with respect. I will not tolerate oafish behavior or failure in social decorum."

For crying out loud.

I had a friend back in high school whose mom would scowl withering glances at me any time I put a foot up on a chair or used the wrong fork at dinner or skipped any minor bit of etiquette. Even my best behavior wasn't enough to satisfy her, as my breeding was evidently lacking. I would never reach whatever bar she set for acceptable manners, and eventually, I just stopped trying. Which is probably why my friend stopped inviting me over, and we never spoke again after graduation.

After several criticisms without any apparent path to improving the situation, this is where I would usually start laying on the sarcasm. Back then, it just meant not being able to mooch awesome dinners off my friend's family, but now, my survival instinct is sounding a klaxon in my ears to keep it civil. The repercussions here could be considerably worse.

"Yes, ma'am. Ms. Greystone, ma'am. Sorry."

I manage to keep the sarcasm out of my voice. Best I can do. Her scowl doesn't change. She measures me suspiciously like she expects sarcasm, as well, but looks willing to resume talking. She starts drifting slightly to the right, and I pivot a little to keep my focus on her.

She folds her arms and looks at me down her nose, which is no easy feat when she is shorter than I am. "As I said, I am your liaison with the police department. I have worked in this capacity for the past sixty years. I am one of the senior department liaisons. I know what I am doing. I have one of the best closure ratings among the liaison pool. You may request my credentials from the captain if you feel it necessary. Just heed my directions, and you will be fine."

I start to take a breath to ask a question, but fortunately, I remember to not interrupt. I file it away in my brain to bring up later.

"I will be attuned to you, beginning tomorrow. Do not abuse this privilege. I am not at your beck and call, and you will be wise to remember that. I will not run your errands, and I will not indulge frivolous requests. I will not tolerate demeaning comments regarding my corporeal state. I will not respond to you outside of working hours unless it is an absolute emergency.

"Are we clear?"

Evidently, one advantage of being dead is you don't have to pause for breath. I wisely keep that observation to myself too.

I take a step away from the chair, moving closer to her to show a false sense of my comfort with her. Since she doesn't pose any immediate threat, my curiosity is taking over. I really can see right through her, though details are distorted a little, hazy. I can't see inside her; I don't see her brain or anything. But being closer to her, I can see individual hairs, all of which are perfectly in place, freckles on her skin, eyelashes. I swallow nervously. This is as close as I want to get. I resist the urge to reach out and try poking her.

"May I ask a few questions, Ms. Greystone? Ma'am."

"If you must," she replies, her arms still folded. She keeps a critical eye on me. I feel like another point has been tallied against me. Somehow not accepting her statement at face value is a failing in liaison partners.

"What is a liaison?"

She closes her eyes and pinches her nose between her fingers, the picture of long-sufferance. With her eyes closed, I take the opportunity to study her face more clearly. She has delicate features, a thin nose, narrow cheeks, deep-set eyes that bulge a little wildly when she is focused on something, but the beauty one might generally find there is marred by lines from the constant scowl she wears. Well, and the whole being able to see through her thing. "Oh dear. Exactly how much has Detective Marsh explained to you?"

"I start tomorrow."

She stares at me again, waiting for me to continue. I raise my eyebrows back at her.

"Ah. I see. You haven't taken your oath then?"

I give her my best blank stare.

"You haven't performed the Loyalty Ceremony? The Strengthening?"

More staring.

"Were you even told that I would be your liaison?"

I'm getting so good at this staring thing.

"This is highly improper. You are woefully unprepared for this responsibility. Well, then, alright. I don't know that I've ever had to explain it before. A liaison is . . . It is your connection to the Police Department and its resources. I can quickly relay information between you and your superiors. I can reconnoiter. You will be able to communicate with me no matter what distance is between us. I have a catalog of information at my disposal, which means it is at your disposal."

"Wow. That's awesome, Ms. Greystone."

She pauses. I think she's trying to tell if I'm humoring her or being condescending to her in any way. I'm trying to make myself look as sincerely as I feel. She's my ghostly smartphone. A smartphone with an attitude and a legitimate disdain towards me. There's going to end up being some kind of drawback, as with everything else about this place. Like she'll suck years off my life or drive me insane. And she'll be able to conveniently keep tabs on me as much as anything, I'm sure. But having someone assigned to answer my questions? Awesome.

"What I am not is your secretary," she continues, though there's maybe slightly less chill in the tone. Maybe. "I am not an encyclopedia to use whenever the mood hits you."

I deflate a little. Dammit, that is exactly what I was hoping for.

"Just because you have a body, living though it may be, does not mean you are the senior partner in this pairing."

Because I have a body? What was it she said earlier? She has no tolerance for comments about her corporeal state?

I raise my hand. She nods, sternly. OK, that might be a little more smart-ass than I need to be showing. I put my hand down.

"Ms. Greystone, what does my having a body have to do with anything? You've been doing this job for sixty years, you said. Why would I act like I'm in charge?"

Well, here's a new one. I've only known Ms. Greystone a couple of minutes, but I'm pretty sure this doesn't happen to her often. She's speechless. Her mouth is even hanging open.

Great, what did I just do?

"Oh dear," she says and disappears.

Chapter 7

IT'S HOURS AFTER MS. GREYSTONE left, and if anything, I'm more anxious than before.

I've had no contact with anyone I know today, given no idea what to expect, no clue what is going on. Would Marsh find me if I left my apartment? Eventually, I stop caring. They have me under some kind of surveillance, so I'm sure they'll track me down.

But I don't fare any better over at Warner's. Even Annabelle avoids me. I sit at the bar to ask Warner a few questions, but he snarls so fiercely I'm worried he will jump the counter to get at me. He doesn't want me scaring other customers away, so I slink back to my corner for a while before leaving.

I wander the streets for a few hours, but I don't find anything that holds my interest. A few times I think I see someone following me, but I can't ever pinpoint who, where, or even if it is true. After a while, I give up and go back to my apartment. Maybe I can get some books or something. No TV to watch, no internet to troll, no news, no forums. No music to listen to. No games to play. No school classes to attend. No friends. No Amber. I don't even have a clock to stare at. The minutes crawl by and become hours.

Right as I begin to doze off, I get startled awake.

"Yo, kid! Get your ass down here!" I hear Marsh's bellow from below, and I realize this may be the first time I've ever looked forward to seeing him. What's wrong with me?

But the wait is over. Finally. I look out the window, down to the street. Marsh is at the curb in front of my building, standing next to an enormous, black horse-drawn coach. Dread rolls off the carriage in waves, poised rather than parked. A vehicle has never filled me with fear before, and I include some very sketchy food trucks on that list. A corpse I don't recognize is sitting on a seat in the front of the coach. Even other people move away from the coach as they pass, staying on the far side of the sidewalk. I shudder. It feels like I can see the stare from those damned horses through the walls of my room. Marsh cups his hands around his mouth and yells even louder, "Shake a leg, dammit!"

I wave that I hear him and give one last glance around my place. I guess I'm ready. I can't believe I'm going to walk towards Marsh rather than run away from him.

I'm wearing the best fitting of the clothes they gave me. It's nearly identical to the suit I was wearing yesterday, just a slightly lighter shade of gray. I have a black, stained tie that I manage to twist and loop into something that passes for a knot. My shoes are slightly too large, made of worn black leather and thin soles, the kind that walked hundreds of miles a lifetime ago.

I don't generally obsess about my appearance. My hair is short enough that it only takes seconds to comb it. I try and shave, not because I want a baby-smooth face, but because I can't stand an itchy beard.

My badge goes into a pocket, but I don't know what I'm supposed to do with the massive sidearm they've given me. I just hold it in one hand and head down the stairs. I'm glad I have it. I turn a corner on my way down and see some of my neighbors making their way up. I resist the urge to run in fear at shambling corpses approaching me in the gloom. I wave with my empty hand, but they can't help but see the gun even in the dim light. I'm not sure if it's the wave or the weapon, but they give me ample room as I pass, glaring sullenly at me. This is about as friendly an interaction as I ever have with my neighbors.

I cross the dust-choked foyer and walk out into the humid night air. The coach Marsh is leaning on is impressive, even bigger than it looked from above. It's tall. I'm pretty sure I could stand upright inside. It's completely enclosed, matte black with ornate black metallic trim. There are no insignias or markings to indicate what it is. It's as wide as a bus, with a set of steps that leads up a single flat-paneled door. The wooden wheels are lined with a metal of some kind and are as big around as I am tall. There is a padded bench on the front, where the driver can sit with room to spare. The driver is wearing a navy-blue uniform with brass buttons and shoulder things. What are those called? Epaulets? He's got a badge similar to mine pinned on his chest. He sits, staring at me with a bored look on his face, holding the reins to the horses. I say hi to him, nod in my best friendly manner, and his expression doesn't change in the slightest.

I take a second look at the horses. All four of them, nearly identical. They're huge. I've been around a few horses in my life. Mostly at state fairs and the like, and I've seen the occasional thoroughbred up close; I know how big they can get. But I've never seen any this massive. They are not just tall, they are solid, muscular, a Clydesdale's big brother. One turns its glowing red eyes to regard me, like it knows I'm looking. Maybe I'm reading more into it, but I'm pretty sure it's not impressed by what it sees. I keep clear and take a step back. It snorts, sounding amused, and dismisses me with a swish of its tail.

Marsh is leaning against the wagon, waiting. He's got an old, dark gray suit on. Maybe these crumpled, stained suits are standard issue here. I don't know if he's wearing the same shirt from last night or not, but it looks familiar and doesn't smell any fresher. He's definitely wearing the same tie, though. The stains are in the same pattern. I didn't realize a fedora could get that wrinkled or crumpled. He's puffing on a cigar, the cloud he's exhaling mixing with the nearby fog. Maybe Warner sells the things; it's got a similar swampy funk to it that I recognize.

This guy has to weigh at least twice what I do. Maybe he's related to the horse. He's wide at the shoulders, and his biceps are about the size of my thighs. His hands could palm my head. And he hasn't gotten any prettier overnight.

"Marsh," I greet him, warily. I have no idea what to expect from tonight.

"Holy Hell, Green. I've seen old women duck-waddle to the crapper faster than you. You ready for this? You're not goin' to wet yourself or embarrass me, are you?"

"Yes. No!" Dammit. "Yes, I'm ready. No, I won't piss myself. Let's go."

He opens the door for me, but as I try to step past him, his hand slams against my chest, stopping me. He pulls my badge out, flips it open and stuffs it back in my suit pocket, so the shield is hanging over the top and visible. He nods, and I pull myself inside. It would be cliché to say I feel like I'm climbing into a coffin. It's dark, uncomfortable, confining. Marsh enters behind me, closes the door. We sit in pitch black for a few seconds before I hear the hiss of gas and an interior light dimly grows brighter. His open eye reflects the light, looking like it's glowing in the gloom. Where do they keep the gas for these things? I'm guessing in a tank underneath the back seat. I try not to think of exactly how big of a bomb I'm sitting on right now.

There are two benches inside the coach, facing each other. Behind the back bench is a large cage made of heavy iron bars. Shackles are bolted to the walls and floor inside it. Part of the seat is attached to the door of the cage, so it can fold up when the door is opened. Marsh sits on the bench facing backward, so I sit opposite him.

He doesn't say anything, just stares at me. I try not to squirm under his scrutiny.

"So," I venture. Marsh puffs on his cigar, filling the space with smoke. I stifle a cough. He might not have to breathe, but I do. However, it's better than the alternative—sitting in a sealed box with just Marsh's corpse stinking it up.

"Look, Marsh. Tell me what is going on."

I don't know what I'm expecting from him. I hate to sound like I'm whining, but seriously I need to wrap my head around this situation. He chews on his cigar a bit, puffs out another cloud. "OK. We got a few minutes to kill. What do you want to know?"

I'm taken off-guard. He's really going to give me some answers? Great, now I don't know where to start. Every single question I've had over the past few weeks comes rushing to me all at once.

After a brief pause, I ask the one that's been bothering me the most. "Where are we? You say I'm working for the Necropolis PD. Is this place called Necropolis?"

Marsh chuckles, a chilling sound that bounces around the inside of the coach, trapped, unable to escape. He knocks on the side of the coach, and we lurch forward as the coach pulls away from the curb. I can't see where we're going, but I can feel the rattle and roll of the vehicle. The motion of the coach mixes with corpse stink and cigar smoke, and it's going to be a miracle if I don't throw up before the ride is over.

"This place has had a lot of names through the years,

kid. It's existed in some form or another for as long as we've needed to hide. Depends on who you ask. I've heard it called Meridian, officially. Though you'll hear folks call it the Boneyard, purgatory, heaven, hell—any other number of places from myth. Necropolis works as good as any."

"Meridian or just Necropolis. OK." I think for a second or two, gather my thoughts. "Where is it?"

His eye twinkles with amusement. Another cloud of smoke streams out. "Now, that's a good question. Let me ask you one. Where did you come from to get here?"

He knows the answer. He's asked me this many times before, but I humor him now. "Nebraska. Downtown Lincoln. I found a door under a bridge. I was dragged down a tunnel that just kept going. I ended up here."

Marsh nods in understanding. "Lincoln. That's one of the open doorways to the Outside."

"Outside? Outside what?"

Marsh leans forward, smoke creeping out both nostrils. He speaks softly, like he's sharing a secret, though the deepness of his voice is enough to rattle the teeth in my jaw.

"This place is outside where you know, kid. It's a part of the world, but nowhere most people can find." He waves the hand holding the cigar expansively. "It exists in between, underneath, and alongside everything that you know. It's made up of forgotten places, dark corners, underground spaces. Unexplored areas of the world, abandoned buildings, and homes. Forests, caves, tunnels, cities below cities below forgotten cities. It's where the dead come to live—the dead who don't die, anyway."

I don't know quite what to say to that. That may be more words than I've ever heard Marsh string together at once. Marsh leans back as the coach turns around a corner. I have to grip the armrest tightly to keep from sliding along the bench.

"Living people ain't supposed to be able to find us here. It's hidden from living eyes. Magic and whatnot. So how you got here," he eyes me suspiciously. "How you got here is a mystery."

We've gone through this line of questioning many times. Clearly, he still doesn't accept my pleas of ignorance.

"Wait. You told me *what* Meridian is. Not where."

Marsh shakes his head. "No, I answered you. It's a mish-mash of forgotten places. Here they are together, but they are miles apart back in your world. You came here through a hidden doorway in Nebraska. But walk a few blocks over in Meridian, and you're at some abandoned buildings no one living could find in Brooklyn. Next to that, there's a whole neighborhood from Paris, or a subway line no one remembers from Cleveland, or a bomb shelter built and forgotten in Moscow. South African slums, shanty towns, swamp villages. Our city here is made up of all the places you living people don't remember no more. Either all record of a place has been lost, or we've helped the process along to claim some places. There are a few doorways out, but they're all hidden with glamours and magicks, or they're guarded by guys like us."

Glamours and magicks. I'd normally think that was a joke, but I am listening to a talking corpse. I'm willing to give him the benefit of the doubt. I'm going to have to accept that just maybe, magic is a real thing.

What else do I want to ask? I've already decided I don't want to know where my food is coming from. I could ask him about glamours or magic, but a few other questions are still looming in my mind. The most important one almost escapes my lips, but I clamp my mouth shut. No. That question . . . that question is too important.

Instead, I ask, "When do I get to go home?"

Marsh smiles and says nothing. I could force the issue, I suppose. Ask again. Pester him until he answers. But his silence pretty much sums up what I feared. I'm not going anywhere.

"What are you going to do to me?" I finally ask.

"Well, now," he says, his smile widening, showing me teeth. "That depends on how good a cop you turn out to be."

The coach slows to a halt, and two knocks sound on the top. We've arrived at wherever he's taking me, and my window for asking questions is over.

"Wait! I still have a lot to ask you. How big is this place? What am I supposed to do? What about magic? How can you possibly think it's a good idea to make me a cop?"

Marsh stands up and extinguishes the light. In the darkness, right before he opens the door, he says, "Just don't screw up. I'll tell you what's what, and hopefully, you'll still be breathing in the morning. Don't sweat it."

Chapter 8

I STEP DOWN INTO A HIGH-WALLED courtyard. It reminds me of a castle. It's full of noise, the stink of horses and bodies, and people shuffling around. The area is maybe as wide and deep as half a football field, but it feels cramped. The walls seem to lean in, looming over us. At the top of the walls, about twenty feet up, officers walk on patrol. They are all carrying guns similar to mine, and a couple also have massive two-handed contraptions that look like rifles attached to a heavy rope net backpack. There are several coaches like the one we used here, some parked, some driving in and out of tunnels leading further into a complex of featureless buildings and bunkers. A group of four officers climbs down out of a coach like ours, only they are holding poles attached to chains and a harness wrapped around a prisoner of some sort. Each pole is about eight feet long and is hooked to some part of this tangle of chains and straps wrapped around the guy in the center. He's struggling, cursing something fierce, but isn't strong enough to resist the four officers steering him into a door on the side of the building.

The building looks like a madhouse run by its patients. It

is falling apart, has broken windows, and doors on the upper stories open out into thin air.

Marsh closes the door to our coach and nods to the driver. It pulls away, headed further into the complex. A few dozen officers are shuffling around, tending horses, guiding groups to doorways, running errands. Hardly anyone pays me any mind, though a few either nod to Marsh or veer out of his way.

I look back through the gateway where we entered. It reaches up to the top of the wall. Two massive doors sit open on either side of the doorway, and they look strong enough to repel an avalanche. They must be a good three feet thick. Outside the gate, a bridge at least one hundred feet long spans a fog-covered river. I can't tell for sure, but I'm pretty sure this place has a moat. As far as I can see, the bridge is the only access to this place.

"Are we at war with somebody?" I ask.

Marsh stops, looks at me puzzled. "What do you mean?"

"I think I just saw a moat." I struggle to put it into words, gesturing around me. "The walls. The gate. The guns. Are there some sieges or something going on?"

Marsh looks at everything I've indicated, then smiles broadly at me. The cigar flares as he sucks in a deep chuckle. "No, but that's a good guess. These walls aren't here to protect us; they're to protect the rest of the city. They're here to keep things IN. We can lock this place down and do our damnedest to make sure nothing gets out."

I stare in trepidation at the large building in front of us. I can't wait to see what's inside.

"Follow me," he says and marches towards the building at the center of the courtyard. We climb a short, broad flight of stone steps and approach the massive Victorian edifice. It's four stories tall, looks like it's a couple hundred years old and should have been torn down decades ago. There are a few barred windows and a portcullis to slam down over the front door, and as we pass through the doorway, I notice the walls are around five feet thick. I swallow nervously and stick close to Marsh. The entrance hall double-doors are wide enough to let four people walk through comfortably, but others have to squeeze through on the sides as Marsh strides confidently through the middle.

I walk across slick, yellow and black checkered tiles following in Marsh's wake. At first, I think he's taking me towards the immense door on the back wall—the one with reinforced bars, locks, and guards in place in front of it. But he swerves to the right, towards less intimidating areas. This main room is tall, expansive, and open. There is a reception counter to our left with a line of people waiting. The place is crowded, with dead bodies packed in tightly, glaring irritably at everyone around them, and with ghosts floating through walls and bodies alike. Even Marsh is forced to slow down as we make our way to a wide polished staircase on the other side and ascend to the second floor.

I wonder again, why do they want me here? They can't possibly think I'd make a good cop. When I first got here, when I was captured and interrogated, they'd asked me what I did. I told them. I'm a student, studying art for now. Digital graphics. That can't possibly be the reason they have given me a job.

Up here on the second floor, it's less crowded. There is one massive room, desks arranged neatly in rows from one side to the other. Each desk has a small gas lamp, one chair behind and two in front, and all are manned. Ghosts float up and down the rows, and no one is freaking out about it. I mean, I want to freak out about it. There are GHOSTS.

Decrepit and decaying officers in suits and ties are sitting at their desks talking to people seated in front of them, some typing, some writing on clipboards. Some have their feet propped up, hat pulled down over their eyes, napping despite the noise. The clacking of typewriter keys is jarring, distracting over the susurration of voices whispering to each other. This is probably the loudest room I've heard since ending up here.

File cabinets line the walls, papers are stacked on every flat surface. Every aisle is narrow enough that two people can't walk side-by-side. If two of them are walking towards each other, one has to duck into an adjoining aisle to let the other slide by. My skin starts to crawl, imagining having to jostle through that crowd of dead bodies shifting around me.

I don't get it. Why is everyone working? I mean, I've always figured that death was the end of all that. I thought . . . I dunno. I thought I'd sit on a cloud in peaceful bliss, staring out over the earth, whatever leisurely activity it is that angels do. But instead, I'm finding out there's more paperwork, more bureaucracy, more structure.

Marsh doesn't pause but leads the way towards some offices located along the back wall. I just follow behind him, ignoring the many stares directed my way. Even here, people pause in their routine to take a look at me.

The offices have windows looking out into the main room, and doors that are mostly open. But there is a lot more space over here, and I let out a sigh of relief. We head to the office at the end of the row, in the corner. Most of these offices look to have several desks in them, common rooms shared by a group of officers. As I noticed downstairs, the ghosts don't always bother with the doors; one floats out of the wall ahead of us. The offices mostly look the same, but the one he takes me to feels vastly different.

It has a closed door, and Marsh knocks and opens it without waiting for a response. He leads me in.

It is much darker here. There is a large window looking out over the bridge leading back to the city. Massive velvet curtains hang on either side of the window, behind an enormous desk made out of some heavy dark wood. It looks as much like an altar as it does a desk. The staining on it is such a dark brown it looks black. It is intricate and ornate, big enough to run laps on. And it only barely distracts me from the room's occupant.

"Hey, Captain, I got him," Marsh announces, clapping a hand down on my shoulder that almost crumples me to the ground. "Jake Green, this is Captain Radu."

The man is standing with his back to me, staring out the window. As he turns to us, my brain recognizes that, while I can see a nice clear reflection of the room in the dark window, and Marsh towering over me and my own wild eyes, what I do not see is a reflection of the captain. I put together that this must mean that the captain is a vampire.

Then I take a good look at the captain, and I realize I already know him. I've met this vampire before. Panic overtakes me. I try to turn and run, but Marsh's hand keeps me rooted in place. I struggle briefly, futilely. The captain moves forward, sweeping his arm towards a comfortable chair in front of his desk, and I lean into Marsh, as far from the captain as possible. The voice crawls into my ears in a thick accent. "*Bienvenu*, Mr. Green. Please have a seat."

He's wearing a blue pin-striped suit that's seen better days. It is patched, faded, soiled. His shirt has stains around the collar, but the blue tie is new, a large red ruby tie-tack keeping it firmly in place.

His head looks a rotting hard-boiled egg, bald and veiny, the ears are pointed, twisted. His pupils are beady red dots in the black sea of his eyes. One eye is weeping blood, a small trickle following the track of dried blood from previous tears. His smile reveals way too many small, sharp, browning teeth. Power radiates off him like heat waves. His frame is slight, slightly hunched, but his presence dwarfs my own and is nearly overpowering.

It's him.

I've seen him before. And I have to squeeze my eyes shut for a second because everything is just too much right now. Too much pain. Too much memory.

It was the captain. The creature. The thing. The thing that dragged me screaming into the darkness and Marsh's waiting hands.

One Month Ago . . .

Marsh has been asking me the same series of questions over and over again for days.

"How did you find the doorway under the bridge?"

When he doesn't like my answer, he leans in ominously closer. He hasn't hurt me. Much. A punch or a slap here or there. But he always feels like he's about to.

"How did you follow Miller?"

I can't answer that one either. Miller is the name of the thing I saw kill the driver. Because I somehow ended up killing him, they think I had planned to do it.

"How long have you known about us?"

It doesn't matter when I protest or declare my innocence as truthfully and earnestly as I can. And it really doesn't help matters when Miller shows up again.

The vampire I thought I killed walks into the room where I am imprisoned. I am tied to a chair, bruised, cold, hurting all over. I thrash against my bonds as much as I can, trying to escape, but Marsh has tied the rope too tightly to allow me to wriggle out of them.

Miller smiles, exposing teeth that could make a shark envious. He seems healthy, uninjured, dead but still mobile, as if I had never jammed a shaft of wood into his chest, his heart. His eyes tell me I will not survive much longer.

"We meet again." He grins wider, impossibly wide.

How? How is this possible? He would have said more, but then another vampire walks in.

All concerns about Marsh vanish. I wish I could scoot my chair away or hide in some way.

"Bon. Explain it to me again," the new vampire commands. *The accent is thick, difficult to understand.*

I blink in confusion, wondering what he means until I realize he isn't talking to me.

"He's a hunter, clearly," Miller begins. "He must have been biding his time, waiting for me. He was on me as soon as I stumbled out into the world. I ran from him, but he managed to follow me somehow."

"Is this true?" Marsh asks me, slapping me on the head. "You some kind of vampire hunter?"

"What? No! Of course not!" I plead. "He's lying!"

"Oh, please! If you hadn't found me when you did, he would have destroyed me for certain."

The vampire clicks his tongue doubtfully. "One so strong as you, Miller?"

I hear the sarcasm in his voice, but Miller seems oblivious to it. "Let's kill him before he can do any more harm!"

The vampire appears to consider the request.

"I swear, I don't know what's going on here," *I plead.* "I'm no hunter. Please, I just want to go home."

They ignore me. Finally, Radu turns to Miller. "Vas-y. Go now. We will decide what to do with this one."

Miller looks like he will argue but glances at Radu and then Marsh and appears to think better of it. He walks uncertainly out of the room.

I wait until the door closes. "He's lying! I just stumbled across him. I wasn't hunting him."

The vampire looks surprised. "Lying? Bien sûr. Of course he's lying. He will be dealt with."

"The Pit?" Marsh asks, and the vampire nods absently.

"Oui. One or two bodies we could have overlooked, but not killing that many."

The vampire focuses on me again. "But I'm curious. Marsh, perhaps we have been asking the wrong questions."

"What do you mean?" Marsh asks, looking sullen that his interrogation techniques are being called into question.

"Tell me, boy. There is something strange about you. Something, comment dit-on? Different. What talents do you have?" the vampire asks me, his English and French both equally confusing to me.

What does he mean?

"Talents?"

He leans closer, and the red spots of his eyes glow more fiercely.

"I can draw OK," I say hesitantly. "I can speak some Spanish. Like that?"

"Go on," the creature says, encouragingly.

"I don't know! Just tell me what you want me to say!"

"What else?" He looms closer. I can't back away.

"I can . . ." I search my mind desperately. "I can play the guitar? I can solve a Rubix Cube in a few minutes. Not a world record or anything, but pretty fast."

"A what?" Marsh mutters.

Radu shrugs. "Yes, good. What else like that?" the captain asks, leaning back like I am finally showing some promise. I am so confused.

"I can do a good Three Card Monte. Some magic tricks."

"Yes?"

What else? What else can I say?

"I have a good bullshit detector," my voice heavy with equal parts sarcasm and desperation.

The vampire turns to Marsh, puzzled. "What is this he says?"

"He means he can tell when someone's lying to him," Marsh explains. *The creature leans closer still, and the smile that blossoms on his face is terrifying.*

"Yes! This is it exactly, I think."

Marsh looks at his companion in confusion. I breathe a sigh of relief, a little of my tension escapes out of me. For the first time, I've given them an answer they seem to approve, though, for the life of me, I don't understand why they like it.

The relief is short-lived. The vampire reaches out so quickly I almost don't see it. He grabs my hair and torques my head painfully to one side. He leans in and bites painfully into my neck.

He drinks.

I thrash and kick until blackness overtakes me.

Chapter 9

My neck throbs, remembered pain lancing me where he had bitten me weeks earlier. I reflexively start to raise the gun in my right hand, but Marsh quickly knocks it back down. The captain looks at me suspiciously. Marsh is staring at me like I'm a puppy who can't figure out the trick he wants me to do. He finally pushes me forward. I slide into the seat, gripping the arm hard with my free hand while trying to balance the gun in my lap. The last time I was in a room alone with these two was unpleasant. And obviously I hadn't made the connection he was the captain.

"Looking good today, Captain. You do something with your hair?" Marsh says with no trace of sarcasm. I look at him like he's crazy.

The captain waves the comment away but looks pleased, like it was a real compliment. "Thank you, Detective." He walks back around the desk and slowly sits back down in his tall-backed chair, keeping his eyes fixed on me the entire time.

"So," he says, contemplating me, head tipping slightly to one side. He says the word slowly, the "s" sounding like a snake's hiss. His accent is so thick I have to concentrate on his every word. "Are you prepared to help us out in our fair city, Mr. Green?"

I nod nervously.

"I actually have a question about that one, Captain," Marsh says. "Why exactly do we need his help? Or even want it?"

The captain is silent for a moment, leaning back in his chair. Finally, he says, "Jacob Green. When you walked through the door under the bridge, what did you see?"

I groan. Not this again. "Look, I've answered these questions already dozens of times."

The captain's smile doesn't reach his eyes. "Humor me, Mr. Green."

Fine. I think back. "The room had some machines. An entrance to the sewers covered by a grate. Oh, yeah, and a stack of bodies piled up against a wall and a couple of vampires trying to kill me."

The captain turns to Marsh as if I had just made his point for him. Marsh looks as confused as I am. Speaking to Marsh, the captain says, "You were given a task to observe the entrances to our city from the outside. *Et alors?* You examined the glamours? They are still intact, yes?"

"Yeah, Captain. They all check out fine. Mortals shouldn't be able to see through 'em."

The captain nods. "*Oui.* As you say, the glamours are intact. The doorways, that pile of bodies, even Miller should not have been visible to him. And yet here he is."

He turns back to me, eyes not blinking, only analyzing. Images of cats and mice flicker across my mind. I'm feeling very much like prey right now. "If my suspicions are correct, he will be crucial to the murders we are investigating. We shall see. In the meantime, let us get him started in his duties. Ms. Greystone?"

Huh? Wait, he's looking past me now. I turn around, and

Greystone floats through the wall behind me, just behind my shoulder. I feel the chill against my back. That's creepy. I didn't hear her at all.

"Let us get you attuned to our new detective here, and we shall see how he does."

Chapter 10

THE ATTUNEMENT PROCESS, OR RITUAL I guess they call it, doesn't take long. When I think of a ritual, I expect to see dark rooms, black robes, candles all over, with choruses of chanting. Like a bad album cover.

It starts here, with Captain Radu asking me to scoot my chair forward and lean closer to his desk. He pulls out a crystal about the size of a softball. It is a milky teal color, rough and blocky, like a hunk of quartz. I expect it to shimmer or glow in some mystical way, but it sits on the desk like a lump of ordinary rock. It's an ugly paperweight more than anything. Ms. Greystone floats next to me, her eyes fixed on the crystal, focusing her entire attention on it. I look at the captain, then at Marsh. What am I supposed to do? Radu elaborately points at the crystal with a ragged, long fingernail.

"Look into the crystal, Mr. Green," he instructs.

I shrug uneasily. "I am looking at it."

"No." He shakes his head slowly, but his eyes never stray from looking at mine. "Look *into* it. Cast your gaze into its depths. *Regarde là-dedans, à l'intérieur.* Not just 'at' it."

Sure. I stare at a crystal on the desk in front of me, trying

not to blink. Maybe if I look long enough, I'll see something
stir to life in its depths. Captain Radu mumbles some words I
don't understand, harsh, guttural sounds. Then comes the expected chanting. I'd like to think it's some magical language,
but for all I know, it could be German or Pig Latin. It lasts
the space of a few blinks. The captain falls silent, appraising
me with a satisfied expression. Ms. Greystone looks smug.
Marsh looks bored. I scan myself internally.

Do I feel any different? No, not really.

"*Voilà.* That is all. It is complete," Radu says, grabbing the
crystal and putting it back into a desk drawer. "From what I
have been able to ascertain, the Ritual of Strengthening and
the Loyalty Ceremony will have no effect on a mortal, so we
will forgo these."

I look down at my hands, flex my fingers. They feel exactly the same as always. I try to hide my disappointment. What
is going on here? I would have felt more bonding if we'd all
put our hands together and shouted, "One for all and all for
one."

Is the room darker than before? Even though the office
has a large window looking out over the city, the clouds are
pretty thick. The black curtains are held back on either side
of the window, heavy folds of thick material pulled out of the
way, so they are not the cause of the office's lack of light. The
gaslights overhead give the room a soft glow, and the kerosene lamp on the desk provides enough light to read by.

Wait.

Out of the corner of my eyes, shadows move around
Radu. But they look normal when I turn my attention to
them. I look away and then look back to him a couple of
times. It seems like shadows are building around him, gathering to him. Then they are gone.

Or maybe I'm just trying to find something that is different no matter how weird it might seem. The captain's eyes

flick away from me. "Detective Marsh, take him to meet the team."

"Wait, what was that supposed to . . ." I start, then stop. As I move, I can sense Ms. Greystone behind me. I know where she is without seeing her. I turn to look at her. Then I close my eyes. Sure enough, I can feel her in my mind. I have a sense of where she is, how she is feeling. This is weird. I open my eyes to see her looking back at me, amused.

She arches her eyebrow at me. She's expecting my next questions, clearly, but I ask them anyway. "Ms. Greystone, what does this mean? Can you read my thoughts? Can I turn it off?"

"We can sense each other's direction and general distance," she explains primly. "If you concentrate, you should be able to sense my demeanor. You'll note that it is not impressed. If you mentally 'shout' at me, I should be able to hear you. It shouldn't take long before we can both fade into the background of each other's thoughts and only be noticeable upon concentration." She pauses and shrugs her shoulders. "Of course, we've never attuned someone to a living mortal before, so there may be some unexpected turns."

Ms. Greystone turns to the captain. "If that will be all, Captain Radu, I'll be away on my tasks." She nods smartly, turns, and floats quickly through the wall and away. All three of us watch her go. Great, a ghost will know where I'm at and how I'm feeling all times of day or night. That can't possibly go wrong somehow.

The leash is back on me, it seems. Any hopes I might have of planning an escape have been dashed. If she can sense where I am at any time, or even what I'm feeling, I'll never be able to get away.

I turn back to Marsh and the captain and realize in surprise that they're both staring at the wall where Greystone just passed through.

"Damn," Marsh mutters. "She is a knockout."

Captain Radu mutters something under his breath, shrugging. I'm guessing vampires have different concerns than the physical appearance of ghosts. Either way, I am totally floored by their reactions.

A ghost? A knockout? I think of Ms. Greystone's hair wrapped in a bun, her plain clothes, and her disapproving scowl. Then there's the chill when she's around, and the involuntary shudder I get from standing next to a ghost. She's attractive, but only under the right conditions, like if there's ever a time when she won't be looking down her nose disdainfully at me. Or creeping the hell out of me. Or if she weren't a ghost.

"How did the kid rate Greystone?" Marsh asks the captain. "Why isn't she going to one of the others in our squad?"

"We do not have enough of the incorporeals strong enough to be liaisons, as you well know. And I wish to see if she can work in that capacity with a mortal. If it is indeed possible, I wanted one of our best liaisons for Mr. Green. There are several questions I'm hoping her years of expertise can answer." He turns his gaze to me and looks at me in a way that makes me feel very uneasy. Calculating. Weighing my worth. I try to deflect their scrutiny.

"Wait, if she's been doing this for a long time," I say, "what happened to her last partner? Where is he at? I'd like to ask him a few questions."

Captain Radu looks at me levelly. Marsh stares. Neither are in any hurry to answer.

"Don't worry about that right now, kid. Let's meet the team."

Marsh grabs me by the shoulder again and steers me out of the room. The captain's eyes bore a hole through me as we leave and walk to an office a few doors down. I sigh in relief to get away from him. I don't realize how tense I am until the captain is out of sight. Greystone is out in the main room, I feel a strange tickling sensation in my brain that lets me know exactly where she is.

We walk into a new office, one with eight desks crammed back-to-back in two rows of four. Papers are piled on desktops. File cabinets line one wall, some with drawers open and stuffed full with files and loose documents. A chalkboard and corkboard are stashed in a corner, ready to be rolled out on a moment's notice—every century or so by the looks of them. Smoke curls lazily in the air from ashtrays heaped with cigar and cigarette butts. Clearly, they don't worry about cancer anymore. Two of the desks are empty. The occupants of the other six all turn to look at us.

"This is Detective Green," Marsh announces, slapping me in the back and almost knocking me off my feet. "Being detectives and all, I'm guessing you've figured out the kid here is a living, breathing mortal. Don't eat him. Let's get this off to a good start."

Detective? People are going to call me Detective Green now? Hopefully, they won't be snickering while they do it. It doesn't even seem real. It is more ironic. Like when my friends would call me genius after I had just done something stupid. Great.

Marsh points at the first pair of detectives. "Burchard and Meints." The first, Burchard, is slightly taller than me, stocky. Like everyone in the room, he has a sour expression on his face, like he's pissed I'm even breathing the air around him. His yellowing eyes have examined me thoroughly, and he's clearly found me wanting. His hair is dark, cut short, his skin is greener than most, pulled taut over his cheeks and jaw. His mustache is thick, almost completely hiding his mouth. He might not be as physically intimidating as Marsh, but he's still plenty scary. He has a vest on underneath his suit coat, a chain attached to a pocket-watch in a pocket. The other,

Meints, is several inches taller than me. He looks older, more distinguished than the others. His gaze is not friendly, which is reinforced by an obvious sneer directed my way. He dismisses me almost as soon as he lays eyes on me. His desk is piled with books on philosophy and various sciences. Where Burchard's skin is smooth, Meints' is wrinkled, like twisting vines. They both grunt and turn back to their desks. Looks like I've managed to give another good first impression.

"Finnegan and Clark," Marsh says, indicating the next two. Clark salutes me with a grin. He's the first person I've seen here who is actually dressed nicely. His suit is clean, pressed, his shirt free of holes and stains. His hair is black, combed and full. If it weren't for the exposed tendon and muscle on his face, where his partially rotted skin is missing, he would pass for a living human. Finnegan is thin. His clothes hang on him like they are on a hanger. His hair is short and so sparse that I can't determine its color against his skin. He looks completely uninterested, fixing me with a bored stare that cuts right through me. My skin crawls. I think he'd have the same look on his face if I were screaming in pain. I keep my nervous smile in place. Neither of them says anything.

"Armstrong and Kim," Marsh introduces the last two. Kim is Asian, about my height, thin. I can't get a good read on his demeanor. He looks at papers on his desk emotionlessly, without care or interest. He just waits. Analyzing. The skin around his left eye has been stripped away, which makes his gaze intense. Armstrong is easier to read. His hair is balding on top, and what remains is long, curly, and almost covers up the patches of skull I can see underneath. He's a big guy, tall and wide. Solid. He's nowhere near the Marsh-side of the size spectrum, but definitely the largest of the other detectives. His hat sits on his desk, crumpled, looking like it has been run over a few times or left out in the rain. It's remarkably similar to Marsh's. On the surface, he isn't paying attention to anything at all. He is scribbling in a notepad. Sketching, I realize. Doodling. I try to see what he's drawing, but he angles it out of the way of my view.

Marsh wanders over to one of the empty desks and sits down in the chair, which groans in protest. The chair has already been reinforced with some steel supports, and it's still having trouble.

"You guys ready?" he asks the others. Not wanting to be the only one standing, I go sit down at what I assume is now my desk. No one complains, so I'm guessing it's alright.

"Remind me why we have to be nice to lunch, here?" Burchard asks, pointing at me. He looks at me coldly.

"Captain's orders," Marsh replies. "So, suck it up, or take it up with him."

Detective Burchard and the others scowl but say nothing further.

"Let's hit it, kid," Marsh says to me. "I've been telling them you know when people are lying to you. Dazzle us."

Eleven Weeks Ago . . .

My eyelids scrape like sandpaper across my eyes, and I blink rapidly in confusion for several seconds. I never expected to wake up again. Some man, some thing had attacked me. My head is still spinning as I blearily look around me, struggling to stand. Attempts to stand repeatedly fail as I fall back into a metal chair. Looking down in confusion, I see ropes tying me down. A single dim bulb high overhead lights the room, and a handful of animated corpses surround me, looming over me, studying me with very unfriendly faces. Seeing a group of dead faces staring at me, that wakes me up fully and instantly.

Sweating, I grip the wobbly folding chair so hard I fear my fingers are going to snap. Babble erupts incoherently from my lips as the monsters shuffle closer to me. I hear my own screaming and crying.

Marsh is here. He towers over the others, a hulking silhouette in the dim light. Occasionally I see a gleam from his one good eye. I want so desperately to get away from him, but there is nowhere I can go.

These walking corpses close in around me and start asking me questions. Their voices wheeze out from dry throats, from behind broken and jagged teeth. Some are debating killing me. Some are sniffing at me, salivating. They are asking all kinds of questions. How did I get here? How had I found my way through the doors? One of them grabs me by the scruff of my neck and picks me up in the air with one arm, letting me dangle still tied to the chair as Marsh leans in close. Marsh clocks me one, and I lose track of time.

"Spill it," Marsh says once the world comes back into focus. He's already bloodied my nose, and it is throbbing with pain. I'd blacked out for a while. I don't know what to say. I can feel my nose pulse with every beat of my heart, taste my blood as it trickles into my open mouth gasping for breath.

They are talking about eating me. Eating my body while I watch. I am in full-blown panic at this point.

"Start talking, or I start eating. You right-handed or left-handed? Which will you miss the least?"

I would say anything right now, anything they want to hear. But something surprises me, driving through even my terror.

Marsh is lying. I'm sure of it.

He has no intention of eating me, regardless of my answer. This confuses me, and the confusion starts in some weird way to calm me down. Why would he lie? I mean, why bother?

But I've always been able to do this, even when I was growing up. Some kids are good at sports, some kids can sing or play music. Others are good at puzzles or math. For me, I've always been able to tell when someone was lying to me. I got so good *at reading people correctly that it just became second nature. I could tell when my brother was lying about breaking one of my toys. I recognized when one of my mom's boyfriends was pulling my leg. I knew when my girlfriend was sleeping with my best friend.*

I even knew when my mom was lying.

Between the pain and the terror, I check out for a minute, thinking back.

Dad was long gone. My older brother was serving his first stint in prison, so it was just my mom and me. I was going to start middle school in the fall, so that made me eleven or twelve. It was a lazy Saturday. The rain outside was intense, so I was sitting on the floor looking at some Aquaman comic. I had cleared myself a small patch of carpet, making it devoid of debris and was quietly reading while my mom was ignoring me nearby on the couch. She was getting cozy with her friend Jack Daniels, the bottle pretty much a constant companion, and was watching some forgettable movie.

We had been sitting like this for some time when, out of the blue, I'd asked, "Do you like having me around, Mom?" No particular reason, just a dumb thing a kid asks to ask to fill the silence in the air as the movie ended.

"Of course, honey," she's said, not paying much attention to me, taking another healthy swallow from her bottle. And I was stunned.

She was lying.

I could tell she didn't mean what she had said. I don't know if it was just the hassles of raising kids by herself, the stress, the holy pain-in-the-ass I was, or the headaches my older brother gave her, but whatever it was, she didn't want it. I was about to ask her whether or not she liked me, but I stopped. Did I really want to know the answer to that? I decided then not to ask, and I never did. I was too scared to ever clarify with her.

I stared at the colors on the page in front of me, not really reading it or even seeing it. Just processing what I'd learned. This was a defining moment in my childhood. I could feel my youth rocketing away behind me as I grew up years in a single moment. My own mother didn't want to be with me. I had never thought of that as even a possibility.

That was when I knew I loved my mom.

I know that sounds weird. Knowing my mom didn't want me around made me realize I loved her. But she could have walked away. She wanted to. But she stuck with me. She stuck it out for me.

She waited a few more years after that, about the time my brother would have made parole. His disappearance robbed her of any joy I remember her having. We barely talked those last couple years. But she stayed.

She gave me until I'd graduated from high school. A few months after I moved out, she picked up and left, got to finally do what she wanted to do. She found some new ex-con to love and ran off to do who-knows-what.

She showed me what love was. Sticking with it, even when you don't want to. She earned my respect. And I learned a valuable lesson at a young age.

Don't ask questions you don't want the answers to.

Thinking of my mom calms me down. It makes me sad to think of her. I wish I could have done something to actually make her like being with me while we were together.

I meet Marsh's gaze, still wincing from the pain. They want answers. But I know he isn't going to kill me, not yet anyway.

"Why aren't you going to eat me?" I ask between gasps. Something changes in his expression. Maybe he realizes he's lost momentum with me. Maybe he thought he's gone too far and I won't recover. But he knows something has changed.

"I guess you didn't hear me right, kid. I AM going to eat

you. I'll chow down on your guts while you sit there and watch if you don't answer my questions."

"Yeah, sure," I say.

I'm light-headed, a little loopy, wondering if I should be saying this to him. I don't want to accidentally change his mind. If he is lying to me, though, that means they want something from me, which means I have at least a little value. It gives me a glimmer of hope. I grasp at that lifeline rather than drown in fear.

Marsh turns to the others and says something to them. There is a low hum at the edge of my hearing that drowns out their whispered conversation. I don't know exactly what he says to them, but they leave. Leaving me alone with Marsh.

He is looking at me strangely.

"You're not going to eat me, are you?" I ask, but I'm confident now. Certain. I'm not sure if it is this question that saves me. It keeps me alive, sure, but that's not necessarily the same thing. But when I knew Marsh was lying, when I confessed to him I knew he was lying, I knew right then I wasn't going to die.

Not that day, anyway.

Chapter 11

"Lie to me," I say.

I'm standing in the middle of another group of animated corpses, these looking no friendlier than the last group. At least Marsh isn't going to work me over with those sledgehammers he calls arms. This group of dead detectives surrounds me, irritated and unimpressed. The only noise I hear from inside the office is the crackle of tobacco burning as Burchard uses a cigar like a snorkel. Hard eyes stare back at me, measuring and assessing. Not a lot of forgiveness in those eyes, not a lot of patience either.

I was able to tell that Marsh was lying. Will I be able to do it here? Can I read dead nervous tics and expressions as well as living ones? My limited experience with cops before now has taught me they are also good at figuring out when people are lying. My little talent might not be so impressive to these guys. I'm not sure what it is supposed to prove, but if I don't blow it, maybe it will help me fit in.

Finnegan snorts derisively. "Seriously? We're going to play a game with the mortal now? What is he, our mascot?"

"I'll start," Burchard says, ignoring the other detective.

His expression doesn't change a bit. He pulls his cigar away from his lips and waves it absently.

Burchard's voice is strong, one of those voices that carry no matter how quietly he speaks. I can detect a subtle accent, British maybe? "Tell me if I'm lying. I've been reprimanded for excessive use of force more times than anyone else here."

His gaze doesn't waver; he stares me right in the eyes as he says it. His face doesn't change expression, even the cigar smoke slowly trickling out of his nostrils partially hides his face. But I'm pretty sure he's lying. Lying, and also still hiding something. I'm not positive, but I'll go with my gut here.

"That's a lie." I try to sound confident when I say it. I don't mention my other observation. I've found people don't like it when you know more about them than they want you to.

Burchard scowls but nods that I am correct. "Yeah. Marsh has me beat."

That information doesn't surprise me at all. Silence in the room. Finally, Marsh says, "Finnegan, you next."

"Fine," Finnegan says. He smiles thinly. His voice is strong, menacing. "I'd like to carve you apart one layer of skin at a time and see how long you last."

I shiver. I don't even have to think about this one. "Truth," I say. It's not the expression on his face that makes me sure of my answer; it's the unwavering attention in his eyes. Finnegan shrugs, dismissively waves an affirmative, and turns back to the papers on his desk.

Kim speaks up next. "If you are feeling confused about anything, feel free to ask me questions any time you want."

No flinch, no conscious indication he's lying, but what he's saying just doesn't sit right with me.

"Lie."

The corner of Kim's mouth turns up in a hint of a smile. He nods in acknowledgment. The room stays silent for a few moments before someone clears their throat.

Detective Meints is looking at me differently than all the others. Most are looking at me like they want to scrape me off the bottom of their shoes, but Meints is looking at me with fascination. He seems very intrigued with me.

"Marsh . . . how does one say it? Marsh 'scores' with more women than anyone in this room," Meints says. His voice is heavily accented. Eastern European somewhere, I can't quite place it. Each word is precisely enunciated and clear.

I look nervously at Marsh, then back. My brain is metaphorically gouging my eyes out at the thought of any of them getting intimate. I hesitate, not wanting to answer. I'm not sure what Marsh will do.

"Lie," I say.

Chuckles from around the room. Mock outrage from Marsh. I've questioned the standards of beauty here before, but I don't believe there is any world where Marsh's mug would attract anything. And his personality isn't doing him any favors either.

Clark pipes up. "A dog licked my testicles once. I licked his back." Groans from around the room. Clark has his feet up on his desk and looks to all the world like this is the most exciting thing he could possibly be doing.

"Dear God, please let that be a lie," Meints says, covering his eyes with his hand. Even Finnegan smiles.

"Lie," I confirm.

"OK, I didn't, but I thought about it."

"Uh, I'll pass on that one," I say, trying to keep my face blank.

Marsh looks around. "Armstrong! Join the party."

Armstrong looks up from behind black curly bangs falling into his face. "This is a waste of time, Marsh. I have important things to be doing."

"He's telling the truth," I confirm, but this just earns me a deeper frown from Armstrong.

Marsh smiles. "Six for six. I told you, boys. The kid's a keeper."

"Marsh?" Meints asks, his eyes locked on to me as he speaks. "This is most unprecedented. We haven't seen something like this for at least two centuries by my count."

"Stow that crap, Meints. He's not some science project. The captain wants his help. We'll keep him alive long enough to give it."

"But—"

Marsh leans forward in his chair. Ominously. Detective Meints relents, but not before dissecting me with his gaze. He starts writing some notes on a notepad.

Grumbles of assent clutter the air, and they all turn back to their work. Marsh turns to me, fixing me with a stare. "OK then. Let's put that talent to work and get you started on your first case."

I don't like the smile that forms on his face at all.

Chapter 12

I LEARN ONE THING QUICKLY ON my first night of work: to the undead here, one's body is more important than anything else. For me, I've taken my body for granted my whole life. I don't mean just my physical appearance, how tall I am, how much I weigh, the color of my hair, that kind of thing. I'm talking about the fact that my heart beats continually, for years without pause. My lungs, inflating, pulling oxygen into my body, pushing carbon dioxide out of my body. Things grow on my body: hair, nails. If I get hurt, my body will heal that damage.

Not so for the majority of the residents that live here.

I've noticed that less importance is placed on their material possessions. They left it all behind once when they died. They can always get more stuff. You steal someone's wallet or their horse, there are hard feelings, sure. But mess with someone's body and people come unhinged. It doesn't matter that the body is rotting, falling apart, if it stinks to high heaven, or if it is missing tissue, limbs or organs. Never mind the state of decay of the skin, what color of green or yellow or pale the pus and fluids that are leaking and oozing in various places.

The people here have survived death with their bodies more or less intact, and they won't risk any threat to the integrity of what they have left.

Which brings me to my current predicament.

The corpse sitting in the chair opposite me now, propping itself against my desk, is stinking up the entire room. And that's saying something sitting in proximity to Marsh. I don't think the funk is ever getting out of that chair.

I appear to be the only one who notices.

Typewriters clack away, and voices curse in the background. Cigarette and cigar smoke come from all corners of the office. Marsh has kept up a steady stream of profanity since we started, smashing keys on his typewriter, slamming drawers in his desk and he shows no signs of letting up. I've no idea what set him off or where exactly his ire is directed. It appears to be focused on wherever his attention happens to go. The other detectives give both of us a wide berth, no one wanting to risk being the target of Marsh's temper or getting pulled into a conversation with me.

I cough, almost gag. How can no one else notice? Maybe they do and don't care. I can't ignore it, but I do my best to power through, my stomach whimpering at the back of my throat in abject misery. I concentrate on the typewriter in front of me. The first thing I realized this morning is that I had never actually used one before and just stared at it in confusion. I've seen them, sure. I know what a typewriter is. But feeding the ribbon, using the carriage return, paying attention to where you get to the end of the page, feeding paper, and carbon copies? Carbon copies! I don't even know how they work. It all baffles me. God help me if I have to use the office mimeograph.

Something that takes getting used to is how much feedback a typewriter gives while I'm typing. Every clack of the keys causes a small tremor across my desk. Stacks of papers flutter each time I return the carriage. If I strike the keys too quickly or with too much force, a pile of papers will tip over, spilling across my desk onto the floor. The pencils on my desktop dance with each keystroke. How did anyone use these things?

I'm used to listening to music when I work. I use it to block out all the background noise. It allows me to concentrate on the task at hand with little interruption. If I'm trying to write, I'll put on something fast and hard, waves of power chords, or something industrial measured in beats per minute. If I'm working on art, modeling or animating something, I'll tend to something more gothic, mellow. But here, without electricity, the closest I can get to music is Finnegan's incessant humming or the various squeaks of gasses escaping dead bodies around me. It's only been a couple hours, and I'm just about out of my mind.

A fly buzzes lazily around the room, passes in front of my face. It hovers for a bit before I swat it away. That's one thing at least, I haven't seen any fast flies here. No need for speed evidently. It flies slowly over to the corpse in front of me and lands on its face, crawling across the bridge of the nose. It walks across the staring, unblinking eye. That's when I realize I'm staring, and this guy wasn't winning any beauty contests before he died.

Grumbling I turn back to the typewriter. My first crime report. I want to be excited, but just can't quite muster it. How many times have you tried to concentrate on something with a dead body staring across at you?

"What's the problem?" the corpse asks me indignantly. "You gonna write down my statement or what?"

"Mmm? What?"

The corpse scowls, flicks the fly off his face, and leans forward. Fluid oozes out of his hands onto the surface of my desk.

"You deaf, all of a sudden? You gonna write down my statement, I said."

I struggle to recall his name. It takes me a couple seconds.

"Mr. D . . . uh . . . Davenport! Mr. Davenport, if you want to file a complaint, then I'll take your statement. That's my job," I say.

"I have to tell you, though, I don't see the seriousness of the situation."

"Not serious?" Davenport yells. Other cold eyes glance up at us for a second before glancing away again. "Maybe because you're still breathin' it don't seem like a big deal to you. You still heal. That idiot put a staple in me! I still have the holes as proof! I got holes!"

He shoves his hand under my nose. I lurch back. My desk doesn't seem nearly big enough to use as a barrier. His hand is putrid; I can almost see the waves of stink rising from it. And sure enough, I can see two little staple holes on the back of his hand.

"You want to file an assault charge. On your boss. For stapling your hand. As you reached to snag a piece of paper from his desk. While he was trying to staple it."

"He should have been more careful!" Davenport says indignantly.

"The paper he was trying to staple was a written warning for your insubordination."

"Hey, that's neither here nor there! He shouldn't have stapled my hand. That's all there is to it."

And so it goes. It doesn't take me long to figure out that Davenport is in here about once a month with some complaint or another, some reason to bemoan his continuing existence. His neighbor's horse carriage is always parked in his spot. His other neighbor is making too much noise. His coffee is too cold. Even death couldn't bring an end to his bitching. You would think that dying would bring sweet release to a life filled with ever-present misfortune and unfairness. But evidently, the desire to complain about it overrides the promise of an end.

It's clear where I rank on the pecking order here. I'm sure I'll be seeing a lot of Davenport in the future. All the crap cases are going to come rolling downhill to me.

"Calm down, Mr. Davenport. I'll take your statement. I'll fill out your complaint. But I have to tell you, it's going to be hard to prove he intended you harm."

I tune out the rest of his ranting as I peck away at type-writer keys.

The rest of the time is more of the same. All the complaints boil down to personal injury. You level someone's building, maybe you'll get a week in the slammer. But break someone's nose, and you're in trouble.

Marsh explains it to me after I finish typing. As much as he can.

"Why do you think we're still alive, Green? Why is my body still moving around after I'm dead? It's about will. Pure, bull-headed determination. Refusing to let even death bring you to an end.

"For some, it's unfinished business that they can't allow to remain behind. Or it's a wrong that needs to be made right, some bastard that can't live without getting what's coming to him. Or it's something you wanted so bad that you never had in life, and you can't bear the thought of never getting it."

He pauses, gathering his thoughts, and I don't interrupt. "Sure, some of it can be called supernatural. Maybe a ritual or a curse yanks you back from whatever hereafter you managed to make it to. Maybe some vamp or some were-animal chows down on you, and you end up here. But even then, it's will that keeps you hanging around," he says.

"The majority of you living assholes, you die, and that's it. Off you go to wherever. But a very small number of us, we have reasons to stick around."

"So, you're saying people who die are quitters?" I ask skeptically.

He shrugs and lets that stand as his answer.

"What I don't get," I say casually, trying not to derail a surprisingly talkative Marsh, "is the different kinds of you. Ghosts, zombies, vampires, I don't know what else—"

"Stop calling us zombies, kid, or I'll beat the snot out of you and make you eat your teeth."

"Right. Not zombies. Um . . ." I trail off.

Marsh finally fills in the silence. "Revenants. Use that word. People will know what you mean."

"So most of you that come back are revenants?"

Marsh shakes his head, exasperated at my questions. "No. Most of those that do come back can only manage to keep their spirit around. Keeping your body together requires more grit."

"Ghosts," I say, thinking of Ms. Greystone and the others I see floating through the precinct.

Marsh nods. "Yeah. Most of them don't remember why they're sticking around. I guess without physical brains, most of them don't keep a hold of their memories so good. They keep going back to where they lived, back in the real world, and we have to send teams to haul 'em back. We don't want any ghost hunters following them back."

"Who ya gonna call?" I quip, smiling.

Marsh scowls at me. "What?"

My smile fades. "Ghostbusters. Who ya gonna call?"

"The hell are you talking about?"

Right. No TV or movies here. I wave away his question with a disappointed sigh and let him continue.

"So those that won't stay here where you folks can't find 'em, those we have to drag back here. If they keep going back to your world, we stuff 'em down in a place we got for them.

Not all are like that though. A small portion of them retains enough sense of self to stick around and be useful."

"Like Ms. Greystone."

"Right again."

"If you come back as a ghost, you end up here?" I interrupt him, but he doesn't seem to mind.

"Not automatically. Ghosts like to haunt a place that's familiar to them. But they're too easy to find there. We like to stay hidden. Safer that way for everyone. So when we find a ghost, we bring them back here, give them a place to hang out."

I nod. Makes sense I suppose. Probably why we only hear about ghosts haunting abandoned and out-of-the-way places. Not in areas with a lot of people. Ghosts are evidently removed from those spaces and brought here.

"So how many are ghosts compared to everyone else?"

Marsh shrugs. "Bout ninety percent, I suppose."

I raise my eyebrows at this. The majority of residents I've seen here have been these revenants. If that's true, where are all the ghosts?

"Ghosts are about ninety percent of you?"

"Right," Marsh says, forging ahead. "Now, those other ten percent, their will is stronger. They can pull together enough form, enough matter, that they can keep their body with them. They can reanimate their body and keep it more-or-less intact. Sure, a vampire virus or zombie bite might help someone cling to their body for a while, but it's only a short-term thing.

"It's a constant struggle. If you lose too much of your body and don't have enough will to put it back together, you lose it.

"Some of us, we can add to our body. Change it. Build it into more than it was in life."

"Like you," I say.

Marsh scowls. "Why the hell do you say that?" he asks, his words dripping with a threat.

"Well, because, you know."

"You think my face isn't naturally this pretty?"

I look at the massive size of him. I find it hard to imagine him as a normal living person of that size. With blood pumping, all his organs intact, he would have to weigh well past 300 pounds, maybe closer to 400. "You, no, you're yes, because you're pretty, handsome, pretty handsome. Go on."

"Anyway," he growls sourly, continuing. "Some of us, we can rebuild our bodies, heal injuries. There aren't many who can, but some.

"And then there's those like the captain. Who is something else entirely."

I hold up my fingers to start ticking them off. "One kind is ghosts. Then revenants, strong revenants, and then the something elses? And the ones that can heal themselves they are the strong revenants and the something elses?"

Marsh nods. "You got it."

I don't bother trying to get a better clarification than that. "You stuck around though. After you died. What kept you around? Was it something supernatural?"

Marsh shakes his head. "No. Nothing like that."

When nothing else is forthcoming, I try another tactic. "How did you die?" I prod him.

The smile he gets on his face gives me shivers and about stops my heart. "How did I die? Not alone."

He shakes his head, lost in thought. "There were some people who needed killing. I got some of them before I died. Plenty more after." He chuckles.

I don't get a chance to ask a follow-up. Ms. Greystone enters the room, casts a disdainful gaze around at the other detectives, finally settling on Marsh and then me. The other detectives in the room stop what they're doing, eyes locked on Greystone. Wait, are they . . . They're totally checking her out. I don't get it. What am I missing?

"Detective Marsh," Ms. Greystone greets coolly. "Detective Green. The captain wants to know how your first night is going."

I shrug. How am I supposed to know? It's not like I have any stick to measure this against.

"The kid's doing alright," Marsh says, his gaze traveling down, then back up Ms. Greystone's body. "Solid first day. He might even last the week."

Ms. Greystone nods like that's what she had expected. While it looks outwardly like she is oblivious to the leers of the other detectives, I can feel her anger at it pulsing out from her. "Then you are to meet the captain down at Pier 12."

Marsh looks surprised. "Pier 12? What's down there? Is that all he said?"

Clearly, she doesn't like to be second-guessed by Marsh any more than she likes it from me. "The captain's exact words were, 'Bring Detective Green and his endlessly-irritating partner down here on the double.'"

She smiles, then sinks through the floor.

"What's Pier 12?" I ask.

Marsh shakes his head, puzzled. "Let's go take a look."

Chapter 13

W E TAKE A COACH OVER to the docks. This time, though, I convince Marsh that I want to ride on the top. I don't want to be confined to a dark box all night; I want to see where we're going. He tells the driver to take a hike, and we both climb up into the driver's bench. Marsh has the reins, of course, which is fine with me as it gives me time to take in the sights. And it spares me having to try and control the horses.

The coach moves at a brisk pace down the center of the roads. It looks like most of the time, the center lane is kept clear for us. Convenient. Now that I'm up in front of the coach, I get a better view of the city. The streets here are very confusing. At first, I thought it was the speed of the coach making the edges of my vision blur, but I've come to the conclusion that it is actually some mystical aspect of the city itself. The streets merge with each other, pavement to cobblestone to dirt to gravel. I don't mean that on one block it's one and on the next block it's different. It's like several roads overlap each other, and in some places, one imposes itself on top of the other. A clogged gutter slowly shifts into an overflowing dirt trench within the space of a few paces. It's less prevalent in the downtown area where I've spent most of my time, but out here in the neighboring areas, it is more common. It doesn't seem to happen as much when I'm down walking at street level; it's like my presence tends to hold one of the super-imposed streets in place. But up here on the coach, moving at a faster pace, I can see the constant shifting. I pull my eyes up from the ground before I get too nauseated.

The crowds shuffle up and down the streets in the over-cast gloom. Now that I've been here a while, and now that I'm starting to understand the differences in the types of bodies, I can see some variety in the corpses walking past. Some are barely lurching, some are just ghosts, but some walk confidently down the streets. Once again, I marvel at what I see: clothing styles several decades to a century or more out of fashion. Along one street I see men wearing top hats and bowlers, walking with canes, wearing suits or work overalls, carrying briefcases and valises. Women with full-length dresses and poofy skirts walk beside others with parasols and slacks. It's like I'm behind the scenes on set at a movie studio, and I'm watching all the extras from various films mingling together.

Marsh notices my interest.

"This is a weird place for you, isn't it, kid? Surrounded by hundreds of walking, talking, thieving, whoring, lifeless, immortal dead people. Some are flesh eaters. Some are blood drinkers, eaters of carrion, offal, and souls," he explains.

"And then there's the nice ones like me, of course." He smiles.

I grunt, nodding. Nice isn't the first word that comes to mind.

We crossed the bridge leading to the precinct early on and are now heading back into the central portion of the city. The crowds are thicker here where the buildings are packed close together. The undead cluster on the sidewalks and loiter against brick walls or even in the gutters. The breeze from riding in the open air is a refreshing change for me.

"Keep your gun handy," Marsh says. He nods towards the crowds lining the sidewalk near my side of the coach. "Most of the folks here, they don't pose you no danger. But some of these folks feed on mortals. Or they would if they could get their hands on some. Here, the pathways to your world are blocked. They don't have any access to living people. But now that you're here with them, well, they might not be able to resist the temptation. You're a bottle of whiskey being paraded in front of a roomful of drunks. You think someone is coming for you, you drop 'em. Understand?"

I look sideways at Marsh and nod. I thought the badge was supposed to help with that, but I guess it's not foolproof. The gun feels a little heavier in my coat pocket.

We take a turn that leads us away from downtown. It is still disorienting to me to see an old Victorian clock tower rising above thatched roofs or junked car salvage yards. Occasionally I'll see the glow of eyes from one of the figures walking near the road we're on, just to give it that extra dose of the surreal. There are a lot more coaches out on this road; it looks like a main thoroughfare from downtown to wherever our destination is located. I can hear the sounds of running water nearby over the tumult. On all sides, I see battered warehouses in a variety of styles. I have more questions, and Marsh can't avoid me for a few more minutes.

"We've gone a couple of miles, now. Even though the sky's never changed, the temperature has. Sometimes it's hot, sometimes cold. Humid then dry. Now humid, again. I've felt a few drops of rain—even a snowflake or two. The buildings are all different. Different styles, ages."

"There a question in there?" Marsh growls.

"Explain it to me. I'd guess, it's just wherever these people come from, they build buildings they're used to. But that doesn't answer it all."

Marsh sighs. "The city. I've told you some of it before. It's made up of places from all over the world. It's not just styles of buildings from around the world. It's actual places. We're moving from one place in the world to a completely different place in the world as we go down the street. For us, it's a single street, but in your world, we just skipped all over the globe, hitting places out of sight. Forgotten places."

He points to a couple run-down buildings as we pass. They look completely unlike each other, even though they are clearly warehouses of some kind. One is faded yellow brick with wooden sills and frames of colorless peeling paint. The other is corrugated steel, rust-colored and flaking.

"Those two buildings are right next to each other here. But in the real world, one could be in the Midwest, the other in China. Our town is folded pockets of reality crammed together. A place for us—one breathing saps like you aren't supposed to find."

"But how? Don't people just wander in?"

"You'd be surprised how much of the world is in front of your eyes, and people just don't see it. No, our Necropolis is made of up of the pieces no one remembers. There are a few doorways that allow passage back and forth, but most of it no longer exists in any living memory."

He sees me struggling to comprehend. He pauses to curse at a slow-moving driver and basically runs him off the road to get around him. I hold on tightly to my seat until we swerve back into the middle of our lane.

"Let me give you an example," he continues like nothing happened. "Remember a place you stumbled across once when you were a kid? Some shop you didn't know, you couldn't remember how you got there? It had stuff you couldn't make sense of inside? Fading what-cha-call-em doilies, glasses in greens and browns, old antiques and other junk? Or maybe it was an alley behind a boarded-up gate, blocked by dumpsters that never get emptied? You snuck back there and saw locked doors leading into dark empty buildings.

"Yeah, those places aren't here because you remember them. I'm talking about forgotten places no one remembers anymore. The people that built them are no longer alive, plans or writings no longer mention them. Boarded over rooms, bricked-up buildings, sewer tunnels that have been closed down and neglected. That's what we've got here."

I think this over. I wonder how many times I've passed by a building or street in my life, a place that I just didn't notice. A business located between two others that completely escaped my notice. Or a turn I failed to realize was there. I think of all the many places I passed every day and never noticed. Then I try and stretch that to every city, in every country in the world. It's dizzying. I wonder how big this place really is. I've never been at a vantage point to look down over it. The world feels like it is getting smaller every day, filling up with more people, satellites exploring nooks and crannies. But even then, how much don't I notice even in my own backyard?

He turns the coach on a wide road filled with large wagons hauling boxes and materials. It's busy here, carts and coaches of all sizes filing past and around us. We join the press and pass through a large gate. Stone pillars rise up on either side of the road, nearly fifteen feet tall. The iron gate is standing wide open. The docks.

The docks are old, with massive wooden pillars holding up piers for a stretch of about a half-mile in either direction along the banks. The docks are all different in style and size. Some look solid; others seem like they'll fall apart with the next wave that crashes into them. But they are all built for receiving ships of various sizes. Fog looms out on the water, making it hard to tell how wide the river is, where it goes, or from where it originates. The water is black, churning, the current swift. There are at least ten long wooden piers, each about 200 feet long. I don't know when they were built, but it looks like they are as old as anything in this city.

There are some boats out in the water, disappearing into the churning mists. One vessel is tied up at the end of the pier that we're approaching. Don't ask me what kind of boat, I don't know. Some are simple sailing craft, fishing boats. But I see at least one steam-ship moored at a nearby pier. A yacht drifts further up in the fog. Behind it, I see a hulking shadow with masts and sails. At the end of the dock we're on, there is a steel cargo ship of some kind. I would expect this pier to be crowded with workers like I can see on other piers. Here, officers are holding the crowd back at the entrance. Down by some large crates at the end, I can see the captain. The air seems darker, more oppressive around him, a concentration of power that he carries around with him. He stands by himself, and even the other officers seem to avoid him. He is standing motionless, studying something on the ground.

Marsh gets down off the coach and clears our way past the cops guarding the entrance. "The captain's standing over running water. He never does that. It's dangerous for him. This must be important. Let's go see what this is about."

I give the horses hooked up to our coach a wide berth as I set out to follow Marsh. I'm conscious of what he said about some people wanting to eat me if they could. I'm even more suspicious of the looks the horses are giving me, now. I don't know how serious he was, but he sure seemed like he wasn't exaggerating. Even though the crowd parts for both of us, are some of them looking at me with more than simple curiosity? Are they gazing at me hungrily? Speculatively? I stick close to Marsh all the way down the length of the pier.

"Detectives," the captain greets without looking up. His

suit hangs loosely off his skinny frame. Its fabric is darker than the shadows swirling around him. At one time, it may have been exquisitely tailored, but now it is rumpled, torn and stained. I initially thought he was wearing a trench coat, but on closer inspection, I realize it's a cloak of some heavy material. It billows slightly, but not in any way that appears affected by the wind. He waves us near with slowly curling fingers on one hand, then leads us over behind some crates nearby and indicates something on the ground, covered by a tarp. "Take a look. Tell me what you see."

Marsh squats, lifts one corner to the tarp, stares down, and doesn't move. His arm holds the tarp, and his scowl gets fiercer.

"Another one?" he whispers.

I look over his shoulder. There is a body on the ground. This body is just lying there. This is a corpse.

I haven't seen dead bodies that didn't move since my first encounter with the captain. At the time, I didn't understand the big deal. I mean, so what? But this is a dead body that used to be undead, and they can't figure it out.

"I don't suppose he's sleeping?" I ask.

"No," the captain replies. "The body is there, but nobody is home."

Marsh is quiet, the way the air in a snowstorm is silent. I don't think I've ever seen Marsh at a loss for words, or at least a rude grunt.

"I don't understand," I admit. I notice only one other thing out of the ordinary, a familiar detail that I have seen before just once, on a similarly dead body. The eyes are gone, like they've been burned out. The sockets are empty, smoking craters.

"Neither will anyone else," the captain sighs. He looks like he ate something foul, his mouth scrunched up in distaste. "This is the fourth one I've found over the past few weeks."

"What?" Marsh looks up in shock. "You've been keeping them from us? I thought there was only the one."

"Non, *malheuresement*. I wanted to keep this contained. I would have brought them to you eventually. I've managed to keep the others covered up, but this one . . . This one was too visible. There's no keeping it quiet now."

Neither Marsh nor I say anything. I keep looking at the body on the ground, over to the captain, then back again.

Finally, the captain snaps, "Don't you understand, Detective Green? For the first time ever in our history, we have murders. And I need your help to solve them."

Ten Weeks Ago . . .

"Craig?" I croak, reaching out for my brother. Then I remember he's long gone, eight years now.

I wake up in the dark. As I struggle to crawl up to consciousness, it feels like something must be draped over my head. Everything feels stuffy, dull; my senses don't give me input the way I'm used to. I struggle for a moment, trying to push away whatever is covering me until I realize nothing is there. Am I leaning against a wall? No, I'm sprawled out on the floor.

Suddenly everything comes rushing in at once, and the avalanche of sensation threatens to drop me back into unconsciousness. I'm in darkness, and I can't immediately see the limits of the room. I'm cold, my clothes in tatters. My joints ache, and I feel bruises all over. There is a ringing in my ear that won't go away. It feels like my ears are stuffed with cotton. I can feel a loose tooth and a sharp stabbing pain in my side.

The floor beneath me is concrete; its damp chill seeps up through me. Where am I?

"Hello?" I call out tentatively, and the words scratch at my throat as they come out. I immediately start coughing. The

sounds echo back around me, giving me the sense I'm in a small room.

My last memory is of Marsh asking me more questions. I may not know where I am, but I'm sure it's not in the same place I last saw Marsh.

There is no response. I feel my way along the wall a few feet until I find a corner where I huddle up to try and keep warm.

I don't know how long I'm there before I nod off back to sleep once more.

I wake up after an indeterminate amount of time. What am I hearing? The ringing is still there, more in my left ear, but there is something else, something external. Whispers?

Yes, I'm hearing whispers, hushed voices around me.

"Hello?" I call again. The voices cease. "Dammit! Please! Is anyone there?"

Wait, there is something else now. I am seeing light from somewhere now. I can make out a slight glow.

A blood-curdling shriek erupts out of the darkness nearby, and a bright figure bursts out of the wall opposite me about eight feet away. The thing flies straight at me, yelling so loudly I think my eardrums will burst. My heart skips several beats.

The ghost stops directly in front of me, staring me in the face from inches away. I can't tell if it's a woman or a man. Its long hair radiates out from a mask of rage and venom. It looms over me for ages, screaming in my face while I huddle in terror and try and keep away from it.

Overhead, more ghosts float through the walls. Their chatter adds to the confusion and pandemonium in the room. Whether they're attracted to the first ghost's noise, I don't know. But they mill around to watch the show—some merely gazing without expression, others swirling around cackling in laughter. There's too many, too much confusion for me to get a good look at any individual.

This goes on for hours. After the initial terror subsides, clarity returns to my mind. I don't know what these ghosts are trying to accomplish, but they are apparently not trying to hurt me. They're trying to terrify me, which is working, but they aren't causing me any physical pain. I'm still too scared to provoke them, but my mind is racing. I make a vow.

Whatever else happens to me, if I have any power over it, I'm going to survive. I'll do whatever I have to in order to get through this. I'll do whatever it is they want me to do. I will not give up.

The ghosts continue their screaming.

Chapter 14

S o."

I don't really know what to say next; I'm just getting uncomfortable with the silence. Marsh hasn't muttered anything since the captain spoke to us about ten minutes ago. The body is covered up and stashed into a closed coach, to be delivered back to the office to some undisclosed room in the bowels of the building.

It's not like there's a morgue.

I'm leaning against the pier's railing, my back to the dark churning water below. The sounds of the water drown out the hushed whispering of the other officers at the scene. It may have been possible to keep the last few bodies quiet, but this one, Captain Radu is right, I don't know how he's going to stop the news of this one from spreading.

I look over the railing at the water. The current is strong, steady, trying its best to yank out the supports of the pier, but this pier has likely been here a hundred years. It's not going anywhere. The railing is worn smooth by hands over countless decades of use. The smell here is refreshing, the salt air blowing away the stench of corpses that constantly clogs my nose. I'm going to have to remember to come back.

"Marsh," I say, finally getting his attention. He turns to me, his face unreadable.

"I'm going to guess you've never investigated anything like this before."

"Got that right," he mumbles.

"I have to ask. Why is this freaking everyone out so much? You've already shown me a dead body before today. You didn't seem bothered then."

Marsh stares at me for a second. A series of emotions flicker across his face, each easily read. First, he wonders how anyone can be as stupid as I am. Then he realizes I am used to things dying. It's what defines being alive in many ways. Being NOT dead. That's not something they have had to think about for decades or centuries. Then I see him reach a decision of some kind. Determination settles over him, and a new fire comes alive in his eyes.

"One body, it's weird, but I can get past it. It's easy to ignore, I guess. But multiple bodies. And it's showing no signs of stopping. After living here as long as I have, kid, nothing was supposed to surprise me anymore. Then you showed up. I still haven't figured out what's going on with you. But this . . . Never seen nothing like this before."

If anything, his scowl gets fiercer. "I told you how someone's will is what keeps them around. Once you make that decision to hang around past death, you can't take it back. It's not a switch you can flip."

I look at him quizzically, and he waves away any question I'm about to ask. He starts walking back to the coach, so if I want to hear an answer, I have to keep up with him.

"The stronger your will, the stronger your body, right? If you're not careful, you can lose your body, but then your spirit sticks around. You can wander around indefinitely as a ghost. You might lose all memory, forget who you are, who you were. You might eventually fade away. But you are still here. You never die."

"Yeah, you covered most of that."

He stops walking and turns to me. I jerk to a halt to keep from crashing into him. I'm pretty sure I would bounce off him.

"OK, genius. But you don't know it all yet."

"Right. Sure." I take a step back to try and get out of arm's reach.

He glares at me for a second, then starts walking again, leaving me scrambling like an idiot after him. "Lots of the ghosts you've seen floating around, they used to have bodies after their death. Many lose their will to hold everything together, you know? They gradually dissipate, like they can't be bothered to hold on to their bodies no more.

"Once you stick around after death, and you find your way here, you're stuck. We don't let you go to the living world, the world outside our walls, because we don't want anyone finding their way back here. And since you already turned away from the bright light or the eternal dark, your path that way is shut.

"You can lose your body, but never your soul. Your soul is rooted here 'til Judgment Day, or whenever things eventually end." He looks back at where the body was laying at the end of the pier. "Except now that's not the case anymore, looks like. We got bodies here with no spirits, no souls. It goes against everything we know."

"Wait, there are a few things I don't understand."

"Just a few?" he mutters.

"Look, I'm going to ask some dumb questions."

"Go ahead," Marsh says like he doesn't expect any other kind. We've reached the coach and climb up into the bench up front. He clacks the reins, and the horses set into motion. We're going slower than on the way here; Marsh is in no hurry to pick a destination.

"OK, here's one. Zombies, spirits, undead things. There is folklore, stories about destroying them. Chopping off the head, exorcisms, silver bullets. Are you saying there's no way to kill you guys?"

Marsh chews over his response for a moment, looking at me with suspicion.

And then he says, "Yes, some of those things work. Exorcisms, ways to force the spirit beyond. The thing is, none of us here can do those things. Even if I wanted to send a spirit on to their great reward—and believe me, there's been plenty—an exorcism would banish everything in earshot, me included. No one here could do it because it would drop them in the attempt. Which means most of us could start an exorcism, but none of us could finish it."

He turns to me with a cruel grin. "One of the reasons we didn't kill you right away is we were sure you didn't have the know-how to do that. If we think for a second you know how to banish or exorcize someone, you won't last two seconds."

"Got it," I say, my mouth dry. I'll make it a point to avoid that topic of conversation in the future.

"Silver bullets will hurt some of us—the more supernatural of us, I guess you'd say. But you aren't going to find any silver here; it's banned. You try chopping off someone's head here, and they're going to get really pissed." He chuckles at the thought. I'm never going to understand this guy.

"So, no death penalty here, then. What do you do with your criminals? You just throw 'em in a cell?"

"Most of them, yeah. The ones that have bodies, anyway. We toss them in a box and let them sweat it out for a few years. When you have all of eternity staring you in the face, you don't want to spend it in a cell."

"What do you do with the ones who don't have bodies?"

Marsh makes up his mind about where he's going,

evidently. He sits up straighter, snaps the reins, and the horses pick up speed. He smiles. "I'll show you."

"It's called the Pit," Marsh explains, squinting against the glare of the energy pouring up from a fissure in the ground.

We're back at the police headquarters. We walked through the massive gate on the main floor, past the guards, the latches and deadbolts locking behind us. We're at the top of some steel stairs, wide enough for about four people to walk side-by-side, winding down around the inside of the walls, around a huge pit in the floor. The room is cavernous, maybe about a football field in length and just as wide. It's kind of like a giant elevator shaft, massive stone blocks fit snugly together to form walls that tower up and disappear into the gloom overhead. It looks like the whole building was built to surround and contain this. The only light comes from the floor, way down below.

I lean out over the rusting railing and look down. The stairs only reach about halfway down, and that is several stories down into the earth. The floor is a good hundred feet farther down from where they end. The stairs stop at a platform, and that is where Marsh is heading. We don't talk much as we make our way down. I don't know that I could walk, talk and take it all in at the same time.

It's crazy loud here, like the roar of a waterfall. I can feel the air being pulled into the floor below. Intense colors flare out from a massive split in the ground. It's like the light is trying to escape, but the pull of force keeps dragging it back in. I can feel the pull from even up here, like something grabbing on to my shirt and tugging.

I pause on the stair I'm on and close my eyes. It reminds me of the beach, standing in the water about knee deep, feeling the pull of the tide trying to tug my feet out and drag me under. It feels like I'm moving, though my brain keeps telling me I'm standing still. I can feel the sand piling up around my feet.

It's like that here, the weight pulling me down to the hole in the ground. I open my eyes and look anxiously at the platform where we're heading. There is an opening in the railing on the end that hangs out over the hole. Seems really easy to get swept off to whatever is down there.

I catch up to Marsh just as he reaches the platform. He walks halfway out and stops, about twenty feet from the edge. I nervously inch out to join him. I try not to think about how easy it would be for Marsh to bump me off and never have to deal with me again.

"What is it?" I yell over the rush of energy pouring past us, visibly getting sucked down into the earth. It's like a tornado of barely-visible colors and lines swirling down.

"Not sure, really," Marsh yells back. "Massive gravity well. Bottomless pit. Scientists and magicians call it different things. It pulls in light, sound, energy. Anything that gets sucked in never comes out."

He slaps one hand on top of his head to hold his hat into place before it gets yanked away. "We bring the ones here who refuse to obey the rules, those that pose a danger to all of us. That won't toe the line. And whether they have a body or not, we toss them in. Bodies get sucked down. Spirits too. Ghosts can't get near this thing, even if a ghost goes in there, it can't come back."

"It kills them?"

Marsh shakes his head. "No. They're still alive down there. Trapped for all time. If we toss a body in there, the force will tear the body apart. But it just pulls the spirit down."

I shiver, trying to imagine being stuck in the bottom of a well for all eternity—too loud to speak, not able to do anything but exist. Whoever is down there, they must be insane. How many souls are pinned down there at the bottom? Do they even know?

"Don't you get too close," he cautions. "If your body gets torn apart, we don't know yet if your spirit will come back."

We both stand there on the platform for a short while, resisting the pull of force trying to lure us down. The roar in my ears discourages talk, but it doesn't stop Marsh.

"I like coming down here to think. The noise, it drowns everything else out."

"This Pit, is it natural? Or did you guys make it?" I ask.

He shrugs and doesn't answer.

I watch streamers of energy swirl past. Closing my eyes, I lose myself in the sensation. I feel a tap on my shoulder, and I open my eyes to see Marsh waving me back.

"Let's go, kid."

Chapter 15

I DON'T KNOW THE FIRST THING about how a detective solves a case. Kind of a major drawback in being a detective as it turns out. But if this is what they want of me, damn it, I'm going to figure out how to do it.

All I can do for now is approach it in the same way I approach projects at school. When I'm building models on my computer, it's all about starting with the basics and slowly working outward. If I want to model a character of any kind, I start out with a simple cube and start extruding one face after another. Squish, stretch, bevel, copy, paste, smooth, pull, and move vertices and faces until everything lines up just right. I'd like to think I can apply that same method here, even though I know this grossly simplifies what I'm in for.

So where do I start? I requested some instruction manuals, training manuals, history books, even doodles on napkins, anything to try and help me get ready for what's ahead of me. They don't have any. Plenty of rules and laws and codes though, rooms full of them. But no step-by-step on how to solve a case.

I'm supposed to provide some special kind of perspective.

They expect this knack I have for sensing lies, or my ability to breathe, is going to be the means of giving them the break-through they want. I'm determined to do a good job here, prove I'm worth keeping alive, but frankly, I don't see how I can pull it off.

We're back in the squad's office. The door is closed, cut-ting out some of the noise from the main room. More impor-tantly, though, it will prevent anyone from overhearing our discussion. Word of the murder has been buzzing around the precinct like a swarm of angry bees. It's all anyone can whis-per about right now, and they're all looking at us for answers. We're all here, all eight detectives on the squad, sitting at our desks in varying states of consternation, confusion and gen-eral pissed-offedness. Even Greystone is here. She's a floating disapproving presence lurking at my shoulder. I can feel her anger in my mind, her irritation, if I didn't already feel it ra-diating off her in waves. She's spent the last half-hour scowl-ing down her nose at the lot of us. I'm not sure what we've done to tick her off, but she's in a snit.

Clark closes the blinds so no one can look in. Marsh eras-es a chalkboard. None of us are talking. Burchard is smoking something that looks like a cigar but smells like a swampy dead dog. Marsh turns to us, opens his mouth, closes it again, and scowls.

Clark shifts in his seat, loosens his green tie, and says, "Well, I'll say it if no one else will. Holy shit! A murder, right?"

He's the only one actually enjoying this. He leans back in his chair, looking around at morose and scowling expres-sions reflecting back at him. "I mean, not many firsts here, are there?"

Finnegan levels his unblinking stare my way. "Except for the breather, here." I'm not sure how he does it, but while his expression doesn't change, I can feel it loading with suspicion, with intent. "It occurs to me that it's a damned coincidence that he shows up right when bodies start dropping. I mean, we never see a single death in this town in its entire history, and it happens the same time he shows up?"

This is bad, isn't it? It feels bad. He's jumping to an incredibly wrong conclusion. I want to debate mistaking correlation for causation, but I don't think it would make much traction.

Armstrong starts tapping a finger on his desk while he growls, "I'm not buying his too-stupid-to-know-anything excuse. I'm with Finnegan. Let's sweat him for some answers."

"That's enough of that," Marsh says quietly, but it cuts through the room. "He's been under surveillance the whole time he's been here. Neither Greystone nor myself have let him out of our sights."

Armstrong continues to tap, Finnegan continues to stare, but I breathe a sigh of relief. I didn't like where the conversation was heading. It's good to know my partner has my back.

"No, that too-stupid-to-know-anything expression of his is real," Marsh continues, ignoring my choke of indignation. "We won't rule out that he's unknowingly connected somehow. But he's definitely not behind it. According to the captain's notes, the first body was found long before Green showed up. So what else have we got?"

Mumbles surround me, coming from everyone except Finnegan, who continues to measure me. I try and ignore him, but I can feel his eyes on me.

"OK, let's start at the beginning. How many are we talking about?"

Burchard reads from a clipboard. "Four. That we can verify."

"Wait," I say. "When Radu found me in that room, right before he dragged me here, I fell onto a whole pile of bodies."

Marsh waves my comment away. "That was back in,

where was it? Nebraska. Those were just dead bodies, mortals. Miller had been killing a bunch for a while. He got a little overzealous in his feeding habits. That was one of the reasons he's in the Pit right now."

"Oh," I say quietly, not knowing if I should feel relieved or concerned.

"These four victims: who are they and how are they connected?" Marsh asks.

Burchard looks at the clipboard again. "Otis Evans. Stephan Thunnel. Charles McRae. Tom Eldredge."

Marsh writes the names up on the board as Detective Meints starts flipping through some files. Meints has a thin folder from a filing cabinet for each of the victims, and they lay open on top of the books strewn across his desk. He glances back and forth between the files and the notes he's written on a pad in his hand, ignores the sighs of impatience around the room, then says, "Nothing stands out about any of them. Eldredge was a bit of a troublemaker, but nothing of great consequence. I can't find anything on the surface that looks strange. No obvious connections between them either."

We stare at the names on the board some more. Finnegan glares suspiciously at me some more. Not a promising start.

A knock sounds at the door, and a guy with a hand truck hauls in four boxes. He parks them, grabs a clipboard and hands it to Marsh to sign. Marsh just stares at him. The guy looks around nervously at the silent room, scribbles something on the paper himself, and hastily leaves. Marsh grabs one of the boxes and slams it down on my desk. Each of the other teams also grabs a box and starts pulling out volumes of paper, files, and photos.

"This is everything we have on each of the four victims," he says. "Let's see what we can find. Anything that looks odd—call it out."

"Wait," I say. "You said there was nothing out of the

ordinary about the four of them. But you have boxes of files. That doesn't make sense."

Detective Kim answers without looking up from the box he's digging through. "We have files on everyone here, Green. You live here long enough, you leave a record."

"You've already got one," Finnegan whispers, passing near me to grab a stack of files out of a box. "But I'm sure there's plenty more we haven't discovered. Yet."

We spend the next couple hours poring over old coffee-stained, type-written reports and lists of former addresses for each victim, previous jobs, hang-outs, and known acquaintances. It's late afternoon when I notice a name that I actually recognize.

"Huh," I say absently. "Marsh, it says here that this Eldredge guy—"

"The one found at the pier," Clark adds helpfully without looking up from his desk.

"Right. It says here he spent a few years working at a newspaper with Jasper Davenport."

Armstrong chuckles derisively. "I don't know that a rag like The Bulletin qualifies as a newspaper." I glance over and notice he's doodling on a sketchpad. It looks remarkably good, but then he catches me staring and hides it from view.

I continue on. "I met with Davenport yesterday. I have his current address in my notes. I can ask him some questions, see if he can give us anything."

Marsh ponders for a second, then shrugs. "Yeah, OK. Why not? Greystone, go fetch him."

The ghost scowls so fiercely I swear I can feel the cold emanating from her increase exponentially. "Excuse me, Detective Marsh?"

"Ms. Greystone, please," I say, jumping in to try and calm her. "I can go if you want to show me the way."

"The kid can't go by himself, Greystone. C'mon, shake a

leg. Go find Davenport for us," Marsh continues, acting unaware of any hostility emanating from the apparition next to me. How he can possibly be ignorant of her state of mind is beyond me.

She glances at me, then back at Marsh, folding her arms in front of her. Then she turns very deliberately to me. "I will inform you when Mr. Davenport has arrived, Detective Green." She floats off through the door.

Marsh shakes his head, smiling but not looking up from the file he's reading. "Can never tell what is going to set her off, kid. I ask her something, and it's like I farted at a baptism."

"You just need to ask her nicely, Marsh. Ms. Greystone's not so bad."

He chuckles, shaking his head. "You've got a lot to learn, kid." He turns back to his stack of papers.

Ms. Greystone returns about an hour later. "Detective Green, Mr. Davenport is in Interview Room One." She turns to go.

"Ms. Greystone!" I say quickly, stopping her. "Two things."

She raises one eyebrow impatiently.

"First, thank you."

She motions with her hand to continue, but despite the fixed expression, I get the sense she is at slightly mollified.

"Second, where is Interview Room One?"

"Oh, for heaven's sake!" she exclaims. She turns to Marsh. "Haven't you shown your partner around the office yet, Detective?"

Marsh is leaning back in his chair, which creaks ominously. He still doesn't look up from the paper in his hand. "He'll figure it out."

She draws herself up and turns back to me. "Follow me, Detective Green."

Grabbing some paper and a pencil, I hurry to follow

after her. I almost run face-first into the first door she passes through. I swear, sometimes I don't know if it's possible for me to look like more of an idiot than I already do.

The interview room is on the same floor, just around the corner and down a dim hallway. I stick close to her all the way there. While technically I'm part of the team here, everyone beyond my squad is still a stranger to me.

I yell out the first time I turn a corner and a ghost passes through me on his way somewhere else. He doesn't even seem to notice me. Greystone stops at the door and indicates that I can go in. I open the door and enter the room, which is much smaller than I was expecting. It's not much bigger than a closet. There's a small table, a chair on either side, and Davenport in one of them. I close the door behind me. Greystone is nowhere in sight.

"Good to see you, Detective! You file charges against my boss yet?" he greets eagerly.

"What? Oh, no, not that. This is something else." I sit down and get ready to take notes. "You remember a guy you used to work with named Tom Eldredge?"

The smile instantly leaves Davenport's face. He sits perfectly still. Interesting.

"What's this about?" he asks, tentatively.

I realize I have no idea what I want to ask him. I have to think for a second.

"Let's start with the last time you saw him," I begin. That's what cops usually ask, right? That sounds like a good cop question.

"I haven't talked to him in ages," Davenport says quickly, but his eyes shift. I have my pencil poised above my notebook, but I don't start writing yet. He's not lying, exactly.

"That's not exactly what I asked, sir. When was the last time you saw him?"

"Look, this doesn't have anything to do with me, right?

I'm actually kind of busy today. I need to get going."

"Mr. Davenport," I say, genuinely surprised. What is going on? "I need you to answer some questions. Just answer me, OK?"

"Look, I worked with Eldredge about four years ago. We collaborated on a few stories. We covered different beats, you know. He dealt with business mostly, me I was into investigations. I quit because my boss was a jackass. You think the guy with the stapler was bad?"

"Davenport."

"You don't know how bad just getting stapled is. You have a living body, with blood pumping through it. You heal. You're what, six feet? Pretty good shape."

"Davenport!" I yell in frustration, cutting him off before he can really get rolling.

"Right. Look, I haven't seen him for about two years. I have no idea what he's been doing or what he's been into. But I get a call from an old source that he's been digging into some of my old notes, looking into a few stories of mine that my good-for-nothing boss was too scared to print. Real good stuff, you know—stuff that would have blown this city wide open. Controversial stuff!"

"Why didn't they get printed?" I ask. He's definitely piqued my curiosity now.

"My old boss didn't have any balls is why. He should see my new boss and get some stapled on. He was too scared of the truth getting out. Actually, that's kind of why I quit. And Eldredge? He wasn't interested in it at the time. But something must have spooked him. 'Cuz I hear he's asking some of my sources the same questions I'd asked. Tracking down some of the same leads."

"What was he looking into? What was your story about?" This is fascinating. What would be controversial here? What could possibly be too sensitive to print?

Davenport leans in closer to me, looks suspiciously around at the empty walls, and whispers, "Demons."

"OK," I say, writing that down on my notepad. "Demons? I don't know what that means, really."

Davenport nods and leans back. He has an internal debate for a second. "Look. I have some notes at my place. The stories never got published, but I never got rid of them. I can give you my notes if it will help. Why are you looking into Eldredge, anyway?"

"He's dead," I reply absently as I write some more notes down.

Davenport laughs, "Ain't we all, pal?"

I look up. "No, really. He's dead. We're trying to figure out what happened."

Davenport stares at me and goes a shade paler. "I see."

I wait. He swallows nervously. "It's demons for sure, then. I can get you my notes. I can be back in an hour."

I nod and show him out. I'm feeling pretty good. I have no idea what his story means, but at least it's something. I walk back over to the squad room.

They are all still there when I return. A few more names are up on the board, a few locations. Not much though.

"Well, kid. What've you got?" Marsh asks. He's humoring me, but I'm feeling pretty good about turning up something useful.

"A lead, at least."

Is this what a lead is?

"Davenport used to do investigative journalism pieces. He worked with Eldredge some time back. Evidently, he thinks Eldredge was working on some story similar to one he worked on a few years ago. A story the paper suppressed. One he seems to think was suppressed for political reasons or something."

"No kidding?" Marsh asks. "What's the story about?"

"According to Davenport, it has something to do with demons."

The room goes totally silent, and they all stare at me for a good five seconds.

And then the room erupts in laughter.

Chapter 16

Armstrong and Meints are hunched over in tears. Clark is pounding his fist on the desk. Finnegan still stares at me, but the corner of his mouth is tweaked in something approaching a smile. Marsh has his eyes closed, pinching the bridge of his nose with a pained expression. This is not exactly the response I had expected.

"This is the guy the captain wants to help us?" Kim asks incredulously, pointing at me between laughs.

I turn to Marsh, still at a loss. "What's going on?"

Marsh scowls at me. "Listen up, kid. I'll say this slowly. There's no such thing as demons."

"But—"

"It's like honest politicians. Bug-eyed aliens. Bigfoot or Elvis sightings."

"Yeah, the King never made it here," Burchard says. I don't know if that's good news or not.

"But Davenport was sure it was demons, and he didn't seem like he was lying," I protest.

"Good to know he hasn't been yanking our chains all these years. He's just insane then," Marsh growls. He leans in uncomfortably close to me, backing me up against my desk. He enunciates each word clearly. "There. Are. No. Demons."

"Wait a minute," I say, frustrated. "You have ghosts, magical rifts of energy, zombies—"

"Stop calling us zombies!"

"—vampires, creepy horses, but you laugh because I believed a story about demons? What's so unbelievable about demons?"

"Oh man, you're hopeless," Clark says, still laughing. "Demons are unbelievable because demons don't exist. Demons, angels—they're just names you mortals use when they've stumbled onto folks like us."

No angels either? I resist the urge to ask this out loud. I don't know what to make of this. I've damaged whatever scraps of credibility I had. But Davenport was so sincere. Looking back on it, I guess this isn't the first time I've been taken in believing someone who was absolutely certain they were speaking the truth. Just because they believe they're speaking the truth, doesn't mean what they are saying is true. It just didn't sound any more far-fetched than anything else I've come across recently. I'm talking to a room full of corpses. Why is it so hard to believe in something like a boogeyman or demon?

"Alright. Fine," I say glumly.

"Look, kid. Go home. Call it a night. We'll pick up again tomorrow," Marsh says, waving me away.

I sigh in frustration. I had been making progress with these guys, and now I'm an even bigger chump than before. I grumble a goodbye, grab my files and notes and start to head home. I walk out the front door and down the steps outside. The courtyard outside is as busy as it was before with coaches streaming in and out along the wide stone bridge connecting us to the mainland. Officers are wrestling resisting detainees, who struggle against the restraints on wrists, ankles, and occasionally around the mouth. The guards along the walls and at the gate notice me pass by but say nothing.

The walk home will take me a while. I could request a coach, but I want to clear my head. And I kind of want to memorize the route to get here.

"Don't let it get to you," Ms. Greystone says at my shoulder, causing me to lurch in surprise. I choke off some choice profanity and give her a strained smile.

I try to ignore the satisfied smile on her face. She's a little bit too pleased that I can still make such an ass out of myself. Greystone floats along beside me, content.

"You don't believe in demons, do you?" I ask her.

"Of course not. Don't be ridiculous."

Right. I walk across the bridge, quiet, keeping my questions to myself. Ms. Greystone accompanies me silently. She is looking up ahead, apparently lost in thought. I have to keep an eye on where I'm going, lest I trip on a pothole or get run over by one of the passing coaches. I swear the horses try and swerve over in my direction.

It is dark, the moonlight dimly lighting the canopy of storm clouds overhead. There are some gaslights along the bridge, but they are spaced relatively far apart. There's no rain yet, but I'm guessing it won't be long in coming. The cool breeze is refreshing. The walk across the bridge back the mainland of the city takes several minutes, but it's nice to just enjoy some real quiet, and some space.

"You are doing tolerably well for your first day as a detective," Ms. Greystone says, breaking our silence.

I look at her in surprise. "How could you possibly think that?"

"None of the others had any more training or experience than you when they started," she says, not looking at me. "I think Marsh destroyed the bodies of half-a-dozen citizens in his first week until they reined in his use of his sidearm. You couldn't pull Meints away from studying the codes and laws for the first several months after he joined. Finnegan just arrested everyone that crossed his path and let other officers sort out their crimes. They are all first-rate detectives now, some of the best the city has seen. When you have all of eternity to learn new skills, we tend to look for aptitude rather than experience. Keep in mind, these men have been doing this job every day for decades. Of course they are going to do it better than you."

I nod. It's nice of her to say, but it doesn't make the pill any less bitter. I'm in over my head, and I don't have any way out. At least I've got some small measure of support from her.

"Now stop looking like such a bloody idiot, and put your mind to your work," she continues. "You have one advantage; you are living. That gives you a different perspective than anyone else here. There may be solutions to problems here that only you will see. You also seem to have a knack for reading people. That is a good skill to have, especially here. You need to develop this. You need to learn to reliably predict when someone is lying to you. Davenport may have thought he was telling the truth, but anyone with half a brain should have been able to determine that his crackpot theories are completely ludicrous."

So much for a shoulder to lean on.

"Yes. Sure. Thanks," I say tiredly. I've had enough motivation. "I'll see you later, Ms. Greystone."

It looks like she has more to say, but my comment definitely signals an end to the conversation. She floats back towards the headquarters, leaving me to find my own way home. The walk takes me just under an hour. Sticking to the main roads, which are clearly lit by street lamps now that I'm back in the city proper, I ignore the crowds and just concentrate on my path. My gaze rests close to the ground most of the walk, watching my feet splash in shallow pools in the cobblestones. I walk through a fine mist and occasional drizzle most of the way. My apartment building finally materializes out of the fog, and I make it all the way up to the front door before I realize I'm not ready to go in yet. I'm restless, depressed. But determined.

"I am going to figure this out," I whisper to myself, fiercely.

There's only one other place I know to go outside of my apartment. I'm guessing I have free reign now to go wherever I want, but I have no desire to stumble into another situation I don't understand and let the world know how dumb I am. So, I turn and walk over to Warner's.

Even though the place is crowded, my usual spot is open. Maybe they think I leave behind germs of mortality wherever I go. I sit down at the table and start spreading out some of my files. I'm going to look at this like I would a piece of art, a character I'm going to model and animate. I'm going to sketch out the broad strokes, get a rough sense of the mood and personality of my subject. I'll create the thumbnails first; then I'll add in the details, zero in on specific features. It sounds easy when I break it down like that.

I just don't even know where the broad strokes start.

A shadow falls on the table, and I look up to meet Annabelle's long-suffering gaze.

"Hi, Annabelle. Coffee please," I ask. She nods and lumbers away. I'm relieved they have coffee. I was worried I would get a blank stare in return to my request.

My determination starts out strong, but after a couple of hours staring at my notes, it's beginning to waver. And the coffee doesn't help; it's so potent I can feel my blood thundering through my veins. I have to sip it slowly, so my heart doesn't explode in my chest.

I'm not seeing anything. Evans. Thunnel. McRae. Eldredge. I can't find anything that connects them. Evans was an artist and painter. A bookbinder. He spent his afterlife in his studio, rarely venturing out. I see photos of some of his work, and while I can appreciate the skill and talent behind them, the subjects don't appear especially relevant to the case.

Thunnel worked on investments and finances. There is some suspicion he ran a protection racket of sorts. Does that have anything to do with it? Could he have crossed someone? But he doesn't have anything to do with Evans.

McRae was a chemist. Some notes say he was an alchemist? I'm not sure what that means. But right now, I'm not in the mood to ask questions that will further prove my ignorance.

Eldredge though, I don't quite understand what he did. After leaving his career in journalism, he switched gears entirely. It looks like he became an architect. But he didn't actually build anything. It's odd, but is it suspicious? Can you build anything here? Or do you just have to pull a forgotten building or structure from the real world here? I'll have to ask Marsh. Even with that, I can't find any evidence that they knew each other existed. I don't see anything in common.

"Hello," a soft voice whispers from the edge of my table. "May I join you?"

I look up, and my breath catches a little in my throat. At first, I swear I'm seeing a living woman, but I quickly realize that no, she's not breathing, but she's definitely beautiful. Gorgeous enough that I think she's alive. She's short; she'd probably only reach my shoulders if I were standing. Blonde hair, pale skin that's not green or desiccated. Red lipstick, thick eye-lashes, and clear eyes that haven't gone yellow or cloudy. I'm stunned.

It takes me a second to recover. Then I feel like a complete dunce. I wonder if my jaw was hanging open. I stand up hastily and point to the bench across from me.

"Of course. Please. Have a seat."

She sits down, leaning forward to slide into the booth, and her breasts strain against her low-cut blouse. I can barely keep from staring. Breasts! Breasts that would look great on a living girl. I can't tell you how much I've missed breasts. I don't leer at women, and I'm usually very polite. I've never been accused of being a gentleman, but I'm not an absolute pig.

I think back to Amber. I remember her body in the dim light of the moon coming in through my bedroom window. The smile on her lips as she takes off her shirt.

I feel a sharp stab of loss and quickly move my eyes to the woman's face. I've never been one to stray at the first sign of attention from a woman, and I don't want to start now.

Let's just say that death doesn't do any favors to a curvy form. On everyone else, that is. I haven't seen any other woman with a low-cut anything since I've been here, and even if they had worn something like this, there wouldn't be anything much to display.

I lock my eyes on her green eyes and force myself not to glance down. Greystone is right; I'm a bloody idiot.

We stare at each other, long enough for it to be a little awkward. But even if I knew what to say, I don't have any confidence it will make me look any less like a raging fool.

"I'm Jessica," she says finally, smiling. She extends her hand. I'm pretty sure she's taking great pleasure in my discomfort.

"Hi. Jacob. Jacob Green." I shake her hand. It feels normal, only slightly dry.

"I know. I've been hoping to meet you here. I heard you like to come here, but I've never actually been able to meet you before."

"Why did you want to meet me?" I ask, genuinely confused. I'm still holding her hand, I realize, finally letting go.

She tucks the corner of her smile behind a white tooth,

chewing seductively on her lower lip. She inhales and cocks her head to the side. "Well, it's not often we see someone like you here. Someone living, I mean."

I pause. Wait a minute. What am I seeing here? My blood thunders a little less, and I start to pick out some details. Her skin is smooth, but no one's skin here is smooth. Yes, there, below the earlobe, a patch of skin missing cover up. She also inhaled. I notice now that she is "breathing," her chest going in and out. Then I notice I'm staring at her chest again and snap my eyes back to her gaze. She is breathing, but it is forced, not natural. Perfume hangs in the air, but it can't quite eliminate the hint of rot underneath it.

"I'm sorry," I say. "I'm being rude. I'm staring. I have no excuse. My mother would be horrified."

She laughs, in genuine delight. "Mother? I haven't heard that word in a long time."

That is like a splash of cold water. It makes me realize how alien my surroundings are. But Jessica continues on, unaware.

"I do hope we can get to know each other better. I have so many questions I would like to ask you."

"Oh," I answer cautiously. "Like what?"

She rests her chin on one hand, placing her elbow on the table. "Well, how about . . . What are you doing?" She glances down at the photos on the table.

I didn't even realize I had all my notes and case photos still out on the table. I make to put them away but then stop. Why bother? She's already seen them.

Annabelle walks up to the table with another cup and some fresh coffee. She pours some for Jessica, who ignores her. Jessica is locking her eyes on me. I'm so distracted by Jessica that I almost miss it when Annabelle says, "Huh."

The waitress has turned to leave when I stop her. "Annabelle! Wait!"

She turns back around, and, out of the corner of my eye,

I notice Jessica flash a look of irritation that my attention has been diverted from her.

"Annabelle, what is it?" I ask her.

"Sorry, Detective. I didn't mean to interrupt," she says, starting to back away again.

"No, please. What?"

Scowling, she points at the photos on the table. "I just haven't seen any of them for a while."

"Wait a minute. All four of them used to come here?"

Annabelle looks at me like I can't grasp a simple concept. "Yes. Just not lately."

Chapter 17

I'M STUNNED. ALL THE WORK and effort put into trying to figure out a connection, and my waitress stumbles onto it with a glance.

"Maybe you should be the detective," I say in exasperation. "What did they do here? Anyone in particular that they talk to?"

The waitress shrugs. "Sure. You'll want to talk to Frank, the guy in the back room. He spoke with them regularly."

"Thank you," I say. Annabelle starts to say something, casts a glance over towards the indicated room, then simply turns and walks away.

"You never did answer my question," Jessica says. I glance up at her, guilty that I'd almost forgotten she was there.

"Question?"

"What are you doing?" she asks again, pointing at the photos and notes strewn across the table.

"Sorry, Jessica, you're going to have to excuse me. I need to go talk to someone." I scoop up all the photos and get up from the table. I make my way through the crowd over to the entrance to Frank's room. I hear Jessica try and get my attention, but I ignore her and keep moving.

In all the times I've been here, I've never really had a reason to speak to Frank before. I've tried saying hi in the past, but he just ignored me and kept his nose in his books until I went away. He has piles of books stacked on the tables of four separate booths and many of the benches, as well. Maps and photos are tacked on the walls all around the room. They don't seem to fit any particular theme. Random postcards faded with age are pinned next to decades-old textbook pictures of animals or tourist maps. The space is cluttered, messy, chaotic. I'm not sure how he managed to convince Warner to give him a room to himself, but there is barely enough room for me to make my way to stand next to him.

Frank is skinny, but not incredibly so. Finnegan is thinner. I notice his fingers are abnormally long, thin, with claw-like nails. He energetically scans the pages of the book in front of him, so engrossed in his reading he doesn't seem to notice me approach. His suit is a little worse for wear, but that hardly stands out here. The pinstripes have nearly faded into the primary color of his suit coat. His scalp shows through the thin hair combed over the top of his head. His skin is a little paler than most, but still, it has a greenish tinge. There's nothing very remarkable about him; he's just the guy that hangs out in the back room at Warner's.

I don't sit down yet; I stand, waiting for him to acknowledge me. On the surface, it looks like he's so lost in his study that he doesn't know I'm there, but now that I'm closer, I'm pretty sure he knows I'm here. He's just pretending to not notice me.

"Excuse me," I say.

"Yes?" he asks, pulling his gaze from his book. I glance at the page, but I don't recognize the language. His eyes keep darting back to his reading, his attention obviously still there rather than on me. "Can I help you?"

"Hi. My name is Detective Green. Can you answer a few questions for me?"

"You want me to answer questions?" he asks, genuinely surprised. "What sort of questions do you think I can answer?"

I nod back over towards the bar. "Annabelle mentioned you might be able to help me out. And I've heard you're kind of an expert on things in town."

He glances through the doorway at her for a second, then back to me. "She did? OK, then."

I hold out the photos of the victims in my folder. "Do you recognize any of these people?"

He makes no move to grab the photos, so I hold them up in front of him.

He looks at each in turn. "I see. Yes. They do look familiar."

I wait. He waits. "Yes?" I finally prod. "Familiar how?"

"Well, they all came in here frequently."

Strange. I know he's being evasive. It's not like he's lying to me, but he's not making any effort to tell me the truth either. All I can tell is that he's intentionally making me work for this. I can't figure out if it's because he's hiding something or if it's just because he's being a dick.

"According to Annabelle, they came in here frequently and spoke with you."

He glares at Annabelle again, then back to me. "Yes, that too."

"Why did they speak to you?"

He mulls over his response for a moment. Finally, he sighs theatrically. "I am afraid it is not terribly interesting, Detective. I am simply somewhat of an unofficial expert on our fair city."

"OK," I reply, waiting.

"I have been here a long time. I spend much of my spare

time exploring the city, learning about it. I know a lot of its history. The origins of neighborhoods and buildings. Past tenants. Gossip. History. That sort of thing."

"I see," I say, mulling my next question. He's acting friendly enough, but something is definitely off. "Was there any particular piece of gossip or history that they were all interested in?"

He chuckles, waving the question away. "Please, Mr. Green. You are trying to read something into this that is not there."

"Am I?"

"Yes, yes. There is no common thread to their questions. They were just questions. I do not recall any of them being related."

"Well, they definitely have something in common now," I say, drily.

"I would like to help you," he says, with that apologetic sound that really isn't apologetic at all.

"Which one of them did you speak to last?" I ask before he can brush me off.

He scowls impatiently, then flicks his hand like he's trying to shoo away an irritating bug. "I do not remember exactly. Eldredge, I think."

"You don't remember for sure? Aren't you supposed to be the history expert?" This guy is pissing me off. All of his answers are calculated, evasive. "What did he want to know?"

"Look, Detective."

"Just tell me, and I'll leave you alone."

He heaves a resigned sigh, flutters his hands and says, "Fine. He wanted to know about the Nursery. He wanted to know who was in charge down there. I told him who I thought was the leader of those wretched souls, and that was the last I heard from him."

"The Nursery?" I ask. "Like, plants and stuff?"

Frank leans forward, fixing me with an intent stare. "No, Detective. Not plants and stuff. Do yourself a favor. Do not go there. I am sure it was nothing. I cannot think of a place I would like to visit less than there. Whatever you do, avoid that place."

He leans back and starts absently fidgeting with the page he was reading. I'm going to ask him something else when I feel a tickling of awareness in my brain. I turn and see Greystone float through the wall by the front door and head straight towards me. Sensing the break in my attention, Frank starts reading again. Guess I'm done asking him questions, then.

"Detective Green," she greets when she gets within earshot. I nod over to my table, and we move that way. Jessica is no longer there. Glancing around, I don't see her at all. She must have given up on me and left.

"Ms. Greystone. What's up?"

"We have a lead," she says. "Detective Marsh asked me to lead you to his location."

"OK," I say, stowing the photos back in the folder in my hands. "Where are we going?"

"A place called the Nursery," she says as she turns away to lead me out. I can't help it. I turn back to look at Frank. I can see his face through the doorway, through the sea of the crowd between us. He is staring right at me, smiling. Like he knows.

"What is going on?" I whisper.

Chapter 18

"THAT'S A BIG FREAKING DOOR," I say, staring up.

The door in question towers over us. Marsh and the others are gathered in front of this massive steel barrier, and I wonder, for the hundredth time since coming here what's going to happen next.

Greystone led me to a carriage, and I traveled for nearly half an hour by myself in silence before arriving here. Plenty of time to stew about Frank warning me specifically not to go to the very place I'm heading.

This place constantly surprises me. My imagination runs crazy trying to picture what I'm going to encounter, and I have to purposely try and keep my expectations neutral. I figure Frank was just trying to mess with me. But what I'm seeing isn't inspiring any confidence.

The rusty steel door is about fifteen feet tall, set into a grime-covered stone wall that completely blocks off the alleyway at the end of an empty street. The wall extends at least thirty feet up and sets flush with the buildings on either side—old tenements, all the windows boarded over. The whole place looks like some surreal war zone. Barbed wire loops line the top of the wall. Four police officers in some kind of metal armor are stationed in front of the door. They're wearing a cross between riot gear and Ren Faire costumes, metal plates and leather straps, helmets that look more like knights than modern headgear. Their guns are considerably larger than the sidearm Greystone insisted I bring along. If I had to give them a name, I'd say they were some kind of shotgun, the ammunition on a belt leading to a backpack. Each slug looks about the size of a soda can. The officers have to use both arms to haul them around, and I'm guessing they are considerably stronger than I am.

Seeing that much firepower outside this door makes me really nervous about what is ahead of me.

All of the detectives are here. They have pieces of protective gear strapped to various parts of their bodies. Arm guards, chest plates. Clark is strutting around making sure everyone gets a look at the armored cod-piece he's strapped on over his suit. Several ghosts are swarming around them. Another group of officers is strapping on metal and leather sleeves and arming themselves with shotguns of some kind— smaller than the backpack-fed ones, but no less lethal.

Marsh waves me over. He slaps some of the metal sleeves into my hand.

"Here, kid. Put these on. Both arms and both legs. Make sure they are tight."

"What the hell is going on, Marsh? Is this the Nursery? What is this place?"

Marsh puts his hand on my shoulder and squeezes painfully. He leans in close to whisper, but his quiet voice still feels like it will shake my molars loose.

"Stick close to me. This is one of the most dangerous places in town. I didn't want to bring you here, but the captain insisted you come and that I protect you. So, for once in your damned life, listen closely and don't ask stupid questions. The things that live here aren't friendly like me. Don't let them get too close. They are going to think we're bringing them a snack, hauling a living person like you in there."

I'm buckling a black leather harness with metal plates onto my arms. It takes some fumbling, but I manage to cinch them tight. Both arms and legs are protected, which leaves me thinking I really wish they had a metal cup like Clark's I could strap on.

Marsh gives my protection a critical glance and nods, satisfied. "Let's go."

We form up into positions. The four guards throw open the door, which screeches and groans loud enough to be heard for a mile. It takes all four of them to struggle with the weight. Once it's open far enough, we run through. A half-dozen officers lead the way, shotguns out. Burchard and Meints trail closely behind them. Clark and Finnegan go next, their side-arms ready. Marsh and I follow, with Armstrong and Kim behind us. Six more officers file in behind us covering the back. The ghosts spread out in all directions.

The gate slams shut behind us, sounding like a blast of thunder.

I've got my gun in my hands, pointed down and to the side. The last thing I need is to accidentally clip one of my coworkers. My palms are sweaty, so I try and keep a solid grip.

Buildings stretch up all around us, more than one teetering precariously to the side. The streets are choked with rubble, debris, garbage. It is dark here: no street lights, no lights behind any of the broken and boarded windows. A fire escape hangs partially attached off the side of one building nearby. It is quiet. All I can hear is our feet walking across the scattered trash and my harsh breathing.

"Contact!" a spectral voice yells up ahead, and three of the officers in front peel off up and around the corner to the left to follow. We keep moving. There are periodically alleyways, so dark I can't see ten feet into them.

I can feel Greystone off to the right somewhere, inside one of the buildings. I don't know what she is thinking, but I can sense flickers of emotion from her. Concentration. Worry.

A soft, slow chuckle echoes from the shadows of a ground-floor interior. It looks like some shop with knocked over shelves and broken out windows. I can't see anyone inside.

A shotgun blast sounds out from behind us, from where the other officers went. Yells and cursing. Another blast.

More laughter, closer this time, from behind a door on our right. One of the officers in back snaps off two shots.

"Stow that!" Marsh bellows. "Save your shots."

I can hear movement all around us now. Silhouettes move in windows up above us. Rocks come whizzing down.

Marsh stops, cups a hand beside his mouth, and shouts out, "Let us through! Send someone to the square!"

A brick comes sailing down and clips Finnegan in the side of the head. He fires a couple shots back in the general direction it came from, all the while clutching his head where he was hit. Holes blossom about a foot across in the walls where he's shot. I can hear things moving all around us now, but I still don't see anyone.

A gunshot claps, and one of the officers in the back goes down screaming. Part of his chest is missing. It isn't until Marsh knocked me to the ground that I realize I was just standing there, staring at the lack of blood and wondering what was wrong.

Gunfire opens up into a full firefight, and we all scatter for cover. I'm glad I have enough wits about me that I don't drop my gun. I dive behind a pile of rocks heaped up next to the wall of the nearest building. It's not going to remove me from the line of sight of the tallest windows, but it's close enough to a wall that hopefully I'm not too exposed.

I see Marsh get hit a couple times as he works his way behind a pillar under a porch. A chunk of his right shoulder goes flying from the impact of one shot. He barely grunts. The body fragments are scattering to dust on the street.

"Marsh, you OK?" I shout over the din.

He waves me off in irritation and starts firing back. Cries of anger bark out as his shots find targets inside apartment windows around us. Shards of glass and particle board are showering down around me as officers return fire.

I still haven't seen who we're shooting at. I would pop off a few shots, but I don't know where to aim them.

A scuff sounds from behind me. I'm about five feet from the mouth of an alley. A little head pokes out around the corner to look at me.

"Holy crap!" I yell in surprise. I can barely make it out in the gloom, but it's a little girl. She can't be more than eight years old. Her stringy matted brown hair hangs down around her dirt-smeared face. Holes and stains cover her clothes.

"Sweetheart, get down!" I yell at her, but she just stares back blankly.

A chunk of brick disintegrates above her head from an errant shot, and I don't even think. I'm up and running at her. A shot sails past my shoulder; the wind tickles the side of my head. I feel a flash of heat on my skin from how close it came.

I grab her around the waist with my arm and slide both of us behind a wrecked dumpster inside the alley. We've got a bit of cover now.

"Are you okay? What are you doing out here?"

I step back so I can examine her, hold her at arm's length, and make sure she's not injured. She smiles at me through broken teeth and bleeding gums.

And then her expression lurches into a rictus of rage;

her fingers claw at my face, and she tries to bite into my arm. My armored sleeves prevent any damage. I just feel pinching from where her teeth are chomping down.

She lunges for my face, and I get my forearm up in time to hold her off. She's flailing wildly with her hands, screaming incoherently, and her ragged nails trace lines across my cheeks where she connects. She's kicking crazily, and even through the armor, I feel one connect with my shin.

"Sonnuva—" I can't keep her off me, and she's way stronger than any little girl I've ever encountered. A slap hits me on the side of my head, and it feels like she's almost torn my ear off. I'm so busy trying to fend her off my face that she is able to kick me in the ankle hard enough to knock me on my ass.

She postures to pounce, and then her head disappears in a spray of bone and brain matter, the body falling on top of me. My ears are ringing from the shot at close range. Someone is shouting near me, and it takes a few seconds for sound to make sense again.

"Suck it up, Green!" Clark snarls, kicking the girl's body off me. He and Marsh both dive behind the cover of the dumpster. The headless body is twitching, but then I see her ghost rising up from the remains. Her face is still contorted in rage, jerking to within inches of my face. She starts screaming at ear-splitting decibels, drowning out the ringing sound in my head.

Greystone appears through the wall opposite me. She looks down at the ghost child, scowls in distaste, and looks at me.

"You are OK?" she asks me. I nod, feeling lost.

"Thanks, Greystone," Marsh says. She fades through the wall again.

"I hate these things," Clark says. I hear snarling in the darkness further down the alley. Two more children come running around a corner, banking off the alley wall. Clark pops up from behind the dumpster and starts firing. The slugs tear through one of them, knocking holes in its body and blowing off one leg below the knee. It hits the ground face-first, looks up and slowly starts dragging itself forward. I've never seen so much fury in a face before.

The other kid hits Clark at full speed, and both go sprawling on the ground.

I have my gun leveled at both of them, but they're thrashing around so much I don't dare take a shot. Marsh reaches over, grabs the kid by the scruff of the neck, and slams it into the wall with one hand. He then immediately follows up with a fist to the kid's face, hitting with so much force it smashes the face flat. Splinters of brick explode off the wall behind the back of the skull.

"The square. Now!" Marsh says, pushing me forward down the alley. The child's body staggers drunkenly around, arms outstretched, flailing blindly for something to grab on to. Clark shoulder-blocks it to the ground and then follows right behind us. Ghosts of children start streaming out of the alley walls around us, howling and wailing at us, swirling in a maelstrom of rage and confusion. We run through the ghosts, trying to ignore them, and head to an intersection in the alley. Just as Marsh gets there, a pack of about a dozen kids comes running from the right. Three or four of them latch on to his legs. He grabs another by a ponytail, swings her around and chucks her down the opposite alley. I lose her in the dark, but I can hear her moving around.

"Start shooting!" Marsh yells at me. Clark doesn't need any prompting; he's up again and already squeezing off rounds into the pack. I don't see what happened to the kid who tackled him.

I bring up my gun, look down the sight, but I can't do it. If it's some big shambling corpse, maybe no problem. But these are kids. At least, they look like kids.

A half dozen are on Marsh now. They aren't able to knock him over, but they're slowing him down. My brain can't quite wrap itself around what is happening. It looks like Marsh is playing with them. I expect to hear giggles and squeals of delight, not the screams of animals—cries of fury and anger. I can't help but wince when I see Marsh hit one so hard its chest collapses, or when he stomps a skull flat into the ground.

Movement sounds from behind us, and I see the rest of the squad moving up the alley.

"Found some friends, Marsh?" Armstrong says, smiling as he unloads shot after shot into a boy no more than twelve, knocking him to the ground. The body looks young, but the eyes contain enough animosity – enough, I don't know, evil—to last a lifetime.

This is a nightmare. I can't get out of here soon enough. I hold my gun in front of me, too scared to use it, too frightened to put it away.

It doesn't take long to scatter the kids; they go scampering back into buildings. We're standing in a four-way intersection of alleys in between the backs of various apartment buildings. From here, there isn't much direct line-of-sight from windows. In the distance, other officers are still exchanging gunfire.

Greystone appears at the mouth of the alley up ahead of us, and she motions us forward.

"OK," Marsh says. I expect him to be breathing heavy, something to indicate he's been exerting himself. Other than a few tears in his clothes, he doesn't look any different than usual. His shoulder where I saw him get hit earlier is writhing, the skin knitting slowly together as it recovers. I shake my head in disbelief. Davenport has staple holes in his hand that are going to last for eternity, but Marsh was practically missing his entire shoulder.

"Marsh, your shoulder."

He ignores me. "The square is up ahead to the right. We'll run for about a block. Once we're there, we're safe. They won't be able to bother us. Even they can't break the compacts in place there.

"And you!" he says, rounding on me and pointing a stubby finger right into my chest.

"Shoot these damned things! They are not children."

"You say that, but—"

"I told you to be careful and shoot anything you see here! I thought even you would be able to follow those instructions. Listen, I know where you come from kids are cute and cuddly. Even when they barf on you, it's roses and rainbows. But these things aren't children anymore. They are endless pits of venom and anger. They have been stuck in their little bodies for centuries. Any kid who sticks around after death has major issues, usually uncontrollable frenzy and anger. And it festers and rots inside them. They respect no laws; they have no boundaries. You cannot trust them. If one gets close to you, you shoot enough holes into it that the body can no longer hold itself together. Am I making myself clear?"

Tears form in the corners of my eyes. I'm not sure my voice won't break, so I just nod my agreement. I feel sick, watching these little creatures getting shot and mangled. Rationally, I understand. Of course I do. But I can't shake the horrified feeling that has gripped me.

I hear my companions ejecting spent bullet casings and loading new rounds into their guns. I don't even know how to do that yet, but it's too much information for my brain to try and process right now. We move forward as a group, running briskly out of the alley opening and down the street. Though this street looks much like the one we came in, no projectiles come at us from the windows overhead. Either they are all over on the other side, or they've had enough fun for one day.

"You're going to want to see this," Greystone announces as we reach a wrought iron fence with the gate hanging askew. I'm surprised to see that it's a cemetery. I realize it's the first one I've seen here. I guess with the dead walking around, there's no need for places like this here. It's not very big, around a couple acres. The fence encompasses it completely. Pathways choked with weeds wind through headstones and mausoleums inside, many toppled over or crumbling.

This must be the square Marsh was talking about; it seems like our destination. We all walk in. Despite what Marsh said about it being safe here, I notice no one is holstering their guns.

"What is it?" Marsh asks, following the ghost. She glides past rows of headstones, over around a mausoleum. She waits for us.

I'm not the first one there, so I hear their curses and mutterings before I round the corner. A body lies on the ground, sprawled spread-eagled on its back. I recognize him.

It's Davenport. And like our four other victims, his eyes are missing, merely smoking craters. It must have happened only moments before we arrived. Even from where I stand, I already know that he's dead.

"Hey, look at it this way, Green," Burchard says, scowling. "No more stapling assaults for you to file."

Chapter 19

"WHAT THE HELL IS DAVENPORT doing here?" I ask. Looking down at the body in this empty place, all I feel is confused. This seems so utterly random to me. It's like showing up on the Moon and seeing my first-grade teacher there. Davenport's corpse is staring up at the sky with empty eye sockets. Like the others, it looks like the eyes have been burned out or melted. I expect him to start laughing, sit up, and admit he's pulling one over on me, but no matter how long I stare at him, he doesn't move.

I turn to Greystone. She's floating in place, not saying anything, just staring down at the body. "You told me we had a lead, Ms. Greystone. That's why we're here. What's the lead?"

She glances up at me; then her face screws up in irritation. "That information wasn't shared with me. Ask your partner."

"But—" She's upset about something again. I don't want to figure it out right now. I step up to Marsh. Before I can ask him anything, though, he's moving.

"Clark, Finnegan, guard our perimeter. Make sure none

of those little bastards sneak up on us," Marsh orders, pointing to corners of the fenced graveyard. More gunshots sound from a few streets over as the two detectives quickly run to their posts. I hear screams that keep going, like air sirens, from somewhere nearby. When you don't have to pause for breath, I guess you can really belt those out.

"How about it, Marsh? What's the lead that brought us here?" I ask when he takes a pause from giving orders.

"We got a letter," Marsh scowls as he says it, like it's a crime that words can be left on paper. "It had some details we didn't think anyone outside the department knew. It was warded against scrying, we couldn't figure out who sent it. So, we thought it was credible. It said to meet here. Now. If we'd known it was only Davenport, I don't think we'd have bothered."

Marsh looks off to the left over my shoulder. I'm about to ask something, when everyone else, almost as one, turns to look in the same direction. I spin, gun in hand, expecting some crazy new creature to be standing there looming behind me.

Nothing is there.

"What the hell?" I ask, confused. And then I hear it.

It's a wailing so high pitched that it barely registers. If there were dogs here, they'd be freaking out right now. It sounds like wind through a field of wheat, a chorus of whispers and distant moans. I try to stare in the same direction everyone else is looking. It takes me a minute, but then I see them.

There are ghosts in the shadows of the windows overhead. The darkness of the windows behind them makes it hard to see, but they are close enough I can discern something inside. They are fuzzy, insubstantial, even for my understanding of ghosts. I can't even determine the gender of most of them. There is a semblance of faces in their shapes, a general outline of body and head, but no specific features. In Greystone's case, every detail is crisp and sharp; individual strands of hair, eyelashes, fingernails. If I couldn't actually see through her, I'd expect to touch her. These things, they're menacing shapes.

And then I notice something that makes my skin crawl. Some of the forms have more than one face. I can't figure out if they are multiple shapes overlapping with each other, or if they swirl in the same mass. I can't tell what is going on.

"Are they merged together?" I ask. I look over at Greystone. She looks nauseous and doesn't answer me.

Kim quietly says, "They're staying in the buildings. They might leave us alone." He doesn't seem like he believes it though.

Marsh shakes his head. "No. We stay here too much longer, and they'll come at us. We're going to have to activate the Ghostbanes. Greystone, tell the rest of your guys it's time to go. Banes are going active in ten."

She scowls at Marsh but doesn't stick around to argue. She races away back towards the gate.

"You know how to activate your Ghostbane, kid?" Marsh asks me.

"I don't even know what you're saying."

"I'll make this quick. Touch your badge and clearly think *'Activate Ghostbane.'* I think it should work for you. We've never tried it with a mortal before, though."

Great. I do as he instructed. *Activate Ghostbane! Activate Ghostbane! Activate Ghostbane!*

Marsh looks at me, studies me a second, then shrugs. I don't feel any different. "Guess we'll see," he says.

He turns to the others. "OK, let's move out. Burchard, Meints, grab Davenport; let's get him out of here."

I follow Marsh as he begins to lead the group back the way we came. Marsh starts speaking to me as we go.

"You're not in any danger from the ghosts, kid. All they can do is annoy you like a pack of bees. But you get a pack of faceless ghosts screaming in your ears and swarming around you, you can't do anything else. Our badges can do a handful of things. This is one of them. It will repel ghosts, keep them about fifty feet away. You just might want to give Greystone warning before you do it, though."

Marsh and Armstrong shoot at anything that moves ahead of us as we run back through the alley and out into the main street. The other two groups of officers are retreating as well, holding off any kids that might feel tempted to attack us from behind. I shiver as I see what looks like a little ten-year-old girl screeching bloody murder, trying to claw us apart. She comes running at us from behind, but she gets torn to shreds by several gunshots that rip apart huge chunks of her body. Her ghost pulls itself out of her crumbling body and continues to come at us, screaming even louder. Then she slams into an invisible force like a wall; I swear she flattens against it. She struggles, clawing at the barrier, trying to get at us, but she starts losing traction, like she's being pulled away from us. She starts moving backward, slowly at first but gathering up speed, until she rockets away from us. I'm guessing it's the Ghostbane at work.

The gate out of the Nursery looms up ahead, and I've never been happier to run through a door in my life.

Four Months Ago . . .

I'm lying on my back in my bed, and Amber is curled in the crook of my arm, her leg draped over mine. We're both naked, and the covers are pulled up over us. We huddle together to stay warm. The air has a cold bite, even inside. My apartment is too old, too drafty to keep warm without paying obscene amounts of money.

"I want you to meet my family," she says.

I chuckle. "Are you sure? They're not going to be very impressed."

She taps me playfully. "They'll love you."

I don't know what to think. I've never been super comfortable around other people's families. My brother has been gone for years. I don't know where my mother is, though I have her phone number but no idea if her phone is even still connected. I don't remember my dad. From how Amber has talked about her family, they are close. That's a dynamic I don't understand.

I haven't had much success with the families of my friends before, either. I was always the one that parents didn't want their kids hanging around. Amber's family will feel the same, I suspect, but for the first time in a long while, I want to make a good impression.

It goes better than I expected. I meet her sister, brother-in-law, and their two young kids. The brother-in-law, Sam, he dismisses me pretty quickly. He's a foreman with a construction company that works on commercial properties. When he hears I'm studying art, he loses interest in me. I'm pretty sure we actually have a few things in common, but I don't get the chance to prove it.

I fare a little better with Amber's sister. She likes me, though I'm sure it's mainly because Amber likes me. I figure I could be the world's biggest loser, but if I treat Amber like a queen and make her happy, I'll be good in her book. I like that a lot.

But where I really excel is with the kids. I've always gotten on well with children, and this time is no exception. I end up spending most of the night playing games with Amber's six-year-old niece and four-year-old nephew while Amber chats with her sister. I end up playing countless games of Go Fish and tic-tac-toe. They ask when I'm going to come over again—always a good sign with kids.

I love kids; I love their enthusiasm and the way they look at the world. Everything is a new and all-consuming experience. I attempt to revert back to that when I work on my art, that wide-eyed fascination with taking in all details. To me, there's nothing better in the world than a child's happiness.

Chapter 20

"IF I NEVER SEE ANOTHER kid again for the rest of my life, it will be too soon," I say with conviction. The other detectives grunt or nod in agreement. I don't know that I'll ever be able to look at a child without fear for the rest of my life.

It's a few hours after our ordeal in the Nursery. The main room is much quieter than usual. One of the officers that had escorted us into the Nursery is now being reassigned as a ghost. His body was too damaged to be repaired. I had imagined there would be a big send-off of some kind—I dunno, a wake or something. But everyone is quiet, subdued, and looking everywhere but the now-empty desk out in the main room where the guy used to sit.

For once, my brain is working just slightly ahead of my mouth. I let the matter drop and don't ask any questions about it. Seeing how everyone treats ghosts, tolerating them at best, flat-out ignoring them most of the time, I recognize it as a sensitive subject. To have your coworker go suddenly from buddy to second-class citizen is probably a lot to process. I don't understand why it should matter, but that seems like a topic for another time.

We close the door to our shared office. None of the detectives were seriously injured on our trip to the Nursery. Marsh got the worst of it with his shoulder injury, but other than tearing a hole in his shirt, he doesn't look any worse for wear. I have a thousand questions I want to ask, any number of directions I could go. It's an itch that I can't scratch. I won't be able to concentrate on anything else if I don't at least ask. Leaning across the desk, I whisper to Marsh, "Your shoulder. It looks like nothing ever happened to it. How is that possible?"

Marsh is leaning back in his chair. He shrugs. "I told you, kid, it's will. I just will my body back into shape."

I understand it's not something everyone can do. Still, I'm curious. "How much damage can you take?"

He sighs loudly. "Look, kid, let me spare you the back and forth. This isn't complicated. I can do something—let's call it, regeneration. Most of us in this room can do it. Except Greystone, of course. It means I can make my body repair itself. From just about anything. I just need time, and I need to concentrate. And it makes me crazy hungry. OK?"

"But, like how badly can you—"

"For the love of . . . What is it with you? I dunno. I haven't met nothing yet I can't walk away from. Bones take longer to regrow than muscle, which takes longer than skin and hair. I break some bones, and it'll take a few hours to heal up. I lose some fingers or toes? Maybe a little longer. It's not exactly something I try and measure."

Man, he looks grumpy about explaining this. I don't know that I've ever seen him this uncomfortable. "Anything else, Green? Any other questions stewing in that damned lump of lard you call a brain?"

"Can you speed it up if you have to?"

"Yeah, sure, if I want to be sick and miserable for days. Or go completely hunger crazed. Or I'll have to re-break it or regrow it again if it don't take right. Now shut it or we'll see how long it takes you to heal a broken jaw!"

He glowers at me, daring me to call his bluff. There are a hundred more questions I want to ask, just off the top of my head. I want to know more about how quickly he can heal. But we have more pressing matters. I lean back and ask another question, but this time, I do it to the whole room, hoping I've found a loophole that will sidestep a serious beating.

"Why don't you put those kids, those things, into the Pit or whatever you call it? Why are they just packed in the Nursery like that?"

"You want to do it, mate, knock yourself out," Burchard snarls. "Best we can do without getting half of us ripped apart is to just contain them there."

Marsh didn't leap over the desk and try and strangle me. Maybe if I address my questions to someone else, he'll calm down. I try another line of inquiries. "Why was Davenport there then? And why was he killed?"

A few shrugs and mutters answer me. I get up and walk over to the chalkboard where we have taped photos of all the bodies. I stare at them. "We just started asking him questions, and he's dead. Maybe someone didn't want us talking to him."

"Don't jump to conclusions," Finnegan snarls. His feet are propped up on his desk, his head propped on his hand, elbow resting on the armrest of his chair. If he were any more relaxed, he'd ooze out of his seat. "Someone could just be pissed he was complaining about being stapled."

"Maybe it was demons," Clark mutters. Snickers and half-hearted laughs sound out around the room.

"We still don't have anything that connects all these victims," Meints points out reasonably.

"Uh, yes I do," I reply, realizing I had never had a chance to fill them in on what Annabelle had pointed out to me earlier.

Stunned silence greets that one.

"So help me if you say demons . . ." Kim starts, but I wave that concern away.

"I spoke with Annabelle down at Warner's. All of our victims used to be regular customers there."

All the detectives relax at that. "I suppose you're going to tell us they all drank beer too," Clark scoffs, shaking his head. "Holy shit, the bartender's been offing the worst tippers in town."

"It *is* Warner's we're talking about," Marsh grumbles, deadpan.

Well, at least they didn't collectively laugh me out of the room this time. I want to tell them about Frank, but rather than get mocked relentlessly, I resolve to go ask him some more questions on my own time.

"Look, I realize it's not much. It's something."

"Right, it's something," Burchard sighs. "Just nothing useful."

I turn and look at the photos on the chalkboard some more. Maybe if I stare at them long enough, something will jump out at me. I hate being the dumbest person in the room. Or, to be fair, the least experienced. It hasn't been conclusively proven I'm the dumbest.

The muttering and comments behind me abruptly go silent, and the temperature drops about ten degrees. I turn to see Captain Radu standing in the doorway, looking in on us. I swear the room is darker than it usually is too. I don't know how he does it, but it feels like he is looking directly at each of us with his undivided attention, all at the same time.

"Another body," he says softly, though everyone hears him just fine. His eyes are glowing red deep in their sockets. "An officer down. And what do you have?"

I sure as hell am not saying anything. No one else does

either.

"I am most displeased," he fumes after a few seconds, then turns and floats away. I can see him moving, but it's like his legs aren't touching the floor; he flows down the hallway.

"Right," Marsh says, looking at all of us from his desk. "Let's hit it again."

Several hours of hitting it pass by with no leads, no progress. Tempers are getting short. We've looked through the files on each of the victims. Except for my "lead," of all the victims frequenting Warner's, nothing seems to tie them together. None of them have been investigated for anything serious, and none of them seem to have known each other. They work in different places, in entirely different fields. They don't belong to any of the same groups, clubs, anything that we can find.

Gradually the other detectives leave to follow up on leads or to just call it a day. Pretty soon it's only Marsh and me.

"C'mon, kid. Let's call it. We'll tackle it again tomorrow," he says.

I lean back in my chair, putting down the pen I've been holding.

"No," I say, seriously. He stares at me, curious. "Marsh, I feel like a joke on this team. I don't have any training, any knowledge. I have no idea why I'm even here."

Marsh shrugs. "The captain wants you on the team. You're on the team. At least until you screw up colossally."

"I'm serious, Marsh. This." I motion to the paperwork. "I think this is the only place I can help. Maybe I'll see something by pouring over notes. Maybe for every nine obvious things I point out, I'll find something that is worth looking into."

He nods, grabs his overcoat and drapes it over his arm. "OK. Fair enough. Greystone will help you get home. I'll see you tomorrow."

The precinct is never closed; there are always people here no matter the hour. But for next little while, I'm alone in the office. There are two or three boxes of files for each victim: notes on prior infractions, logs of past surveillance and reports, interviews with friends and family. And I can't find anything that stands out.

At least this time I sense her coming.

"You're still here, Detective Green," Greystone says as she floats into the office. "Your body needs sleep, unlike most everyone else here."

"I'm trying to find a way to pull my weight around here."

"A laudable goal," she replies, nodding. She floats over to the board, looking at the bodies, studying them. "Have you made any progress?"

I sigh heavily. "No. The only thing I see is the connection to Warner's. I think there's something there, but the others keep dismissing it as trivial. And there's something off about that guy in the back room."

She turns to look at me, her regard is severe and matter-of-fact. It's slightly unnerving, but I try not to let it show on my face or in my feelings. "The captain assigned you to this team for a reason, Detective. Never before has a living person found their way here. Not once in all our history. And you just walked in. You have skills and abilities we have not seen before. If you think something merits your attention, I would advise you to listen to that instinct."

I'm getting a pep talk from a ghost. I don't know whether to feel proud or depressed. If someone dead is trying to cheer me up, I don't know how much further down I can go.

I need a break, so I change the subject.

"Ms. Greystone, how is that officer doing? The one whose body was destroyed today."

She stiffens up. "Why?"

"Because I'm curious how he is adjusting," I reply,

puzzled. "I know I don't understand all the implications, the nuances of everything that is going on, but it seems like a tough adjustment to make."

She doesn't move, but stares at me, quietly. "Officer Jenkins is having a difficult time. Not all can cope with the transition. If he can accept his place on our team, he will be an invaluable asset to the police force. But it is a rare thing."

"I don't understand why. You all are working towards the same goal. We're a team. Why the hostility to ghosts?"

"It, forgive me, this is difficult to discuss. It is not a polite topic of conversation. I am not used to serious inquiries about the matter. I suppose for most of the returned in the city, it implies a lack of willpower. If we were stronger, we could form our bodies. That we can't . . ."

I nod, pretending like I understand. This damned link between us though, I'm pretty sure she knows I don't get it, but she doesn't elaborate.

"Well, let me know if there's anything I can do to help," I say. "Maybe he wasn't directly in charge of protecting me, but he went in to help us. I'd like to repay that in some way if I can."

I register the shock coming from Greystone; she is surprised at my offer. I continue on, a little embarrassed.

"What do you think, Ms. Greystone? Davenport was in here all the time. He has boxes of complaints and charges he's filed over the years. You think it could be a reaction to one of those?"

She chuckles. "Davenport was an odd one, wasn't he? He used to drive Detective Olsen crazy."

"Detective Olsen? Who's that?" I ask.

Greystone is silent. She is staring down at the floor. "I was his liaison for nearly twenty years."

Oh, wow. This is the mysterious partner that I've heard about.

"If you don't mind, Detective. I'll be going." She turns and starts to float away.

The thought hits me so hard I jerk violently, almost leaping out of my chair.

"Wait!"

Greystone turns in surprise. She tucks a stray strand of hair behind her ear in an unconscious manner that speaks to something she must have done all the time she was alive. Her hair certainly doesn't fall out of place now.

"Ms. Greystone, this Detective Olsen. He dealt with Davenport?"

"Yes, as I said. Many times."

"So, Olsen would have filed reports on Davenport?"

Greystone sighs patiently. "Again, yes. Davenport filed numerous complaints with Detective Olsen."

"None of them are here," I say confidently. "There are no files about Davenport filed by Olsen."

She cocks her head slightly to the side, confused. "You must be mistaken, Detective."

"No, I'm not," I say, careful not to interrupt her twice in a row. I'm relieved she let me get away with it the first time. "I've been through these boxes all day. I've read every report, every complaint Davenport filed. None of them are from Olsen."

"But that doesn't make any sense."

"Where is Detective Olsen? Can we ask him?"

Greystone's expression doesn't change, but she says very quietly, "Detective Olsen is no longer here."

Before I can ask a follow-up question, she continues. "He is," she pauses, and I watch her swirl a little, "in the Pit."

That would make it hard to speak to him. I'll have to ask about that later. But I'm too excited to let that stop me.

"Did he keep notes or files? Anything?"

She thinks this over for a moment. "Yes, he did keep

notes. Follow me, if they are not here, then they will be in our storage room."

She is floating quickly, and I have to hurry to keep up. She at least does me the courtesy of not floating through any walls along the way. We make our way down numerous flights of stairs to I-don't-know-what sublevel. I'm surprised at how far down this place goes. We're at least five floors underground when she exits the stairwell and leads me into a maze of dark hallways. We pass dozens of identical doors evenly spaced in the featureless corridor. Greystone better not lose me down here, or I might not be able to find my way back. She leads me to a dimly lit doorway in a little-used hall. I open the door, and Greystone has to wait while I light an oil lamp. I look at a massive storage room with shelves piled to the high ceiling with boxes of files. It's like a Home Depot in here. And it's one of their storerooms. How many dozens of doors did we walk past that lead to rooms just like this one?

Following Ms. Greystone's instructions, I start digging through the contents of the room. It takes the better part of a half hour, but we finally find Olsen's boxes.

Right away, I notice something. I feel it in the pit of my stomach that this is going to be bad news. All the boxes we've seen in here are covered with layers of dust. This entire shelf that I've been searching through for the past several minutes is devoted exclusively to Olsen's case files. And there, at the bottom, are three boxes newly cleared of dust.

I can feel it as soon as I touch the box. I throw the lid off to look at its empty contents. There is nothing in the box.

"This doesn't make any sense," Greystone says. "I know for a fact the files were in there. I accompanied Detective Olsen here every time he moved these boxes to storage. Based on the time stamp on the box label, these must be the boxes that contained files pertaining to Mr. Davenport."

I'm afraid I know the answer to this, but I ask it anyway. "Ms. Greystone, what does this mean?"

She looks at me, and while it's not fear I see in her eyes, it is definitely uncertainty. "The only people that have access to these rooms are officers from our unit."

Dammit. I was afraid of that. I hear Finnegan's voice in my head again, warning about jumping to conclusions. But I don't think there can be any other possibility. "This means that either someone on our team removed these files or, at least, let someone else in here to do it. We've got a mole on the force, don't we?"

Chapter 21

I'M TOTALLY SCREWED NOW.

Greystone has been gone a few hours in the hopes that I would go home and get some sleep. But I'm still at my desk, alone in the office, and my brain is working a million miles an hour. I'm not entirely sure of my position in this place yet, whether or not I have a safety net of any kind. How could anyone believe I would work out as a detective, something for which I'm absolutely not qualified? I barely passed as a digital art student a few months ago. I could play computer games, draw pictures, and make 3-D models. Now, I'm supposed to enforce the law in a town where the natural order of things, as I understand them, is completely backward. And only then because they made me. Because they didn't offer me any other options. I haven't dared ask what will happen if I ever try to refuse. As far as I can tell, provoking Captain Radu would be suicidal since he seems to be in charge of things. Does he report to anyone above him? Are there politicians here? Kings? Archmagi? Grand Poobahs? I have no idea.

If he ever decides that I'm more effort than I'm worth,

I'll just disappear one day. No one will ever find me—even if they knew in which part of the world to look.

The only thing I can think to do right now is to work the best I can at the job they've assigned me. As a detective. I need to prove my worth, validate that this mysterious faith they have in me is well founded. But what do I get as my first real case? An impossible crime. Murders—something never seen before in this place. People are freaking out. The undead are spooked. I don't know what I'm supposed to do, and I'm responsible for helping to figure it all out.

I only know a few people here, and most of them don't like me. Or they would rather eat me than talk to me. But they are my only support here. And now I've found out that one of them may be actively working against us. It would be so easy for one of them to get close to me and make me disappear. I shiver, covered in a cold sweat. Each day seems to find new and exciting ways to terrify me.

It's nearly dawn, hours past when my shift was supposed to end, but I know I'm not going to get any sleep. I put the box back on its shelf in the storeroom and close the door. I don't want anyone to know what I've stumbled on to. By necessity, I'm going to have to trust Ms. Greystone. For one, I know she can't have physically removed the files, as a ghost she can't grab anything. In my mind, I can feel her, and if I understand the impressions from the bond they formed between us, she's as confused and worried about this as I am. She hasn't left the precinct either; she's just giving me space.

Following the sense I have of her, I walk in her direction. She is on the main floor, talking to a few of the other ghosts. They all appear in sharp detail, though a couple of them, like Greystone, also fade out around their feet. Like the undead here with bodies, they appear dressed in fashions that are decades out of style. There are around a half-dozen of them, men and women. All scowl at me as I come down the stairs.

They disperse as they see me approaching, leaving Greystone alone, waiting for me.

"Ms. Greystone, I'd like to go home now. Would you mind coming with me? I think we need to make some decisions."

She nods. "Of course, Detective. I'll have a coach summoned."

I don't recognize the officer driving. He ignores my greeting, just staring straight ahead over the top of the horses. I climb into the coach. Greystone sits on the bench across from me. We make the trip home in silence. A gaslight burns inside providing light. As a ghost, Greystone glows slightly but not enough that I can see clearly to do anything. I'm curious how she's sitting, how she travels with the coach as it moves, but I'm too tired to bother asking for an explanation.

The coach drops us off outside my apartment building, the driver ignoring the both of us as we get out. I resist the urge to flip him off as he leaves. I trudge up the stairway, dimly lit by flickering gaslights at each landing. The shadows almost hide the mold and stains on the walls. Shuffling and whispers sound from behind other doors, echoing in the stillness of the halls.

I find my door, open it and enter *chez moi*. It does nothing to brighten my mood. I hold the door open for Ms. Greystone then curse my stupidity. Still, it only seems polite, and she actually nods in appreciation. Not a smile, exactly, but not a frosty glare, so I count it as a win.

I grab what passes for a beer out of my fridge and sit down on the sofa.

"Ms. Greystone, what are we going to do? I'm so out of my depth here it's not funny."

She floats in the air before me and looks down on me with sympathy. "The important action here is to not inform the wrong person. We should take this straight to the captain."

I start to say something, stop, try again. Finally, "This may be the craziest thing I've ever said, but, no. I don't want to involve Captain Radu."

Greystone waits patiently, I'm guessing she can tell I've got more to say.

"If I'm going to pull my weight at all on this job, if I'm going to figure out why I'm worth keeping around, I have to show I can do something. I don't know the captain as well as you do, but my guess is that if I bring this to him, he'll just ask me to figure it out. He's not going to want another problem; he's going to want answers. Besides, whoever took those files has managed to keep it hidden so far from the captain."

She floats over near me and "sits" on the couch next to me. She sits ramrod straight, knees together, hands clasped together on her lap. I still don't see her feet, but if they were visible, they would be tucked up against the base of the couch. "I think you may be right. But it could be safer if he knows."

"We're assuming he's not the one responsible. I doubt he is, but I don't know. I can't even ask Marsh. Since I arrived here, Marsh has been the only thing keeping me alive. But what if it is him? Someone in the room where I'm working is hiding something about these murders. Right now, I think the only thing that's keeping me safe is my complete cluelessness."

Greystone sighs sympathetically. I know she's acting supportive in the only way she knows how, so I resist the urge to scoot away from the chill radiating out of her so close to me.

"Seriously, though," I continue. "The second whoever it is thinks I might be suspicious, how easy will it be to make me disappear? No one who knows me knows I'm here. My friends, my family probably think I'm dead already."

"One problem at a time, Detective," Greystone suggests softly.

"How do I know this place is clean?" I ask, changing the subject. I wave my arms around to indicate the entire room.

"Clean?" Greystone looks at me in confusion. Her face, as she glances around my apartment, says plainly that "clean" is never a word she would use to describe where I live.

"Clean. No bugs." I clarify.

"No bugs? You want to get rid of insects right now?"

"Not bugs. Listening devices. You guys gave me this apartment. How do I know I'm not under surveillance?"

"Ah, I understand," Greystone replies, nodding. "You have nothing to worry about. This is one of the advantages of having a ghost working with you. I believe you are still assuming electronic equipment will work here. It will not. My mere presence would short it out."

"What about magic?" I ask, my cheeks turning red at the sheer stupidity of saying something like that out loud to an adult.

She pauses, obviously trying to choose her words with care. "You are closer to the mark with this question. To one who knows the arts, they could scry your words out of the air. This isn't as foolish a question as you seem to think."

"Are you serious right now?" I was half hoping she would have ridiculed my question and I could forget about it.

"Yes, but while I cannot prevent someone from scrying you in my presence, I can sense when it is being done. While we discuss these things, I will know if anyone attempts to overhear our words."

I think this over, trying to poke holes in her logic. But it seems pretty safe. One thing, at least, is that I feel secure speaking to Greystone. I may not have any experience in being a real detective, but I've seen enough spy thrillers and horror movies to know that most people who get caught in conspiracies always end up trusting the wrong person before everything goes to hell. I have no choice but to put my faith in Greystone, and I think I'm relatively safe in doing so. We'll see how catastrophically stupid this decision may or may not be.

I try to put it into words. "OK, so just to review: we're investigating murders, and someone has clearly removed evidence from a storeroom—evidence relating to one of our victims."

Greystone nods.

"The only people that have access to that storeroom are people from our unit."

Greystone nods again.

"Could anyone else have gained access? Copied a key or something?"

She shakes her head firmly. "No. It isn't a physical lock. Only people from our unit can enter."

"And who sets that up?"

"Captain Radu," she says. "He is the only one."

I hate asking questions that must seem obvious to anyone who lives here. But the sooner I understand this stuff, the better.

"And it's keyed to what? Our bodies?" I ask.

She shakes her head again. "No, to your badge."

"To my badge." I ponder this for a moment. Is there anything there?

"To answer your next question," Greystone says, pushing her glasses up her nose. This makes me smile. Her glasses are part of her physical form. I'm guessing it must be some habit she had when she was alive that she's carried over. "No one but you can use your badge. The badge is attuned to a specific individual."

"So, no one but our unit then, in any obvious way, can access the storeroom. Which means we'll need to start by looking at everyone in our unit."

Captain Radu. Marsh. Meints. Burchard. Clark.

Finnegan. Armstrong. Kim. Ms. Greystone. And me. I know very little about them outside of my interactions with them at work. I've tried asking about their lives back when they were mortal, but universally, the people here are reluctant to talk about that time, if they even remember much of it at all. For many here, mortality was literally lifetimes ago. It's like a distant dream—only barely recalled. When they get to Meridian, many of them leave their old selves behind and start anew, reinventing themselves to be better or worse than when they were alive. They could have been doctors, priests, or mass-murderers before they put on badges and began enforcing the law.

I think I can safely discount me. I don't remember killing anyone. So that leaves nine other possible conspirators. Something else occurs to me. "I've been assuming there's only one, but I guess that doesn't have to be the case."

Greystone nods grimly. "That is true. There could be more. I also had not thought of that."

"Well, we're going to rule out you, and me, and Captain Radu for the time being." But I'll keep Radu as a long-shot suspect, just in case. "That leaves seven possibilities. I barely know anything about any of the people I work with. You've worked with them. Can you tell me what you know about them?"

She nods, reluctantly.

"Tell me about Detective Burchard," I ask.

Greystone shifts uncomfortably. I'm essentially asking her to spill whatever gossip she knows, asking her to talk about her coworkers behind their backs. But she recognizes the need for it. "Detective Burchard—these are merely my observations, you understand—he has been on the force longer than I, nearly seventy-five years. He is quick to spot details that most others miss, and he finds the anomalies in the patterns of his investigations. There have been many cases solved because of his attention to detail. He will spend hours looking at photos and reports, sifting and sorting information."

I nod. That all matches with what I've observed as well.

She continues. "If you can catch him in the mood, he's actually quite witty."

Now that's where her observations differ from mine. Burchard's usually got a serious expression on his face when he's not glaring in anger. If he has a sense of humor, I have yet to see any evidence of it. Unless you count the wicked zingers and verbal barbs he tosses out without any apparent effort. Burchard hasn't been overtly hostile but hasn't said anything nice to me either. As long as I stay out of his way, he doesn't seem to care about me.

"Detective Burchard isn't prone to excessive violence but has proven very competent in carrying it out when necessary," she continues. "He is the best shot in the squad by far. I get the impression he has a history of killing. A soldier, perhaps."

I can see that. No telling if he still craves it. If he were working against us, he would be methodical, ruthless, and violently unstoppable.

"What can you tell me about Detective Meints?" All I know about him is that he's tall, the tallest detective on our squad. He's got an older and wiser air around him.

"He is certainly the most well-read," Greystone says. "I have yet to come up with a general topic he doesn't know at least something about. He is an expert in philosophy and most of the sciences. I've heard a few of his peers call him 'professor' from time to time, and I doubt it was meant ironically."

A professor. That makes sense. Like most professors I know, he has no tolerance for incompetence or laziness. When I make mistakes, his voice is usually the first and loudest to point it out. I've tried asking him questions about various things, and while he clearly could answer, he won't bother responding to me.

"He's supposedly written multiple volumes of esoteric and historical research, but I haven't managed to find time to read any yet. He's extremely clever. And logical. There's not much that he can't deduce or ferret out."

I heave a depressed sigh. If Meints is behind this, he'll stay several steps ahead of us the whole time.

"What about Detective Finnegan?"

She presses her lips together in disapproval. "A psychotic, vicious man. He enjoys inflicting pain and misery." She stops, surprised at herself.

I nod, encouraging her to continue. "I'd guess he's a serial killer before I'd think a detective. For all I know, that's what he was before he joined the squad."

Greystone composes herself. She really doesn't like to dish the dirt on the detectives in the squad. I'm guessing she went too far in expressing her dislike of Finnegan because she's intent, now, on keeping the observations proper. "He's thin but with a wiry, cruel strength. He knows his way around chemicals; he's the expert on anything related to this area of research. Bombs, magical spell components—he spent many decades in forensics before moving up to his role as a detective. The forensics team still regularly consults with him to help understand any complex information they can't figure out."

He's had it in for me since he set eyes on me. I think he just wants to slice me open to see how I tick. Peel me open slowly, with deliberate care, to great satisfaction. I can feel his eyes on me any time I'm in the same room, like he's preparing for my dissection. Regardless of whether he's working against us or not, I don't want to find myself alone with him. Marsh's presence is all that keeps Finnegan from tearing me apart. Part of me hopes Finnegan's the one, just to get him away from me. But if it really is him, I don't see things ending without a lot of blood.

"Then there is Detective Clark," Greystone says. He's been the friendliest of the group so far, but I think it's only because I amuse him. I work at trying to be a cop, and he thinks it's funny. I almost expect him to give me a treat every time I talk.

"Detective Clark manages not to allow the stresses inherent with the job to get him down. He is independently wealthy; he doesn't need to live off his salary like the rest of the squad. He works the job because he's quite skilled in following paper trails. Of the entire group, he is the one who best knows the laws and codes we live by."

"Wait a minute. Back up a second."

Greystone waits patiently while I try to put this into words.

"We get paid?"

She smirks, chuckling silently. "Of course you do, Detective. Hasn't Marsh told you yet?"

Oh, we're going to have some words.

"As I was saying," she arches an eyebrow at me, asking permission to continue. I nod eagerly.

"Don't tell him you heard this from me, but I happen to know Clark does work for at least two charities in town."

"Charities?" I can't wrap my head around that. I don't even try. He dresses the best of us. His suit is always cleaned, pressed. The color seems more vibrant than anything we're wearing. Not louder. We all wear clothes that are dark and subdued, but his just radiate more color. Rich. Charity worker. Anywhere else, I'd say he's a nice guy. Here though, it seems like too much compensation. Something's definitely up. Since he's the only one that treats me with any degree of civility, I hope it's not him. He's way more perceptive than he lets on too. I can see in his eyes that he reaches conclusions ahead of most of us but holds it back. He definitely hides things from us. I just don't know how malicious his deceit is. Is it dangerous or just cautious? If it's Clark, I don't think we'll ever see it coming.

"I'm afraid I don't know too much about Detective Kim. He keeps to himself, doesn't betray a lot of emotion. He has only been working for the precinct for twenty years. Until you, he was considered the rookie."

Of the group, he's the one who seems to most expect me to fail. It's hard to read his expression, but I imagine he has scorn written all over his face whenever he decides to look my way. When he deigns to speak to or about me, his words are always derisive, pointing out my flaws. He's just waiting for me to fall on my face as if it is inevitable like day follows night. Given how guarded he is though and that even Greystone hasn't discovered much about him, if Kim is the suspect, I won't find out until it is too late.

"Then there is Detective Armstrong. He is quiet but calculating, not shy. He's perceptive. He keeps to himself a lot but rarely lets anything escape his attention. You will have noticed him sketching or doodling in his notepad, but don't let that fool you. He's soaking everything in around him."

He's solid as a rock too, judging by the couple times he's body checked me when I've run into him going around a corner. I'm pretty sure he spent a lot of time as hired muscle. I've been bounced by enough bouncers at rough bars to recognize the demeanor. To him, I'm a distraction he's trying to get rid of. I wouldn't expect him to go out of his way to help me.

"While Detective Meints might know math and science, Detective Armstrong has his ear to the ground. He has contacts throughout the city: informants, friends, sources of information about any facet of the city or people in it. Any fact, detail, historical anecdote, or piece of gossip that's passed by us, Detective Armstrong can recall at a moment's notice. If he is behind this, Detective Green, he'll disappear somewhere no one will ever find him long before we get close to catching him. In a city made up of all the forgotten detritus of the world, he can find places forgotten by everyone else here."

I don't even want to ask about the final member of our squad.

"What can you tell me about Marsh?" I ask in a whisper.

She hesitates. "It can't be Detective Marsh. He's the senior detective in the precinct. He's been working this job for over a century. He might not exhibit the learning or education of the other detectives, but he has good instincts, he can read people well. And when he can't, well, he's virtually unstoppable."

Detective Marsh. Dear God, please don't let it be Marsh. If it's Marsh, we won't be able to stop him. He'll set it up to look like me. No way he'll take a fall when he's positioning the perfect patsy to take one for him. I know it's not rational, but I just can't picture this being Marsh.

How do I feel about Marsh, really? I don't know that I can answer that question, even to myself. For weeks I lived in terror of him. But I also know that he kept me from getting killed by some of the hungrier denizens here. Do I like him? I don't. I want to get as far away from him as possible, but while I'm stuck here, I don't dare. He may be the best insurance I have for staying alive.

It's dangerous to eliminate him as a suspect; I get that. I'll be risking my life. But I just can't bring myself to believe it's him. I'll look at him last—after I've exhausted all other avenues.

"Where would you like to start, Detective?" Greystone asks softly.

I close my eyes and rest the beer bottle against my forehead. I wish it were colder; it's not helping hold off a killer headache that's building.

I just don't know. "No one sticks out. I'm hoping it can't possibly be any of them. I barely know these guys, but I can't picture any of them doing this. If this person finds out I'm looking into him, he'll kill me before I get close. Of course, if anyone on the team finds out I'm seriously investigating them, half of them would kill me on principle. Or if it's Finnegan, he'll just kill me for fun.

"If we pick wrong," I start, but my voice gives out. I clear my throat and try again. "Ms. Greystone, if we mess this up, if I get killed making the wrong decision, you'll let the captain know what happened?"

"Do not tread down that line of thought, Detective Green," she says sternly. "We need to approach this problem with the intention of solving it, not being defeated by it."

I nod and think for another minute, then make up my mind. "Let's just start with one at random. Saving Marsh for last."

Greystone nods. "OK."

"Let's start with Armstrong."

She hesitates. "I'm not certain what more you think I can tell you, Detective."

I gesticulate with my arms, as if that will explain more clearly. "I don't know. You've known him longer than I have. You've had more experience with him."

"I think you overestimate my status. Being incorporeal, I am not seen as a peer among many of the others in the precinct."

I grunt in understanding. That stupid corpse versus ghost thing again. I don't think a ghost floating next to me, chill radiating off her causing goosebumps to break out on my flesh, is any weirder than speaking to the walking corpses that surround me. Then something occurs to me.

"What about the detective you were linked to before me? Did he have any experiences with Armstrong?"

"Detective Olsen? Yes, I suppose that he did."

She thinks for several moments. Finally, "Perhaps there is something from my observations of the two of them together that I can share, though I'm not sure what you are hoping to learn from it."

"Again, I don't know. Can you just tell me something, anything, about how this Olsen guy got along with Armstrong?"

"Very well," she says.

Detectives Olsen and Armstrong

"A year ago, Captain Radu instructed Detective Olsen to meet up with Detective Armstrong to investigate suspicions that someone had either created or found a tear in one of the veils hiding our city from the rest of the world. The two of them had worked together before, but Detective Armstrong typically worked with Detective Kim on most cases, and Detective Olsen would work with Detective Marsh. But in this instance, Detective Marsh was busy on some other project.

"Something you must know about Detective Olsen is that he was very methodical. Very logical. He was meticulous in his gathering of evidence, and when he reached a conclusion on one of his cases, he was rarely mistaken. He worked well with Detective Marsh, as Detective Marsh would follow Detective Olsen's findings and would generally remove any obstacles that presented themselves.

"Detective Armstrong was the polar opposite of Detective Olsen. Detective Armstrong followed hunches, intuition, flashes of insight, and visions. Detective Olsen admired the man's results, but they did not typically enjoy working together, as their approaches were so fundamentally different.

"Normally, a case such as this would be handled by the Retrievals Office, as tears in the veils of the city generally meant that residents were escaping into the real world. But that wasn't what was happening in this case, at least not entirely.

"When there is fighting and there is warfare in the mortal world, especially on a large scale, it can damage the barriers that separate us. And some conflict in Afghanistan, I believe it was, created tears that allowed a group of residents here to reach out and pull mortals through, to bring them here and, well, to consume them.

"It had been going on for several weeks before word reached Captain Radu. We knew it was happening, but we didn't know where the tears were located. They were too ephemeral, too elusive for us to track.

"The detectives spent the next few days asking questions around town, tracking down leads. Detective Armstrong knew who to ask, and once they found someone, Detective Olsen would question them. This is where Olsen excelled; he was good at ferreting out information from people, even information they didn't realize they knew. Eventually, they followed leads that guided them to someone who was involved.

"This is where Detective Armstrong began to use one of his unique talents. He began to draw.

"You must understand, his talent for drawing is supernatural, something beyond the abilities of mortals. When he draws, he channels some force that pulls detail into his work. If you ever get the chance to see his sketches, you will see that they move; they are living on the page.

"Once they located someone who knew about the tears, Detective Armstrong started to draw images of them, and the background of the illustrations pointed to where we could find them, even though the detective had never been there before.

"The two detectives found the location of the tear, a garage in an empty building, where piles of the remains of corpses were stashed. The tear itself was a shimmering energy that flickered in the air, like a window that looked onto some other place.

"They entered the building, and a firefight ensued. The detectives wounded and detained five individuals, who had taken advantage of the tear to feed on mortals.

"Detective Olsen was certain that at least one person eluded them. But with the five apprehended and shipped to the Pit for incarceration, there was nothing further they could do. Forensics arrived to re-seal the tear, and no further information was uncovered.

"Now that I think about it, Detective Olsen was bothered about the case. Besides the fact that he felt someone had escaped them, it was something to do with the corpses, I believe. He didn't share his concerns, but he spent a good deal of time examining the remains of the victims.

"I will need to reflect on that some, perhaps."

Greystone is silent for several minutes, thinking back.

Finally, I break the silence. "That's interesting, Ms. Greystone. But what does it have to do with Armstrong?"

She frowns at me, redirecting her attention and her ire to me.

"Returning to the subject of Detective Armstrong, you will need to exercise great caution. I do not know the extent of his precognitive abilities or if his sketches will warn him of your plans. Presumably, he has already drawn you and who knows what he may have already deduced. When you believe that he is not paying attention, he is undoubtedly receiving visions and flashes of intuition. He is not to be taken lightly."

Chapter 22

How do you act inconspicuous when you stand out like the blazing light of the sun in a darkened room? I'm different than everyone in this entire city—and different in an incredibly obvious and glaring way. I'm the only one that needs to breathe. Others eat. They drink. But I'm the only one that has a beating heart that pumps my own blood to keep me alive. My body is warm. I'm a curiosity—a freak, in that I'm normal adrift in a sea of odd.

How on earth am I going to be able to trail Armstrong without him knowing? Even the most clueless idiot would realize that conversations pause whenever I'm around; people stop what they're doing to observe me. And I work with some of the sharpest and most observant people here. If I'm going to seriously try and spy on my coworkers without them knowing, I've got to come up with a better plan than simply bumbling around and hoping I don't get seen.

Greystone leaves around two in the afternoon. I have five hours before I need to start getting ready for work again. My body needs sleep.

An hour passes. I'm still just as awake as when I started.

My window is open, but rather than cooling the room down, it lazily pushes the warm air around, smothering me more than refreshing me. Noises sound from outside on the street: the shuffling of feet, the clomping of horse hooves as they trot past pulling carriages and carts, the occasional coarse laugh or curse of passersby. A few flies buzz around. My mind won't turn off.

If I don't find out who is killing corpses, I'm not adding any value to the team. And Radu has made it clear that's the only reason I'm still alive. He thinks I may bring something they haven't seen before. Why he believes this, I have no idea, and I can feel panic clawing at the edge of my mind when I think about it for too long.

If I don't uncover which member of my squad is trying to conceal evidence, this person may realize I know about him. The longer I investigate, the more likely I'll give something away or be discovered. I can't make a single slipup. Whoever is doing this, he has apparently kept it quiet for this long without the others in the squad catching on. He'll be alert to any snooping.

If my coworker finds me out before I find him, I'm dead. If I don't figure out who is responsible for these killings, I'm dead. And others are going to die.

So, what do I do? Dammit. I sit up.

Well, the first thing I do is give up on sleep and put some clean clothes on. I shuffle over to my icebox, open it, grimace, and close it again. I could sit on my couch and drink some beer, but I'm feeling restless, and my mind is just running in circles. I decide to make my way over to Warner's. They have food there I can eat, and if I don't actually ask about where it comes from, I probably won't throw it up.

Fifteen minutes later, I'm pushing open Warner's door. I've never been here at this hour before. I'm kind of expecting it to be slow this time of the day, but then I remind myself that even though some of these folks sleep, not all of them do. The place is as packed as always. I find my way over to a booth that's open, ignoring the talk around me.

I see Frank glaring at me from the back room. He tracks my movement the second I come into his line of sight. I look at him quizzically, and he just turns away and concentrates on the book he's reading. Strange. I've been meaning to speak to him about my experiences in the Nursery, but I can't summon the energy right now.

I'm expecting some quiet time to myself, but no sooner do I plant my butt on the bench than someone scoots in right next to me. Surprisingly, she is familiar. I recall the green eyes and her nearly living appearance.

"Um, hi," I begin, trying to remember her name. Jen, Jamie, Jane, Jessica . . . Jessica! She doesn't even bother with sitting across from me this time. I slide over, but she has me trapped in the booth, pinned between her and the wall. She's facing me, smiling. She's breathtaking, there's no denying that, but I don't like being trapped. Unfortunately, unless I'm willing to crawl under or over the table, she's got my undivided attention for a while.

"We were interrupted last time, Detective Green," Jessica says, smiling eagerly. She places a hand on my forearm, and I'm aware just how close she is to me. She's undoubtedly the most beautiful dead girl I've run into here. Normally, I would love to chat with a beautiful girl who seems kind of into me. But the fact that she is dead is too big a hurdle for me to clear. I would prefer to figure some things out about this case. Unfortunately, she doesn't look like she's going to give me the opportunity.

On the other hand, she's the only person who actually wants to talk to me. She isn't obligated to associate with me in order to keep her job.

Fine. I can try to forget my troubles for a little while.

Let's chat with the closest thing to a living girl I'll meet here.

"You're right, Jessica. I'm sorry. You have my complete attention tonight." I signal to the waitress to bring over a couple of coffees. I don't recognize her. I guess Annabelle isn't working this shift.

"Good," Jessica replies brightly. "I want to know all about you."

"Why?" I ask suspiciously. What's her angle here? Does she really want to get to know me, or is this something else?

She smiles playfully and, as best I can tell, sincerely. "Do I need a reason to want to know about my first living neighbor in town?"

Fair enough, but I'm still wary. "I've been answering a lot of questions since I got here," I say. "To be fair, this is a friendlier interrogation than I've experienced so far."

Her face registers shock. "No, Jacob! I'm not interrogating you, truly." She starts to say more but hesitates as our waitress arrives and sets down two mugs of what passes for coffee here.

Jessica waits until the waitress has left before she continues. "You don't have to tell me anything you don't want to. I'm not trying to dig secrets out of you. I just want to get to know you better. Tell me about you."

She doesn't seem to be lying about this. I guess this is what it appears to be, for whatever reason she might have. I hate that I'm suspicious of every person I meet here, but so far, my experience has proven this to be a healthy decision.

What do you tell a dead person that they would find interesting? Blood type? My BMI? This whole situation seems completely ridiculous, but at the same time, I can't help myself. For the first time in months, someone wants to hear about my life without beating the information out of me.

Before I know it, I'm spilling every little thing about my life that pops into my head. I tell her about going to school in Nebraska. I describe living in a place where you can see sky from horizon to horizon, where life revolves around college football, Runzas, and a live music scene.

All of it is completely foreign to her. She is fascinated when I mention suffering from allergies, something with which no one here has problems. She asks me what I study in school. She understands being an artist, but when I tell her about creating 3-D models and animating characters on computers, about vertex lighting, rigging, what I know about light maps and texture maps, I can tell it all sounds like gibberish to her. Even so, she smiles and nods in polite interest.

She asks about my family. That takes all of about twenty seconds, so then I start to talk about Amber, but she quickly steers the conversation another way. She pays rapt attention to everything I say whether she understood what I was talking about or not, and I have to say that's never happened to me before. I also can't help but notice that she hasn't moved her hand off my forearm. Which is nice. But it would be nicer if her hand had warmth, if it didn't feel so stiff and cold. It's just a constant reminder of how different she is than what I'm used to.

"What about you?" I ask her. I don't want to be a total bore, and I'm genuinely curious about her. No one talks about how they got here, who they were before or what they used to be. To them, it's another life.

Jessica shrugs, glancing away, giving me the opportunity to surreptitiously examine her. Her skin is pale, like the last time I saw her, but again I can see the edges where the cover-up doesn't completely hide. She is still doing her fake breathing. I wonder if she does it all day or if she's merely doing it for my benefit. Even covered with flowery perfume, the smell of decay still tickles my nose.

"What do you want to know?" she asks.

I pause. What *do* I want to know?

Guardedly, I say, "I'm not sure what questions might be impolite here."

"Oh, don't worry about that. I'm curious what questions you would ask me."

Here goes nothing. "How long have you lived here? In this place, I mean? Is that a rude question, like asking how old you are?"

She laughs. "No, it's fine. I've been here nearly one hundred years."

The mug pauses partway to my lips.

"Ah." Well, that blew any follow-up questions out of my mind. "Hmm, what do you do?"

"I sing. I run a theater troupe. I observe."

I nod, and I try to manage a genuine smile. An actress—that I can understand. She continues. "My group and I, we try and emulate the living. We call ourselves Those That Came Before to sound all mysterious. You should come and see some of our performances."

"I'd like that," I reply. It's true; I would like to experience something normal, and I'd like to see her perform. "Performances of the living. What's that like?"

She shrugs nonchalantly. "We do things that living people do. Eat, sleep, dream. One of our most popular bits is portraying how you mortals get ready in the morning. Bathing, grooming, dressing. We have to keep security on hand; sometimes we do such a good job the hungrier ones in the audience try and grab a snack."

"Heh," I chuckle and take another sip from my mug.

"Could you tell I was not a living girl when you met me?" she asks, turning serious. I pause, keeping the cup in front of my mouth. I don't want my expression to betray me. Of course, I knew she was dead. The skin, the fake breathing, the slight smell of rot, the eyes. Maybe from a distance, maybe I'd be fooled. Up close, even though she's the closest I've seen to living, she's still a long way off. No point crushing her though as she clearly goes to a great deal of effort to appear to be alive.

"I had a hard time at first, of course," I say, cautiously. She beams back at me, pleased.

I open my mouth to ask another question, and I completely freeze. A thunderbolt of an idea has just hit me.

"Jake? What is it?"

I set my mug carefully down on the table. I think about it a little. Am I crazy? Yes, but maybe—hmm . . .

"How would you like to help me do some undercover work?" I ask, the words out before I can worry about the wisdom of this action.

"Oh, yes, please!" she gushes, grabbing my forearm with both hands, leaning close. "How can I help?"

An hour later, we're walking into my apartment. Jessica is the first corporeal girl I've brought home here. Weird. All the times Greystone has been here, I've never felt that I was in my place with a girl. The two of us, a ghost and I, are we friends? No, not friends. Coworkers.

With Jessica, though, it's definitely different. It seems more intimate.

I don't have enough belongings for things to get messy in my apartment, so it's passably clean. No stray clothes laying around, no trash piled up. It's easy to keep the place tidy when you don't own anything.

"You live here?" she asks, the smile on her face a little forced.

"What? Is there something wrong?"

She hesitates, setting down two boxes full of makeup, a garment bag with some clothes, and other materials I haven't been able to identify. "Well, it's just . . ."

"Yes?"

"It's just that I expected you to be somewhere a bit nicer," she says. "Not that there's anything wrong with your place!" she adds quickly. Her eyes linger on the cot, canvas stretched across a splintered wooden frame, torn stained sheets and a blanket bunched on top.

I frown, looking around again. She can tell I'm not understanding.

"Have you been to any of the other detectives' homes?"

"No. Why?"

"You should. They live in places nicer than this. A lot nicer actually. Estates, penthouse suites, that kind of thing. I'm surprised you're in this area; it's mostly criminals and such."

"Sonnuva... Marsh!" I grumble quietly. I'll have to bring this up with him soon.

Jessica pushes me back into my lone chair. A stray spring digs into my spine. I start to lean forward and stop myself just in time. Jessica is bending down to reach one of her boxes behind me on a table, and I just about plunged my face into her chest. By her smile, I don't think she would have minded. Still, she's uncomfortably close as she reaches past me. Finally, she gets what she needs and leans back.

"OK. I think I have everything we need here. I brought some of my stage makeup, a change of clothes for you, and I have my materials for a glamour."

"Wait, a what?" I ask.

She looks at me quizzically.

"What do you mean, a glamour?" I reply. This may be the first time I have an actual opportunity to get an answer on this.

She thinks I'm kidding at first, but her smile fades as she realizes I'm serious. "Oh, I see. People don't use glamours in the mortal world." She looks vexed at having to explain, reluctant.

"It's magic," she says finally. "It makes people see what

you want them to see. They rely on a combination of words, materials, gestures, and artistry. Not everyone can do them, and most of us only specialize in a very limited number. My glamours alter one's appearance, and I generally alter them in a specific way. Others make glamours to hide and conceal things or create illusions. Basically, anything that alters a way you perceive people and the environment around you."

I smile like I understand what she's saying. "What makes someone good at them? Could I do them?"

"Possibly," she says with a forced smile, which I read to mean: not at all likely. "One of the biggest factors in one's ability to create glamours is one's willpower. Most mortals who have the willpower to do it are also the ones who have enough willpower to persist past death and make their way here. Then for those who can create them, imagination is also important. It makes them more believable. Magic isn't merely logic or learning; it involves those and many other factors."

"Magic. Glamours. This glamour you're putting on me—this will make people think I'm dead?"

She nods. "Yes. I have a passable ability in this. Usually, I'm trying to do it the other way around, trying to make someone who's dead pass as living. But I shouldn't have too much trouble. With the makeup and the glamour, you'll look like a regular resident here unless you're observed with anything other than casual scrutiny. Don't do anything out of the ordinary, and even your detectives shouldn't notice you.

"Now, lean forward, let's get started."

She leans over me, our knees touching, her eyes gazing into mine and about my face. It takes about another half hour. And then I look dead. Or so Jessica tells me. I study myself in the mirror, and it just looks like I've got green foundation smeared on my face. I think it's ridiculous.

"I really pass for dead looking like this?" I ask her. I don't understand how this magic works, I'll just have to take her word for it.

"Of course. Can't you tell? The glamour is working. Some of my best work, if I do say so myself."

I shrug. OK, then. Now to step two.

Ms. Greystone, can you hear me?

I'm "thinking" as loud as I can, directing it towards where I sense the ghost in my mind.

"*. . . Det..tive . . . Gr . . . n?*" I hear the words in my head. Fuzzy, faint, garbled, but I can make them out. I hope this isn't the best it will ever get.

I'm going to follow up some leads on my own, I think at her.

"*Are . . . you sure? You should . . . someone . . . with you . . .*"

I nod, then realize how stupid that is. I hope she doesn't know I did that, or she won't let me hear the end of it.

Yes. I've got someone with me. Tell Marsh, I'll check in later. I'll need your help in a little bit. But until then . . . Um . . . Green, out.

I can't tell if I hear the sigh of exasperation in my head, or if I just imagined it. I open my eyes and turn to Jessica.

"OK, let's go." She grabs my hand and pulls me out the door. She's much more excited about this than I am.

Jessica and I loiter around the bridge leading to the police precinct. There is a lot of foot traffic going in and out. Since this is the only way to enter or leave the precinct, this is probably the best place to try and start following him without being obvious about it. It's not like I've ever done this before. I lean against the wall of a nearby building, something I would expect to see in some European town, giving me a clear view of the front gate.

After about an hour I see Armstrong walk across the bridge and start marching into town, the collar of his coat upturned against the wind. About time. I'm freezing my ass off. It was plenty warm outside my apartment, but here, it's at least forty degrees colder. Jessica doesn't seem fazed by the temperature. When I asked her about the change in weather, she admits she doesn't understand it either. That's just how it works here. I'll never figure it out.

I let Armstrong get about a block ahead of us and then start out after him. To better blend in with the crowd, Jessica insists on holding onto my arm and walking with our hips almost touching.

We follow him for the next several hours. He wanders all over town. He doesn't seem to be doing any police work, per se. He walks along the main river that bisects the downtown area—the River Styx, appropriately, though Jessica assures me no one really thinks it's the actual river from legend. It runs through a deep canal, the current strong and churning, the water dark. Buildings butt up right to the edge of the path lining the canal. The walls and buildings provide a nice buffer to the wind, and the temperature is considerably warmer. The river is loud, and it meanders through the town, under several bridges. This path is very popular; we pass numerous people, helping us blend in. At one point, I think I see something under the surface of the water and lean out over the side of the path. Jessica quickly yanks me back away from the edge and shakes her head. I'm confused, but later see a large shadow under the water pull away from the shore, and I shiver at what might be down there.

We see Armstrong speak to several people along his walk: shopkeepers, people walking on the street, the occasional person hanging out at a corner. I'm not close enough to ever hear what he says, but he never speaks to anyone for long. Most of the time he merely nods or waves as he passes by.

Eventually, we follow Armstrong over near the docks. He spends an hour on a bench by the pier, a clipboard in his lap with paper clipped on it to repel the occasional gusts of wind, sketching pictures of birds and the waves. Later, back in a business area in the middle of a pedestrian district, he gets lunch at a cart on an alley corner. I have no idea what kind of meat is slapped between the slabs of bread he gets, and I don't really want to know. Some sort of condiment squirts out from the sandwich when he takes a bite; I hope to God it's mustard, but it's not any color of anything I've ever seen before on a sandwich. It doesn't escape my notice that he slipped the cart vendor a thick envelope, but they don't appear to talk about it any.

A few times he glances over his shoulder, and my heart stops, but he doesn't seem to take any interest in us. Finally, he ducks into some bar called Giuseppe's Place. By going in, we significantly increase the chance he'll see us, but I want to know what he's doing. We wander in shortly after and see Armstrong sitting down with a trio of unsavory types. I don't recognize any of them, but their hatchet faces and massive arms probably don't come from soft living. We manage to find a booth nearby but out of line of sight. Jessica orders a couple drinks for us while I concentrate on listening to what Armstrong is saying.

"Antonio, you know how it is," Armstrong whispers as we get our drinks. "If I give you too much, suspicion will come right down on me. You may not know Radu, but believe me, you don't want to catch his attention."

"That's not our deal, and you know it," one of the men responds. Maybe this is Antonio? "We're paying you good money."

Armstrong interrupts. "All I'm saying is, I'll give you what I can. I haven't steered you wrong yet, have I?"

"We've got a big shipment coming in tomorrow. Our guys have a lot riding on this one."

"And I'm telling you," Armstrong says, "that if you bring it in at Pier 14, I'll make sure the Port Authorities are busy somewhere else."

I whisper to Jessica, "Are you hearing any of this?" She shakes her head, shrugging helplessly. "I'll tell you when we leave."

I don't know what to make of this. Armstrong doesn't say anything related to the murders, but he talks to Antonio and his friends for several minutes about a shipment of something coming in and how he'll help them get it past the authorities.

The conversation turns to talk about some kind of sport I can't identify; then they finish up and part. We get up and follow soon after.

He travels to a park—at least, what passes for a park here. A battered gazebo sits in the center of weeds clustered on bare dirt. A few paths crisscross in between pockets of dead trees. Some shrubs nearby have actual greenery on them, though it barely covers the wicked barbed thorns that poke out everywhere. Here the detective meets with a corpse so old it looks like it will collapse into dust at any moment. We hear only snatches of conversation from the bench we're sitting on. To get any closer would be too obvious. Again, he discusses details about helping him smuggle some stuff into the city. I'm relatively sure he's not talking about the murders.

We have found a park bench tucked near the entrance, and we're trying to look as uninteresting as we can. Jessica is holding my hand, sitting close to me, leaning into me so we can both hear what is being said. She's a little closer than I'm comfortable with, but when I try and scoot away, she just moves right back up to me.

Armstrong nods to the fossil he's talking to, and then turns around and starts heading right for us. There's nowhere to go without obviously avoiding him, and the path is going to take him right next to us. I panic, not sure what to do.

Jessica grabs my chin in her hand, turns my head towards

her, and she plants one on me, nearly climbing into my lap. She kisses me hard, her other hand sliding behind my head so I can't back away. Her head blocks Armstrong's view of my face, so I close my eyes and pray he's too busy staring at Jessica's curves to notice the lucky stiff she's latched on to.

Any other time, having a beautiful woman throwing herself at me is something I dream about but never really expect to happen. But this . . .

Her lips are locked onto mine; her tongue darts into my mouth. I feel her breasts pressed firmly up against me, and it's all I can do to suppress a shudder of revulsion. The lips are dry, leathery. I can taste a wave of rot and decay breathing out of her mouth. A trickle of fluid leaks from her mouth into mine, and it's not saliva. Her tongue is as dry as a stick, with a rough sandpaper texture. Instead of sliding up against my tongue it snags on it. I can't hear her breathing, which is wildly disconcerting. With my eyes closed, all I can picture is a corpse wrestling with my lips and biting my face. I feel panic building, and it's all I can do not to scream.

"Jake?" It takes me a second to realize Jessica is speaking to me. I open my eyes, and she's looking at me with concern. Her nose is pressed against mine, her eyes filling my vision. "Are you OK?"

I look around before looking back to her. Armstrong is gone. Even if I could pick up his trail, I'm not sure I want to right now. I lick my lips nervously, still tasting a tinge of decay, and I suppress a shudder. "Hmm? Yes, sure, of course."

She slides away from me but retains a grip on my arm. "Did I do something wrong?" I look at her, and I see the distress on her face, the fear. A wave of emotion crosses her stiff face. She's teetering on an edge, worried I am genuinely repulsed, and if she thinks that, it will mean she's not as living as she is attempting to be. Maybe she doesn't care what the rest of the dead in this town think of her but, me, a living person, my opinion matters.

I don't want to hurt her feelings. She can't change who she is, she hasn't done anything wrong, and I'm not going to cause her pain because of my hang-ups. Even if up until a few months ago, necrophilia was a perfectly legitimate hang-up by any definition.

I force a smile onto my face and urge it to look reassuring. "Of course not, Jessica. You took me by surprise, and I was worried about Armstrong seeing me." I squeeze her hand.

A few seconds pass uncomfortably, but I must have been convincing because she smiles at me, and I can almost visibly see the tension release from her shoulders.

"C'mon," I say, standing up and pulling her up to start walking with me. Even though we don't have the pretense of needing to act to try and look inconspicuous, she continues to hold my hand. "Let's go. I need to go back to the precinct and speak to my captain."

Chapter 23

Back at my apartment, I hand Jessica her supplies. "Thank you so much. You've been a tremendous help."

"Of course, Jake," she smiles. Her hands linger on mine as she takes the supplies from me. "I'm happy to do what I can."

Hmm. She makes no move to leave, so I have to try and usher her out. "I have to get cleaned up. And, um, get to the office."

Jessica leans in close and drags one finger up my arm. "You don't have to go in yet, do you?"

My smile is a little forced. I back over to the door and open it up. "Sorry, duty calls. I really must go."

She pouts, but mercifully, she walks out into the hallway. "See me again soon, Jake. I want to hear what you find out."

I nod, mumble a goodbye, and close the door. I don't think I've ever breathed as big a sigh of relief as I do right now. I hurry and strip down, heading to the shower, and work on washing the makeup off my face.

Once I've dressed again, I think, *Ms. Greystone, can you come visit me, please?*

It doesn't take me long to bring Greystone up to speed on what I have been doing. She is not happy I involved Jessica, but grudgingly admits it may have been useful. But she is really not happy about how I followed Detective Armstrong around without her help. She's floating laps around my small living room, her version of pacing.

"How has he managed to keep this a secret?" she asks out loud. I'm pretty sure she doesn't expect me to know the answer, so I don't bother with a reply. "Even if he doesn't have a liaison bonded to him, it's staggering he has been able to do this without anyone discovering it."

The gloom outside is gradually brightening, indicating somewhere above the perpetual cloud cover outside the sun is rising. People are shuffling along on the sidewalks below, going to and from destinations in their eternal restless existence. Talk about The City That Never Sleeps. I look longingly at the crappy little cot, wishing I could spare just an hour or two. While most everyone else here doesn't have to worry about it, I need sleep, but this isn't going to wait.

"We're going to have to talk to someone about this, aren't we?" I ask, morose. I can't see any way around it.

Greystone nods in sympathy. "I'm afraid so."

Who am I going to trust with my life? "We're going to have to assume that Captain Radu is not the guilty party."

Ms. Greystone sighs in relief. "I can't believe the captain would commit acts of murder then turn around and assign his best squad to investigate them."

I can't find a hole in her logic. Unfortunately. On the bright side, if he's not the killer, then he may not kill me for discovering a mole on the team. All I have to do is tell the captain that a member of his squad is on the take. I'm sure he won't take it out on me at all.

"Yeah. Great. If we're wrong, what's the worst that can happen to me? I'll just become like everyone else here."

Greystone floats alongside me as we enter the precinct. I'm used to getting a lot of stares everywhere I go, but today, they seem exceptionally suspicious. That's got to be in my head. Right? Conversations aren't stopping more often than usual as I go past. Looks of hostility and hunger are no more common than before. I keep telling myself that as we go up the crowded stairway to the second floor.

One of the ghosts that floats past me in a hallway looks familiar to me. I can't quite place him until he is nearly beside me.

"Officer Jenkins?" I ask. Yes, I'm right. He looks at me, not at all happy. Not exactly hostile, but not pleased I've called attention to him. The last time I'd seen him, he had an actual body. A rotting, decaying body, sure, but one made out of real flesh. Now he is transparent and slightly green. Unlike most of the other ghosts I've seen, his body looks like it is a rotting corpse instead of a normal human. It's odd, to be sure. He has a full body, unlike Greystone who fades out below the knees. He's still wearing his police uniform, still has his badge on his chest. I can even see stains on his translucent shirt. With the exception of being able to see through him, he looks just like he did when we went out into the Nursery.

"What do you want?" he demands, defensive.

I hold up my hands, placating. "Nothing, just . . . How are you doing?"

"You telling a joke?" he asks, scowling at me even more fiercely. Leave it to me to make someone mad by trying to be friendly. "Is this funny to you?"

I look to Ms. Greystone for support, but she merely shrugs. "Of course not! I was genuinely interested. Never mind then."

Muttering, he stalks off. It's strange that I don't hear the stomping of his feet. I think it is disorienting for him as well.

I see him reach his hand out to slam a door open right before his hand passes through the doorknob.

I make my way through the main squad room and walk past my desk. The door of Captain Radu's office looms closer, ominously closer. Out of the corner of my eye, I see Marsh notice me as I go by. He stares at me curiously. I try to ignore him.

Bracing myself, I knock on the captain's door. It's too dark for me to see if he's in his office, but I can feel him in there. Not in the same way I can sense Greystone. With her, I just know where she is, like I know my hand is sweating and clenched nervously in my pocket. With the captain, it's more of a sense of dread, a lump in my stomach, a flight-response screaming at my body to run away as fast as I can.

"Enter," the gravelly voice says from behind the door. No avoiding it now. I open the door and walk in. Ms. Greystone doesn't look any more eager than I to go in.

The captain is seated behind his enormous desk. He is alone in the room. The shadows seem darker in here than anywhere else. I smell something metallic, foul. Some kind of blood, probably. An oil lamp on his desk and two more in the corners illuminate the room. One elbow is propped on the desktop; his chin is resting in his hand, the index finger extended along the side of his temple. His bald head doesn't move, but his red eyes track our movements as we approach.

"Detective Green. Ms. Greystone. To what do I owe this pleasure?" he greets. He doesn't look at all pleased.

My mouth is dry. I'm taking too long to answer, and Greystone isn't in any hurry to jump out there.

"Captain," I nod. I try to gather some words together. "I've found . . . we've found something."

His eyebrow slowly arching is his only reply.

"It started when we noticed some files missing. From the file room. They were all the files Detective Olsen had gathered from his interactions with Davenport."

The captain slowly sits up straighter, his scowl getting fiercer. "What?"

Greystone finally speaks. "It's true, Captain. We're missing files. We found evidence that they had been removed."

"There's no telling how long the files have been gone, but it looks like those files were specifically targeted. No other files were touched. We came to the only conclusion possible," I say.

The captain answers for me. "Someone on the team is involved." The shadows are gathering behind him, getting angry. The shadows, I mean. They are getting angry, not just the captain. I try and ignore them, but they are too unsettling.

"Exactly," I nod, struggling to keep my gaze on him. "But where do we start? We can't just accuse someone of this. So . . . well, we decided to . . . kind of take a look at what some of the squad were doing."

The corner of Radu's mouth twitches into a grin, though none of the humor travels to his eyes. I decide I like the scowl better. "You started spying on your fellows."

Greystone says, "Yes," at the same time I say, "No, not really." We look at each other, and I grimace.

Radu asks, "Did you find out who it is?"

"Not exactly," I confess, and Radu slouches back down in his chair. "We decided to start with one of the members of the squad, so we started with Armstrong."

"Armstrong? *Pourquoi?* Why start with him?"

"We picked someone at random." I look at Greystone. I'm feeling less sure about this now than I did this morning.

"And?" Radu demands.

"I haven't found anything linking him to this case, but we did discover something that we felt needed to be brought to your attention."

Here we go. I describe all of the actions we'd seen

Armstrong engaged in over the past day. I leave out Jessica's involvement in the affair, and Greystone doesn't correct me on it. I'm not sure how Radu will react to me bringing her into all this. I talk about Armstrong's meeting with Antonio and others in the bar, then meeting with the old man in the park.

Radu's scowl gets fiercer, and his eyes start blazing as I recount all the details I can remember. He sits silently for a minute after I'm finished. I shift uncomfortably from one foot to the other.

Finally, he shifts his gaze to my companion. "Ms. Greystone, get Detective Armstrong in here. Now."

Shit. I start looking around for escape routes. I wonder if I can jump through the window out into the courtyard below or if I'll just bounce off the glass.

"Yes sir," she mumbles and hurries out. Captain Radu stares at me for the next couple of minutes. It's the longest two minutes I've ever lived. He sits as motionless as if he were carved in stone. It's unnerving.

Greystone mercifully returns through the door a few seconds before a knock sounds and Armstrong enters.

"You wanted to see me, Captain?" he says, giving me a curious look.

"Come in. Close the door. Sit down."

Sure, he gets offered a seat. I've had to stand this whole time.

"Detective Green here has just told me some interesting things," Radu says, the words slither out of his mouth.

"OK," Armstrong replies, more curious than alarmed. "I'm all ears."

Radu leans forward, fixing Armstrong with his stare. "It seems Detective Green saw you meeting with Antonio Cusmano. Not only that, he was close enough to hear you negotiating smuggling items into the city."

Armstrong sits up in alarm. "What?"

"And then," Radu continues, more loudly, enunciating his words more clearly. "He saw you meet with Frederick Stone in the park."

Armstrong is looking at me uncomprehendingly while I've got the same look on my face looking at the captain.

"How did you know all these names?" I ask. I sure as hell don't know any of them.

Radu ignores me. "You assured me, Detective Armstrong, when you began these negotiations, that there was no way you would be discovered. That no one would be able to uncover your actions. This assurance was the only reason you were allowed to go forward with this plan."

"Wait, what?" I'm totally confused now. I don't wait for an invitation. I sit down in one of the chairs opposite the captain's desk.

"But that's not possible," Armstrong says, sagging back in his chair. "I swear, Captain. I used all the proper glamours and veils. I've been careful. No one could have followed me or known what I was doing."

"And yet here we are, Detective."

"Wait, you knew about this?" I ask. Each of us in the room seems to be baffled about completely different things. Armstrong is confused how he was followed, and I'm confused that the captain is in on the situation. Greystone is probably confused about how I've gotten so far in my life being this stupid.

Armstrong is looking at me with frustration and anger. Radu is staring at Armstrong with a similar look.

"How the hell did you see me?" he asked. "How did you even get close enough to hear me? The veils I used are supposed to muffle sound to within a few paces."

I shrug uncomfortably.

Radu speaks to me while still glaring at Armstrong. "A

few years ago, Armstrong approached me with a unique suggestion to feed information to some of our local crime figures. Make himself seem disenfranchised. We let a few petty crimes slide in order to use the information to make bigger collars down the line. It's worked well for a while.

"But now . . ."

Armstrong spins back to the captain. "You're not shutting it down?"

Radu's fixed stare reveals nothing. "We can't allow this to become common knowledge, Detective. Surely you can understand that?"

"But—"

"I'll think about it," Radu cuts him off, then waves him away. "Go. Return to your duties. I'll consider allowing this to remain."

Detective Armstrong stands, glares murder at me, then storms out of the office.

"This doesn't clear him of suspicion regarding the missing files," the captain states, analyzing me again. I feel like a clever mouse cornered in front of a hungry cat. "But I don't want you distracted by thinking Detective Armstrong is dirty either."

I nod, sighing. "Sure, great. But I can't apologize to him, not without everyone asking what's going on. I don't want to blow his cover if he's keeping it a secret. And I don't want to jeopardize his underworld contacts." I want to make a joke about underworld contacts in a city of the dead, but I wisely decide to save that for a later time.

Radu steeples his fingers in front of him. He is concentrating. "Armstrong is unlikely to let his guard down, now. I doubt you'll be able to spy on his activities for some time."

"True," I agree glumly. I look over at Greystone. She shrugs. No help there.

"I think you are right in that we have someone on the

team working against us. This would explain many things. You can't follow Armstrong anymore. You will need to investigate one of the others. Who will you look into next?"

I pause in surprise. "You want me to continue?"

Radu nods. "I continue to believe you may be uniquely suited to this. In a short time, you discovered a secret that a room full of experienced detectives had not noticed."

He doesn't answer my quizzical stare.

"Well," I start, thinking it over. "If I have to pick a likely suspect, I guess I'm going to pick the one I most want it to be."

I look at Greystone.

"Detective Finnegan," we say together.

Instead of heading into the office with the other detectives, I turn the other way and walk down a hallway. I open the first unmarked door I find. A supply closet. Perfect.

Ms. Greystone, could you come speak with me, please? I could talk to her in my mind, but I still feel more comfortable talking to someone face-to-face.

"Of course."

I don't need to tell her where to find me; she floats through the wall, illuminating the small space we're standing in.

"Before we start trying to spy on someone else, what can you tell me about Finnegan?" I ask her. "Was there any interaction Detective Olsen had with him that might be of interest?"

She hesitates. "Detective Olsen did not enjoy working with Detective Finnegan. He was clearly suspicious of Detective Finnegan, but he never shared the nature of those suspicions with me. I only know he reluctantly accompanied Detective Finnegan on a case because he was ordered to do so."

"Please tell me," I ask, and it says something about how

distracted I am that I barely notice how closely we're crammed together in this space as I listen to her begin to speak.

Detectives Olsen and Finnegan

"There had been reports of an illicit substance being distributed in the Underneath. The Underneath is an area of Meridian where the detectives do not like to go. It is a warren of rooms, tunnels, and caves that meander throughout the area below the city. We would block it off altogether if we could, but the network of passages is so extensive it is a hopeless endeavor.

"The substance in question was a euphoric comprised partly of the blood of mortals that let one experience their recent memories. Where they were getting their supply of mortal blood, and who exactly was responsible, were unknown to us.

"'Very clever,' Detective Finnegan had said when we found a sample of the drug to examine. 'An intriguing mixture of chemical and alchemical components combined with the mortal blood. Whoever is creating this knows their stuff.'

"Detective Finnegan was very knowledgeable of all matters relating to mind-altering substances and their chemical properties. He spent a great deal of time researching materials both mundane and arcane. Stumbling across a new drug intrigued him no small degree. He spent a few days studying its properties by testing it on himself.

"Detective Olsen met with little success finding the source of the mortal blood. He spent those same days searching the streets for more samples of the drug while Detective Finnegan studied the substance itself. Usually, I found Detective Olsen to be methodical in his approach to searching for clues, but this time he seemed distracted.

"'I'm glad you're enjoying this,' Detective Olsen said.

'But we're wasting time. We're no closer to finding those responsible.'

"'Actually,' Detective Finnegan replied with a lazy smile, 'I figured that out a couple of days ago.'

"'We might not know where the blood is coming from,' he said, 'but the other ingredients are a different matter.'

"Detective Finnegan was able to isolate some of the compounds used and track them to their distributors.

"These other ingredients weren't illegal, per se. They were mainly base components used in a variety of alchemical concoctions. That did not stop Detective Finnegan from using enthusiastic forms of persuasion to find out those who were purchasing these ingredients.

"'It's the pleasure in his eyes,' Detective Olsen mentioned to me, once, while watching Detective Finnegan question a suspect. 'The pleasure he takes in inflicting pain. It is unsettling.'

"The screams were quite loud, but they did not last long before the suspect told the detectives everything they wished to know. Moreover, the suspect they questioned was drafted into working for Detective Finnegan as an informant and released. The information that he provided, the names of those who were purchasing supplies from him, gave Detective Olsen a wealth of information to sift through.

"Shortly thereafter, Detective Olsen was able to map out the patterns of distribution of the substances until, finally, they located one of the major suppliers of the drug. A Mr. Carlyle. Once they had his name, it was short work to find him.

"Where he was hiding, though, it was quite odd.

"Normally, if a suspect is illegally escaping the city to go into the mortal world, especially if they are killing mortals and endangering the secret of our existence, the suspects are terrified of being apprehended. The prospect of spending all of eternity in the Pit is a deterrent to most.

"Mr. Carlyle, however, seemed relieved that we found him. Several used vials surrounded him, now drained of the blood drug that Detective Finnegan was calling Daydream. Mr. Carlyle smiled and wept as the detectives picked him up.

"Detective Finnegan was most thorough in questioning Mr. Carlyle. They found the passageway he had been using to gain access to the mortal world and sealed it. He had been solely responsible for creating and distributing the drug, so the supply of Daydream was eliminated.

"The case was closed, and the sentence carried out. It was to be the Pit for Mr. Carlyle. But I sensed that Detective Olsen was troubled.

"I asked what his concern was, but Detective Olsen struggled to convey his thoughts to me.

'It was the memories in the blood of the last batch of Daydream," Detective Olsen said. "Carlyle hadn't distributed them to anyone; he kept them all to himself and kept taking more and more of the drug derived from that victim.'

"Detective Olsen told me that Carlyle just kept repeating the same things: 'Their eyes,' Carlyle had said. And, 'They are coming for me.'

"Typical rantings of an abuser of mind-altering substances, I had argued. And Detective Olsen nodded but seemed unconvinced.

"When Mr. Carlyle was brought before the Pit, there was relief in his eyes. I expect that it was a relief to be out of the hands of Detective Finnegan, at last. He whispered something to Detective Olsen, right before he was cast in. When I asked the detective about it, about what Mr. Carlyle had said to him, Detective Olsen looked troubled.

"'He said that he would finally be safe,' Detective Olsen told me. 'That they couldn't follow him in there.'"

On that note, Ms. Greystone falls silent, pondering her own story.

"That's interesting, Ms. Greystone. What is it supposed to tell me about Finnegan?"

She gazed levelly at me. "To use caution, Detective Green. Mr. Carlyle preferred being thrown into the Pit for all eternity rather than spend another minute in the care of Detective Finnegan. Whatever else you do, be extremely careful."

Chapter 24

I SIT DOWN AT MY DESK across from Marsh. He's leaning back in his chair, legs crossed with one ankle resting on his other knee, hands folded across his belly. He's staring at me. I shuffle a few pieces of paper, moving them from a stack on the right to the left side of my desk.

He's still staring. Finally, I meet his gaze. "What?" I ask.

Marsh shrugs. "Anything you want to tell me?"

"No," I reply irritably.

"OK, then." He continues staring.

I can only take it for about ten seconds. "Seriously, Marsh?"

"Hey, you don't wanna talk, don't talk. What the hell do I care?"

I glance away and notice Armstrong is glaring at me. Wow, I always thought *shooting daggers with your eyes* was a dumb expression, but I've never seen anyone look at me like this before. I look at the other detectives. Meints and Burchard are studiously NOT looking in my direction in a way that tells me they are paying attention to nothing else. Kim is looking curiously between Armstrong and me.

Finnegan notices everyone looking at me, frowns in disgust, and turns away. Clark looks like he wants popcorn to enjoy the show.

I turn back to Marsh, who is still staring at me. His face is expressionless, but I can tell he's enjoying my discomfort. "Have you found out anything about the case?" I ask him.

"Nope. What about you?" he replies, smirking.

"No," I stammer, trying to play it cool. I think about the missing files that one of the men in this room is responsible for making disappear. One of them is related, in some way, to this case, this murder case. I swallow nervously. "No, nothing."

"Well, then," Marsh says, not moving an inch, "looks like we've got some work ahead of us, don't we?"

"Right," I mumble, digging into some more files.

The hours drag slowly by. Nothing of interest jumps out of the files I study. No one comes running into the office confessing to the crimes. Finally, I can't take any more. I make a lame excuse, and I duck out a few hours early.

Ms. Greystone, can you find Jessica for me? I ask her with my mind as I'm walking back home.

"If I must."

That's the spirit, Ms. Greystone, I think to myself. At least, I hope it was just to myself. I pause and listen in my head, but I don't hear an angry huff, so I must have kept that private.

Ask her to meet me at my apartment again if you don't mind. We're going to go undercover again.

I'm hoping for a little bit of time to rest, but Jessica is waiting for me inside my apartment when I get there.

"I hope you don't mind," she explains, standing up from the chair where she was sitting. "You don't keep it locked."

"No, it's alright. I can't imagine anyone wanting to spend effort trying to move anything out of here. I, uh . . ."

She walks over to me and hugs me fiercely, crushing me

to her chest, and she kisses me on the cheek. "Thank you for calling me," she breathes huskily. She doesn't immediately let go, but Ms. Greystone floats through the nearby wall, giving me the excuse I need to shuffle out of Jessica's grip. Jessica smiles, ignoring the scowl coming from the ghost.

"We need to follow someone else now," I stammer, walking over to the chair and sitting down.

Jessica walks over to get her materials. "Someone else? What happened to what's-his-name, Armstrong?"

"Turned out to be nothing. We got it all cleared with my captain," I answer evasively. The situation with Armstrong is confidential, and I've messed it up enough already. I don't want to potentially complicate it further. "We're going to follow another of my coworkers."

"Must be serious," Jessica muses as she picks up a small box. "You guys are even investigating each other now."

I really wish I didn't need her help, but I have to admit, her disguise, that glamour she put on me, really worked. "Something like that," I agree.

I'm sunk in my chair as Jessica walks over to me, sets her box down on the floor, and she abruptly sits on my legs, straddling me, resting her arms on my shoulders, clasping her hands together behind my neck, and arching an eyebrow. "How much of a hurry are we in?"

"Big hurry!" I gasp, squirming.

"Really, Miss Everin," Greystone says, disapprovingly.

"Hush, you," Jessica responds without even looking at her. She leans in closer to me, brushing her lips against mine. The only way I can get away is to dump Jessica on the floor, and I'm about two seconds from doing that when she leans back pouting.

"Fine," she says, picking up her supplies and starting to work. "I'm doing this out of generosity for you. I want to help. But a guy needs to be nice to a lady. I certainly wouldn't mind some appreciation."

I force a smile. "Of course. I'm sure I can find a way to make this up to you."

I'm hating Finnegan more and more by the minute.

Everything goes on more quickly as Jessica is more familiar with what she's doing this time around. As we're finishing up, I turn to Greystone.

"Ms. Greystone, can you locate Finnegan? Let us know where he's at, and we'll meet you there."

Greystone gives a suspicious glance at Jessica while replying to me. "Certainly."

Greystone floats out the door, which I quickly open and escort Jessica through. I don't want to get stuck with her alone in my apartment, not until I can figure some way out of communicating my disinterest without losing her willingness to help me out.

It's warmer tonight. More humid. If there were a breeze, it would be almost pleasant. Jessica holds my hand as we walk, and she chats about the play she and her troupe are working on. It seems like such a normal conversation I almost forget where I am, the foreign weirdness of it all. After wandering the streets heading in the general direction of the precinct, I hear from Greystone.

"We may have a problem," she says.

What's up? I ask, think, whatever.

"I can't explain it, entirely. Let me come to you."

There is a bookstore up ahead, so we duck into there. I nod at the clerk who gives us a disinterested glance as we slowly weave our way through a labyrinth of shelves and books stacked to the ceiling. I'm curious what passes for written entertainment here, but Greystone shows up before I can start digging into what surrounds us. I'll have to remember to come back here later.

"What's the problem, Ms. Greystone?" I ask quietly.

We've found a corner of the store where we are alone.

Greystone has her arms folded across her chest, and her brows are furrowed in concentration. It's distracting that I can read the titles of the spines on the books behind her as I look through her.

"Detective Finnegan is able to sense me somehow."

I frown, confused. "Is he attuned to you like I am?"

"No, definitely not."

Jessica wraps her arms around mine and pulls close to me. "How do you know he can sense you?" she asks.

Greystone looks like she isn't going to answer for a second but reluctantly concedes. "As soon as I get him in sight, he stops what he is doing and looks around. Within a couple seconds each time, he is able to see me."

"It sounds like a Ward," Jessica laments.

"Of some kind, yes," Greystone responds, and before I can open my mouth to ask, she continues, "Wards are a means of preventing actions from affecting the Ward's owner."

"Magic," I say.

Jessica waves away the term. "Yes, if he has a Ward against surveillance, it may even stand up to my glamour. My glamour makes others see us how I want them to, but it doesn't prevent them from seeing us all together."

"He saw me even when I was invisible," Greystone mutters.

"You can turn invisible?" I ask. Why am I always a few steps behind every conversation I get into? I hurry with a follow-up question to make me seem a bit smarter. "How does he get this Ward thing?"

Greystone shrugs, her scowl deepening. Jessica explains, "It is most likely an object or totem of some kind on him. They are expensive, delicate items. I find it surprising that he has one that can survive the rigors of his job."

"Like a necklace or bracelet or something?"

"Yes, or a ring or tablet. Really anything that can hold an image engraved on its surface."

"Tattoo?" I ask.

Jessica hesitates. "It's possible to do that, but unlikely. Too risky. A tattoo would continually drain energy, and to power something like a Ward, it would eventually drain him of his life force. It would leave him conscious but trapped in a husk of a physical body."

"It has to be an object of some kind? He can't just wave his hands and cast a spell?"

Greystone answers this one. "Yes, technically he can, but again, the amount of power required makes this impractical. Most Wards of this kind require the creator to remain motionless, in a state of constant concentration. To be able to cast a Ward against surveillance while walking around would only be possible for the most powerful of practitioners to perform."

"And Finnegan isn't a practitioner?" I question. I can't believe I'm having a serious conversation about magic—the practicalities and intricacies of casting spells and maintaining them. I've had conversations like this with people when I'm playing computer games. In the context of a video game, this isn't strange at all. But talking about someone in real life, actually casting spells? It's hard to wrap my brain around.

"No, he would have to register as such," Greystone replies. "A practitioner is different than someone who can merely cast spells or create glamours. Practitioners are mages of the highest order who have spent decades or centuries perfecting their craft. And the guilds would have claimed him decades ago if they had detected him capable of such levels of power with the Art."

"OK, so in order to follow him, we're going to have to find that object of his," I say, hoping one of them will contradict me.

They don't.

Chapter 25

A WEEK LATER, AND I HATE Finnegan more than I thought possible. A full week of him staying one step ahead of me the entire time, without even knowing he is doing it. The case is going slowly, and we haven't turned up anything new. No new bodies, fortunately, but no new clues either. Every spare second I can find, I try and tail Finnegan. And no matter what methods we try, he immediately knows he's being followed.

Greystone had to quit after the second day. Finnegan is suspicious on the best of days, and even the dimmest person is going to notice a familiar ghost tailing you every time you turn around. Each time she got him in sight, he would stop whatever he was doing and start looking around until he saw her. The first few times, Greystone would tell him some inane bit of work-related information, but that wasn't going to hold up for long. She had to call it before he started looking into what was going on.

Jessica and I didn't have much more luck on our own. We would get Finnegan in sight, and almost immediately he would pause what he was doing. He would surreptitiously start looking into window reflections to see behind him or cast random glances back over his shoulder. At least twice by my count, he identified Jessica. Both times she gave him a flirtatious batting of her eyelashes, but he would just scowl and walk away. He must not have been able to see through the glamour Jessica put on me because he never confronted me at work about following him and didn't treat me any lousier than he usually did.

And what did he do during this time?

Absolutely nothing that I could see. An entire week of playing pool against various people he didn't seem to know and playing card games with people who didn't like him. He's skinny, wiry, and pretty quiet. He shouldn't be that intimidating, especially not when compared to some of the really creepy folks that can be found around here, but he's the one who sends shivers up my spine more than anyone else. I dread getting caught alone by him. He never yells at anyone, never pushes anyone around. If something goes wrong, he just stares at a person, and they back down. I saw at least one heated altercation while he was playing cards—some big guy yelling in his face. Finnegan just stared at the stiff until the other guy backed down and hastily apologized. I'm telling you, creepy.

We only observed him for a few seconds at a time. That was as much as I could glimpse before he'd start looking around to see who was so interested in him. I could never put an actual distance to his awareness; he just seemed to know he was being scrutinized as soon as we got him in our line of sight.

"This isn't working," I say to Jessica after ducking into an alley, so Finnegan doesn't see us. "We can't even peek around a corner before he senses we're here."

Jessica pouts, leaning her head on my shoulder. "Have you found his totem?"

I shake my head in frustration, trying to ignore her squeezing up between me and the wall. "I haven't seen anything. He doesn't have any rings, any jewelry. Not even a watch. From what you and Greystone tell me, it can't be anything flimsy like clothing or paper."

"This is true," she verifies absently.

I'm going to have to come up with a new plan. "C'mon. If we try any more, he's going to search us out. We're pushing our luck with him not noticing us yet."

We get back to my apartment. I walk straight over to the refrigerator and grab two bottles of beer. They're slightly colder than room temperature, which is distressingly warm. I'll never be able to sleep in this heat.

I turn around to offer a beer to Jessica, and I see her a few feet away dropping her blouse to the floor.

"Uh," I say, trying to set the beer in my hands on the counter. I have to try a couple times; I keep missing the counter. My eyes are riveted on what I'm seeing in front of me. Jessica doesn't have anything on underneath her blouse. She's leaning forward, her hands clasped behind her back. She licks her lips, slowly walking towards me.

"I know something that will take our minds off our problems," she says softly.

I have had several vivid fantasies that are remarkably similar to this, except for the glaring fact that the beautiful woman coming towards me is usually not dead. Jessica's makeup covering the blemishes on her face doesn't extend below her chest. I can see green, wrinkled skin and a couple of holes peering into blackness in her torso.

My stomach roils sickly, and I can taste bile. I try to step around her, but she pushes me down onto my chair and sits on me again, straddling me. She hooks one elbow behind my neck and kisses me soundly, her dry tongue scraping against my teeth. I taste her in the back of my throat. Her lips chafe against mine. I try to say something, but my voice is muffled into her mouth, and by making noise I only encourage her. She grabs my hand and places it around her breast, holding it in place over the top of a firm nipple which presses into my palm. Her breast is solid, leathery, not at all what I'm familiar with. I pull my hand away and put my hands on her shoulders, intending to push her away, but she moans eagerly as I grab her, and she starts fumbling with my belt. Her fingers scratching at the belt sound like the skittering of an insect across the floor, making me shiver.

"No!" I gasp, tearing my lips away from hers, turning away from her. I pick her up and stand both of us up so I can hold her at arm's reach. My strength surprises even me. "Jessica, no."

She exhales in frustration. "Yes!"

She looks at me with eyes wide open and realizes this isn't some game or form of teasing. She leans back angrily. "Why not? What is wrong?"

"Look," I try to explain, but I can't form any words that make sense of this at all. What possible reason could I have to spurn the advances of an eager woman I like? I end up helplessly shrugging my shoulders.

"I see," she says tersely. She stares at me intently, her lips pressed firmly together. Then she spins on her heel and picks up her shirt. Her back to me, a back that has bruises and open sores, she slips back into her shirt and begins to button it up.

"Jessica, I'm sorry, it's just—"

She spins fiercely, her eyes furious. "Don't! I don't want to hear it." She grabs her makeup and materials from my table and marches out, slamming the door behind her without looking back.

Time screeches to a halt, and I stand in place for nearly a minute, completely dumb-founded and speechless. I've hurt her feelings. I've offended one of the few people here that seems to actually like me, and that makes me a bad person. This might make me an even worse person, but I am also incredibly relieved. I've been dreading the night she made her move, and now it's over. I'll have to find a way to apologize, obviously, but hopefully, this means she won't make similar attempts in the future.

Then it hits me.

"Crap," I say out loud. With Jessica gone, I have no way of disguising myself. She's the only person I know that can help me. Now I'm up the proverbial creek. The second I leave my apartment, I will be instantly recognizable. No way will I be able to follow anyone like that. This glamour on me right now is the last one I'll have for who knows how long.

Hmm.

Ms. Greystone, are you there? I think/broadcast.

"*Yes, I'm here, Detective Green. Is there something you need that Miss Everin can't provide?*" I can actually hear the snark in her voice.

Um, well, Jessica will no longer be helping us, I think guiltily.

"*How on earth did you manage that? I had assumed she was rather smitten with you.*"

I'd rather not go into it. I need your help.

"*Yes?*"

The glamour I have on me now is the last I'm going to get, so this is my last chance to try and see what Finnegan might be up to. Can you tell me where he is? I'll give this one more shot.

"*Detective Green, I'm not going to allow you to follow a suspect without any backup. And if I'm with you, Finnegan will sense me regardless of your glamour.*"

Look, if you can tell me where he is, I'll follow him. You hang back and follow me. Maybe he won't sense you if you're not looking for him. You'll just be looking at me.

"*I believe your logic to be flawed,*" she thinks in an amused tone. "*But I will help you if you want to make one more attempt.*"

I put my two bottles of beer back in the fridge, wondering why I bother trying to cool them down. Looking around this hole I call home, I think back to Jessica's surprise at me living here. I need to remember to ask Marsh about that. Honestly, I'd be happy with a bed. Well, a bed and an internet connection. But one step at a time. I grab my badge and my gun. Then I head out the door and start walking in Greystone's general direction.

A few minutes later, Greystone says, "*I've found him. He's leaving a bar called Wiechert's and is heading in your direction. In fact, if you stay where you are he'll probably walk right past you.*"

OK, hang back. Once I see Finnegan, you can start following me.

I find a doorway to some non-descript building, lean my shoulder against one side of the frame, and try and hide in the gloom. Barely a minute passes before I see him striding quickly down the opposite side of the street. He glances once over his shoulder, then looks around. His eyes look over at me and then right past me. Whatever this glamour on me is making me look like, it must not be very interesting.

He slows down almost directly across the street from me and stops. He looks around, again, confused. I will myself to be invisible in the shadows. Still, he doesn't seem to notice me. I hardly dare breathe right now. I'm puzzled. Why doesn't he see me? But he can't. Is this part of the glamour at work? I wish I knew more about them. Every time we followed him before, was it Jessica or Greystone he was sensing and not me? Maybe the fact I'm alive is messing with his sense somehow? I don't try to figure it out; I just need to capitalize on my luck.

The street is relatively empty. Finnegan waits for a few people to walk past him, then begins making complex gestures with his hands, uttering weird syllables under his breath that I can't make out. I see a dim puff of light in front of him, like he lit a match. Then he turns and quickly strides away down a nearby alley. I let him get a short lead on me and then follow him.

"*Detective, what are you doing?*" Greystone asks.

What do you mean? I'm following Finnegan.

"*No, I see Finnegan walking down the street towards me, back the way he came.*" I can sense where Greystone is, and it's nowhere near where I'm at right now.

What the hell? No, I'm telling you, I'm following him down this alley.

"*This is most confusing. He just walked past me and didn't notice me at all.*"

We're talking about magic, so I have no idea what is or is not possible. Did he make an illusion? Did he fool me or did he fool Greystone? Does he have a twin? All I know is that I see him disappearing into the shadows of the alley opposite me, and I'm not going to lose him.

Look, Ms. Greystone. You can follow that one if you want. But I can see Finnegan cutting through alleys and down some back streets. I need to keep him in sight.

"*Keep going, Detective. I'll catch up to you. Please be careful.*"

Finnegan is moving so fast he's almost running, and I follow through alleys choked with debris; I have to watch my footing, so I don't slip or make a loud crash knocking things over. The gaslights from the streets barely reach back here, I can't move nearly as quickly as I would like, and Finnegan seems to know them well.

I'm getting farther away from the sounds of people. Most of the buildings I'm walking past are industrial in nature. The occasional light shines from a lone window, but most of them look abandoned. I have to slow down around several smashed-in metal garbage cans and mangled shopping carts. Coming around the corner, I realize I've lost Finnegan. I curse loudly in my mind, and by the sharp jab of disapproval I feel from Greystone, I must have broadcast that one.

Sorry, I mumble mentally.

I'm looking down a road of packed dirt and gravel, lined by several large abandoned brick buildings. No lights shine in any of the broken-out and boarded-over windows. I jog quickly down the road, trying not to trip over the washboard grooves in the earth, glancing in doorways and alcoves as I go.

I'm two strides past a boarded-over metal freight door when I see a flicker of light through a crack in the frame. I quietly sneak over. The freight door is about eight feet tall, boarded over and chained up. It would normally slide to the side along rails at the top of the frame, but it is sitting off the tracks. The door is leaning up against the wall, and there is enough space for a skinny, sneaky bastard to slip through the gap and enter the building.

It's a little tough for me to wedge my way through, but I manage. I feel horribly exposed as I struggle to squeeze through, expecting Finnegan to pounce on me as I am helplessly pinned, but I crawl across some gravel on my hands and knees, and I finally get inside.

The interior is full of junk and garbage. The inside space is enormous—maybe a couple of hundred feet square, open to the two stories above. A walkway encircles the exposed area on the upper stories, leading to some dark offices. The stairs are open, and the walkways are made of steel grating. Large chains hang from steel beams up in the rafters; at one time, no doubt, they were used to move heavy equipment to the higher levels. Part of the upper floor has collapsed in the far corner. The glow of moonlight, what little of it trickles through the clouds, barely illuminates the upper floors, but it is almost pitch dark where I'm at on the ground. I see the pale afterimage of light moving down a broad stairwell to my left, so I follow cautiously, trying to pick my path around debris on the floor.

The stairs descend into darkness. The light ahead of me is just enough that I can keep up as it moves farther down the brick walls lining either side winding around to the right. There's enough distance that I can't see Finnegan directly, but the dim glow from whatever light he's using allows me to barely make out the stairs in front of my feet.

I reach the basement level after a handful of turns and end up in front of an open workspace. It looks like it used to house machinery of some kind. The room is massive, the ceilings about twenty feet high. There are rows of large furnaces or engines like nothing I've ever seen before. I have no idea what they would be used for; they are big metal boxes with dials, gears and levers on the front with pipes leading up and out over the ceiling above. Were they operational, they would likely make an incredible amount of noise. Now, they are silent and cold. In between the husks of these steel giants, the room is full of workbenches, at least twenty or so, with tools, vices, and scraps of wood scattered throughout. On all the tables, I see beakers, vials, glass tubes, Bunsen burners, propane tanks and other materials I remember from my science classes back in middle school. Bags of some sort of crystals, rough rock pebbles like quartz are wrapped up on one table. Dozens of vials containing something that looks like blood are stacked next to them. Dust hangs in the air everywhere. There are ventilation fans in the barred windows high up in the wall, but they aren't spinning. Probably not much call for helping people with breathing.

Meth lab? I think to Greystone. *Can I "think" you what I'm seeing?*

Evidently, it works. That's good to know.

"Get out of there!" Greystone shouts in my mind. *"This is bad, Detective. You are in great danger!"*

The hairs on my neck stand up, and I know I'm not alone. A cold lump forms in my stomach. I never knew where the "pit" of my stomach was, but I'm pretty sure I'm feeling it now. I pull out my gun and hold the heavy weight of it with both hands. From my position, where I'm crouching down behind a table, I try to get a vantage point where I can see the whole room. For all the good it does me. At right about the same instant that I realize I can't see Finnegan anywhere, I hear the scuff of a shoe behind me.

I spin around, and Finnegan is staring at me from about ten feet away. He has his gun drawn as well, but he's holding it down at his side.

"Who the blazes are you supposed to be?" he snarls and snaps his fingers. A ball of blue light appears above and behind his head, lighting the room up in a weird blue tone that makes it look like we're underwater. The globe crackles, expanding and contracting in a pulsing pattern, softly buzzing with energy. He didn't chant, read a spell, meditate or anything in a way I expect magic to be done. He just snapped his fingers. That is ominously frightening.

Finnegan is pissed, royally pissed, that much I can tell. But I also realize he has no idea who I am.

"You're in a world of trouble, asshole," Finnegan says. He's looking around to see if there is anyone else here but me. I notice the close proximity of any number of steel tools he can use in excruciatingly painful ways.

That blue light, does he need a totem for that too? I ask.

Greystone's voice in my head is a few octaves higher than usual. *"No! Only arcane practitioners can even create Eldritch energy, Detective Green. If he can cast it instantly, without ritual, it shows he is a mage of the highest order."*

The information is slowly penetrating my brain. If

Greystone is freaking out, I could be royally screwed, here. Finnegan isn't going to just be mad about this; I'm in real danger.

So he doesn't have a totem-thingy powering his Ward? I ask bleakly. *He's just casting it while walking around? But you said he isn't a practitioner.*

"He can't be. It's simply not possible. Unless he has some means of boosting his reserves of arcane energy."

Like how?

"I don't have time to explain, you need to get out of there!" Greystone says, urgently.

"I'm only going to ask you once. Who are you? What are you doing here?" Finnegan asks.

My mouth is dry, and my mind is racing. Do I tell him who I am? He may kill me if I don't, but will telling him keep me alive? He has me cornered. I don't think I can get past him and I'm terrified any sudden movements on my part will end up with painful consequences. I open my mouth to respond by saying something incredibly witty to buy me time, and I inhale some of the dust floating around. I choke and start coughing.

"The hell?" Finnegan mutters, and then his eyes narrow further. "Green? You asshole, is that you?"

He doesn't wait for me to answer. "You're coughing. You're the only person that needs to breathe down here. No wonder I couldn't figure out who was following me; I didn't bother trying to track a mortal. How the hell did you get a glamour?"

I'm still coughing. It's winding down, but I can't answer yet. I glance around, trying to find some way out of this mess, but nothing is presenting itself. I'm pretty sure he'll perforate me with his gun before I make it two steps.

"Ah, it's that little tart that's been following me around the last couple of days. I just figured she was a cop groupie.

But she was with you, wasn't she? Well, this is unfortunate."

"She's available now, if you're interested," I wheeze, slowly standing up.

He chuckles, but it's a sound that sends a chill down my spine. He keeps a close eye on me, allowing me to stand but making it clear I can't try anything else.

"Well, I suppose I'll have to track her down after I get rid of you. She'll only be marginally harder to kill than you. Is Marsh here with you?"

I feel cold. Any small hope I had of walking away from this just died. "Uh, wait a minute. Get rid of me?"

Finnegan raises both arms and waves them over his head. Though I notice the gun stays relatively pointed in my direction. "Are you kidding me? Do you have any idea what you've found here? How stupid are you?"

"I dunno, how stupid am I, Finnegan? What did I find?"

He gets ready to reply, then pauses. He puts his arms down and regards me coolly, his eyes calculating. "Interesting. You're stalling. That means that ghostly bitch must be on her way."

On cue, Greystone comes streaking through the ceiling above the stairway, her ghostly form illuminating the doorway as she aims at Finnegan. She screams, loudly, an unearthly wail that rises in pitch and starts rattling my teeth. Some of the beakers and dust on the tables start shaking, vibrations radiating from Greystone's howl.

Finnegan hardly even glances at her. He waves his hand like he's brushing away a fly, and a cage of crackling energy surrounds Greystone. It's made of the same stuff as the globe, which doesn't flicker or change in any discernable way. Screeching to a halt, she ricochets off the bars of power and hangs in the air, the energy completely encircling her. Her scream instantly goes quiet, cut off mid-wail. While she's silent in the room, I can hear her screaming in my mind. Her mouth is open in a rictus of pain, shrinking back from making contact with any portion of the cage around her.

"Greystone?" I ask, taking a step towards her. She doesn't appear to hear me or is in so much pain she can't respond. Her screaming won't stop in my brain. "What did you do to her?"

He shrugs. "What do you care?"

"You've been killing people to cover up what? Drugs?"

"Killing?" He looks genuinely confused. "You think I'm the one murdering people? That's why you've been following me? Unbelievable. You are the worst detective I've ever met, Green. I'll be doing everyone a favor."

"You're the only one I'm going to murder."

Finnegan raises his gun and fires.

I don't know how it doesn't kill me. I take a step backward in surprise, tripping over some debris at my feet. Something hits my left shoulder, and it feels like hundreds of tiny ant bites stinging me. I spin around and slam to the ground on my back.

The walls are standing at a strange angle that I can't make sense of. Finnegan takes a step towards me, a thin smile on his lips, the gun leveled at my face. I lift my hand slightly, straining at the weight of the gun in my hand, and pull the trigger. I don't even know if it's aimed at him. The gun kicks back and slams into my face. I squint through the pain and see a shield of energy flare to life in front of the Finnegan, catching the brunt of whatever projectile I just shot out. He's completely unhurt, but the force from the shot is still enough to pick him up off his feet and toss him back several yards. He slams into a workbench, and glasses and beakers shatter and go flying in all directions, scattering their contents across the floor and tables. Dust, powder, and liquids spray all around him.

I scramble across the floor on one arm and my knees, zigzagging through workbenches, trying to put some space between us. My left arm is hanging uselessly. I can't feel anything below my shoulder. I'm pretty sure the building is spinning in circles because I can't seem to figure out which way is up. The blood thundering in my head drowns out Greystone's continuing screams.

Finnegan rolls over on the ground and laughs. "That hurt, you dick!" He slowly stands up and dusts himself off. His gun is a few feet away from him. He reaches down, casually picks it up, and starts to walk towards me again. I duck around the corner of one of the large metal cases, blocking him from my view. I look down and see the smear of blood I'm leaving as I'm dragging my shoulder across the floor. Who knows what kinds of dirt and debris I'm grinding into my open wounds as I struggle to move.

He yells out at me from the other side of the machine, circling towards me from the other side. "I'm going to enjoy tearing you apart. I don't normally eat mortals, Green, but for you, I'll make an exception. You're going to die watching me take a bite out of your throat, and you'll never even know what you stumbled on."

I lean my right shoulder on the ground, manage to barely lift the gun off the ground. I aim at where I expect him to come around the corner. As soon as I detect a flicker of motion, I pull the trigger again. The shot is loud enough it almost covers up Greystone's unrelenting crying inside my head. The round tears a metal vice off the corner of a nearby table. Both the vice and my bullet glance off Finnegan's shield, making him stagger but not stopping his advance. I really hate that smile on his face right now.

The blue sphere of light moves from behind him and flies over above my head, marking my location. He's taking his time. I can see the blue light sparkling off the gleam of his teeth through his narrow grin. I try lifting my weapon to fire again, but I'm moving too slowly. Finnegan easily catches up and steps on my hand, pinning my gun to the ground.

This is not looking good. His smile widens, and he aims his gun at my head.

"Hey, Finnegan," a deep voice snarls from the stairway. A gunshot explodes in the silence. The energy shield flares to life on Finnegan's side as he is, again, lifted off his feet and thrown against a table, smashing into it with his stomach, grunting and cursing.

Marsh walks calmly out of the doorway, firing another shot that knocks the skinny detective down. Finnegan crashes to the floor a few feet away from me, his gun clattering off under a table. Marsh might be the one shooting him, but Finnegan glares murderously at me.

"I think you've got some explaining to do," Marsh says smugly, advancing towards the both of us. Greystone is still in her cage, screaming in my head, and blackness is bleeding into the edges of my vision. Somehow, I muster the strength to push myself backward across the floor with my legs and try to put some distance between Finnegan and myself.

Marsh rounds the corner of the aisle of worktables we're behind. The light cuts out for a second, until I shake my head and blink fiercely. The glowing blue ball is still there, so I guess I blacked out for a moment. Marsh is several strides closer now, gun pointed at Finnegan.

Out of the corner of my eye, I notice the blue sphere of energy starting to grow larger. I look at it more closely. Am I blacking out again? No, it really is getting bigger.

"Marsh," I croak hoarsely.

The sphere explodes into a ball of blazing blue fire nearly ten feet across. It starts pulling in the air around it in a blazing vortex of heat and flame. I feel myself slide a few inches towards it before it rockets towards Marsh and detonates right in his face. My partner staggers back and drops to his knees. He is at the center of an inferno of blue flames. Licks of fire spit out in all directions, lighting up items on top of nearby tables. Some of the beakers start exploding from the heat, spraying boiling liquid out.

I can't hear anything over the roaring of the fire. Finnegan gets up and turns to me. I can't move out of the way as he takes three quick strides and kicks me as hard as he can in my stomach. Pain blazes in my midsection, and I try and curl up around the waves of agony. He kicks me again, and then a third time. I start vomiting after that one. I hear Marsh howling curses as his flesh sizzles away.

Somehow, I manage to hold on to my gun. This time I line him up squarely in my sights, and I pull the trigger. I don't blow my own head off. Things go black again. After a few beats I manage to open my eyes enough to see Finnegan slumping against the table next to me. Fluid is leaking from a fist-sized hole in his side.

He takes a lurching step towards me, slips in my puke on the floor, and drops to one knee. My ears are ringing too loudly to hear what he says, but I see his lips mouth out, "This isn't over."

Finnegan stumbles away out the door and up the stairs.

I lay weakly on the floor. I feel blood on my body, vomit congealing on my face. Blue flames reach up from the mass of Marsh about twenty feet away. Flames are licking the ceiling. I can feel the heat. The smell threatens to make me vomit again. The mass in the center of the flames moves, shifts, and slowly stands up.

"Kid . . . you gotta get . . . outta here," Marsh says with a tortured voice, staggering to the side. An arm grabs a table to steady himself and beakers explode from the heat. How is he still alive? I mean, not alive, but not dead. I can see bone underneath the flames.

I look over to the stairway. It's a long way away. I'm pretty sure it has gotten farther away than when I entered the room.

"Can't . . ." I whisper, blinking.

I open my eyes, realizing Marsh is yelling at me. ". . . up! Wake up, Green. I can't grab you without frying you." Some of the crystal rocks start exploding, either from the heat or the flames.

Suddenly, the room goes dark. This time I'm pretty sure my eyes are still open. The place is mercifully silent, just the occasional pop of something exploding or falling from a table tells me I haven't gone deaf.

"Huh," I hear Marsh grunt, the sound of his flesh sizzling loud in the sudden silence. "Guess his spell finally gave out."

A dim glow gradually increases, lighting the room up with green radiance.

"Detective Green," Greystone says, floating above me. She's free from her cage, and she's the source of the light. Her form is flickering slightly, like she isn't tuned into the right channel. She looks positively distraught. "Detective Green, are you OK?"

I nod, waving away her concern. "Shurr . . ."

I see Marsh walk over to me, squatting down nearby. He's a smoking, smoldering ruin. His flesh is charred black, burned and blistered. Every time he moves his flesh tears and oozes various fluids. His clothes are either gone or fused with his skin. He's smiling though, and his eyes are clear. He doesn't smell better cooked than normal.

"That was pretty badass, Green. Slowing down his feet with your stomach like that."

"Shut . . ." I cough weakly. "Shut up."

Chapter 26

A COUPLE HOURS LATER AND THE squad is still crawling all over the warehouse. The forensics team is cataloging everything in the lab, taking notes, marking things in chalk, bagging vials, beakers, and chemicals into canvas bags. I say it's a forensics team, but it's nothing like I've ever seen before. Instead of magnifying glasses, digital cameras—I don't know, actual science equipment—there are a couple guys who are unofficially called sniffers.

And yeah, that's what they're doing; they are smelling the area like hound dogs. One of them occasionally crouches down on all fours to get a closer sniff at something or other. I imagine he's going to be high as a kite by the end of this, with all the powders and dust in the air.

A handful of others are walking around with their eyes closed while assistants take notes. Those are the scryers. They are talking about the things they "see" in their mind, impressions of the area. There are some photographers, but they are using old cameras with powder-flare flashes, using honest-to-goodness single exposure plates of some kind. It's something I'd expect to see in those Old West, turn-of-the-century shows. The place is crowded, with probably twenty folks or so in the lab with more upstairs and throughout the warehouse. Officers are upstairs going through all the offices, desks, and debris seeing if there is anything else of note here.

I'm not sure exactly when others got here; I passed out for about an hour. I'm barely coherent now.

Marsh and I are over in a corner while everything goes on around us. He's healing rapidly, having stopped smoldering about thirty minutes ago. Thankfully, someone found a blanket he could wrap around himself, so I don't have to watch his flesh reknit. He's been eating nonstop to replenish his energy, and that's a sight I can go without seeing again. But in between bites, Marsh is standing in front of me, guarding me. It turns out that actual human blood smeared all over the floor drives some of these guys crazy. One of the new officers went blood crazed and launched himself at me when he smelled me. Marsh caught him, and the officer is off healing broken bones while Marsh's glower has been discouraging that from happening again.

As near as I can tell, this regeneration process Marsh is going through is fairly consistent. His skin and muscle actually writhe and twitch as they reform. Closing a single bullet hole will take roughly a minute, unless he has to go in and dig the bullet out. Something like a shotgun blast will take longer. The fire caused significantly more damage and will likely take several hours to fully heal.

And while he can recover from just about anything, it does nothing for the pain. He still feels everything; his brain still processes pain in the same way it did while he was alive. He's just had decades of practice coping with it.

They had a "doctor" fuss over me, but frankly, he wasn't much help. He wasn't used to healing actual living bodies. He did some magic on me that got my arm moving and feeling again. My whole shoulder is bruised and sore, but I shouldn't experience any permanent damage. Bandages were wrapped around the wound, and someone gave me a spare shirt to wear.

The room looks a lot different now, with gaslights and torches illuminating the space instead of that weird blue globe of energy Finnegan had. I almost don't recognize the place. It looks smaller now. I can't believe I almost died in this dump. A shadow somehow passes in front of all the light in the room, in all directions at once, and Captain Radu strides into the room from the stairway that was empty only seconds ago. He marches straight toward us. The other members of our squad gather around while everyone else quickly finds somewhere else to be.

"Update," Radu orders. The command demands obedience.

Marsh absently scratches his scalp behind one ear, showering out flakes of burnt skin as he speaks. "Looks like Finnegan had a little side business going on."

Meints steps forward, looking at his notepad. He has been taking copious notes, detailing every beaker, vial, glass or container—including sketching out complex chemical diagrams. "Alchemical-grade dust, refined and purified. Some of the strongest I've ever seen. We haven't been able to break down the formula yet; it keeps shifting as we examine it. It's the street drug Arcane. Also several vials of Daydream."

Burchard stands next to him, hands in his pockets. He says, "Not surprising. Finnegan was always a shifty bastard."

Clark nods, on the other side of Radu. "No telling how much of this stuff has hit the streets; judging by the scope of the setup here, I'd say he's been peddling this crap for years."

Marsh interjects, "It would explain a lot of things, actually. Some of the breaches into the mortal world, the increase of spirits in the Nursery. And, frankly, how Finnegan was displaying practitioner-level skill in magic without being registered. Who knows how much of this gunk he's been taking himself."

Radu glowers. It looks like he's been sucking on something sour. Finally, "*C'est tout? Is this all of it?*"

Meints shrugs, looks at Burchard who shrugs as well, and says, "No way of knowing that, Captain. This could be one of several labs. I'd like to think it's just this one, but nothing is ever easy with that guy."

Radu turns to me. His eyes are blazing furiously, and the rest of the room seems to fade into darkness as the captain becomes the sole focus of attention.

"*Messieurs,* I am not pleased with your progress. Instead of tracking down this killer, we are no closer now than we were before, and we're down a member of the squad. *Merde!* Detective Green, do you have any reason to suspect it was Finnegan who is behind these killings? Are his dealings with these drugs the cause of all this?"

That's a damned good question. I frown. "No, I don't think so. Finnegan seemed genuinely surprised I thought he might be behind it all. And since he was getting ready to kill me, I don't have any reason to think he was lying."

"Captain," Kim interrupts bravely. Radu's focus shifts to the detective. Kim tries not to look uncomfortable as he continues. "Why was Green following Finnegan in the first place? Are you investigating us? What's going on?"

The captain stares expressionlessly. Everyone's gaze, mine included, are on him.

Crap, I'm dead. I'm so dead, I think, not caring if Greystone overhears.

"*Trust the captain,*" Greystone thinks back reassuringly.

"Detective Green, tell them what you found."

I hesitate. "But Captain . . ."

He turns back to me and arches an eyebrow threateningly. More danger is conveyed in that single movement than cocking a gun at me by anyone else. I spill.

"Ms. Greystone and I were digging through some old notes related to the murders and realized there were case files missing." I pause, but no one says anything. Reluctantly, I continue. "We discovered that someone had removed files from storage."

"But we're the only ones that have access to storage," Armstrong says. He opens his mouth to continue and then stops as realization hits. I see similar expressions around the group.

"Yeah." I swallow nervously and force myself to continue. "Someone in this group removed those files. So, for whatever reason, one of us is blocking this investigation."

Greystone speaks quietly, "I agreed to help Detective Green look into this. He was afraid, and rightly so. I believed that if his suspicions were made known, his life would be in jeopardy."

"Did you know about this, Captain?" Marsh asks. All eyes move from me to the captain.

"*Oui*. Only after Green's investigation exposed an undercover operation that Armstrong had been working on for a couple years."

"Captain!" Armstrong protests, but Radu waves him into silence.

"No. No more secrets. I want everything out in the open. We find who is doing this; we uncover what is going on no, matter the cost; and we pick up the pieces later."

Armstrong clenches his teeth but nods his assent. Then something else occurs to him. "Wait a minute. Green, you thought I was the murderer? What the hell for?"

I shift my feet uncomfortably. "I had to start somewhere. I just picked someone at random."

"I thought you stumbled across me," he accuses me heatedly. "But you were following me to see if I was out killing people?"

Radu cuts him off angrily. "Instead, he discovered your operation with crime figures you managed to keep hidden from the rest of the group for years. He then shifted his focus to Finnegan and discovered this."

Marsh regards me thoughtfully. Maybe calculating is a better way to describe it because it's not particularly friendly.

"Uh, I hate to point this out," Burchard says. "But none of this has uncovered who took those files."

"Sweet," Clark grimaces. "That's just great."

"*Alors,* here is where we stand," Radu summarizes. "One of us, myself included, is suspect in, at the very least, trying to hinder the investigation into these murders. At worst, they are committing the murders themselves. Armstrong's undercover work is blown. Finnegan is operating a drug ring that has been causing us headaches for who knows how long. And we still have no idea who is behind this.

"The only one of us we can rule out as a suspect," Radu continues, "is Detective Green. He wasn't here when the murders began."

"That would be great if he weren't so clueless," Burchard grumbles.

"Or hopelessly incompetent," Armstrong adds.

Meints stares at me suspiciously, writing notes down in his journal.

"I vote for useless," Clark adds.

"Enough!" Radu whispers fiercely. "Inexperienced he may be, and yes, his results may have set us back more than they have helped thus far. But he has been getting results. I expect all of you to keep him alive. Let's train him how to be competent and hope that can be accomplished in a single lifetime. I need results."

Radu gives us all one last stern glance and then walks away. The rest of us stand silently, appraising each other. The look is the same on all of our faces: one of us is working against the rest; we just don't know who.

"Go, team!" Clark says.

Chapter 27

MARSH HAS FINALLY STOPPED SMOLDERING, though his skin is blistered, scabbed over and oozing in a few places. If he smiles, he might split open some newly healed skin, but I doubt we'll have to worry about that happening.

Someone brought him a spare suit, so he's mercifully clothed now. He adjusts the skinny, plain, black tie, knotted sloppily around his open collar. I see some fluid stains start to spread out immediately in spots on his shoulders.

"Let's take a walk," he says and starts going up the stairs, expecting me to follow. He's walking without a stitch in his step, which is more than I can say for me. I hate that he assumes I'll just follow, but I only hesitate a second before hurrying after him. I try and match his stride as we go up the stairway to the main floor. Every step feels like a hill. I hurt all over. My stomach is killing me where Finnegan treated me like a soccer ball. The stairway is wide enough for us to walk side by side, but I let Marsh proceed a few steps ahead of me. We weave through a few officers on the ground floor, but Marsh doesn't walk through the front. He heads towards an exit in the back of the building.

"Detective Green, are you OK?" Greystone asks in my mind.

I think so. If I scream in panic, come running. That's the best system we've come up with so far.

He marches past the line of officers cordoning off the area and walks casually up the alley out toward the main street. We leave the crowd of officers and onlookers behind.

"How did you know to come look for me?" I ask.

"Greystone," he says. He chews on something, spits it out, and continues on without turning to me. "So. You thought someone on the team might be working against us. And you decided to not tell me."

"Marsh . . ."

"I'm mad, but I'm impressed," he keeps going, ignoring my attempt to explain. "I'm impressed you didn't just assume I'm not guilty. That's good instincts."

He halts abruptly and turns to me. As I stop to stay with him, he pokes me in the chest with a single finger. Hard. "Ow!"

"But I'm pissed, Green. I'm your partner. I've got your back. The captain put me in charge of keeping you alive, and I take that seriously. You could have been killed."

"Yeah, well."

"Until you get proof I'm blocking this investigation, you keep me in the loop, dammit. Starting right the hell now. Am I clear?"

"Righ. OK! I trust you. At least I trust you now, anyways—unlike a couple weeks ago where you were beating the crap out of me."

Marsh waves my comment away. "Old news."

"But it's not like you're up front with me on everything."

He looks at me quizzically. "What do you mean?"

"My apartment, for starters. I found out you put me in a dump."

He chuckles, threatening to tear his lips. "You got me there. That place is a real shithole. It's where we park suspects."

"And I'm supposed to be getting paid!"

He shrugs. "Let's call you an unpaid intern for now."

I look around. The alley is empty except for a few pieces of trash blowing around in the breeze. The mortar on the brick walls nearby is crumbling in places, a few bricks missing. I could be standing anywhere in the world; the place is that nondescript. The buildings loom up around us. Down at the mouth of the alley, I can see people walking and riding horses on the main road. The familiar and unfamiliar mix together in a way I still can't quite understand. The hulking, burned monstrosity of an animated corpse standing next to me claims to be eager to protect. But only weeks ago, he was torturing me, interrogating me relentlessly—the greatest source of fear and terror I've ever experienced. A few weeks earlier, I wanted nothing more than to be as far away from him as the earth could allow, and now, my life seems to depend on keeping him close.

"Look, Marsh," I say finally. "I trust you, I do. But that also makes you the most dangerous person here to me. If you were behind this, it would be really easy for you to make me disappear. I would just be gone. If it means anything, I didn't start investigating you because I thought you were the least likely to be the culprit."

He slaps a thunderous hand down on my shoulder—the one that isn't shot, thankfully. "You're all right, Green. I'll talk to the captain about getting you a new place to live, something a little better suited for you. A little safer. Maybe there's a place open where we stick our parolees."

We start walking towards the mouth of the alley.

"So, now what?" I ask. "Do we go after Finnegan? Do we try digging into someone else on the team? Or do we start looking somewhere else?"

I never hear his answer. Marsh opens his mouth to respond, but whatever he was going to say is drowned out by the screeching, deafening howl roaring towards us as we reach the opening onto the road. A meteor is streaking down out of the sky heading straight at our feet. A figure stands on top of the building across the street directing the meteor, but I can't focus on anything but the ball of fire heading right at me. The air is sucked out of my lungs, and my eyes dry out. My teeth are rattling from the force of the oncoming projectile.

Marsh barrels into me, wrapping me in a bear hug that nearly breaks my back. We crash into the brick wall of the nearby building as the fireball explodes at our feet. The next few seconds are spotty; I black out at least twice. I'm not sure which way is up. I'm gasping for air and choking on ashes. I'm being crushed, a massive weight is on my chest.

"*Detective!*" I hear Greystone's voice in my head, but I can barely concentrate on it over the ringing in my ears.

I dimly realize the weight on my chest is Marsh. It's his ashes I'm choking on, the back half of his body is scorched away. I can see bones and internal organs. Again. He's out cold, a dead weight on top of me. I struggle to slide out from under him, panicking. I am coughing uncontrollably. Looking around me, I'm surprised to see that I'm inside the building I had been outside of a few seconds earlier. There is a huge, gaping hole in the brick wall where the combined force of Marsh and the explosion broke through.

Over the ringing in my ears, I can hear Finnegan's mocking voice from across the street. "You still alive in there, Green?"

Son of a bitch! I snarl in my head. I manage to push Marsh off of me. He's completely unresponsive; I've no idea if he's been destroyed or what. I stagger to my feet and start a lurching, faltering run out into the alley. Without even thinking, I draw my gun and run out the hole in the wall. I have to hold one arm up over my mouth to filter the smoke out from the flames burning around the entrance. I'm still coughing out a mouthful of Marsh's ash.

People are scattering in all directions trying to run away from the flames. Finnegan is standing on the third-story roof across the street, one leg propped up on the ledge, arms leaning on his upraised knee.

"Damn, Green, for a living guy, you're pretty tough to kill," he yells, smiling evilly.

I raise my gun and fire. I'm not a marksman by any stretch. But the nice thing about these guns is the projectiles they fire are massive, and the impact covers a large area. I only have to point in the general vicinity of my target, and I'll usually hit it.

General vicinity I can do.

That electrical force shields him from my shot, the same field he used earlier. He barely flinches.

"Green, you idiot. You can't hurt me with that thing." A ball of fire starts to materialize in the air above him. I'm guessing this will be meteor number two.

Finnegan only needs to hit me once. And he's right, that shield of his, whatever it is, seems to protect him. I could blast at it all day, and it wouldn't scratch him.

The ledge he's standing on, however, is another story entirely.

I ignore him and pull the trigger again. My second shot disintegrates the bricks. He's not hurt from my shot, but as the ledge he's leaning on crumbles, he loses his balance. His arms pinwheel frantically before he pitches headfirst over the edge, the ball of fire flickering out of existence. He spins head over heels a few times on the way down, smacking off the side of the building at least once.

Bones shatter and break when he hits the sidewalk. His

scream of pain and rage would normally have sent me running away in terror, but I'm too angry. I keep my gun aimed at him and start walking forward.

I squeeze off two more shots at him for good measure, shield or no shield.

It looks like he has to concentrate on maintaining that shield because this time nothing stops my shots. The first one tears a sizable chunk out of his midsection, leaving a smear of fluid along the ground. The second shot manages to wing him, ripping some skin off his face.

I hear some footsteps running up behind me, and I glance back. Kim and Armstrong come running full steam out of the alley entrance. Behind them, I see Meints and some other officers going through the hole blown into the alley wall.

"What the hell is going on?" Kim asks, quickly assessing the street.

I'm still moving towards Finnegan but looking over my shoulder back at my two companions. Kim's eyes widen as he looks past me. I turn back around to see a cloud of smoke erupt where Finnegan is struggling to get up. Through the haze, I see Finnegan's shadow spring up and take off.

Dammit!

"C'mon!" I yell, running after him.

Finnegan sprints up the street. Even with part of his torso chewed away and blood streaming from his face, he's moving as fast as I can run at top speed. There are too many people on the street for me to take another shot. And I don't remember how many shots my gun holds. He bulldozes through the crowd, tossing people out of the way. They look around in confusion, picking themselves off the ground as I run past.

He turns a corner, and I'm about thirty feet behind him. As I round the corner, I look back and see both Kim and Armstrong running after me, confusion on their faces.

"Where are you going?" Armstrong yells.

I don't understand what the problem is, so I don't bother to reply and keep running. Finnegan knocks a few people down, and I have to scramble around them. He puts some distance between us. I know I'm not in peak condition at the best of times, and I'm coughing from the smoke and Marsh I inhaled earlier. My side is cramping up. He's pulling away as he turns another corner into another alley.

As I go barreling into the alleyway, a few things happen at once. The sky darkens, even more than moving into a narrow alley would account for. Captain Radu drops from the air right in front of me. I don't mean he falls; I mean, it's like he takes a step down, only that step must have been from at least fifty feet up. He lands as casually as if he'd stepped off his front porch. Shadows writhe and swirl around him, and his red eyes are blazing as I pull up short. He holds out his hand to block me.

"Stop!" he intones, and my knees buckle at the command. Behind him, Finnegan throws open a rusted metal door at the end of the alley. Finnegan gives me a glare full of venom, a threat in a glance, and runs into the darkness beyond the door.

"Captain, we can catch him! He went into that building right back there!" I say, willing myself to run around him, but my feet staying oddly in the same spot.

Radu turns his bald head and looks behind him. No other part of his body moves; he stares at the doorway for a second. I hear pounding footsteps behind him as Armstrong and Kim run up.

"Green, what—" Armstrong starts, but Kim interrupts him.

"Captain?"

Captain Radu turns his gaze back to me, but he's looking at me quizzically.

"Where did he go, Detective Green?" he asks quietly.

I look at him like he's gone crazy. "Through that door-way right there!" I say, pointing behind him. The steel door whines loudly as it slams shut.

Kim looks at me strangely. "What doorway?"

"What are you talking about?" I'm screaming at them. "The only doorway in this alley!"

"Green," Armstrong says slowly, like he's speaking to a slow child. "There's no doorway in this alley. It dead-ends in a pile of trash."

I look back to where the alley ends. The rusted door is closed. There is some litter and refuse for sure, but not enough to hide the door. The door couldn't be more obvious if it had a neon sign over its head pointing at it. Finnegan has a massive lead on us now.

"What the hell, you guys?" I snarl in frustration.

I get blank looks back from Armstrong and Kim. Radu looks at me with a lot more interest.

"Curious" is all he says.

Chapter 28

Marsh gets worked over by what passes for medics here. He's fine once he comes to, maybe crankier than usual. He has to lie on his stomach for the remainder of that day and the next while his back regrows itself. With Finnegan on the loose, I'm not allowed to go anywhere by myself. Even Greystone going with me isn't enough as she can't physically do anything to protect me.

I'm relieved from duty for the next few days. That's what they tell me, but it amounts to house arrest. Two officers are stationed outside my door. I recognize them from the precinct, but I don't know their names. They don't bother to introduce themselves, and I can't care enough to ask. We leave it at that for the time being.

Greystone pops in from time to time over my two days of incarceration. She fills me on the case's progress—or its lack thereof. Finnegan is nowhere to be found.

I need something to take my mind off things for a while.

"Tell me about some of the other detectives," I ask Greystone one afternoon.

She doesn't bother asking for more details; she's used to

these questions by now. A minute passes in silence before she responds.

"Unless you are interested in a specific colleague, I thought I'd relate a story that involves both detectives Clark and Meints. It took place roughly eight months ago."

I nod for her to continue.

Detectives Olsen, Clark, and Meints

"Detective Olsen had been asked to follow up on some missing persons. Ordinarily, this is the responsibility of the Retrievals Department, those responsible for finding citizens of our city that escape to the mortal world. There were a few citizens that had been missing for some time, and no evidence had been uncovered that they had left the city.

"He spent some time reviewing case files, revisiting the last locations of those missing, reexamining witnesses. I was surprised, actually. Usually, Detective Olsen was very efficient in matters such as these, but he seemed distracted. Unfocused. I would come across him multiple times staring into space, lost in thought. He wouldn't share with me what was on his mind.

"'I need a break,' he declared one day and went to visit Detective Meints at his home. I'd never known Detective Olsen to get side-tracked or stalled in an investigation. Concerned, I accompanied him.

"When we arrived at Detective Meints' home, Detective Olsen didn't have any questions relating to the missing persons. Or at least his questions didn't appear to directly relate to the problem at hand.

"He was asking about the origins of Meridian, about when the city was founded, how it was founded, and when it first grew from being a small refuge for the undead to become an actual city.

"It was quite fascinating information, really. Detective Meints had done extensive research on the subject. He may not be the expert on the subject, like that scholar in the bar you frequent so much, but he knew a great deal about it. Detective Meints spent many hours answering Detective Olsen's questions, expounded on his findings and opinions, patiently explaining his thoughts. The thing I found the most interesting was Detective Meints' observation that mortals are primarily concerned with where they are going after this life whereas the undead are more concerned with from where they came.

"I had no idea why Detective Olsen was so interested in this subject. He would not answer any of my pleas to explain. Detective Meints gave him a copy of some notes he had written, and over the following week, Detective Olsen studied them diligently.

"While glancing through them at the precinct, Detective Clark saw what he was reading. After his predictable derisive comments and mocking observations, Detective Clark paused.

"'You're really interested in this stuff?' he asked. 'I know a guy who might be able to give you some more information if you still have some questions.'

"'Let me introduce you to Davenport,' he said, and the smile on his face should have tipped off Detective Olsen that he was being set up for something. 'I'll have Chuck go get him.'

"I thought that initial meeting with Mr. Davenport was a disaster; the man was clearly delusional and obsessed with gaining attention and special treatment. It lasted for hours. I later found out that the regular officers dealt with him on numerous occasions over the years and had forbidden him from returning to the precinct except under the most dire of circumstances.

"Now that there was a detective giving him attention, he couldn't be turned away anymore. Even by Detective Clark's standards, this was a prank of sizeable proportions. Davenport could return to the precinct for the most trivial of reasons. And he would ask for Detective Olsen exclusively.

"This should have been a major annoyance. Mr. Davenport arrived with pages of tightly written grievances he wished to address. Detective Clark was quite pleased with himself. I saw him and this Chuck—one of the officers, Officer Charles Abayomi—laughing about it at length. But quickly Detective Olsen began to meet with Mr. Davenport in private. I do not know what they spoke about. Detective Olsen would never share with me what they discussed. I only knew he took extensive notes.

"Detective Olsen never found the missing persons, despite the captain's multiple attempts to follow up with him. Detective Olsen stopped speaking to me entirely. The disappearances increased, and Detective Olsen no longer seemed interested in investigating the case."

Ms. Greystone stops speaking. I wait patiently for the conclusion to the story, or even a point of some kind.

"And?" I prompt, exasperated.

She looks at me quizzically. "And what, Detective?"

I raise both hands above my head in frustration. "What do you mean, 'And what?' You didn't tell me anything about Clark or Meints! Meints is a genius. He knows everything about everything. I knew that. Clark is Mr. Congeniality. He knows people everywhere, and he's a smart-ass."

Greystone scowls, not impressed with my mood. "I can see that you are growing irritable being confined to your home. I will leave you to your solitude."

She floats through my wall then, leaving me more confused than enlightened.

Chapter 29

Between you and me," Greystone confides in me the following afternoon while I eat something at my counter that may have once been a hamburger, "Captain Radu is sure that Detective Finnegan has escaped back to the mortal world."

"That door I saw him go through?"

She shakes her head. "No, Detective. As we have told you repeatedly, there was no doorway. You may have suffered from a concussion or hallucinated."

"Whatever," I snap. I know what I saw. Finnegan walked through an open door into the darkness beyond. It appears that I'm the only one who saw it. Or at least the only one who will admit to seeing it. I suspect that Captain Radu saw it, as well. I just don't know why he would lie about it. He wouldn't let me enter the alley to prove it either. Any time I tried moving in that direction, my limbs would seize up. I don't know what whammy the captain hit me with, but I had no option but to return with him.

"Why do you think he's gone back to the real world—as you call it?" I ask sourly.

She shrugs. "The ghosts have been combing the city for

any trace of him. Our best scryers have been looking cease-lessly. Our trackers have been searching through the sewers and tunnels below the streets. If he were still in the city, they would have tracked him down by now. Even if he could ob-scure his exact location, we would find some trace. The only explanation we can come to is that he has managed to escape the confines of the city."

Greystone continues, uneasily. "Anyway, the captain is certain Detective Finnegan is gone for the time being, but since we have no way of knowing where he is, we can't let you go around unescorted. When Detective Marsh has re-covered, he will accompany you again."

I don't respond, so we spend the next several minutes pointedly ignoring each other. I pick up my sketch pad and start drawing a masterpiece of Finnegan mangled on the ground after falling and being shot a few times. It is my fond-est recent memory.

But I'm curious. There are paths, exits from this city—ways to go back home. Clearly, there must be if they think Finnegan used one. Was that the doorway he used? Could my way home be that close? Was that why Radu kept me away from it?

I want nothing more than to drop everything and just run, go home, leave all this insanity behind me. Let me go back to art classes, admire young coeds, hork down ramen noodles, and get some crappy job behind a convenience store counter.

And Amber. I want to see Amber again if she hasn't al-ready moved on. It's times like this I wish I could speak to my brother again. He gave the worst advice in the world, but at least he'd listen to me.

Without some way to hide there, though, someone would follow after me to either drag me back or just kill me. The only thing worse than living with this insanity here would be to bring it back home with me.

And that just makes everything worse—knowing I can find a way back and knowing with equal certainty that I can't use it. Greystone is just irritating me now. It's nothing she's doing; in fact, she seems to be uncharacteristically nice today, but even looking at her just drives home the point how alien everything is. I childishly ignore her questions. After some time, she realizes she can't shake me out of my foul mood, so she makes some excuse to leave and departs.

The days crawl by. I don't exactly have much to do. No TV, no phone, no radio. No social media or internet. I doodle some sketches of people I've met here, but none of them are good enough to make me want to finish them.

Reading a couple of books kills some time. Marsh gave them to me a while back. One is on the history of a bayou and the forgotten parts of it that tie to this city. Written in nearly illegible scrawling cursive and broken English using colloquialisms from about a century earlier, it doesn't hold my attention long. The other book is worse, but it has pictures of horses, so I stare at it for a few hours.

On the third day, I wake to someone knocking on the front door so hard I'm afraid it's going to rattle off the hinges. I stagger over to the door and open it. An ugly face grins at me.

"Hey, Marsh," I greet, rubbing my eyes. "C'mon in."

"No," he says. "Your place is a dump. Let's go."

I choke back a curse, mildly irritated. "You're the one who put me here!"

"Which is why I know how bad it is," he agrees. "Let's hit Warner's."

"Fine. Give me a sec." I splash some water on my face, put on a clean shirt, and join him out on the stairwell. My definition of a clean shirt has changed a great deal in my time here. There are laundry services, but for people who aren't bothered much by the stench of decay, spring-scented clothing isn't a high priority. If it's not overpowering and it doesn't walk away on its own, I'll call it good.

"How are you feeling?" I ask as we walk down the stairs. I notice the officers aren't outside my door anymore. Good riddance.

"Not bad. Back's almost normal. I can stretch without splitting the skin. And I didn't see any reason to try and speed up the healing, so it's almost as good as new."

"Speed up the healing? Why don't you always do that then?"

He shrugs. "I can do it, but it's not always a good idea. Stuff doesn't always heal right. If I need a short-term fix, I can get things to work well enough, but I almost always have to rip pieces off and try again. It has to be an emergency for me to want to do it, and you cooling your heels for a couple days didn't seem like an earth-shattering problem to me."

I nod and pause for a second. There's been something I've wanted to say, but not sure how I should do it. Sighing, I plunge forward. "I just wanted to say thanks, Marsh. You saved my life back there."

Marsh waves away my words with a swish of his hand. "No sweat."

"No, seriously, Marsh. That fireball thing Finnegan threw at me would have killed me. Thank you."

He nods but doesn't say anything, which means we're done talking about it, I guess. We walk the rest of the way to the bar in silence.

We find a booth inside Warner's. The place is relatively empty. I guess every bar has a lull. Some guy is at the piano playing a semi-upbeat tune, which sounds oddly out of place. Someone stops beside our table, and I glance up. I almost shriek out loud as I look at one of the most repulsive faces I've seen in my life. Not to be cruel, but the girl standing at our table looks like her head was run over by a bulldozer. Her short black hair is sticking up every which way. Her nose is smashed flat to her face and crooked like it's been broken in two to three places. She has two large teeth protruding out of a mouth with no other teeth to be found.

I cough awkwardly to cover my reaction. Marsh gives me a curious glance. "Hey, gorgeous," he says to her without a trace of irony. "Can we get some breakfast?"

"No," she says, shifting uncomfortably.

Marsh and I both raise our eyebrows.

"Uh, look," Marsh says patiently. "You're new here . . . ?"

"Maude," the waitress supplies her name quietly.

"You're new here, Maude," Marsh continues. "So maybe you don't know how this waitressing thing works. But generally—and I'll admit I've never done it, myself, so I could be wrong—I tell you something I want to eat, you go get it for me, and if you don't screw that up too bad, I'll give you something nice for your trouble."

"It's not that," she says haltingly.

We both stare at her waiting.

"We found something out back. Warner wants you to come see."

"That's not something you want to hear from someone who's going to cook your food," Marsh says, getting up. "Lead the way."

"So, Maude," I ask as I follow them back through the door leading into the kitchen. "I haven't seen Annabelle lately. What's she up to?"

Maude lurches a bit but keeps going, shoulders slouched. "Ask Warner," she says.

We go through the kitchen, and that horror show will stay burned in my brain until the day I die. Let's just say, sanitary food preparation isn't too important here. I'm not sure what creatures were quivering and cawing before being hacked apart by cleavers, but I decide to not look too closely. The steel countertops are blackened with grime and mold. The grill has a layer of sludge covering it. It's amazing I haven't been killed just by eating the food here.

Maude weaves her way past the two short-order cooks and out the back door. The alleyway is clogged with garbage and debris, and the stench is devastating. I can't help but cover my nose with my hand, and I struggle to keep the contents of my stomach down. Some of the piles of trash are taller than I am. Clearly, the garbage men don't get around here too often. But then, if I had enough willpower to overcome the grip of death to continue living, I don't think I'd take that opportunity to clean up other people's garbage either.

Warner is standing next to an open dumpster. He looks pissed, impatient as he waits for us. His black clothes are actually a solid, deep black; they aren't faded out like most people wear. Even with the grim set to his face and morose expression, he looks out of place here in the garbage and refuse behind his place. Despite everything, I've always thought of Warner as a class act.

"Finally. Our city's finest. What took you assholes so long?" Warner asks, arms crossed, glowering at us.

Never mind. He's a dick.

"Any reason we're standing out here instead of eating our breakfast?" Marsh asks.

Warner grinds his teeth, calculating his answer. Finally, he waves away what he wanted to say and settles for, "Yes, and I don't know what to make of it. We wouldn't have discovered it if it weren't for the smell."

"Seriously?" I ask, gesturing to our surroundings and trying not to gag. "What could possibly smell worse than this?"

"See for yourselves," Warner says, stepping back from the dumpster to give us room.

Marsh and I step up to the dumpster and look in.

Annabelle's corpse looks back at us, half-buried under several bags of trash. Not her corpse laying down where she decided to take a nap, but her lifeless, totally dead corpse with burned out eyes, laying where it had been dumped.

I swear.

"No kidding," Marsh agrees, frowning. "She was the best waitress in town."

Maude harrumphs and returns back inside.

Another murder. This time someone I know. And of the very few people I know in this town, one of the ones I sort of liked. She was cranky, only spoke to me when absolutely necessary, probably wouldn't have cared if I'd lived or died, but I knew her. I pound my fist against the dumpster in frustration.

"Marsh, we've got to find who's doing this."

"No wonder you're a detective, with that brilliant insight of yours." Marsh turns to Warner. "Tell me about her. She have any friends? Enemies? Cranky customers?"

Warner shrugs sadly. His cantankerousness is gone now, uncertainty mellowing his mood. "I don't know too much about her. She is . . . *was* a good worker. She never had any problems with nobody." He opens his mouth to say more, then just shrugs helplessly again.

I remember back a few weeks ago, to the last conversation I had with her. "I know someone who knows her," I say absently, more to myself than anyone else.

"Who's that?" Marsh asks, surprised. Like I'm not allowed to know anyone besides him.

"What's-his-name, the scholar in back."

"Frank?" Warner offers.

"Yeah. I want to ask him a few questions. You want to come with me, Marsh?"

He shakes his head. "Nah. That guy pisses me off. You can deal with him. Just don't leave the bar."

I nod and head back inside, trying to wipe some of the grime off my shoes on a thoroughly useless mat outside the door.

"And tell Greystone to send a crew out here to clean this mess up," he calls after me.

I nod again and weave my way through the kitchen, trying to keep my eyes locked on the door ahead. The cooks ignore me, and I ignore what they're cooking. I think that our relationship is exactly as it should be. I return to the bar and head over to the back room where Frank is typing up some notes.

"Hello, Frank," I greet him as I approach the open door.

He doesn't look up from his typewriter and continues clacking away, but at least he responds. "Detective," he says, politely.

"I've got a few questions for you if you don't mind," I say as I step inside the room.

Frank doesn't stop typing, but nods. "Of course. Anything I can do to help," he says.

It irritates me that he won't stop what he's doing, but I'll let it slide for now. "I'd like to ask you a few questions about Annabelle."

He tsks sadly. "Yes, poor soul. Just awful what happened to her." He glances over at the piles of notes stacked by the typewriter. Sure, they stay neatly stacked for him; they'd be all over the floor if I was typing.

I get ready to ask him a question, but I pause. Something's off here. My brain can't decide what it is yet. He's not being rude; he even seems reasonably helpful. There's no reason I should suspect him of anything. But something about him is bothering me. What is it?

"Detective?" he asks, glancing up at me.

I shake my head, like the act will actually clear my mind of its confusion. "When was the last time you saw her?" I meet his gaze, but it makes me uncomfortable. It's not crazy, but it's intense. I lean against his table as he continues to type. He's watching my expression now instead of his hands.

"The last time I saw Annabelle, I believe, was the last time we spoke, you and I. She finished her shift here. I did not see her after that."

"Did you ever see her outside of work?"

He shakes his head and looks back down at his hands as he continues plunking on keys. "No, not really. I spend most of my time here working on my research."

What is going on here? Something is really distracting me now. It's his typing. Unlike many here in Meridian, I don't have years of experience in using archaic contraptions and forgotten inventions. But one thing I've become intimately familiar with during my short time as a detective is working through mountains of paperwork on a typewriter. I know how the machine feels in front of me, the tactile sensation of keys underneath my fingers.

Whatever Frank is doing, it doesn't ring true.

"Detective? Is something wrong?" he asks, but I ignore him now. I watch his fingers as he types, and then it clicks.

I don't feel anything when he presses a key. I hear the clacking of the keys, I hear the bell chime when he reaches the edge of the page, and I see him use the carriage return to start a new line, but there is no vibration from the typewriter. My wrists are still sore from endless hours of that vibration, but I feel none of that here.

If the typewriter isn't working, what exactly is he typing? I look closely and blink in surprise. There are no letters on the page. Actually, the keys don't move at all when he types. How is this possible? I'm leaning against the table, but I'm not feeling any tremors or feedback. What the hell?

Frank stops typing, or feigning typing, or whatever it is he is doing. The sound of the keys clacking lasts a few more seconds before fading out. I look back up to see Frank staring at me intently.

"Well," he says, surprised. "No one has been able to do that, not for a very long time."

"Been able to do what?" I ask, confused.

"See through my glamour. And it is a very powerful glamour, Detective Green." Frank seems to be mulling something over. Reaching a decision, he abruptly stands up.

He walks around the table and over to the entrance of the room. He quietly closes the doors, shutting off sound from the bar outside. At least, it looked like he closed the door, but I swear it seemed like his hand wasn't actually touching it. I don't spend too much time dwelling on it because it occurs to me that we're alone in the room together, and the space feels much too small. Suddenly the stacks of books, papers, and photos pinned to the walls feel like they are closing in on me.

He walks about halfway back towards me and stops, sizing me up.

"I had hoped to avoid this. Ever since I saw you here, I feared you might be a problem."

I definitely don't like the direction this conversation is taking. I make sure to stay out of arm's reach. He must have seen my concern on my face as he waves an arm dismissively. "Do not be concerned, Detective. I have no intention of harming you today. I am merely deciding how to proceed."

He has no intention of harming me. *Today.* Don't think I didn't hear that part of it. "How about you just get to the point, Frank."

He smiles mischievously. "Very well. I will, as you say, get to the point. I know who is responsible for the demise of our poor, beautiful waitress."

I stare at him. "OK, I'll bite. Who?"

"Well, I do not know their identity specifically. But I

know who it was, as in a group. But I am afraid you are not going to like the answer."

I think I know where this is going now. "You're going to say it's demons, aren't you?"

His face lights up in delight. "You are extremely perceptive, Detective."

"Look," I say, getting a little angry. "I don't need you wasting my time."

"Whatever do you mean?" he asks, innocently.

"It might be funny to mess with the lone living guy. I know I've still got a lot to learn, but at least I know there's no such thing as demons. So why don't you quit stalling and tell me what you know."

"I see. Very well. I am more than happy to cooperate with you. You have my word."

He extends his hand to me. "Shake on it?" he asks, again grinning.

I'm irritated, but if it gains his cooperation, I'll play along. "Sure," I say, reaching out to shake his hand. I'm ready for any sudden moves.

My hand passes right through his. I don't mean I missed; I mean, where I expected his hand to be a solid, physical thing, my hand met nothing. I stand there, staring uncomprehendingly, passing my hand back through his again, trying to figure out what this means. He's not a ghost, at least none like I've ever seen. He looks solid, but he's clearly not.

He's grinning from ear to ear, delighting in my confusion.

"Have you figured it out yet, Detective?" he asks. He leans in closer and speaks in a whisper.

"How does it feel, meeting your very first demon?"

Chapter 30

G*HOSTBANE! ACTIVATE GHOSTBANE! ACTIVATE GHOST-BANE!* I scream at my badge. Nothing happens. Frank is still in front of me, smiling, uncomfortably close.

My brain isn't working really well right now. There are a few gears that are slipping.

Shit. I'm terrified. I've just stepped off a ledge, and I'm looking at a long drop.

"Detective Green? Are you OK?" I can hear the alarm in Greystone's voice.

Yes. No. Maybe? I don't know what the hell . . . Not hell, I mean heck! Dammit. I'm fine. I'm . . . Leave me alone. Over and out.

Awesome. That was smooth. I'm not ready to get Greystone involved in this yet until I understand how much danger I'm looking at.

Frank is still smiling at me. I expect to see canary feathers peeking out from his cat's grin. He's just waiting, reading my reactions.

"A demon," I finally say.

"Yes."

"I don't know what that means," I admit. "Wait, are you going to try and possess me?"

He leans back a bit, raising his eyebrows. "Would you allow me to do that?" He says it as a joke, but I can hear the yearning hidden behind the words.

"No. Of course not."

"Then you need not worry, Jake. I can only enter where I am invited. That includes bodies. I cannot have one of my own, but I can take one that is freely given to me."

"Only enter where you're invited in? That sounds like vampires."

"What are vampires, Jake? What do you know of them really? They are demons that have taken over some poor soul's body. Well, a demon of sorts."

"So, you're like Satan or Beelzebub, those guys?"

Frank shakes his head dismissively. "They are the ones that got me into this mess, yes. But I have not spoken to them in millennia."

That stops me again. I was kidding. Kind of.

Crap.

I've never considered Satan or Beelzebub to be real beings. They have always been figures in a story, one that I more or less believed, but in the abstract. I never expected to actually meet them.

"Mess?" I ask, trying to reign in my panicked thoughts.

"Kicked out of the presence of God. Cast into Eternal Darkness. Exiled into the torturous bowels of hell for all of eternity. That mess."

I'm feeling a little dizzy. "Do you mind if I sit?"

"Be my guest," he offers, with an amused smile. "It is not like I can use it."

I sit, dropping a little more quickly than I expected. My mind doesn't want to believe this. I'm talking to a demon. And I believe what he's telling me, which goes against everything my mom and every pastor I've ever heard warned me against.

"How did you get out of hell?"

He sighs theatrically. "Hell is not a specific place, you understand. Sure, we congregate in some places, so we can all be miserable together. But hell is anywhere God is not. My rebellion, my sins were so egregious that He has completely cast me aside. I got suckered by the sweet words of the Morning Star and made a mistake from which I will never be able to recover.

"I did not get out of hell, as you say, because I can never escape it. It is everywhere with me. It has been this way for millions of years. It will be the same for millions upon millions more."

Again, he puts levity to the words, but they are forced. I'm about to ask another question, but I recognize in his eyes that he *knows* I can hear the longing in his words. I see the first flash of anger cross his gaze.

"Jacob Green, we could spend the remainder of your life discussing things that you do not understand. I was created millions of years ago. I have lived and observed humans throughout the entirety of their existence. I have seen every possible human drama, scheme, thought, and desire. None of it interests me anymore. So a person dies and goes to God a few years earlier than you feel is fair. What does that matter against the millions of years I have waited? And you lot, no matter how poorly you blunder through your existence, you can pass on to Him. Killing you before you can sin too badly would be a gift to you—from an eternal perspective—do you not think?"

He is suddenly an arm's length away from me. He moved across the room in the space of a blink. "I have found a place where I can pass the dreary years away in relative obscurity and peace. And you are threatening that."

"Me?" I ask in confusion. Just once, I wish I knew what was going on! "How do I threaten you? I barely even know you."

"It is because of what you are."

I wait. "You're going to make me ask it, aren't you?"

Frank chuckles. I hear actual amusement. "I must admit, it has been many centuries since I have met someone who entertains me as much as you."

"Thanks?"

"Of course, I think that was a monkey I met last time, so maybe it is not quite the same."

"Nice. What am I that threatens you so much?"

He leans in so that he is only inches from my face, "You, Jacob Green, are a Seer."

Frank looks at me intently, but I just stare back at him. I'm not going to give him the satisfaction of asking a question this time.

He smiles and takes a step back as he continues. "A Seer is someone who is able to perceive the truth of things. Not simply knowing when someone is lying, though undoubtedly that is the most common aspect you experience."

"Sure," I say, placating him, waiting for him to continue.

"You can see the true face of things. Glamours do not work on you. You can detect the meaning behind words. You can perceive the intent of a message. You can detect deception regardless of how it is presented."

I think about this. OK. It makes sense; it explains a lot. But so do horoscopes. Someone says anything generally enough and you can convince yourself it applies to you. "A Seer, you said?"

"Yes. A gifted individual, you stumbled into our city because you could see through all the glamours that keep it hidden from mortal eyes."

"You think that's how I found my way to this place? This

city?"

He snorts derisively. "For a start. Glamours are everywhere here. Everyone you have met thus far has them. And for those like me—"

"Demons, you mean."

"Yes, for demons like me, we can create the strongest glamours of all. We have been living here for centuries, undetected, unsuspected. Because our glamours cannot be detected by anything."

"Except me," I say slowly.

"Exactly." He smiles at me, but I don't sense anything friendly from it. "Except for Seers."

I pinch the bridge of my nose, closing my eyes. A shiver travels up my spine. I can't sense Frank's presence at all. There's no way to accurately explain it. When you're in a room with someone, you can feel that they are there. Whether it's a comforting feeling or a terrifying one, you at least acknowledge that someone else is nearby in some way. I don't get anything like that from Frank. He is completely silent. There isn't a scuff of a boot on the floor, no sound from the shift of leaning on one foot to another, no creak of joints as the body shifts. No breathing. Nothing.

I open my eyes to make sure he's still there. Yup, he's staring back at me. Staring at me with eyes that have seen millions of years pass them by, eyes that don't exist in a physical sense but in some spiritual form.

"How do you look so real then? If you don't have a body? If I can see through glamours, why can I see you?"

He shakes his head. "You see me in my natural form, Jacob Green. You alone out of everyone here. I could change my form so that you see something else, but it requires more effort. We need to hurry this up, Jacob. I do not like being out of sight for this long."

"Why?"

Frank just smiles. "One more question. A freebie. I might not even lie to you."

"I'll know if you lie," I reply confidently.

"Of course you will. I have only been lying for millions of years. I have been surrounded by the vilest and most evil creatures in creation. I am sure I will not be able to get one past you."

Dammit. I swallow uneasily. One question and an answer I probably won't be able to trust. I could ask about the case, I suppose.

"So, you've seen God then? He really exists?" I sneak in two.

Frank's smile fades away. His eyes lose focus. He doesn't say anything.

"Yes," he finally says, quietly. "I remember Him. I hated Him all the time I was with Him, hated Him so much. Always with the rules. Work to do. And then Lucifer—with his tantalizing words and plans—was it any wonder I was led astray? And then He cast me out for my rebellion. And now, now all I want is to go back."

He shakes his head quickly and snaps his gaze back to mine. I think of my brother, and another question comes to mind, but I dare not ask it. I couldn't trust the answer, no matter what he said.

"Enough of my problems," he says. "As if I could even confide in you. Your mind cannot possibly comprehend the complexity of my situation. And you should not believe anything I tell you anyway."

"I'm pretty sure I will know most of the lies—even if you manage to get a few past me," I say.

"That is the beauty of lying," he says, turning away from me, walking back around the table to sit down in front of the typewriter again. "I will tell you this secret: a good liar never lies all the time. Then no one trusts anything you say. But if you lie one time out of four? One time out of ten? Then you people start to listen. Such knowledge can be yours, and it is right most of the time. Except when it is so disastrously wrong." He starts laughing.

I already hate this guy. The trick is going to be making sure he doesn't hate me. Because I'm pretty sure he could cause me some trouble. Who am I kidding? I'm in crazy trouble right now. I'm talking to a demon!

"You have strong glamours, you say?" I ask him.

"Oh, yes."

"So, if I try and convince my coworkers about you—"

"I would strongly advise against that, Jacob. They will not believe you, and you will not be able to prove it. You will look more foolish than you already are."

"Great," I mutter.

"But more importantly," he continues, and his grin widens impossibly even further. "If you start talking about demons, then others like me will know you know. And if they know a Seer exists, they will take immediate measures to eliminate you. You are the greatest threat we face."

"Oh. But if I'm your greatest threat, why are you helping me?"

He laughs. "That is precious. You think I am helping you? Maybe, in this case, telling you the truth is going to do you the most harm."

"What?"

"Jacob, you are a Seer. You are likely the first one that has ever been to this place. Your kind were hunted to near extinction by supernatural beings throughout history. Even I do not know how few of you there are left, nor how you became one. But I do know that very few people here will welcome your presence if they know the truth."

I groan and close my eyes. Wait a minute.

"You're lying," I say, opening my eyes and standing up.

"Am I?" He leans back in his chair.

"What you just said. Seers were hunted, there are few left, I won't be welcomed here—something isn't right."

Frank shrugs. "Perhaps. Maybe you should try telling everyone that you are a Seer. See what happens."

And back to where I started. Dammit again.

"OK. Enough with the games. You're clever, I'm stupid, and I pose some kind of threat to you and your friends—"

He hisses sharply. "NOT my friends! None of us are friends. My kind are unified in our misery, but do not mistake that for affection or even cooperation amongst ourselves."

"Fine!" I snap. "I get it."

"No, sadly, you do not get it. And I do not care to spend the eons necessary to explain it to you."

I clench my fists and recognize how futile the gesture is. What am I going to do, hit him?

"You said you know who is killing these people. Just tell me so I can get out of here."

Frank stands back up and slowly saunters over to me, completely invading my space. He's almost nose-to-nose with me again. "This is where we need to make what you would call a deal."

"A deal. With a demon."

Frank nods. "I will tell you what I know. And you will not tell what you know about me to your coworkers."

I mull that over for a second. "That sounds deceptively straightforward."

He chuckles. "It always does, does it not? Would you prefer to draft a contract? Sign it in your blood?"

I scowl at him as he continues. "No, my dear Jacob. If you want to hear what I know, you will agree to these terms. And if you break them, I will turn the full fury of my attention onto you. And I doubt you will survive it long."

I'm sure he's not lying. Swell.

I nod.

"I am not the only one of my kind in this sad little city—this place that has tucked itself away from the rest of the world. The creatures here, so assured of their safety, cut themselves away from humanity, and fill up the forgotten cracks and fissures of the world. They imagine themselves immune to the dangers posed by the mundane world. But despite their silly beliefs, they are still mortal. Mortal immortals, ha."

Frank laughs to himself, like he's forgotten I'm in the room with him. He sits back down, leaning back with a self-satisfied air. His eyes blaze with a frightening intensity, the focus of his gaze far away. "We are the true immortals; we have days without end before us. Your undead friends are mere blinks in my lifetime."

He focuses his attention back to me, all humor and warmth gone from his eyes. "I am content to hide here and idle away my time. But others of my kind, they find amusement wherever they can. And another has found it here. I wish to be alone, so I will help you."

Frank pauses, sizing me up. I don't know what I would say at this point, so I wait patiently. Finally, he leans forward, and his next words are barely more than a whisper. "Do you think that these undead neighbors of yours will never pass on to the judgment they deserve? Eventually, they will. And another demon has decided to speed that process along."

"But how is he doing it?" I ask. Frank likes to talk, and I want to wrap this up.

"How do this city's residents become undead in the first place, Jacob? What have they told you?"

I think back for a minute. "They say it has something to do with willpower."

"Correct," Frank nods. "Willpower is what keeps their souls tied to this plane. So, how do we then make them leave this plane and move on to the next?"

"Take away their willpower?" I answer, not even knowing what that means.

"Exactly. Now you understand."

"Huh? No, I don't understand. You haven't told me anything."

"Have I not? I disagree. I have told you everything."

I blink, and he's standing next to me, whispering in my ear. "Remember our deal, Jacob Green."

I blink again, and he's gone. I'm alone.

Chapter 31

Wʜᴀᴛ ᴅᴏ I ᴅᴏ ɴᴏᴡ?

I can't process this clearly. More than any other time since I found myself here, I feel helpless and alone. I desperately want to talk to someone. But I have no family, no friends I can turn to.

I'm still in Frank's room, alone. Dust and neglect cover everything. It's all I can do to keep from shivering despite the heat. With the doors closed and Frank gone, the room looks abandoned, uninhabited.

"Are you OK, Detective?" Greystone says to me in my mind.

I shouldn't confide my thoughts to anyone here. Not even to Greystone. I'm not one of them. They're treating me as somewhat of an equal right now, but it could be a temporary attitude that may change at any time. If I'm not careful, I could reveal secrets I've managed to keep hidden—even after all that Marsh put me through during my weeks of torment. I could endanger family and friends.

For the first time, I can't dredge up the resolve to care enough to stay silent.

What do you know about me, Ms. Greystone?

"*Detective? Should I come find you? Are you in danger?*"

I'm fine, Ms. Greystone. Please. What do you know about me?

She pauses for a moment. "*We know what you have told us. You were a college student. You came here from Nebraska.*"

What about people close to me? What do you know?

"*You had a girlfriend.*"

Have. I have a girlfriend, I stress.

"*Of course,*" Greystone amends, and I can hear the puzzlement in her voice in my head. "*You have a girlfriend. And a mother, though you know not where she currently resides.*"

Did you know I had a brother?

"*I believe you did mention that, yes. You had a brother who died a few years back.*"

I'm silent, pondering the question that is tearing me apart. A tear forms in the corner of my eye.

Did he though, Ms. Greystone? My brother? Is my brother here?

Twelve Years Ago . . .

It's fall; I'm thirteen and in my final year of middle school. I idolize my older brother, more so now than any other time. Craig is four years older than me, and in my mind, he can do no wrong. Even as young as I am, I know that he gets into trouble all the time, but that just makes him so much cooler. He's had girlfriends for years, and his bad-boy attitude drives them crazy. He loves heavy metal music and hardcore punk—anything fast, loud and angry. I can't get enough of it.

The feeling isn't always mutual. He doesn't like his little brother hanging around him all the time. But just because he picks on me at times doesn't mean he's OK with anyone else doing it. It's OK when he gives me grief. Even if I hate the words at the time, I love the attention. But heaven help anyone else if he catches them giving me a hard time.

Will Fenkle is the biggest asshole of the eighth grade. He delights in the misery of others, especially if he's the one to make them miserable. No one—no boy or girl, teacher or kid—is safe from his attention. Unfortunately, this includes me. I'm not necessarily popular, but I am well liked by most. I get along with just about anybody. But something about me just rubs him the wrong way.

We hate each other from the first time we meet.

I wish I could say I step up and stop him from picking on other kids because of some noble desire to protect others. The truth is, I don't want to attract his attention any more than anyone else does.

I ignore him as he makes life miserable for a few other kids in the hall. I'm glad it isn't me. When he does turn his attention to me, I just keep my head down and a smile on my face like it's all a big joke and try to weather it as best I can. If I don't put up too much of a fight, usually the worst I have to deal with is having my books knocked out of my hands or having to listen to some half-witted attempts to insult my mom.

But then a few weeks into the semester, he starts picking on Dylan Anderson.

Dylan is a pain in the ass. It's not his fault; he's developmentally challenged, but thirteen-year-olds aren't usually known for their patience and understanding. He lashes out at anyone who tries to talk to him. He can only say a few words and generally behaves at about a five-year-old's level. He's in special classes; we only see him during lunch and gym, and for the most part, he keeps to himself.

Of course, this makes him a prime target for Will.

But Dylan's mom is friends with my mom. I grew up hanging out with Dylan. We're not friends; I'm not sure Dylan knows how to have friends, or that he will ever want a friend, *but he doesn't lash out at me, and I try and help him out when I can.*

And when I see Will start tripping Dylan, laughing at him, bringing Dylan to tears, I lose it. The next thing I know, I'm spinning Will around. Will's surprise at someone attacking him is probably the only reason things go the way they do.

I land the first punch, hit him square in the nose with everything I have. His knees buckle as blood starts gushing from both nostrils, but I don't stop. I keep hitting him, over and over in the face. When he drops to the ground, I start kicking him as hard as I can.

I don't stop until some teachers pull me off him.

I am suspended for a few days. The principal hears how it started, hears what Will was doing to Dylan, and she has no sympathy for him. She suspends him, too. I think she'd like to give me a pass, but I did go kind of crazy, and she has to administer some form of punishment. Given the circumstances, I get off pretty light.

You know that theory that says all you have to do to stop a bully is to stand up to him? It doesn't work out like that all the time. That might work if said bully doesn't have an older brother who is even worse than he is.

My first day back, after school, Will is waiting for me with his brother and some of his brother's friends.

It does not go well for me. They break one of my fingers. I get a concussion and a black eye.

But unfortunately for them, I have an older brother too. And my brother is way scarier than Will's.

I stagger home and explain to my mom what happened. She has to take me to our doctor. My brother listens to everything I say from the other room but doesn't say a word. As my mother hustles me out to the car, I look over at Craig. He nods to me, grabbing his keys. As my mom drives down the street, I look in the side mirror and see Craig hop into his car and drive away in the other direction.

He beats the tar out of those kids. Hospitalizes most of them. Only one of the boys who hurt me manages to get away before the police catch up to my brother. He paid special attention to Will and his brother. They spend weeks recovering, Will never did walk right after that.

My brother Craig goes to jail. He used a baseball bat, so he gets extra time for using a weapon. This was his second offense.

I think about what my brother did a lot. It occupies my thoughts many nights after this event. I'm proud, in a way, that my brother protected me the way he did, regardless of the consequences. But another part of me is just sad for my brother. I don't think Craig knows what to do with himself. He is scared of the future, of growing up, and just lashes out at anything and everything.

Craig is sentenced to five years, but we know he should probably get out earlier if he can behave himself. He never gets the chance. Three months in he disappears from prison. Foul play is suspected, but nothing is ever proven.

I never see him again.

I sometimes wonder if he was protecting me that day, or if he finally saw an out from his responsibilities—a way to escape the whole process of maturing, getting a job, everything that comes with growing up.

I love my brother, but this is not what I want for myself. I want to be someone; I want to have a purpose in life. It would be easy to throw away responsibilities and follow my brother down his path. But anytime I'm giving up on something in life, if a challenge is too hard, I think about my brother. He is my hero, but I don't want to follow in his footsteps.

I wait to hear an answer, dread pooling in my stomach. I feel raw, exposed, terrified.

"No, detective," Greystone answers at last. *"Your brother is*

not here. At least, not that I am aware."

I gasp, but whether it is in disappointment or relief, I can't really say. A weight is off my shoulders, one I didn't know was there. I can't explain why I even thought he might be here, I just needed to know he wasn't stuck here like me.

I don't know if there is anyone I can trust here in this godforsaken place, but for all her disdain, I think Greystone is the one I can distrust the least. Have I made an error? Have I given them something that will be used against me later?

I still don't know what happened to Craig. He disappeared from the world, like I have. But I can take comfort that I really am alone in this place. It's scant solace.

"Why would you believe he is here?" Greystone asks.

I don't know how to answer that.

I need a moment to myself—if you don't mind.

"Of course, Detective Green."

I struggle to compose myself and return to the colossal problems at hand.

Chapter 32

Wʜᴀᴛ ᴛʜᴇ ʜᴇʟʟ ᴅᴏ I do now?

I've got answers. More answers than I know what to do with. More than I can safely handle assuming I can believe anything Frank just told me.

He's a demon. A demon!

I have to accept that much at face value. And I'm pretty sure it isn't just a misunderstanding that we have thousands of years of historical records claiming that demons are evil and corrupt creatures that want the worst for any humans that cross their paths. Demons are bad. I'm going to accept that one as truth. I'm also going to assume that Frank was lying as much as he was telling the truth. Or telling the truth but implying a different meaning—just messing me over in any number of ways. I'm not sure what his angle is, but I have to count on the fact he has one.

I'm usually good at reading people. I can tell by their mannerisms, their evasiveness, the inflection of their words—whether or not they are telling the truth. But Frank didn't have a real body. There were no natural mannerisms to read, only those he chose to visually display. So, even if I felt he's lying about something, it could be because he wanted me to assume he was lying.

I have no idea.

I can turn this thing in circles all day.

The information I have at hand is limited. Frank claims a demon is behind everything, which I know from experience is going to be greeted by heaps of ridicule. He says I'm something called a Seer and if people here find out about it they're going to want to kill me—which most of my neighbors want to do anyway. He says he gave me the answer, but I don't see it. I'm going to need help to figure this stuff out, but I have to do it without outing Frank. Because if I do, even on accident, I'm going to have a demon give me his personal attention and devote the entirety of his evil to making sure my life is as miserable as possible. And he's been doing this stuff for as long as humans have been around.

This is going to suck.

After several minutes of chasing my thoughts around in my mind, I open the doors and to reveal the main room of the bar. My world has been rocked, again. Each time I think I have a grasp on the situation around me, a new doorway opens up onto something bigger and more terrifying. My knees are a little shaky, and I walk through the door and into the main room to see Marsh, with Greystone floating beside him, waiting for me. They are both staring at the doorway I exit. They are whispering fiercely with each other, but quiet down once I get near.

"Green," Marsh greets, his eyes narrowed suspiciously. "Where ya been, buddy?"

"Um. In here." I point needlessly at the room behind me.

"You said you were going to talk to Frank."

I nod. "Yes."

"So, what did you do instead?"

I look at him, confused. "What do you mean?"

Marsh folds his arms in front of his chest, his shoulders looming over me. "Well, see, I'm a detective. Which means I notice little details like when the guy you tell me you're going to talk to is sitting over there at the bar, drunk, singing off-key tunes to Warner the whole time."

I look over at the bar. Sure enough, Frank is there. He glances up at me right when I look over, raising his glass to me, smiling.

"He was here the whole time?" I repeat, stupidly.

"Yeah. Or didn't you think I'd notice that?" Marsh is irritated, but Greystone is looking at me in concern.

"Are you alright, Detective?" she asks.

I close my eyes, pinching the bridge of my nose. Frank was in both places at once. While it makes me look like an idiot or a liar to my companions, it does help cover up where I got my information. I'm going to have to be very careful how I ask my questions. Marsh might not look like it, but he's smart. He'll know if I'm obviously trying to hide something.

"Fine. I'm fine. I just needed some time alone to think. Look, I need to tell you both something in private."

"What you got?" Marsh questions.

"Can we go somewhere in private, please?"

"Alright, alright, princess. Don't get your knickers in a bunch. We're done here. Let's grab a carriage, and you can spill your secrets to us."

We have to close Warner's down first, to Warner's obvious dismay. I can tell his heart isn't in it, though. He's going through the motions of being pissed about our heavy-handedness, but I think he's relieved to be able to go home for a while. I just hope he's still going to let me back in once he reopens.

Once Warner's is behind us, the three of us are inside a carriage lit by gaslight and Greystone's dim luminescence. Marsh just told the driver to drive with no real destination yet. Both Marsh and Greystone are waiting for me to get talking, but I realize I don't know how to say this.

"Marsh," I say slowly. "You were mad that I didn't share my suspicions about the squad with you. I told you I'll trust you."

He nods, saying nothing.

"I'm going to trust you now. I think what I'm about to tell you could put my life in danger again."

"Damn, Green. Why is everything about you? We're supposed to be solving a string of murders."

"This is related," I assure him. I take a deep breath. I need to keep Frank out of this. "Have you ever heard of someone called a Seer?"

I can see Marsh roll his eyes in the gloom. "Oh, for fuc—"

"Detective Marsh!" Greystone scolds, then turns to me. "A Seer? Where did you hear this term?"

I wave dismissively. "Around."

"And you think a Seer may be responsible for the murders?"

"No. Just, what can you tell me about Seers?"

Marsh adjusts the hat on this head, crosses his arms and scowls. Greystone thinks for a moment. "There haven't been reports of Seers for decades, if not in over a hundred years, Detective Green," she says. "Seers were those who saw the truths of things. Mortals often related them to fortune-tellers and psychics, but they were more than that. They were dangerous to all of us since they saw through our glamours. They could see our true faces. They used to be employed by the aristocracies in various European courts; they were witches and shamans in tribal cultures. They started churches and religions in the Americas."

"Or corporations," Marsh sneers.

Greystone ignores the interruption and continues. "They were systematically hunted down and exterminated a long time ago. Why would you think a Seer is involved in this, Detective Green?"

Here goes.

"I think . . . I think I'm a Seer."

I might as well have said I was from Mars. Both of them strain to keep straight faces.

"Why do you think that, buddy?" Marsh asks, the tone that of an adult dealing with an imaginative child.

Greystone continues patiently. "That is highly unlikely. Being a Seer isn't something you can learn, Detective Green. It can't be taught. It is a gift one is born with. You would have to come from a line of Seers. It may skip generations—I understand—but there would be a record of it. If someone has told you that you can become a Seer, they are making a jest."

"Let's just say I think I am, OK? How would we know?"

"For one, to be a Seer, you would be able to detect lies," Greystone says. She pauses as she sees Marsh stiffen beside her. "What?"

"I'm pretty good at that," I confess.

"But that's just a party trick," Marsh mutters, looking at me strangely.

"Secondly," Greystone ticks off on her finger, "you would be able to see through glamours. Can you do that?"

Frank said I could, I want to say. Instead, I waffle. "I don't know. Where's a glamour that I can see through?"

Greystone chuckles. "Well, Detective, they are everywhere."

Marsh points at Greystone. "She has one, I bet."

"Detective Marsh!" Greystone objects, offended. Evidently, that is some kind of undead etiquette faux pas.

"How would I see through it?" I ask him.

"Why are you asking me? I dunno. What do you see when you look at Greystone here?"

I look at Greystone. She is looking back at me with a

strange expression, is it nervousness? Dread?

"No. If it's something she doesn't want to discuss, I won't say it. Ms. Greystone, I won't—" I start to say, but she interrupts me.

"It's OK, Detective Green," she says like she's swallowing something vile. "What do you see?"

"Don't worry," I assure her. I stare at her, looking her over. Her body is floating on the seat, seated but not really touching it. As a matter of fact, how does she keep pace with the moving carriage? I still haven't figured that one out. "I'm sure it's nothing. I don't see anything strange. You look the same as you always do. Your hair is gathered up in a bun, and I see a sensible tweed business suit of some kind. Old-fashioned, but nice. Obviously, I can't see any color, you're all greenish-blue to me. You have a blouse of some kind buttoned to the neck, your glasses are horn-rimmed; I think that's what they're called . . ."

I trail off. As I describe her, Greystone's eyes have been growing wider, her expression angrier. I look in confusion between her and Marsh. He's looking right back at me, as confused as I am.

"Oh my God," she snarls and simply disappears.

"What's going on, Marsh?" I ask, dumbfounded. The only sound I hear is the rattle of the carriage wheels on the cobblestones outside. Marsh's mouth is hanging open.

"That's seriously what you see?" Marsh asks me.

"Of course, that's how she's always looked. Wait, why? What do you see?"

"Greystone is a total hard-on-inducing, drop-dead gorgeous bombshell, you knucklehead. She drives half the office crazy wishing she had a body of flesh. I thought there was something wrong with you that you weren't drooling all the time or walking around with a permanent boner."

"I thought it was just a dead thing, you thinking she was

so stunning."

"She's really a bowzer, huh? That's disappointing."

"No! She *is* beautiful. She just evidently looks different to me than she does to everyone else," I say, feeling dirty for saying it. Greystone is my . . . Well, she's my friend, I guess. It doesn't feel right to talk about her that way. "Look, I've always thought she was attractive, but I figured it wasn't appropriate to dwell on it. I mean, I'm like a stray dog you guys have adopted. What good would it do to pine after her?"

Ms. Greystone? I think. *I'm sorry, I didn't mean to offend you.*

"Please leave me alone, Detective." I hear her think back, followed by a sensation of a door slamming shut in my mind.

I sigh loudly. "I'm so confused."

Marsh shakes his head ruefully. "I still can't believe that's how you've always seen her."

"So how are you supposed to look?" I ask him.

"What do you mean?"

"I mean, do you have a glamour on?"

"Nope. What you see is what you get, kid," he says proudly.

"I guess that makes sense. No one would choose to look like that on purpose."

I see his fist coming just in time to roll with it as he punches my shoulder.

"What does this mean?" I ask him, switching back to a serious tone again, while rubbing feeling back into my shoulder. "The seeing through glamours?"

Marsh considers silently for a moment. We hang on as the carriage rounds a corner, and I recognize the sound of the bridge leading back to the precinct.

"We're going to have to speak to the captain."

What was it Frank said? *What are vampires, Jake? They are demons that have taken over some poor soul's body.* But is that true? Will letting the captain know I'm a Seer be a death sentence?

"Marsh, are you sure we have to? Didn't Greystone just say Seers were hunted down and killed?"

"I'm sure she exaggerated. You're alive, aren't you?"

I shrug. Barely alive.

"Oh!" Marsh says excitedly as the carriage comes to a stop. "Tell me quick. The captain. What does he look like?"

Hesitantly, I say, "Bald. Veiny. Red eyes. Gathers shadows around him. Kind of short."

"Holy shit, Green!" he laughs as he opens the door. "You might want to keep that to yourself from now on. He doesn't look that way to me at all!"

Great. I'm not going to die at all in the next few minutes or anything. Everything's going to be fine.

"Let's go talk to the captain," I say, resigned.

Chapter 33

MARSH KNOCKS ON THE CAPTAIN'S door, then opens it and walks in without waiting for an answer. I follow nervously in his wake. The captain's chair is behind his desk but facing away from us. The back is tall enough that we can't see if he's sitting there or not. It is facing the large window behind his desk, overlooking the city under a dark, cloud-covered sky.

"Captain, need to talk to you," Marsh says to the back of the chair.

The chair slowly spins around. Radu is there, after all, his hands clasped below his chin, fingertips touching in a steeple over his lips.

As if on cue, as my worry rises, the door behind us swings closed on its own.

"Please, Detectives, *entrez*. Do come in," Captain Radu says, his tone dripping with displeasure.

Marsh just stands there, looking smugly at the captain. He appears to be in no hurry to speak. I glance at him uncertainly, but he ignores me.

Great. I guess it's up to me then.

"Captain, what do you know about Seers?" I ask.

One eyebrow arches slightly. He lowers both hands to clutch the armrests of his chair, and he leans back a bit. "What do you know about them, Detective?"

"They see the truth of things. They see through glamours. Detect lies."

I pause.

"Go on," Radu encourages.

"They were thought to have been killed off. You guys, well, supernatural creatures, I mean. You killed them all off. Thought they were a danger."

Radu nods. "Yes. Continue. This has bearing to the case why?"

"Well, because I think I am one. A Seer, I mean."

He doesn't blink or react in any way. I stand uncomfortably, waiting. Marsh looks amused.

"Yes, obviously you are a Seer, Green," Radu says with no emotion as if I'd told him the sky is blue. Well, cloudy in our case.

"You knew?" Marsh and I say in unison.

"Of course, I knew. I could smell it in his blood when we first met. I have tasted the blood of enough Seers in my time to recognize its scent. Had I not known he was a Seer, I would have killed him immediately to protect the existence of our city."

This statement does not put me at ease.

"Given the situation we are experiencing, I thought the presence of a Seer would be to our advantage. We have traditionally slaughtered Seers in the past to protect against the knowledge of our existence becoming widely known. Detective Green here is already in our city. There's no reason to keep knowledge from him now that he is here and cannot leave."

I can't decide whether to be relieved or terrified right now. "If you've known all this time, why didn't you say something, sir?" I ask.

He stares impassively. "As I've said, I've met many Seers in my time. And while it is a natural gift that is passed down through family lines, merely having the gift is not enough. Plenty of Seers went mad with their insights, or ignored them, or misinterpreted them for their convenience. Not all Seers have the same sorts of abilities. I suppose someone can explain it to you at some point in the future.

"You needed to understand what you can do. I have been waiting to see if you would be able to put it to use or not. And you have definitely proven yourself more pragmatic than many of your ilk. You tend to accept things at face value, without prejudice. I believe you will make a valuable, permanent addition to the squad."

He pauses, weighing his words. I don't know why he bothers choosing his words carefully; it's not like he's been anything but blunt so far.

"We will need to take care that news of your gift does not become too widespread. Many still fear Seers, and rightly so. People with your gift were responsible for hunting down and exterminating many of our kind. There are still those here who remember those times and were directly affected by them. You could be killed simply for being who you are, which is ironic since that is what your kind did to us down through the ages."

I nod dumbly. What is there to say? I'm not responsible for what my ancestors may have done. It's a stupid reason for someone to hate you. But what can I do other than just try to prove them wrong?

"Well, we've managed to figure out that I can see through these glamours you guys use. I can I hear lies told. Most of the time."

Radu nods. "You've figured out that what you see isn't necessarily what the rest of us see?"

"Yes, exactly."

"That's what drove many of you Seers insane, seeing things that no one else could. Seeing doors where others saw none, for example."

I knew it! I'd shout out loud if it wouldn't attract attention. I'd shout in my head, but I think I've done enough to upset Greystone.

"But the more pressing question: are you feeling insane, Detective?"

"I'm standing next to a hulking corpse, I'm friends with a ghost, and I'm talking to a vampire. Even you have to admit, that's a little crazy."

I see a corner of Radu's mouth twitch. That's probably as close to a smile as I've ever seen on him. "Very well, Detective Green. I'll accept that you aren't currently insane. And you should accept that you will see things differently from the rest of us.

"Out of curiosity, which one of you finally figured it out? You being a Seer I mean? Detective Meints has known for the better part of a week now."

Marsh scowls at this. I'm too embarrassed to admit that I didn't figure out, Frank had to point it out to me.

Finally, Marsh nods his head towards me. "The kid started asking questions about Seers. He connected the dots."

"I see," Radu says. "So, we have established that you are a Seer. What now?"

"What now?" Marsh repeats back, confused. "We thought you should know . . . what you already know, I guess."

Well, here goes nothing.

"Actually, I do have something to bring up," I say, swallowing nervously. How do I talk about this without revealing Frank?

Radu sits up and cocks his head curiously. "Detective, your heart rate just elevated. You're nervous. No, scared.

What is it?"

"I think I know who is committing these murders."

"What the what?" Marsh exclaims, turning on me. "And you're just saying this now?"

"Yes, Detective?" Radu prompts.

I'm having a hard time saying it, but I finally force it out. "It's a demon. I mean, I'm pretty sure. A demon."

Marsh is staring at me with his mouth hanging open. Twice in one night, I should write it down. He speaks to the captain while still looking at me. "Uh, captain, I swear I didn't know he was going to—"

Radu waves his hand to silence Marsh. "Hush, Marsh. *Vas-y*. Continue, Detective Green."

"I've been doing some digging on my own, and I'm pretty sure that a demon is doing these killings. He's forcing the spirits out of the bodies somehow."

"A demon. Interesting," the captain says, deep in thought.

"Heh. A demon. Right, kid. See, like I told you earlier, there's no such thing as demons."

"Of course there are, Detective," Radu interrupts, leaning back in his chair. "And I fear Detective Green might be on to something here."

"What's that now?" Marsh asks, confused.

"Demons do exist, I can assure you. We are just overlooked, immune from their attention. Or at least, I had assumed so for centuries. But if you are correct, Detective Green, this would explain a lot."

Marsh's gears are still spinning, trying to wrap his head around this revelation. Captain Radu leans forward in his chair, pinning me with his gaze. "But what this doesn't explain is why Detective Green's heart rate jumped as he prepared to explain this to me. What else is there?"

I really wish I could run out of here and never come back. My head spins trying to come up with a convincing lie. I can't tell them that I'm terrified I might accidentally say something that reveals Frank's true nature, and then he'll persecute me to death in retaliation. I can't say anything that even leads suspicion to Frank. But I do have another worry, close at hand, that may help me to conceal the truth of my concern.

"Well, sir. Vampires . . . aren't they— Well, aren't they demons, sir?"

A flurry of thoughts pass through the captain's eyes, but he relaxes and leans back again. "I am beginning to see the problem here. You fear I am a demon. And a demon is responsible for the killings. You fear that I am somehow involved or wish to keep it a secret and that I will work in some way to silence you."

He stares at me intently. I try to speak, but can't, so I just nod instead.

"We are sometimes referred to as demons, or our bloodthirst is attributed to unholy forces. But I assure you, Detective, I am not a body housing a demon. I want to solve this series of murders and bring it to a stop."

I have a hard time reading the captain sometimes, but this time I can tell he is radiating absolute sincerity. Not to say he isn't dangerous or that he won't kill me if he decides to. But he doesn't appear to be working against us.

"This is crazy," Marsh mutters.

"Detective Green is correct, we may be looking at a demon here. So, what does that mean to the case?"

I think about this for a minute. I've been mulling over some possibilities ever since I had my conversation with Frank.

"I don't think anyone on our squad is a demon, sir," I explain. "I think I can recognize them or spot them."

"Seriously?" Marsh asks. I'll admit it, I feel a little smug seeing Marsh trying to keep up with things for once.

I nod and continue. As I was able to sense something off with Frank, maybe I can look for similar oddities around others to flush them out. "But I think someone may be working with him. I don't know why, but someone has removed those files from our file room. I think we need to figure out who is working against us on the team before we can make any progress on tracking down the killer."

Radu stares at me intently. "Yes. This makes sense. How do you propose to do this?"

The way he asks it makes me think he already knows the answer. But I answer anyway. "I'll need to ask them."

"You are going to interrogate the fellow members of your squad?" the captain asks.

"Yes," I sigh. "I'm going to ask each of them—one at a time, point-blank—if they stole the files."

"Detective Green, if the wrong person finds out that you are a Seer, your life could be in great danger," the captain cautions.

I look over at Marsh. He nods back at me. "Don't worry, kid. I've got your back."

"Let's do it," I say.

Radu grins, a genuine smile, exposing sharp fangs and making his eyes blaze red. It's terrifying.

"I'll start calling them in," he says eagerly.

Chapter 34

I'VE HAD SOME LONG DAYS recently, but none have felt longer than today.

We have a plan. Captain Radu will call in each member of the squad, and we'll confront each of them individually. Marsh will do the questioning, and I'll read their responses and ask any necessary follow-ups. Radu will glower menacingly.

I'm supposed to know if someone is guilty. If I think someone is guilty, I'll let Radu know afterward, so we can try and confront him while his guard is down. The captain is pretty confident he can tell when I'm lying since I'm still living—something about the scent of my sweat and the rhythm of my heart—so he'll make sure I don't frame anyone. And that's apparently all the evidence we need.

Greystone floats through the door without knocking. She doesn't say anything and avoids my gaze. Radu called her in to help. I want to talk to her, but I can tell she really doesn't want to speak to me right now. Sighing, I resign to put it off until later.

"Who's first, captain?" Marsh asks. He starts to lean

against the captain's desk, catches Radu's expression, and quickly changes his mind. We have three chairs set up, one facing the other two. Radu will oversee from behind his desk. Even with the large piece of furniture between us, he feels uncomfortably close.

"You are, Marsh," the captain says, ominously.

"Eh, what?"

"Before I drag the whole squad through this, a squad of men I have personally vetted myself and trust absolutely, I want to make sure neither of you is obfuscating the truth. Detective Green, start asking him questions."

Marsh turns to me, crosses his arms across his chest, scowling. "Yeah, kid, knock yourself out."

Great.

"Detective Marsh," I begin. I glance at Greystone, but she is still determinedly avoiding my gaze. No help there. "Did you take any files from the storage room?"

Marsh meets my gaze without flinching. "No."

"Do you have any involvement with the murders that have been happening around town?"

"Just trying to find the bastard that did it."

"Are you a jackass all the time, or just around me?"

"It's all for you, buddy."

I glance at Captain Radu and see him scowling. I hastily ask, "Any other questions?"

"That depends on how truthfully you feel he answered," the captain replies, his eyes boring into mine.

My mouth is a little dry. "Well, he answered the first two questions honestly. The last one, he wasn't telling the truth on that one."

"Heh," Marsh chuckles.

"Very well, Detectives. Let's begin. Since we've already had him in here, let's bring in Armstrong first. Ms. Greystone, if you would be so kind?"

She nods and floats out. I move over to the chair next to Marsh. I open up a notebook, grab a pencil, and doodle nervously while I wait. After an incredibly long stretch of about thirty seconds, Greystone returns followed by Armstrong.

Armstrong stops on the threshold of the office and eyes us suspiciously. He stares at me a little longer than everyone else.

"Captain. What's this?"

"Enter, Detective Armstrong. Have a seat. These detectives have some questions for you."

He grumbles as he walks over to the seat. "Want to try and blow my cover on something else now?"

Armstrong sits down, folds his arms across his chest, and stares expectantly at me.

Marsh gets his attention. "We're going to ask you a couple things, Armstrong. Just tell us the truth, and you can get out of here."

"The truth, is it? Are you sure that's what you're after?" He glares at me accusingly.

"Calm down, Armstrong. It ain't like that," Marsh tries to placate him.

"Really? Maybe you can explain what it's like then."

"Look. You know the storeroom? You remember those files that have gone missing. You the one that took them?"

"What files?" Armstrong asks cautiously.

"If you took the files, you'd know what files, genius."

Marsh has an interesting interrogation technique—I'll give him that. I glance over at Radu, but the captain is focused on reading Armstrong.

"I don't know anything about any missing files. We haven't figured out which ones are missing yet."

"OK. You sure?"

A level stare is all he gets in return.

"Fine. You're sure. Here's another one. You kill anyone

and leave their soulless corpse spoiling on the sidewalk?"

"What? No!"

"You doing anything to impede the investigation? Other than just general incompetence?"

"Of course not!"

Marsh turns to the captain. "That's all I've got."

Everyone turns to look at me. I shrug. "I don't have any questions for him."

Radu nods at me, then turns back to Armstrong. "You are dismissed, Detective."

Armstrong sits motionless for a few seconds, then he looks at each of us in turn. "You guys are crazy," he finally declares. "Let me know if you need any more of my help. Maybe I can give you some more obvious answers you can pretend to need."

The captain turns to Ms. Greystone. "Send Detective Burchard in."

While Greystone is gone, Marsh turns to me. "Well, Sherlock? Is Armstrong our guy?"

I shake my head. "No. He's telling the truth. I'm sure he's not involved. He definitely doesn't like either of us, though."

Marsh shrugs and says, "Cry me a river," as Burchard walks in the room. I haven't worked much with Detective Burchard yet. He manages to avoid me whenever possible. He is cautious when he enters the room, and as he scans the three of us and notices Greystone floating in behind him, he gets very suspicious. His guard goes up; I swear I can almost see it lock into place behind his eyes.

"What's going on?" he asks.

"You may sit, Detective," Radu says, glancing at the empty seat. He is still leaning back in his high-backed chair behind the desk. Shadows are more concentrated around him, his side of the room is darker, but his eyes are so piercingly bright they almost glow. Burchard sits down across from us, crosses one leg so his ankle is resting on the other knee, and folds his arms defiantly.

"Detective Marsh, Detective Green, ask your questions," Radu commands.

Burchard looks at us warily, expectantly.

Marsh gets right to it. "Some files were stolen from the storage room. You know anything about it?"

"News to me until Green told us," Burchard replies, not moving an inch.

"You know which files are gone?" Marsh continues.

"I don't think I need to. They're files relating to the killings. You think I have something to do with this?"

"Do you?" Marsh counters.

"Hell no, I don't." Burchard's scowl deepens. "And screw you for thinking so."

"You kill any corpses lately?"

"Only after you buggered them. Is this really what I'm in here for? A fishing expedition?"

Radu's voice drifts out from his chair. "Just answer the questions, Detective. We're asking everyone."

"No, I haven't been killing people. I haven't done that since living here." He looks pointedly at me. "Back in the real world, I killed plenty of people. We all did. I was very good at it. I enjoyed it. I still would. But I'm not killing your kind back in your world," he says, indicating toward me. "I'm not killing our kind here. And I'm not working with anyone who is."

Yikes. He's telling the truth, which means I'm sitting in a room full of people who have killed before. I glance uncomfortably at Marsh and Radu, and I swallow nervously. In Radu's case, I'm going to guess he did it a lot. I feel Radu's gaze swivel my way as if he knows the direction of the turn my thoughts have taken.

Marsh looks at me. "You got anything to add, Green?" I

shake my head, not trusting my voice right now.

"That will be all, Detective Burchard," Radu says. Burchard stays seated for a moment, glaring at us, waiting for something else. When he's sure we're truly done, he gets up and leaves without a word.

After he leaves, and Greystone goes to fetch the next of our coworkers, I whisper to Marsh and Radu, "He feels clean to me too."

"You sure?" Marsh asks.

I shake my head again. "He doesn't feel right for it. I'm sure."

Clark walks in the room. This ought to be good.

"Woah, what's this then?" he asks, smiling. He walks quickly over to the open chair, sits, and then scoots it closer to me so that our toes are nearly touching. He leans forward expectantly.

"These detectives have some questions for you, Detective Clark," Radu says, frowning. It always looks like Radu is biting down on tinfoil when he speaks to Clark, a grimace of displeasure.

"Sure, sure. Let me have it."

Marsh leans forward, and Clark glances over at him. "You ever take any files out of the storage room?"

"Oh, sure," Clark answers. We all blink at him. His smile never wavers. "Wait, you mean like steal them? Then no. Not really. Maybe? Wait. Nope, I'm sure."

"Clark, it's a simple question," Marsh says.

"Yeah, I know."

"You're sure you've never taken any files out of there?"

"Yeah, yeah."

"Because some of them went missing recently."

"Green mentioned that."

"Important files," Marsh continues, clearly starting to get irritated.

"Right."

"Look, Clark. Files relating to the murders have gone missing. That means one of us took them."

"Yeah, Marsh. I get that. I'm a detective, remember? So, who did it?"

"You tell me."

"You think it was me?"

"That's why I'm asking."

"Detectives," Radu says, glacially. I can almost feel the temperature drop in the room. "Is this getting us anywhere?"

Clark shrugs. "I dunno. He's asking the questions."

"Are you committing murders, Clark?" Marsh asks.

"Nope. Well, yeah, in the line of duty."

"What? We don't kill people; we can't."

"Oh right. So, then no."

"You working with anyone who is committing the murders?"

"I don't think so."

"You don't think so?" Marsh says, his teeth grating.

"I'm pretty sure I'd remember."

"So that's a no?"

"Yes."

I'm no mind reader, but I can practically see the desire to reach out and strangle Clark radiating from Marsh's head.

"What do you mean, 'yes?'"

"Yes, that's a no. Do you think I'm confessing to something?"

I raise my hand to get Clark's attention. "Detective Clark," I interrupt, hoping Marsh will cool down. "Do you have any guesses as to who would have taken the files?"

Clark grins even wider at me. "Sure. Someone who doesn't want us to figure out who's committing these murders. If you were smarter, I would figure you for doing it. But I think we're pretty safe there."

"Right," I agree slowly.

I don't know anything else to ask him. Marsh is glowering, his teeth clenched. After a few seconds of silence—where Clark glances first at me, then at Marsh, then back again—Captain Radu finally speaks. "You can go, Detective Clark."

Clark nods to us all. "OK, sure. Thanks, guys. Let me know if I can help out again." He gets up and leaves the room. The door closes behind him, and Radu motions for Greystone to stay where she is for a moment.

"For the love of God, please tell me it's him," Marsh pleads.

I shrug. "I don't know," I admit.

"What?" Marsh demands.

"I'm sorry, Marsh. He sounded like he was telling the truth the whole time."

"How is that possible? He answered each question every way possible."

"And I'm telling you, I can't tell if any of his answers are wrong. Not without reasonable doubt."

"Dammit, Green! I don't know if I hate you more than Clark right now or not."

"Was he deliberately trying to hide something? Or was he just being a pain in the ass?" I turn to Captain Radu. "You know more about this than I do. Is there some way he can fool this thing I can do?"

Radu shrugs slightly. "It is possible, I suppose. There are charms or wards one could craft to confuse certain tells a body makes when disguising the truth. But they are usually powerful wards, and I would have detected them on him. I wouldn't know specifically what they were for, but I'd know if he had some. And he doesn't appear to possess any."

"But he was being deliberately evasive. You have to admit, that's suspicious. Can we detain him anyway?" Marsh pleads.

Captain Radu ignores Marsh and turns to Greystone. "Let's continue. Send in Detective Kim, please."

"Dammit," Marsh grumbles. He turns to me and pokes me hard in the chest, almost knocking me out of my chair. "Get it right this time, Green. We only have one shot at this. I don't think we can keep calling them in to ask them point-blank questions."

I'm still rubbing my chest, trying to take some of the sting out of it, when Kim walks in. He glances at all of us and remains standing, casual but alert.

"Have a seat, Detective," Radu stretches out his hand, pointing at the empty seat. "These detectives have a few questions for you."

Kim doesn't say anything. He sits down, his back straight, and he stares at us without expression.

"OK, Kim," Marsh starts, still pissed. "Maybe you'll be less of a smart-ass than Clark."

"Undoubtedly," Kim responds while Marsh is preparing his next words.

"Here we go," Marsh growls. "Kim, we're missing some files from the storage room."

Kim's expression doesn't waiver. He waits a few seconds. "Is there a question there?"

"Did you take the files that are missing from the storage room?"

"No."

Marsh stares at him a few seconds but gets no reaction. "Do you know anything about the missing files?"

"No."

"You know who took them?"

"No."

"Don't talk me to death, for crying out loud," Marsh says. Kim continues to stare.

"Fine," Marsh continues. "We think the files are related

to the murders being committed. Which means someone on the squad might be involved. You know who that might be?"

"No."

"You know who is committing the murders?"

"No."

All of Kim's answers are direct, confident, and absolutely true. Marsh looks like he's gathering steam for another round, so I jump in. "Thanks, Detective Kim. That's all we needed."

Kim looks at everyone, seeing if anyone is going to contradict me. When no one does, he stands up. "If that is all. Captain. Detectives." He turns and leaves the room.

I just shake my head at the questioning looks the others give me. "Of everyone so far, he's the clearest read. He's definitely not involved."

"So that just leaves Meints," Marsh declares. "He's a shifty bastard. Let's get him in here."

Shifty? Marsh is just spoiling for a fight now. Detective Meints walks in a few minutes later. He's wary, probably sensed the mood from everyone else walking out of the room.

"Hello, Captain. What do you need?" he asks, addressing Radu and ignoring us.

Radu nods his head towards the empty seat. "These detectives have a few questions for you. Just answer them truthfully."

As Meints takes a seat, I study his face. His stubble is peppered with gray. The beard actually makes it harder for me to read his expressions. But behind it, I can see he is nervous, much more so than anyone else so far today.

"Hey, Meints. How they hanging?" Marsh asks. I think he senses Meints' nervousness as well.

"Fine."

Marsh just waits, silently observing the other detective. Meints glances back and forth between the two of us.

"What?" he asks.

"Hmm? Oh, nothing," Marsh says, looking down at his hands. "You ever take any files out of the storage room?"

Pause. Hesitation. "No," he lies. "Uh, I mean, not without authorization." Lie again.

"You were authorized to steal files?" Marsh presses.

"No! I didn't steal any files." Another lie. "I mean, what files are you looking for?"

"Missing ones, Meints. Missing files that might relate to the murders."

"Oh." Meints swallows nervously. "Those. I don't know anything about those files." Again, he's lying, but something isn't quite right about it.

"You aren't doing anything that would hinder our investigation, are you?"

"Absolutely not!"

"Wait a minute," I interrupt. Meints looks at me as Marsh scowls. "Detective, these files you didn't steal without authorization. What were they related to?"

Meints hesitates. Radu leans forward a few inches. The detective answers slowly, "I borrow cold case files. To study. On my own time."

Interesting. "But you return those files?"

He shrugs. "Eventually."

"Are they specific cold cases? Or any that happen to be lying around?"

Meints is clearly uncomfortable. "Look. I study cold cases, OK. I figure I can maybe solve a few."

I think I understand what I'm seeing here. He isn't lying so much as he feels guilty or ashamed. He's doing things he doesn't want us to know about, but not necessarily anything illegal. Marsh looks at me questioningly, and I shake my head. I don't have any more questions for him.

Radu's voice interrupts my thoughts. "Detectives, do you have any more questions for Detective Meints?"

We both shake our heads.

"You are dismissed, Detective," Radu says.

"Uh, OK. Good day." He gets up and walks out of the room. The door closes on its own after he passes the threshold.

Marsh chuckles. "Well, I think we got our guy."

Captain Radu continues to stare at me. "Detective Green, do you agree with your partner's assessment?"

I ponder this a bit. I think back to how everyone answered their questions. Clark was the most evasive, but Meints is certainly the guiltiest; I just don't think he's guilty of what we're looking for.

"I don't think it's Meints," I say.

"What?" Marsh is incredulous. "That guy's practically got thief written on his face."

"Exactly. 'Thief,' not 'murderer,'" I shoot back.

Marsh sneers at me for being a smart-ass, but Captain Radu's gaze doesn't leave me. "Continue, Detective."

"Meints feels guilty, but not of this. I think he just has a guilt complex. It just didn't ring right."

Marsh stands and fumbles through his pockets, coming up with a cigar and a lighter. "So," he lights it, takes a deep drag, and begins to pace angrily around the room. "You're saying that the guy you think feels guilty doesn't feel like the right kind of guilty? Am I understanding this right?" Marsh stops directly in front of my chair, his knees crashing into mine, and he towers over me with a menacing sneer. "OK, genius. *Who is* our guilty guy then?"

I glance over at Greystone. She was looking at me but averts her eyes quickly. I've damaged that relationship; I'll have to fix it soon.

"There's one that didn't sit right with me. I want to look into Clark."

Marsh leans in even closer to me, and the grin he is wearing is terrifying. "Now, we're talking!"

Chapter 35

Y OU SURE THIS IS THE place?" I ask pointlessly. Marsh snarls something that I take to be assent.

"Yes, Detective," Greystone says, patiently. "This is where your friend Miss Everin, resides."

"He has friends?" Marsh mutters, not expecting a reply. We're outside a three-story building in the heart of Meridian. The two lower floors are some kind of nightclub. A saxophone cuts through the murmur of the crowd packing the space inside and spilling out into the street. The upper level is mostly glass where I'm guessing there are a few apartments. Pretty swank digs, all in all. Given that most of the people here wear somber colors and live in dim lighting, a bank of windows lit up brightly from inside is a little out-of-place. There are some nearby buildings that are taller, that are more what I expect from abandoned tenements, but Jessica's building looks positively classy.

It's strange. From what I know of how the city works, these are buildings and portions of cities that have been forgotten in the real world. Overlooked, abandoned, concealed with glamours, and completely written out of history. But this building is almost modern; it would fit in downtown LA or New York just fine. How does something like this become completely forgotten about by everyone ever involved with it? Where this could have dropped off the map is beyond me.

The crowds around here are larger than I've ever seen in this town. There are a lot of people walking the streets and going in and out of buildings, clustered together in pairs and groups. Evidently, this is the hip part of this dead town. People shuffle past us, constantly bumping into me but wisely giving Marsh a wide berth.

I'm not looking forward to this. Jessica was upset the last time we spoke. I spurned her advances, and she was severely offended. Now that I know I see the world differently than everyone else, I understand what's going on. She must have a doozy of a glamour on her, which I can see through. To me, she looks like a corpse, and no matter how attractive it might be, a corpse is not going to turn me on. But she thought I was seeing a living, breathing woman. From her perspective, it has to be something about her personality I'm rejecting. Any way I look at it, I don't think I can explain it without flat out telling her the problem.

But do I trust her with my life? Does smoothing over her hurt feelings justify putting my life in her hands? Captain Radu, Marsh, and Greystone have all adamantly insisted I not tell anyone that I am this thing they call a Seer. But how else do I explain it?

We don't get a lot of friendly looks as we start moving through. Marsh leads the way, his foul mood written on his face. Most everyone who sees his scowl quickly scoots out of his path. Marsh walks past the front entrance to the club, stays on the sidewalk, and heads over to a door on the side of the building. He reaches up to pull on the handle, but it is locked. He snarls, annoyed. He knocks on the door. Hard. It sounds like gunshots as he hammers on the door a good dozen times.

An eye-plate covering a peephole opens on the door, revealing suspicious eyes glaring at us from inside.

"Residents only," the voice behind the eyes declares before firmly shutting the plate.

"Really?" Marsh mutters, not amused in the slightest. This time he knocks so loud I'm surprised he's not denting the door.

"I could just enter and explain to him if you like, Detective Marsh," Greystone offers, but he waves her away.

"Nah. I'm good."

The eye-plate opens again. "Residents only. Do not make me come out there."

Marsh flashes his badge. "You're welcome to try, pal. Necropolis PD. Let us in."

The eyes study the badge for a few moments; then they turn to regard the three of us. They stare a few more moments, and then the eye-plate slams shut again. We look at each other. Seconds tick by. The scowl on Marsh's face deepens. I take a step back, giving Marsh more space.

We hear a lock turning on the other side of the door, and the door swings open. I peer over Marsh's shoulder but don't see anyone on the inside. I'm confused until I hear the voice coming from down below me.

"Please enter, gentlemen. Madam."

The doorman is roughly four feet tall, and that's being generous. The inside of the door has a ladder built into it so he can reach the peephole. He is dressed in a sharp dark suit with a crisp white shirt and red tie. None of the colors are faded, and there are no holes or split seams; even his shoes are polished. I don't think I've seen anyone dressed this nicely since I've been here. His skin is even relatively close to a healthy living skin tone, a dark brown rather than green or grey. His hair is colored a dark black, which surprises me. I'm used to pale, colorless hair, brittle and dry. His is combed and styled. I can tell he is dead, but he's the liveliest person I've seen here.

"Thanks for being so quick, big guy," Marsh says, walking brusquely past him. Greystone floats past, nodding to him but not saying anything. The doorman is clearly put out by having to let us in.

"Thanks," I say nicely, trying to smooth things over. As I step around him, I see him do a double take.

"Sir?" he says, reaching out to stop me. He grabs me by the sleeve. I expect him to say more, but he's staring in fascination at my hand. He hasn't let go of me, I notice.

"Sir, you're alive?" he asks, his other hand now tentatively touching mine.

I hesitate.

Marsh is halfway up the first flight of stairs. Greystone is floating up behind him, and she turns around in alarm.

"Alive. And warm." The doorman looks up at me now, and his eyes focus sharply. Deviously.

Hungrily.

"Hey, now!" I protest, trying to pull my hand back as Greystone yells out, "Detective Marsh!"

And the little guy chomps down on the palm of my left hand. I scream in pain and try and shake him off, but both his hands are latched onto my wrist. I slam him into the wall, but he doesn't let go, and his teeth break my skin. As my blood hits his tongue, I can feel him start convulsing in pleasure.

That's when a freight train plows into him, tearing him off my arm and smashing him into the door. The door is knocked completely off its hinges as Marsh lands on him out in the street. His teeth were biting down on me when he was tackled, and he ripped a nice chunk out of my palm when he was torn away. I can't help it; I cry out in pain.

Out on the sidewalk, the crowd scatters as Marsh sits up

and pins the doorman beneath one knee and starts smashing fist after fist into the guy's upturned face. I see my red blood spraying out of his mouth along with splatters of his own blackish ichor. After about half-a-dozen hammer blows, the guy isn't even twitching. My partner adds a few more for good measure.

Marsh gets up and turns back to me. "Green, you OK?"

I'm sitting on the bottom step, clutching my hand. I nod shakily, holding my hand against my shirt, trying to stem to flow of blood.

Marsh turns back to the doorman, who is starting to stir. Marsh picks him up and kicks him. I'm talking he holds him at waist level and launches him like an NFL punter. The doorman sails across the street, slams into a bench on the other side of the road, and crumples to the ground. Some of the bones don't look like they are pointing the right way.

Marsh walks back to me. "C'mon. Let's get up to this lady's place and get you inside."

The crowd peers in the stairway curiously as we make our way up to the third floor. Marsh has to help me navigate the stairs. I'm not in danger of blacking out, but I'm weaving a little bit, and he keeps me from falling back down.

We turn the corner, out into the hallway on the third floor. There are four doors up here: two of them are open, their residents out in the landing to investigate the noise. Jessica is outside her door, looking at us in confusion.

"Back in your homes. Nothing to see," Marsh says, walking in front of me. One of the bystanders doesn't clear the way fast enough and Marsh elbows them to the side, nearly denting the wall. He points at Jessica.

"You! You're Jessica Everin?"

She nods. "Yes, what—"

"Good. We're coming in," he says, shooing her back inside as I stumble after.

"Hey!" she protests, futilely. I bump into her in the hallway as I try to squeeze past. Marsh slams the door behind us and locks it.

"You can't do . . ." she starts to lay into Marsh, but then she notices the blood on me, the blood that's still leaking out of my hand and onto her floor. "Jake, are you OK?"

I nod and move past her. I need to sit down. I walk into her front room and I'm halfway to sitting in an easy chair before I realize there are other people in the room with me. Two other men and a woman are sitting on the couch, and a third man in the chair matching my own. All of them are openly gawking at the blood oozing between my fingers. Bottles of wine and half-empty glasses are on the coffee table, and cigarette smoke hangs in a cloud over the room.

"Don't mind me," I say wearily, pinching my injured hand harder, holding it against my stomach. "But if any of you want a bite, remember I'm armed."

"Hold on, Jake," Jessica says firmly and runs into the back of the apartment. Marsh walks into the doorway to the room, blocking the exit. He eyes everyone suspiciously. Greystone floats over to me.

"Detective Green, how are you feeling?" she asks.

I take a moment to try and calm down. The last thing I want to do is snap at her after she's finally willing to speak to me again. I'm not hurt too badly. I'm bleeding, sure, and I can feel a piece missing from the bottom of my left palm. It hurts like hell. And no telling what kind of infection I'm going to be looking at. Was that a zombie? Will I turn into a zombie?

"You won't turn into a zombie," she reassures me mentally. I must have broadcast that last worry. Or she's starting to get to know me.

I attempt a shaky smile at her. "I'll be fine."

"If he can keep from being torn apart by little kids and

doormen for two seconds," Marsh grumbles.

Jessica returns with an armful of bandages, rubbing alcohol and scissors. I raise my eyebrows in surprise.

In response to my look, she explains, "We use them to appear more alive. Nothing like a bleeding injury to make it seem like we're one of the living." She sits on the arm of my chair, puts my hand on her lap, and starts to clean the blood off.

One of Jessica's guests stands up. "Miss Everin, it looks like you and your guests need some time. We'll be going if you don't mind."

Marsh answers for her. "Woah, now. Slow down. Have a seat." He folds his arms and firmly plants himself in front of the exit. "We won't take up too much of your time, pal."

The man holds up his hands in surrender and sits back down.

Marsh points at Jessica. "You're Miss Everin." He waits for her nod of assent before he continues. "Who are you guys?"

The four look at each other a bit before the man who attempted to leave answers, "My name is Harold Mayweather. This beautiful woman beside me is my wife, Genevieve."

Something about him distracts me from Jessica's work on my palm. Harold looks normal enough. His clothes are well made, though about a century out of fashion. He would look more at home in a Victorian parlor than hanging out above a nightclub. He's wearing a pinstriped suit with tails, a gray vest, high-collared shirt, and carrying a cane with a decorative gold knob. Everything is pressed, wrinkle free. I think he even has a pocket watch on the end of a fob. He must be one of Jessica's actor friends. His wispy black hair is slicked back in a comb-over that attempts to cover a hole in the side of his head. His wife, Genevieve, wears what I can only call a dressing gown. It's long, velvet, and she's wearing gloves that reach her biceps. Her hair is wrapped in some intricate braid around her head.

I'm not sure what it is that caught my attention. He looks strange, but no stranger than anyone else here. He glances at me, catches my eye, then quickly looks away. His wife notices his reaction and looks over at me curiously.

The man on the other side of Genevieve is wearing an honest-to-god top hat and monocle. He has a thick mustache that has been waxed into curls. I'm pretty sure it's fake. With his wrinkled skin and slightly heavy body, I can only think *Mr. Peanut* as he says, "I'm Ferdinand Calhoun."

Greystone chokes back a laugh. I must have broadcast that out through our contact. I may be a little bit loopier than I thought.

The last man is leaning back in his chair, a glass of wine in one hand and a cigar in the other. His face is chiseled tough, the lines hard. His skin looks solid and worn instead of the soft leathery skin I'm used to seeing. He glares at all of us. "Mr. Dean."

I don't know if they are supposed to be important people or not. I've never heard their names, and Marsh wouldn't be impressed if God himself appeared in front of us.

Marsh makes a note of all the names in a small notebook. He continues scribbling without looking up. "What do you guys do then?"

"I say, is this important somehow?" Mr. Peanut asks.

"Humor me," Marsh says, glancing up. Jessica is finishing up wrapping my hand in gauze. It is snug and has stopped the bleeding. I look up at her, smiling thanks, but she only returns a frown. Well, that hospitality was short lived.

"Well, we are actors, sir. Surely, you know this."

Marsh nods towards the chiseled-out-of-stone Mr. Dean. "What about you? You don't look like one for much acting."

Dean takes a swallow from his wine glass, keeping his

eyes locked on Marsh. Finally, he growls, "I am the financier."

"Detectives, why are you here?" Jessica asks in exasperation. She moves my hand off her lap and starts cleaning up her supplies. "I have no desire to spend any more time than necessary with Detective Green."

"Jessica," I say, but Marsh's laugh interrupts me.

"I know how you feel, lady. Wow, Green, you've got a real gift with the girls."

She is putting her supplies back in a box, shoving them in harder than is strictly necessary. I stand up and approach her. I can see that she knows I am coming closer to her, but she doesn't turn around.

"Jessica, we need your help," I explain as sincerely as I can.

She turns to face me, arms crossed in front of her chest. She stares at me resolutely. "I'm sorry to disappoint you, but I have no interest in helping you anymore."

I spread my arms, about to make some kind of a point, but I have no idea what it is. Instead, my arms fall to my sides, and I turn to Marsh. "You need these people to answer any more questions?"

He shakes his head. "I just needed to know who they were. They can go now."

All four of Jessica's guests start to stand up, but Jessica gestures for them to stay. "No, they don't need to leave. You'll be leaving now since there's nothing left to discuss."

They look uncertainly at each other, then start to sit back down.

Marsh snarls at them. "Don't get comfortable."

Jessica turns to Mr. Mayweather. "Harold, don't let these detectives intimidate you."

Mayweather raises his hands from his lap. "Please, we don't want to get in the center of this."

Again, something about him is strange. I take an unconscious step forward and look at him more closely. He glances at me and quickly averts his gaze again.

Mr. Calhoun fidgets uncomfortably. "Detectives, please. Is this really necessary? What possible help could a troupe of actors be to you?"

"My thoughts exactly," Marsh mutters.

I turn again imploringly to Jessica. "Please, Jessica, just hear me out."

She ignores me and turns back to her guests. "Harold, what were you saying before we were interrupted? Your wife has some sort of opportunity she wishes to discuss with us?"

Harold waves away the question, putting on an air of false modesty. "Please, Jessica. We don't need to talk about this now, we can come back . . . er . . . What are you doing?" he asks me as he finishes. As he's been talking, I've been slowly getting closer. I'm staring at his face. What is going on?

There is something different about his face. I can't explain it. His expressions are unlike anyone else's I've come across. Maybe it's because he's an actor, but there's a nagging in my gut that says this isn't the case.

"Don't mind me," I say, absently, still staring at his face. "Go on."

"Really, Detective," Genevieve complains indignantly. "This is quite rude."

Mayweather continues, slightly flustered. "I was just saying, I don't know why you're bothering to ask us anything."

I ignore his words, instead concentrating on his face, his eyes. What is it?

"Detective Green, what do you see?" Greystone asks me inside my head.

I can't explain it, Ms. Greystone. It's like . . . It's like . . . The words coming out of his mouth don't match the expression on his face as he's saying the words. The sentiment isn't lining up with the meaning. His face is just a—I dunno—a mask for whatever is inside.

It's like what's inside him doesn't match the outside. When I think of me, I think of both how I look, my body, and that inner part of me that makes up my personality. If I had to put a word to it, I'd say my spirit, I guess. I can separate them in my mind, but they are two halves of the whole that represent me in my mind's eye. With Mayweather, it's like those two pieces are different halves that are somehow out of sync. But how does that even make sense? How could you have something different on the inside? Like someone switched bodies? Or took possession.

Realization hits me. My eyes go wide. "Holy crap!" I whisper.

Harold Mayweather is a body playing host to a demon.

At the same moment that my eyes flare open in understanding, Harold's face undergoes an instant transformation. He realizes he's been made. His eyes blaze with surging energy, and his mouth splits into an insane grin. He leaps up from the couch and rams both of his fists into my chest. I don't even have time to react. It feels like I've just been hit by a truck. I go sailing over the top of the kitchen counter behind me and slam into the upper cupboards. My back destroys the cabinet I hit, shattering dishes and glasses around me as I bounce off the shelves and hit the ground.

Around the counter, I can still see what is happening, but I'm too dazed to move. Marsh drops his notebook and draws his gun in one smooth motion. Before he can get a bead on Mayweather, though, the demon reaches down, seizes a leg of the glass and mahogany coffee table, and swings the entire piece of furniture into Marsh's face. The force of the blow shatters the table around Marsh's head, sending his gun flying and knocking him into a tangle with the bar stools in front of the counter.

"What—?" Calhoun staggers up in confusion, his mouth hanging open in shock. Next to him, Harold's wife turns to

Calhoun, her mouth a grim line, her eyes glaring manically. She grabs his head in both her hands and twists.

Calhoun's neck snaps loudly over the noise of Marsh trying to extricate himself from the stools. She wrenches it so hard his face is blinking in confusion, looking from where it has been twisted completely backward on his body. He convulses into a heap on the couch.

Genevieve turns to her husband and shouts, "Run, Master!" She throws herself on top of Marsh, her fingers extended like claws. Jessica looks on in horror.

Master? That's an odd way to address your husband.

Unless she's speaking to the thing inside him.

Harold Mayweather looks at me, laughing to match his wild grin. I've never heard a laugh like that before. It cuts through the noise of the dishes that continue to fall down from the mess of cabinets and cupboards to crash around me. Mayweather steps towards me, his arms extended. I'm screaming at my body to move, to do something, but I can only manage spasmodic twitches.

"I haven't killed a living person for some time now," Mayweather says, smiling. Out of the corner of my eye, I see Marsh toss his attacker off him like she were a child and move for his gun.

Fingertips are scraping across my cheek when a clap of thunder erupts in the room. Marsh's gun goes off and nearly blows Mayweather in half at the midsection. He drops to the floor, howling not in pain, but in fury. The blast knocked him about an arm's length from me, and he starts to pull his body across the floor towards me, trailing viscera behind him. Marsh shoots again, removing one of the demon's arms at the shoulder.

Mayweather tips his head back and screams, a sound that trails ice down my spine. It is a sound filled with rage, malice, and pure hate. He is still entirely too close to me for my comfort. The shriek continues to grow in volume, and it takes me a second to realize I'm seeing a visible glow emanate from his eyes. Fiery energy begins to roar from his eye sockets, a blaze of magnesium that flares out blindingly.

The scream cuts out suddenly, and Mayweather's body rests in a heap on the ground, smoke curling up from empty eye sockets. The corpse is truly dead.

Marsh pulls himself up from the floor and takes stock of the room. Jessica hasn't moved, tears in her eyes, hands clutched in front of her face in horror. Mr. Dean hasn't moved. He's still sitting calmly in his chair, sipping from his glass. Mr. Peanut is twitching. Mrs. Mayweather is glaring at us in fury.

Alien eyes peer out from her face. The demon has found a new home.

"It will do you no good!" she gloats, grinning the grin that moments before I had seen on her husband's face. "You have one body, I have many!"

She turns and runs at the large picture window. Marsh stares at her in confusion, his gun still trained on her husband's body a few feet from me. She crashes through the pane, arms held wide, not bothering to protect her face, jumping out over the street three stories below. Her laugh hangs in the air behind her.

A punch bowl bounces off my head painfully, and somehow manages not to break, but just rolls around on the floor. Greystone streaks over to the gaping hole in the wall. "She hit the ground running!"

Marsh pulls himself off the floor and takes stock of the room. I can't take my eyes off Harold Mayweather's body so close to me. Smoke dances from his empty eyes. His blackened teeth grin back at us from an expressionless face. The body is now an empty husk, discarded on the floor.

Sounds from the crowds milling below carry up to us.

Glassware spills from the counter and crashes on the floor near me.

"I say," a weak voice squeaks from over by the couch, from Calhoun's face, pressed down into the cushions. "Can I get some help over here?"

The room starts spinning, and blackness flickers at the edge of my vision. I hear Mr. Dean chuckle, "Now, there's something you don't see every day."

Chapter 36

I FLICKER IN AND OUT OF consciousness. Dishes crash on the floor nearby, the noise startlingly loud but not enough to fully wake me up.

"Are you sure you wish to hear about Detectives Kim and Burchard right now, Detective Green?" Greystone asks in my head.

That's odd. Why would she want to speak about this now? But then it occurs to me we've already had this conversation. It happened several days ago while I was stuck in my apartment while Marsh was healing.

We already talked about this, Ms. Greystone, I reply. I sense confusion from her in my mind. Wait, it's the memory of her question I'm thinking about. Does that mean she's answering now?

It's too confusing to try and sort out right now. I drift, and in drifting I return to Greystone's earlier words.

Detectives Olsen, Kim, and Burchard

"Seven months ago," Greystone begins. "Detectives Kim and

Burchard were assigned to help Detective Olsen. It wasn't so much that the captain felt Olsen required aid in finding the missing persons, rather he had the impression Detective Olsen needed assistance in wanting to.

"Something had changed in Detective Olsen over the course of this investigation. He no longer spoke with me. In fact, he had all but severed the link that we had formed when I became his liaison. I could only locate him through extreme effort. More people had disappeared, and both detectives Kim and Burchard were certain this was connected to the other disappearances. But Detective Olsen made no efforts to investigate them on his own.

"Between them, these three detectives were the most analytical of the squad, meticulous in their investigations. Detective Kim accompanied Detective Olsen at all times. He didn't find anything that Detective Olsen was overlooking. On the surface, everything appeared to be normal.

"Detective Burchard spent much of his time reviewing the case files that Detective Olsen had already poured over. And Detective Kim spent the majority of his time watching Detective Olsen himself.

"You'll have to forgive me, I find it difficult to speak of this time. Suffice it to say, while Detective Kim kept an eye on Detective Olsen, Detective Burchard made some startling discoveries.

"He uncovered the fact that Detective Olsen wasn't attempting to locate the missing persons at all. He had diverted his investigation into other areas. He went through the motions of appearing to search for them while other detectives accompanied him, but on his own time, he was working on something completely different.

"It was Detective Burchard that finally discovered what he was up to. He found the stash of plans Detective Olsen had been using to build Ghost Cages. It makes me sick even speaking of these devices. These are abhorrent constructs of energy and are only used by practitioners of magicks. They are forbidden here in Meridian. But they are used to bind ghosts. You saw one example when Detective Finnegan cast one around me in that cellar. Perhaps the plans alone could have been explained away as research into a theory, a motive behind the disappearances. But he had the materials there as well. It was clear that not only was he building these devices, he was also using them.

"Detectives Kim and Burchard followed Detective Olsen after hours and observed firsthand what he was doing. Detective Olsen approached a person in said person's home and shot him multiple times, destroying the body. As the victim's spirit emerged, he activated the cage, capturing the ghost. I don't know if he had been behind the disappearances the entire time, but he was indeed responsible for several of them in the most recent weeks.

"I trailed Detectives Kim and Burchard as they entered the room where Detective Olsen was standing over the remains of the body. Not taking any chances, they had their weapons raised.

"'It's over, Olsen,' Detective Burchard said, his weapon unwavering and aimed at the other detective.

"'No, it's not,' he replied. He was sizing up the two guns aimed at him, and I feared he was going to try and shoot his way out. 'Don't you see? I'm trying to stop it.'

"Detective Kim held out restraints with one hand, his gun never wavering in the other. Detective Olsen stood where he was, becoming more agitated.

"'I can't believe you don't see it! You two are usually the most reliable. The patterns! Don't you see the patterns?'

"It didn't take long for them to uncover the truth from him, now that he had been apprehended. At some point during his investigations, Detective Olsen became convinced that he needed to stop the perpetrators who were making people disappear. But they couldn't be captured by normal means, and this was the method he had devised to root them out. He had been destroying the bodies of those he believed were responsible, capturing their ghosts as they fled the remains of their bodies, and throwing the spirits into the Pit.

"It was a gross violation of the vows he had taken as an officer of the law for the city. And truly, it still makes no sense to me. If he had discovered who was responsible, the squad would have captured them and thrown them into the Pit. But that wasn't enough for Detective Olsen. He believed there was a greater conspiracy going on, and only he could see it.

"'Wake up!' he screamed at us as the cuffs were put on and he was led back to the precinct where he used to serve. 'They are still out there! Stop them! You have to stop them! Wake up!'"

"Wake up!"

Huh? The words rattle painfully around my skull. Where am I?

"Detective Green, wake up!" Greystone is saying the words out loud, not just in my head. My eyes flutter open. She is hovering in the air above me.

I'm still laying on the floor in Jessica's apartment. Broken dishes surround me, and I can hear noise from outside through the hole in the wall where a window used to be.

"Are you OK, Detective?" Greystone asks me.

"Yeah, yeah, sure," I say with little conviction. Am I OK, really? Probably not. Alive, but far from OK. My hand throbs in agony. My ears are ringing. Blood flows from cuts on my face. I feel a stabbing sensation in my back where I hit the top of the upper counter.

But I'm still breathing. I smile and give Greystone a thumbs-up.

Chapter 37

A FEW MINUTES LATER, I'M SITTING down in the chair again. Jessica had to get her first aid supplies out for me once more. She's patching up various cuts and scrapes from dishware shattering on and around me. Her hands are shaking; she's trying to stay composed, but she's clearly rattled.

"OK. What the hell is going on here?" Marsh asks as he twists Calhoun's head back on straight with a sharp jerk. The grinding of bone sends a chill dancing down my spine. Calhoun's mustache is hanging askew, and he uses both hands to adjust the angle his head is perched atop his neck.

Mr. Dean has refilled his wineglass. He sips casually, staring out the broken window with a slight grin on his lips. He says nothing. Calhoun is busy clearing his throat, trying to see if it still functions correctly.

"I don't know," Jessica says, hoarsely. She's keeping her eyes focused on my injuries, not meeting anyone's eyes. "Harold has always been eccentric. But tonight, even before you arrived, he was acting strangely."

"How long have you known the Mayweathers?" I ask her.

She thinks it over for a second while she cleans a cut on

my wrist. "I've worked with them for several years. This . . . I can't wrap my head around what I just saw."

She finally looks up at me. "Jake, what happened to him? To her?"

I glance at Marsh. He shrugs. Of course, no help there. He's leaving it up to me to decide what to tell her. And I need her cooperation.

"Jessica, I don't think that was Harold Mayweather."

"What?"

"And whatever it was, whatever Mrs. Mayweather is now, she was conspiring with it."

Jessica opens her mouth to say something, but nothing comes out. She sighs in confusion.

"Look," I explain. "This is sensitive information. But that wasn't your friend Harold anymore. He's been taken over by something else."

She looks at me, still puzzled. I think in my mind how to explain it, but then Mr. Dean starts speaking.

"Don't be dim, Jessica. They're talking about demons." There is something inherently smug about this guy that I just don't like.

"What do you know about it?" Marsh asks him suspiciously.

Dean laughs, but there is little humor in it. "Detective. You don't become the richest man in this town by being stupid. It's a simple observation. You mention Mayweather isn't himself. You are clearly here to speak to Ms. Everin about helping you in this investigation into the murders that have been happening."

"Demons?" Calhoun squeaks in alarm. He clears his throat and tries again. "Demons are real? What do they want with us?"

"That's an excellent question," I say, grabbing Jessica's hand in mine. She lets me hold her hand while I speak.

"What do they want with you? Jessica, you mentioned the Mayweathers were eccentric. What do you mean?"

She shrugs, looking down. "He and his wife have always been interested in matters of the occult. Secret societies, rituals, even ways of contacting those that have passed on."

Marsh chuckles quietly. "Seriously? That's ridiculous."

I don't understand why that is any stranger than other things I've encountered here, but I let it pass.

"OK. Dabbling in the occult here is considered eccentric. And magic and glamours are OK. I'll have to ask you to clarify that later. But then you mentioned he'd been acting strangely?"

"Yes," she says, squeezing my hand a bit tighter. I try to keep from wincing. "He started missing rehearsals, and he couldn't remember his lines." She turns to face me, her face grim. "Harold *never* missed rehearsals, and he was always prepared. His wife was different too. Before, she couldn't be forced to touch him, and then recently she was constantly doting on him, hovering around him, answering questions for him, never leaving his side."

"This is all very fascinating," Calhoun interrupts. "But demons? Was that a demon?"

All eyes turn to me. I debate for all of about a second. *Screw it.*

"Yes. That was a demon."

"Harold Mayweather was the killer? He's been killing people in town?" Jessica asks incredulously.

"And now it's in his wife's body, it seems," I say.

Mr. Dean clears his throat. "A more interesting question, how did you know he was a demon?" He takes another swig of wine, staring at me intently.

I say nothing. Marsh snaps back at him. "The kid's sharp. We've been tracking this guy for some time now."

Dean sets his glass down, rests his elbows on the armrests

of the chair, and stares at me fixedly. "I don't doubt Detective Green's intuition, but I don't think that explains everything we just saw, does it?"

He does something. I can see on his face that he's concentrating on something; his body tenses up. We're all looking at him. What is he doing?

All of a sudden, everyone else in the room jumps back from Dean. Marsh reaches for his gun. Calhoun and Jessica both gasp and reel back in shock. Even Greystone jerks in surprise. What is going on?

Dean relaxes, leaning back in his chair. The others are now looking at him in confusion.

Greystone, what's going on? I ask her.

"*You didn't see that?*" She counters. "*Oh, of course, you wouldn't have seen . . . Oh no.*"

Dean is smiling smugly again. "Detective Green is a Seer."

"What?" Marsh says, feigning surprise while reholstering his gun. "Green? Please, this guy couldn't find his way out of an outhouse. Just because he couldn't care less that your face went all crazy."

"Detective Green is a Seer. He couldn't see the change to my glamour because he can see through them. I've encountered his kind before, just not in a few centuries. I thought we had killed you all off."

I see Jessica's eyes widen in alarm. If she were alive, I'd expect the color to have drained from her face. "A Seer? He can see through . . . through glamours?" Tears start welling up in the corners of her eyes. I wasn't even sure it was possible for them to cry. She stands up and pushes me away, looking at me with a nauseated expression on her face. "Excuse me, please."

Jessica stands up and runs from the room, closing the door to her bedroom behind her.

"I'll go speak to her," Greystone offers and floats from

the room, through the door to the bedroom.

Marsh scowls at Mr. Dean. "OK, Einstein. You've got it all figured out. Enlighten us. What's going on?"

Mr. Dean shrugs, his point made. "How should I know, detectives? That's your job."

"If we're done here, I have appointments," Dean says, standing.

Marsh steps forward and knocks a hand to his chest. "Hold on, pal. We need to get some things straight. First, no talk of demons outside this room. We don't need folks panicking any more than necessary."

"That won't be a problem," Dean says with a slight grin. "No one would take it seriously even if I were to risk speaking of it."

"Second," Marsh continues like he hadn't heard. "No speculating on your crazy theory that Green here is a Seer. We all know it's crazy, but someone might believe you or think there's something to it. You start telling people that, it could make things dangerous for him. And that would be dangerous for *you*. You endanger my partner, and you'll go from being the richest man in town to the richest man in The Pit."

Dean chuckles, unconcerned at the threat. "I'll make you a deal, detectives. I'll keep my wild stories to myself if I can borrow Detective Green for the occasional business deal." He turns toward me, a sly smile creeping across his face. "You will be well compensated for your time, I can assure you."

"Well..." I say, confused. I'm not unsure what the implications of this are, one way or the other.

"Besides," Dean meets Marsh's glare without backing down. "It wouldn't be in my interest for information like this to get out. In my business, the more you know than your opponent, the better position you're in, and if my rivals found out there was a Seer running around Meridian, they might want him for themselves. If you're worried about someone who can't keep a secret, I'd keep my eye on the actor over there."

"Who, me?" Calhoun squeaks.

Marsh grinds his teeth in frustration. He looks from Dean to Calhoun and then back. "I'll send a pair of officers to watch you. We don't know why Mayweather was here yet. We don't know if he was here for all of you or just one. He could have been here for you, Dean."

Dean nods. "It seems likely."

Calhoun huffs.

Dean raises a knuckle to his forehead in farewell. "Good day, Detectives. I'll wait below for some officers to take me home." He levels a smirk in my direction, and I want so badly to hit him in his smug face. Or let Marsh do it for me. "I'll be in touch when I require your services."

Marsh makes no further objections, so Mr. Dean steps around us and out the front door. Marsh and I look at Calhoun.

"What?" the actor protests. "I certainly won't tell anyone. Demons? Seers? Please, I'd be laughed off every stage in town."

The bedroom door opens, and Jessica returns, Greystone following behind her. Jessica's eyes are downcast, and she dabs at them with a handkerchief. She walks up to me, about an arm's length away, and stops. She darts a glance at me, her expression miserable. "All this time, you could see me. What I really look like. And you never said anything."

"I didn't know," I say as gently as I can. "I didn't know any different."

She nods. "I know. I know. I just couldn't understand why you weren't interested."

I raise my hand to stall her. "Jessica, please. It's not that I'm not interested. You're one of the few friends I have here.

You're not my friend because of how you look. You're my friend because of who you are. All of you are. Except for Marsh."

"My looks get me places," Marsh says without changing expression.

Jessica has regained her composure a bit. She meets my gaze now and smiles bashfully.

"Well," she says, wiping the last tear out of her eye. "You came over for my help. What do you need?"

"Yes!" I say. I'd kind of forgotten the reason for our visit. "We were hoping you could disguise me again. I need to follow someone, and none of us can get close."

"Sure, why not?" she agrees, a rueful smile on her lips. She has me sit at one of the bar stools and gets out her kit of supplies. She performs her magic again, putting makeup and whatever glamour on my face. Mercifully, she doesn't straddle me this time while doing it.

Marsh whistles. "Damn, Green. This is the best you've looked in all the time I've known you."

"Thanks, Marsh."

"Wow, you even sound different. Less whiny and pathetic. You should really think about having her make this permanent."

We review our hastily made plan again. I'll follow Clark around to see if he's up to anything. The rest will follow several blocks behind, Greystone keeping tabs on me through our link. We'll keep Calhoun and Jessica with us for now, for their own safety.

Greystone flies over to the precinct, gets Clark's location from the captain, and fills him in on what's been going on. Unfortunately, Clark hasn't been at the precinct for hours.

After some further digging, we learn that Clark is following up some leads over in an underground club not far from us. The four of us walk over there in silence. Jessica has no great interest in speaking to me right now, and Calhoun is so confused and bewildered he doesn't know what to say. Marsh just scowls. It's the longest twenty-minute walk I've had in a while.

We meet Greystone at the entrance. The place is in the basement of an old packing plant. The thumping of music in the ground vibrates my bones. Every once and a while, the door will open, and the music will blast out. I hear horns, an upright bass, drums, but my brain can't put any melody to it.

The streets leading here are dark, narrow and twisted. You can't see far in any direction. One lane just merges into another at all different angles. The buildings that loom over me blend from one to the other as well. It's not that they are built next to each other; it's like they have been slammed together and patched up. There is a light fog on the ground, and the air is damp and chill. The bright lights of Jessica's building are far behind us.

Greystone verifies Clark is inside, so I wait out on the street with Jessica and Calhoun while Marsh and Greystone go farther down the street, out of sight. I'm glad not to go into the club. It's small, sparsely populated, and I'm afraid I'll stand out too much. I don't know if this glamour can stand up to close scrutiny from a crowd. And if Clark is questioning people in there, he may work his way to me. Fortunately, I don't have to wait too long. He comes up the stairs after we've been there for about twenty minutes. He's leafing through a small notebook, barely looking up as he walks down the street away from me.

I let him get about a block away, and then I start after him, Jessica at my side. We leave Calhoun behind to meet up with Marsh. Greystone will follow a little behind me. I'm worried the whole group of us would attract too much attention, so we have to spread out like this. There are a few people out on the streets, but it's not empty enough that I worry about him spotting me. He's not walking particularly quickly, so I don't have a hard time keeping him close. But the way these streets twist and turn, I can't let him get too far ahead, or I will lose track of him.

Clark turns a corner up ahead, stepping around a broken carriage in the gutter. I make the turn and see him further up, still leafing through his notebook. He makes an abrupt left, skirting the outside of an empty store-front.

I hold onto Jessica's hand and pull her along with me. We get to the edge of the street and peek around the store to see him taking another turn ahead of us, his shoes echoing on the cobblestones. We reach the corner and make the same turn, but I don't see him any longer. I can't even hear his steps anymore. I let go of Jessica's hand and take a few steps away from her.

Nothing.

I jog down the road, closing the space to the next road. At the intersection, I take a look down each of the alleys. It's hard to see anything in the darkness, but I think I see him to my left, so I go that way. Jessica jogs after me, struggling to keep up.

But at the next intersection, I don't see him again. If it was even him I was following in the first place. He's gone.

Dammit. I lost him.

"I relayed that to Marsh. I will spare you his response," Greystone replies.

I'm clearly not good at this. I wait pointlessly at the corner with Jessica for a few minutes. I have no idea where we are, exactly. The streets here are barely wide enough to be considered alleys. There are gas lampposts at each corner, but they barely provide enough light to see something directly underneath them.

I see Marsh's shadow loom out of the fog, followed by Greystone's glow, and then Calhoun closely behind her.

We're going to have to start all over again and try and find Clark.

"Smooth, Green," Marsh growls. He looks back over his shoulder to make sure the others are all with him.

"Sorry about that—" I start to say more, but as Marsh turns back to me, his eyes widen in surprise.

"Hey, Green," a voice whispers in my ear from behind me.

A shotgun blast louder than God goes off next to me. A hole the size of my head erupts in Marsh's chest, and he drops so hard I almost feel the earth shake.

My ears ring so loud I can barely hear his screamed curses. There's movement to my right, and suddenly Clark is standing next to me, a shotgun smoking in his hands. It's double-barreled, but each barrel is about six inches wide. He's smiling his same mischievous grin.

"What's going on, you guys?" his grin widens as he cocks back the hammer of his gun.

Chapter 38

REACH FOR THE GUN AT my waist. I don't know why I'm trying, Clark has his shotgun pointed right at me. But it's all I can think to do. He looks even more amused; I can hear his chuckle over the ringing in my ears. Greystone screams my name as Clark raises his gun to point it right in my face. The barrels are dark and endlessly deep. But instead of pulling the trigger, he slams the end of the barrel straight into my nose.

My vision explodes into bright colors. Pain blinds me, and I drop to the ground. My right wrist suddenly erupts in agony, but my brain can't process why. Tears flood my eyes, and once I manage to open them, I can hardly make sense of what I'm seeing. My gun is in my right hand. But . . . Yes, I think I'm lying on the street. Clark is standing on my wrist, grinding it into the ground as he's casually reloading his weapon. My fingers spasm from the pain; the gun falls out of my hand and Clark kicks it away.

"Wow, Green. If you'd have lived long enough, you would have made a hell of a detective. Who would have thought it? I didn't expect to get caught for a couple more years at least." He slams the shotgun shut. The tears from my eyes mingle with the blood that is running freely from my nose. Shaking my head, I try to clear my vision and focus on my surroundings.

There is someone else here. To my side, I see Jessica being restrained by another officer. I don't know him; he doesn't look familiar to me at all. He's behind her, holding her arms together. She's struggling fiercely, trying to shake him off, but he's got her elbows pinned behind her back, and for all her efforts, he doesn't appear particularly stressed. Greystone is floating over Marsh, trying to determine how badly he is hurt. I can see some twitching in his limbs, but nothing co-ordinated. Clark is looking at Calhoun. The actor is swallowing nervously, looking back and forth between Clark and the other officer.

Clark is still laughing. "What?" he asks Calhoun. When the actor doesn't respond, he turns to the officer with him. "What do you think, Abayomi? Should I just let this guy go?"

I recognize the name from one of Greystone's stories. What is his name? Charles?

The officer shrugs. "Give him a chance, at least. Might be fun."

Clark nods and turns back to Calhoun. "Off you go then."

The actor stares at him in confusion, his mouth opening and closing without making any noise.

"You're not even going to try to run?"

Calhoun takes a tentative step back. Smiling, Clark waves him along. "Go on."

With a look at Officer Abayomi, Calhoun turns and starts to run. He's not particularly graceful. It looks like more of a waddle than a sprint. Clark lets him get about ten paces before firing. The shot shears the actor's right leg off at the knee. Calhoun spins and hits the ground, howling in as much surprise as pain.

"What do you want?" Calhoun wails as Clark approaches him. Clark isn't in a hurry, he takes his time. He gets right up next to him. Calhoun continues his pleas. "What do you want? I can give you money. I won't tell anyone about this. I promise!"

"Oh, I know you won't," Clark says, pulling the trigger. Calhoun's head evaporates in a spray of chunks and fluid. He cracks open the shotgun again, ejects the spent shells, and starts loading in two new ones. "Man, you'd think an actor would have more memorable last words."

"Detective Clark, you can't possibly think you'll get away with this!" Greystone yells, furious.

"What, are you going to haunt me? Oh, wait, I have something here for you," he says, reaching into his pocket. He pulls out a small, gray stone that fits into the palm of his hand.

"Detective Green, you've got to get out of here!"

What..? I'm useless; I can barely stand. Dizzy.

"NO!"

He tosses it at the ground underneath Greystone. It sparks when it hits the stone street, and light blasts out of it, enveloping Greystone. She screams in pain and fear as the light glows brighter. In another second, the light explodes. I shade my eyes and try and blink away the afterimage of Greystone.

As my vision clears, Greystone is gone.

"What—?" I say out loud this time.

"Banishment Stone. She'll be gone for a while. Jesus, don't they tell you anything, Green? You never really stood a chance here, did you? We should have killed you when we found you, but you were just so damned hilarious. If I'd have known sooner that you were a Seer, I would have. What a pain in the ass."

"Hey, Clark," Abayomi says, slapping cuffs on Jessica. "Marsh is starting to move around some more. We really don't want him coming after us. He heals pretty fast."

Clark considers Marsh, laughing as my partner struggles on the ground. "Yeah, I suppose you're right. We'll have to come back for him, though. It'll take both of us to lug him back to the precinct."

Clark walks over to Marsh, staying just out of arm's reach, and levels the shotgun at Marsh's head.

"Clark, no!" I yell uselessly. A twin explosion and Marsh's head just vaporizes above his jaw. The twitching stops.

"How long you think that will keep him down?" Abayomi asks.

Clark shrugs. "Dunno. A day at least. He's never come back from missing a head before, no matter how small a brain he carries around."

I realize about two steps into it that I'm on my feet and staggering over to Clark. He turns to me in surprise, still grinning. "You asshole!" I yell, but he just sidesteps the punch I throw at him. He sticks a foot out, and I go sprawling in the gore on the street. Will Marsh become a ghost now? Will Calhoun? I don't see them appearing yet.

"Why are you doing this?" I ask, trying to get my bearings enough to stand up.

"Because it's funny, Green," he says, looking at me intently, smiling. Studying me. "A demon possessing dead bodies. How crazy is that? The total and complete denial of everyone in this place—they think they beat death somehow because we're all still here. It's hilarious."

"Clark, you're killing people. And who knows what the demon wants," I say, pretty sure my words are coming out slurred.

"Jake!" Jessica struggles, but the officer holding her spins her around and drives his fist into the side of her face. She falls to the ground, and I see Abayomi start kicking her for all he's worth.

Smeared gore on the ground causes me to slip as I try to sit up, and I fall to my elbows. "C'mon, Green. Let's go. Time to wrap this up. You should have been dead a long time ago."

His grinning face is the last thing I see before the butt of his shotgun slams down into the back of my head, and everything goes black.

I've gone deaf and blind. Colors flicker in darkness. A rushing roar of noise drowns out all thought. My teeth are rattling, and there is a metallic taste in my mouth. I blink a few times and try to move, but everything hurts. Even turning my head makes me nauseous.

It takes me a few seconds after fluttering my eyelids, but things start to come into focus. My cheek is lying against a metal grate. A maelstrom of color is being sucked into a hole in the air, and I realize where I am.

We're at the Pit, inside the precinct.

"You're awake!" Clark says, pleased. He's leaning against the railing at the edge of the grate, next to the gate that opens out into the Pit. Even one step past the threshold is a one-way trip to oblivion. It is uncomfortably close; I'm lying about six feet from the opening.

"You can't even begin to guess how many bodies I've tossed into this place," Clark says casually. "I found a back way in here almost no one remembers, and it's been a bitch keeping the glamour up to hide it. Totally worth it though. It's easy to just drag people in here and toss them away. Like you, Green. No one will even know what happened to you."

I feel movement on the grate, and slowly turn my head to look behind me. Jessica is lying face down near me, and Calhoun is draped over the top of her. His leg and head are still missing. Officer Abayomi has closed the door up above and is walking back to us.

"What?" I mumble, my brain working furiously to make sense of what he is saying.

"The demon needed me to dispose of the bodies," Clark answers. He's looking over his shoulder at the energies being pulled into the Pit. "I mean, you saw how the captain's hackles raised when we were finding a couple of bodies. If he'd have seen dozens or hundreds piling up, he would have looked into it a lot sooner."

"Why are you helping it?" I ask.

"Hey, I'm not running around killing people! At least, not much. Do I look like a psycho to you?" He grins at me again. "I'm just cleaning up the mess. I mean, this demon, he burns through the bodies so fast. They don't last long; he's got to find more."

Clark stands up and stretches then walks, stepping over me, to Calhoun. He and the other officer each take an arm and drag him back over to the railing. I see a ghostly shape of a head forming where the actual skull should be. It looks like the ghost of Calhoun is frantically trying to pull free of his body.

"At least they're lasting a lot longer now. This demon, it's almost got the hang of it, I'm betting."

Calhoun's struggles are in vain. Clark and the officer count to three and then hurl Calhoun's body out over the edge. The force of the Pit grabs it and sucks it hungrily into the vortex of energy. And just like that, Calhoun is gone.

"They last a lot longer in human bodies, I'm told. But the living are harder to control. Now that the demon has figured out a way to kick the spirit out of the dead body it inhabits, it has a body with no one else fighting to take charge."

He chuckles. "A demon with an immortal body. Now, that's something I can't wait to see."

Clark turns to Abayomi. "What do you think, Chuck?

Girl next?"

"Aw," he says, disappointed. "I was hoping we could spend a little more time with her."

Clark shakes his head. "I wish you could too, man. You have a real talent in that area, but we've got to get back to Marsh before that big lug comes around."

"You think he can heal a missing head? I never seen that before. But I suppose you're right." They both walk over me to grab Jessica. She's starting to come around as they lift her arms like they did Calhoun's. I'm still groggy; every movement causes me more misery and nausea, but no way in hell I'm just going to sit here.

"Jake . . . ?" she slurs.

I start to sit up, but Chuck knees me in the face. My head slams back against the grate, rebounding off the metal. Both he and Clark laugh and step over me. I can barely twitch a finger right now, much less fight off two officers. I'm fighting to stay conscious, willing my body to move and trying to shut out the sudden shrill noise that's getting louder by the second. But then I notice Clark and Abayomi both pause and look around in confusion, like they can hear it too.

There is an unearthly shriek, and Greystone bursts up from beneath the metal grate, screaming for all she's worth. I can hear her over the noise coming from the Pit.

Clark merely rolls his eyes, but it startles Officer Abayomi enough that he jerks back and drops Jessica's body.

Clark laughs harder, snorting. "Chuck, you just got spooked by a ghost."

I'm not going to get a better chance. I lurch up while Chuck is yelling at Greystone. I teeter awkwardly on my feet. I flop forward and slam into Chuck's back. I take a couple groggy steps with him before shoving him out, off the edge. Not much force, but it was enough to make him take that one fatal step. I don't see him get dragged into the Pit; I just hear his scream fade away as I fall down onto my hands and knees and start vomiting.

"Holy shit, Green!" Clark says, and I can picture that smile still on his face. "Look at you, almost saving the day." He punches me hard in the ear. I didn't think I could hurt more, but he proves me wrong.

Clark turns to Greystone and looks at her critically. I glance up, helpless. I'm trying to see what he's seeing. It takes me a second, but then I realize what's happening.

Greystone is slowly being dragged towards the Pit. Her ghostly form can't resist the pull. By the look on her face, she knows it too, but she's still trying to protect me.

"Stay away from him!" Greystone snarls at Clark.

"What, seriously? Greystone, you can't stop me. What is this now, the second officer in a row that you've failed? You might have distracted that idiot Chuck, but you've thrown your life away. What did you hope to accomplish here?"

She grins fiercely, defiantly. "A distraction."

Then I feel it. A pounding, getting closer, rattling my teeth through the metal grate. I look over my shoulder. Clark does as well, and I see the smirk vanish from his face.

Marsh plows into Clark at top speed, crushing his massive shoulder into the other man's chest. It's not perfectly lined up though, and Clark grazes off him and slams back into the railing. I hear the bones in his back crack. The metal railing bends back toward the Pit, but it supports his weight.

Marsh looks like ten kinds of hell. Half his face is still missing. The right half of his skull above the jaw isn't there. Brain matter and bone are exposed. He is glaring out of a single left eye. I can actually see through a hole in his body, see the spine and ribs revealed under the flesh that is still dripping gore. He is holding some kind of organ—a lung?—inside with his left hand.

"Hey, Marsh," Clark wheezes, trying to stand. "You heal

fast."

Marsh's knee slams into Clark's face, throwing him back against the railing. Marsh pummels him with his right hand. Again. And again. I see teeth flying.

Marsh jerks him upright. Marsh's face is something out of nightmares, his single eye glaring with palpable fury. Clark is standing in front of the opening in the railing. He teeters, windmilling his arms. Clark looks at Marsh, then at me.

"Well then," he says, the smile returning.

Marsh doesn't say anything, I'm not sure he can. He just lets go of Clark's shirt and kicks him square in the chest. Clark's body flies out. If the force of the Pit weren't so strong, he might have actually sailed over it. I see the hungry pull of the vortex drag Clark down, laughing hysterically all the way. His laughter hangs in the air for several seconds after his body is gone.

"Greystone," Marsh chokes, falling to his knees. It looks like he's no longer conscious as he topples over on the platform. I stand up and move towards Greystone. She's about three paces from the edge, and slowly getting pulled closer every second.

I try to yell to her, but my head is still swimming, and my words come out in an unintelligible mess. Desperate, I shout to her in my mind.

Ms. Greystone! Come on, you need to move away.

She smiles sadly at me, stretching out her hand to brush my cheek. There is a tingling sensation, the barest whisper of a touch. *"I can't, Jacob Green. I'm too close."*

"No!" I slur as loudly as I can.

"It was worth it. I enjoyed our brief time together. I'll be OK."

No! Now you listen to me. I need you to stay with me.

She just continues to smile at me, resigned. It takes all my strength to stay standing, everything is spinning around me.

Don't give up! Please! I know you can escape this.

"*You'll learn your way here,*" she says, ignoring my pleas. She is two paces away now. "*You will find your place.*"

Just listen! You said that the difference between ghosts and those with bodies is just a matter of willpower.

"*Jacob, you don't—*"

Dammit, Greystone! Listen! I'm a Seer. You may know what it means, and I don't. Not yet. But I know you. I can see the truth of you. You can do this. Do you understand? I can see the strength in you. You can do this.

"*Do what?*" She asks sadly. She is another step closer now. I reach out to her. *Take my hand.*

She shakes her head. "*It doesn't work like that.*"

Take. My. Hand. Or I swear to God I'll step off this platform with you.

She hesitates. In my current state, she rightly fears I'll follow through on my claim. She reaches out and grabs at my hand. Her hand passes right through me.

Concentrate! Don't worry about your whole body. Just your hand. Your fingers. One finger. Touch my hand. Hold it. Just for a second.

She is now out past the platform. My toes are at the edge. I use my other hand to grab the railing.

Just your fingers, Greystone. Stay with me!

There. The whisper of a feeling. Her fingers are touching mine.

That's it, Greystone. More!

It's not much, but she's no longer being pulled into the Pit. She's there, at the end of my arm, holding onto my hand. I take a tentative step back, and I feel resistance on my fingers. There is just enough tangibility. I pull her with me. Her face is furrowed in concentration, her eyes closed. She doesn't realize we're moving in a new direction now.

Don't look, Greystone. Just concentrate on me. I take a few more steps back. *That's it.*

Gradually, walking and weaving backward, I walk back across the platform, careful to avoid Marsh's body. I keep going, up the steps towards the door. My legs are shaking. I'm covered in my own blood and vomit. I don't know how far away will be safe for her, but I'm not taking any chances, no matter how wildly the walls are twisting in my vertigo. I keep a hand on the wall to steady me, and I keep an even pace up the steps until I reach the door, and carefully, I open it up, stepping out into the precinct. The room's commotion comes to a grinding halt. If my ears weren't ringing so badly, I'd swear you could hear a pin drop. The officers out there stop what they're doing, stunned.

The ghost of Officer Jenkins is there, staring at me slack-jawed. "Greystone! Green?"

The room explodes into motion. Officers start rushing over to me, barraging me with questions, racing past me to go down the stairs for Marsh and Jessica. I hear multiple shouts for the captain.

I don't pay any attention to it. I feel Greystone's fingers on mine. She's here. I finally sigh in relief and stop, and my emotions must have traveled through our link. She opens her eyes and looks around, startled. The sensation of her fingers disappears as she returns to her normal state. But she did it. She did it long enough.

You're safe, Ms. Greystone. We did it. You did it.

My legs give out from under me. It's just too much for me to stand any more. I close my eyes, lean back against the wall, and shut out all the noise around me.

Chapter 39

MY EYELIDS DRAG SLOWLY ACROSS my eyeballs. My tongue is dry and swollen. Even the dim light from the cloud-covered sky outside the window causes me to flinch as I open my eyes. I try to move my left hand to shield my eyes, but it doesn't seem to budge.

"Jake?" I hear Jessica's voice nearby, but it sounds muffled. "Don't try to move."

I take a look around me now. I'm in a plain room on a narrow bed of some kind. Judging by the noise outside the door, I must be in the precinct building somewhere. Jessica is in a chair next to the bed. She's not wearing anything covering her face that would make her voice sound so strange, which makes me realize the problem is with my ears, not her voice.

"What's going on?" I ask. My voice is weak, tinny in my ears.

"Shh," she whispers, grabbing hold of my right hand. I look down at my body, and I won't lie. It's a mess. My left arm is in a cast and secured to the bed. It appears that I'm not wearing any clothes. The sheet is pulled up to my chest, but I can see bruises on my skin almost everywhere it isn't covered.

"Everything is OK," Jessica says. "You've been out for nearly two days."

"Two days?" I shout and immediately start coughing, which triggers a crazy headache. My vision swims a bit. I feel her hand on my chest, holding me down.

"Jake, you need to rest. You were severely injured. You have a concussion, and Jake . . ."

Her voice fades out, along with my vision, and I go floating in the black again.

The next time I wake up, it is darker outside. My stomach rumbles loudly. I glance around the room, seeing nothing but shadows, hearing nothing but a few voices from far off beyond the closed door. Which is why I about crap myself when a voice whispers from the corner of the room.

"*Bonsoir*, Detective Green," the voice slithers into my ear.

My heart is hammering crazily in my chest, but I let a breath out once I realize I recognize the speaker. "Hey, Captain Radu."

The far corner of the room is blanketed in darkness. I don't see the captain there at first, but he gradually coalesces into a recognizable form as he walks out of the shadows. I see his blazing red eyes first, followed by the veiny bald head, the crooked protruding teeth. The freaking scary expression on his face. He does the whole moving-across-the-room-without-actually-moving-his-feet thing and reaches the side of my bed.

The chair that Jessica was seated in before is against the wall, but it suddenly slides across the floor until it is behind Radu. He sits down, back straight, feet and knees together, hands clasped in his lap.

"How are you feeling, Detective?" the captain asks. He studies me, his eyes fixed not on mine, but on my throat.

I nod uneasily. "Like I got hit by a truck."

Radu makes a *tsk* sound in his throat. "Understandable."

"Wait," I say, struggling to sit up. "What about everyone else? How's Marsh? Greystone?"

The captain holds up his hand in a calming motion. "*Calme toi*. Relax, Detective. They are fine. Marsh recovers considerably faster than you do, though even he had a tough go of it. He's been up and around for the past day. Ms. Greystone is likewise doing well."

He looks at me curiously. "She tells me something quite remarkable. You saved her from the Pit. What she describes is unprecedented. She has stationed herself outside your room the entire time you have been recovering."

"What?" I say, confused. "Why doesn't she come in?"

"She has been guarding your door. She is worried that our adversary might have other operatives working inside the precinct. No one that she doesn't recognize has been able to get close to this room."

You've been guarding my room, I think to her.

"*Oh! Detective, you're awake. How are you feeling?*"

I'll tell you in a minute, I reply. *I'm talking to Captain Radu right now.*

"What's the status of the case?" I ask.

Radu smiles, pleased that is one of the first thoughts to my waking mind. "Now that we know it was Clark who was working against us, we should be able to make some progress in tracking down our suspect. This woman you encountered at Miss Everin's home, I understand you got a good look at her."

I shrug, then wince at the pain it causes. "Well, kind of. I figured out who she was. Who it was. I know what shell it's wearing right now. No telling if it's still inside Mrs. Mayweather."

Radu shakes his head. "We found Mrs. Mayweather's

corpse the day after your encounter. My question to you is, can you find it again? The being inside?"

I have to think about that. I think back to what I saw, how the demon didn't look natural in the body he was wearing. Hesitantly, I nod my head. "I think so."

Radu smiles widely. He has a lot of sharp, pointy teeth. "Excellent."

Radu nods and stands up. "Take the rest of the day to recuperate. Tomorrow, meet with Detective Marsh, and get caught up on the case."

The door to the room opens on its own and Radu glides over to it. He pauses at the threshold. "I'm glad you survived, Detective Green. You are an asset to our staff. I trust that will continue."

He steps out, and the door closes behind him.

Huh. I think the captain is starting to like me.

"That's not a good sign, Detective. That's when he's the most dangerous," Greystone warns.

What? Are you serious?

I hear snickering in my mind, and I relax. If Greystone is cracking jokes, I must be doing OK.

Thank you for watching my door.

"No one will get past me, Detective. Get some sleep."

I close my eyes again, and I have the most peaceful night's sleep I've had since arriving here.

A knock sounds at the door to my room the following evening. I've just finished putting on a button-up shirt, and I'm trying to wrangle a tie into place. Seriously, why do people use these things? The cast on my arm was gone when I woke up. I have a few bruises left, but the major damage seems to have been healed by what passes for a medical staff here. I'm still a little stiff, moving slowly. I'm not sure who did what to me to speed the healing along so quickly—more magic than medicine, I'd guess. Frankly, I'd rather just keep that one a mystery.

The door opens, and Detectives Burchard and Meints enter. They both look irritated, but Detective Burchard definitely more so. "C'mon, Green. Let's go," he says. He frowns at me as I struggle to finish up tying my tie. Actually, I don't know that I've ever seen an expression that wasn't a frown or scowl on his face. I've heard him laughing from the other room before, but by the time I enter, it vanishes without a trace.

Detective Meints is standing with his arms folded, diligently not looking at me. He looks like he ate something sour. When he finally speaks, he's still staring the other way. "Detective Green. There's something I've been meaning to ask you."

I wait, then sigh when nothing more is forthcoming. "What?"

He clears his throat. "It is true, then? You are one of these Seers? That's confirmed?"

Burchard snorts derisively.

I nod. "Yes," I reply, seeing no reason to deny it now. Burchard rolls his eyes.

"Incredible," Meints exclaims, and I swear his fingers start twitching like he wants to start taking notes. "I have many questions. To date, I've only ever been able to study your kind in books and tomes. In stories."

"I don't know that I'll be much help, Meints. I barely know anything about it."

"True, but you must have a guess as to the extent of your abilities. From my studies, I know we are unlikely to be able to lie to you. I was suspicious when you performed your stunt for us when we first met you. But it couldn't possibly be what it appeared, could it? We thought Seers were all but extinct."

I shrug as I grab my badge and gun and get ready to go.

"You probably know more about it than I do, Meints."

"Obviously. What I'm asking is," he holds up his hand, motioning me to wait. "When you and Marsh questioned us all before the captain . . . we thought it was the captain who was gauging whether we were lying or not. I was sweating bullets wondering what the captain was up to. But it was you, then. Wasn't it?"

"Yeah. It was me. And I'll be honest, you stood out from the rest. I don't think I've ever seen anyone mess up so spectacularly trying to answer questions truthfully."

I get a chuckle out of Burchard on that one even though the scowl never leaves his face.

"Hey!" Meints protests, looking at me now. "I get nervous around the captain."

"I get that. But why were you so guilty about everything? I mean, you were second-guessing every answer you gave."

Burchard speaks up, quiet but serious, "Yeah, he does that. His guilt hangs over him like a cloud. Past sins and all, right, Meints? He probably flubbed every answer he gave, questioned himself. Tripped every magical lie detector you've got. But despite all that, Green, you went after Clark."

There's no question there, so I don't respond. Burchard nods to me, then, to his partner. "Looks like you're scared of the wrong guy, Meints."

Meints waves that away. "Him? As opposed to the captain? Bah. I'm not scared of Green."

"I'm just saying maybe you should be," Burchard continues, and I swear, just for a microsecond, there was a grudging flicker of a smile on his face as he falls in beside me.

"And I don't feel guilty," he grouses. I don't know who he's trying to convince; we all just stare at him.

Burchard shakes his head and starts walking to the door, and I fall into step beside him. Meints catches up on the stairwell and flanks me on the other side. I guess they're guarding me wherever we're going because normally they would leave me in the dust.

"Actually, since we have a Seer here," Detective Burchard says with such forced casualness that it instantly gets my attention. "We could ask each other questions and find out the real truth, couldn't we?"

I shrug, uncomfortable with the direction his question is leading. "I dunno."

"I mean, hypothetically, I could ask you something like telling me what really happened with that girl on the Andersen case—"

Meints spins and jabs a finger at Burchard across me. "I told you already. Nothing happened! Give it a rest!"

Hmm. That's interesting. I open my mouth to respond and Meints rounds on me. "Nothing. Happened. End of story." He glares intently at me, and I concede and keep my mouth closed.

We take a long, quiet coach ride to Clark's apartment. Greystone is waiting for me outside the building on the street. The steel-gray clouds cover the sky again. What I wouldn't give for a few hours of sunshine, but I'm guessing it would be lethal to half the inhabitants of this place.

I pause on the sidewalk next to Greystone. Now, I'm scowling as I look at the building where Clark lived. Ms. Greystone is looking at me curiously. The other two detectives are trying to figure out what's going on.

"Is there a problem, Green?" Meints asks. He's looking irritated at me. Burchard is scanning the streets nearby. There are a few people out, looking our way out of curiosity. But most are steering clear from the handful of Meridian's finest guarding the entrance to a large stone building. The building is clean, sturdy, the windows intact, the paint fresh. The double-door entryway is open, inviting. I'm pretty sure I can see marble tile inside.

"What the hell, you guys?" I finally manage to articulate. They all look at me in confusion.

"Have you seen the dump I live in? And you guys live in places like this? Seriously?"

Meints smiles. Burchard shrugs his shoulders and stares at me impatiently. "This place is a dump compared to where Meints lives. He has his own butler and everything. Don't worry about it. Let's go in and talk to Marsh."

Grumbling, I follow them inside. Clark's place is up one flight of stairs. We pass a few more officers on the way up. I'm getting a few hostile glares from the other men. I can only assume they blame me for some reason, blame me for Clark's involvement or in his dismissal.

Perfect. Because it's totally my fault he teamed up with a demon to start a murder spree.

The door to the apartment is open. Marsh is standing in the main room, looking at some items on a bookshelf. He grins when he sees me walk in.

"Green! How ya feelin', buddy?"

Armstrong and Kim are here as well, searching other rooms. Yeah. Other rooms. This place is big enough to have rooms. The ceilings are high; the rooms clean. The floor tiles are gleaming where they show around thick, colorful rugs. Meints and Burchard wander back out into the hallway.

"I'm feeling a lot better, thanks." I glance around the room we're in. It's neat. Tidy. In fact, I notice that there is hardly a single item out of place. It barely looks lived in. There are ashtrays on the coffee table, but they are empty. I'm sure Clark wasn't a smoker; that's something I would have noticed. All the dishes are put away. There's nothing in the sink.

Marsh notices where I'm looking. "Don't overthink it. Clark had a maid. Unfortunately, she stopped by a few days back, already threw out a bunch of stuff. We've been searching for anything obvious, but we haven't uncovered anything yet."

He smiles and turns to Greystone. "But now that you're here, Greystone, you can do your thing."

"Her thing?" I ask. "She has a thing?"

"That she does."

"What's her thing, then?"

"I'm standing right here, Detective."

"What's this thing of yours then, Ms. Greystone?" I ask out loud.

"I'm very observant," she explains as she floats backward away from me, arching her eyebrows. She passes through the wall into the bedroom.

"Well, that cleared it up. Thanks," I mutter.

Marsh laughs, clapping me on the back. This time I was ready for it and braced myself against the impact, so I don't go sprawling. "She's one of the best crime scene whatcha-ma-callums . . . analysts. We spend a few hours looking at all the stuff sitting out, easy to find. Then she spends a few minutes."

"I thought we have scryers and sniffers. Those guys you used back at Finnegan's lab."

"Oh sure, we've got those guys too. And they'll get their chance. And they'll be more thorough than Greystone can be. But their work takes time. Greystone on the other hand."

He stops as Greystone floats out of the bedroom, across the main room and into the second bedroom, which I take to be a study of some kind. Marsh waits until she's out of sight.

"You really can't see how smoking hot she is?" he whispers to me.

"She's very attractive, Marsh. I just don't see the same thing you do."

"That's a shame."

"Marsh, what's she doing? How does she analyze things?"

He smiles and holds up his hand in a placating gesture. "Just wait."

It doesn't take long. Greystone floats back into the main room, over to us. I don't know exactly what Marsh is seeing when he looks at her. I still see the conservative business suit, the glasses, her hair gathered up in curls on her head. She sees me watching her float up to us. She smiles at me, and I'm relieved to see it is a smile that is completely devoid of self-consciousness. She knows that I can see her how she truly is, and while that irritated her for some reason before, it no longer bothers her. When I look at her, I see someone I trust, someone I like to be around. A friend.

I guess there's nothing like several near-death experiences to help you focus on what's important.

"There is a wall safe in the bedroom behind the photo of the cat," she says.

"A cat photo? Really?" I ask Marsh.

"There is a stash in the floor under false floorboards near the dresser," Greystone continues. "And in the study, there is a fake panel in the desk on the back."

"On it," Kim says, going to the study. Armstrong walks over to the bedroom.

"How?" I start to ask, then think about it. She can just float through objects. She can look behind walls and floors. Handy.

Marsh and I go over to the couch and sit down, and soon, Armstrong and Kim join us with what they've found.

Kim slams a stack of books and papers down on the coffee table that he found in the desk. Armstrong has two armloads of things. He sets a stash of gold and silver bricks down, wrapped in clear plastic.

"The metal was in the floor, but these were in the safe," he explains as he sets down a black ledger and a few photos.

We start to pour through our new clues. The gold we

don't need to worry about right now. I mean, it's a lot of gold; don't get me wrong. But gold doesn't do me a whole lot of good right now. I wouldn't even know what to do with it. What kind of value does it have here? Is it equivalent to what I'm used to, or maybe it's used in magic rituals in some way? The silver has definite value for magical items and is definitely contraband. I'm much more interested in the other things he had.

The books and papers are all about demons. It's bizarre. We're talking actual demonology books, like instructions on how to summon them, lists of demon names, descriptions of their natures, stories of past exploits. Books written in Latin and German with annotated notes in English. And these demon names, I now know that they represent real creatures, actual beings I could run into here, not characters from some story. It's good information but doesn't necessarily give us any clues to help us now. Armstrong is glancing through it.

"Hmm," he says, stopping on a page.

"What?" Marsh asks. Then, before Armstrong can respond, he says, "And don't say any of the freaking demons' names! The last thing we need is calling their attention to us."

"I wasn't going to say any names," Armstrong explains patiently.

"Well, Green here would probably say the names out loud. So you," he points at me. "Do not say any demon names out loud."

"Does that really work?" I ask.

Armstrong and Kim shrug. Marsh throws his hands up in the air, as if I've just proven his point. "What the hell do I know? Let's not take any chances, OK?"

"As I was saying," Armstrong harrumphs. "There is a name circled here. But, a few pages earlier, there were a couple other names circled."

"Demon names?" Marsh asks.

Armstrong nods. "I count around half a dozen or so. Maybe ones he was interested in or trying to summon?"

"But which one did he summon? If it was even him that summoned the thing?" I wonder.

The ledger proves to be more interesting. It has a list of names, not demon names, but the names of regular people. I recognize some of the names on this list as being names of our victims we've been investigating.

"I think it's his kill list," Kim says. "Or at least his list of bodies he's gotten rid of."

My jaw drops. "But there are hundreds of names on this list."

Kim's expression doesn't change; it's still the same flat stoic stare. He continues. "There are also some photos."

He lays the photos on the table. They're of me. Then some other people. Then some of Jessica with me. Marsh points to me in one of the photos with Jessica standing next to me. "Who's this?"

I think Marsh is making a joke.

"*Detective Green! That's you,*" Greystone says.

What? Of course, it's me. I can see that.

"*But it doesn't look like you. When Miss Everin put that glamour on you. You looked different, like another person entirely.*"

Oh. Interesting. I can't see the glamour in the photograph.

"I recognize that guy," Armstrong says. "He was following me around a while back. You think he's one of Clark's conspirators?"

"Um . . ." I say.

Kim ignores me. "We can ask Everin back at the station. We've got her there in protective custody. She can tell us who this is."

I raise my hand uncomfortably. Marsh raises an eyebrow. "Yes, Green?" he asks patiently.

"It's me. In the photo. That's me."

"Yes, Green. We can see he has some photos of you."

"No, I mean that one," pointing to the photo of Jessica and the glamoured version of me. "That's me next to Jessica. That's me with a glamour she put on me."

Armstrong glowers at me. He glances at Kim, who merely shrugs his shoulders again. A few uncomfortable moments of silence pass. Then Armstrong breaks into a smile. "Well, that explains it then! Damn, Green, we couldn't for the life of us figure out how you were watching us."

"That was back when I didn't know who was working against us," I explain, trying to defend myself.

Armstrong laughs away my words. "Don't worry about it. We just wanted to know how you were doing it." Kim nods.

"So, Clark had Jessica and I under surveillance," I say.

Marsh sifts through the photos. "And they knew what you looked like when you were glamoured. That must have been how he knew you were following him when he ambushed us."

"Who are these others?"

Greystone interrupts from over near the window. "One of the men in the photo. He's across the street."

I resist the urge to rush over and stare out the window. What I need to do is be more circumspect. I casually walk over to the window's edge and peek my eye out of the corner.

"Real subtle," Marsh snickers, but I ignore him. I spot the guy immediately, on the other side of the street, in a crowd of a half-dozen others. He is watching what is going on at Clark's building. It's hard to explain what is so different about him. Where I see everyone else walking around normally, he looks to me like he is trapped inside a costume, or like he's concentrating on manipulating each piece of his body separately instead of just moving. Regardless of the body he's wearing, I can easily see him now that I know what I'm looking for. I wasn't sure I would be able to spot the demon when I told Captain Radu I could, but I didn't want to admit that.

The demon is in the man's body. One of the people in the photos on the table is now an empty shell, standing across the street from us. I don't know who it is. He's speaking to one of the people next to him, laughing. I've never seen the second man either.

"Well, share with the class, Green," Marsh says. "Is the guy out there?"

"Yes," I answer, still looking out the window. "But the demon is wearing his skin."

Stunned silence hangs in the air behind me. I turn to see Armstrong and Kim looking at each other, gauging each other skeptically. Kim finally nods, Armstrong shrugs, and Marsh punches his fist into his open palm. "Let's get him," Marsh says.

I glance back out the window and see the demon staring right at me from the street.

"Crap."

Greystone's voice whispers fearfully. "He knows. He's looking at us now."

"Go! Go!" Marsh bellows at the other detectives. "Green, who are we looking for?" he yells over his shoulder.

"White hair, green suit, black tie!" I yell back. I follow more slowly. I might be healed from most of the damage done to me, but I'm far from being in top form. Burchard and Meints fall into step beside me, their guns drawn. I look at them strangely.

"Captain's orders," Burchard explains as we hurry down the stairs. "He's tired of you getting used for punching bags and target practice."

"Marsh threatened to cut our balls off if we let you get hurt again," Meints adds. "Burchard might know what that feels like; he's married, but I don't want to live for eternity without them."

By the time I get to the street, he's long gone. Marsh is organizing officers to fan out looking for him.

It only takes about ten minutes to locate him. I catch up to Marsh, who is swearing up a storm. We find the body face down in a gutter about four blocks away. Green suit, crumpled shirt, eyes empty—the corpse vacant, a hollow shell. The demon has jumped bodies. We lost it again.

Chapter 40

We're back to the drawing board. Again. We've hit another dead end, short of me scouring this whole city trying to look at every single soul that lives here. Meridian is made up of forgotten things. Every building, alleyway, room, and hole is something that has been thoroughly scrubbed from the collective memory of the world.

Even here, no one truly knows every corner. There are doorways hidden from view, buildings tucked into folds in reality, probably whole neighborhoods that can only be found by walking the correct steps in hidden paths. There are no maps of Meridian; at best, there are only guides who know those paths that they themselves have walked.

I have been looking at our case files all morning. We know that the demon has been jumping bodies. We know Clark was working with it to conceal evidence of its actions. We suspect a group of zealots has been helping them as well. Was Clark involved with them? No way to tell in the evidence we've found so far. If Clark was working with others, he didn't keep a record of it. We know he worked with officer Chuck, but even Chuck's partner didn't know anything about it. I questioned him personally, and he was telling the truth; he just thought it was official business any time Clark came by to talk in secretive conversations.

The members of the squad have been treating me marginally better, though. Now that we all know Clark was actively working against us, my "suspicions" proven justified, they are more accepting of me. They protect me because the captain has ordered them to. But I'd like to think they don't actually mean me harm anymore.

"Yo, Green!" Burchard hollers from the doorway to the office. "Someone here to see you."

He ducks out before I can ask who. I'm a little puzzled. Jessica is in one of the rooms upstairs, under protection until this all gets sorted out. She has free reign to come down and check in on us. On me. Outside of her, I don't know anyone who would want to come to see me.

I walk out of our office into the squad room. The place is as busy as I've ever seen it. A little loud, to be honest, which is unusual here. Dead detectives and officers shuffling from desk to desk. Typewriters clacking away. Raised voices calling to each other. I look around for Burchard and see him waving to get my attention up by the front desk. I don't see anyone with him.

"What's going on, Burchard?"

Detective Burchard points down, in front of the long wood counter. "This guy is asking for you by name. You figure it out."

I have to lean over the desk to see who it is. There, his head barely peeking over the top, is the doorman of Jessica's building. The one who took a bite out of my hand a few days ago. I lurch back quickly, out of reach.

"What the hell?" I say, slightly panicked, reaching for my gun—which I realize I left on my desk, so I end up slapping at my waist like an idiot.

The doorman is dressed in a black suit, red velvet vest, and is holding a dark fedora in his hands over his chest. He is clutching it tightly.

"Detective Green. My name is Archibald Smith." He bows his head slightly. I calm down a little bit when I realize he's not trying to snack on me again. "I've come to turn myself in."

"Eh, what's that?" I ask, confused.

He bows his head again, struggling to meet my eyes. But he does look at me, and I can tell he is mortified.

"I've come to turn myself in for assaulting an officer. My behavior was deplorable, and I offer no excuse for my actions."

I take a good look at him. He doesn't appear to be poised to attack me again. It also doesn't escape my attention that he looks fully healed from the beating he took from Marsh. He might be little, but clearly, there's more to him than meets the eye. "Well, you did take a good chunk out of my hand."

He closes his eyes and looks absolutely guilt-ridden. "I apologize most profusely. I was not prepared to meet a living person. I like to pride myself on my iron will and self-control, which obviously are not words you would apply to my actions. I hope you understand that my actions are wholly my own and should not reflect poorly on the integrity of the building where I work."

I shift uncomfortably from one foot to the other. I can tell without a doubt that he is very sincere in his apology. I'd be able to tell if he were not.

"Look, come back with me to my office where we can talk in a bit more privacy."

He nods, relieved, and steps up to my side, keeping his eyes focused in front of him. We weave our way through the press of officers and go back to the office. Burchard follows a few steps behind us. I glance at Smith out of the corner of my eye, just to make sure he doesn't try to sucker punch me or take another bite, but he keeps his attention focused forward and never even peeks over at me. Interesting. The other detectives look up as we enter.

"The hell are you doing back here?" Marsh demands loudly of my guest, standing up quickly.

Archibald flinches and attempts a bow. "Detective Marsh, I believe? As I informed your partner, Detective Green, I am here to turn myself in for my actions the other night. You have my deepest and most profound apology, and I intend to pay to the fullest extent for my crime."

Marsh looks frozen in place. He eventually relaxes, slightly confused. "Uh, OK then."

The other four detectives are looking on curiously. Archibald again explains his surprise at seeing a living person in front of him and his little lapse in willpower that caused him to try and eat me.

"I assure you, Detectives, that it will not happen again."

"Well, I might still be a little skittish around you, Mr. Smith. But I'm willing to let this go."

"Not going to happen," Marsh says firmly. He points at the doorman. "You're just lucky he's a little fella. We can't let folks around here think there's no harm in taking a little nibble off you whenever it tickles their fancy."

"Your partner is quite right, Detective Green. I must insist that I be punished for my crime. And I sincerely hope that there were not too many people in the crowd who witnessed my shameful actions. At least none of the building's residents were witness to it."

I nod, embarrassed. "OK."

"When my sentence is complete, I will go search out the residents of the building and their guests that day and extend my apologies. I will have to beg Miss Everin to allow me to contact all six of her guests from that day. I need to assure them they will not see me lapse in that manner again."

I look at Marsh, my brain trying to process what I just heard. Burchard beats me to saying it.

"Wait a minute. Back up. Six guests?"

"Well, yes. I keep track of everyone I let into the building, the times they leave and return. It's part of the expectations of my job."

Marsh walks up and towers over Mr. Smith. "Burchard's right. We only counted four people, not six: Calhoun, Dean, and the Mayweathers."

"Well, yes," Archibald says, leaning back from Marsh nervously. "They were the four guests who were with Miss Everin at the time of my incident. But surely their two friends who arrived with them would have heard about it by now. Even though they left shortly beforehand."

Archibald looks around and realizes we're all staring at him.

"Which. Two. Friends?" Marsh asks firmly.

"Mr. Daniel Cortez and Mr. Francis Goldman. They had been arriving with the Mayweathers regularly over the past few months."

"They wouldn't happen to be any of these guys would they?" I ask, pointing at the photos we recovered from Clark's apartment. We've tacked them up on a corkboard in our office.

Smith glances and the photos and nods. He points at two of them. "Yes. This one is Mr. Cortez, and this one is Mr. Goldman."

And just like that, we have a new lead. Sometimes you earn them. Sometimes they just fall in your lap. Sometimes they come when someone snacks on you.

I take Mr. Smith up to one of the officers outside to book him on his charge for assaulting an officer, but I make a point to put in a good word for him and stress his help in an ongoing investigation. Smith bows to me and, his chin up, resolves himself to accept his judgment.

I get back to our office to hear Meints arguing with Marsh.

"What good is it going to do to just charge out and grab these guys?" Meints asks.

"What, we just ignore them? Is that what we do now?"

"No! Of course not. Marsh, hold it a second. Think this through. We can't just toss them in a cell. If one of them is this demon, then that will be useless. We can't just kill their bodies."

Everyone mulls this over. Meints is right; we can't just grab them and hope our problems are over. We need to have more of a plan.

"The Pit," Marsh says, simply.

"Maybe. Who knows? I'm just saying we need a plan!"

I clear my throat. I already have a plan; it's just not one I can share. "I need to go to Warner's."

The group looks at me curiously. "Uh, now's not a good time to hit the bottle, buddy," Marsh advises.

"There's someone I need to talk to. I need to do it now. Can I go by myself, or does someone need to come with me?"

Both Burchard and Meints shake their heads. "No way, we had our turn," Burchard says. "Someone else gets to take this bullet."

"Fine," Armstrong decides, standing up. Kim stands up with him. "We'll take you. Let's just make it quick."

Kim shoots Marsh a serious look. "Wait for us to return."

With my protection on either side, we make our way over to Warner's. I have a few questions I need to run past Frank.

The crowd at Warner's is quiet tonight, withdrawn. We allowed it to open up again, but the vibe hasn't been the same since. The mood's been grim ever since Annabelle's body was found. It's a little depressing, but right now, I have bigger problems. I still haven't figured out a good way to ditch the two detectives so that I can speak to Frank in confidence.

"Yeah, I suppose so," Armstrong says. He and Kim are looking at something next to them. But I can't for the life of me figure out what it is. We're barely inside the door, looking at the crowd. "Let's do that."

The two of them start walking towards a booth near the back. I hear Kim chuckle at something. "You said it, Green." That's weird. Kim never laughs at anything.

"What the hell?" I mutter. They are supposed to be guarding me, but they just ditched me at the door.

A voice whispers in my ear, "They think they are still with you."

I jump and barely stifle a scream from erupting from my throat. Frank is standing right beside me. I glance over to the room at the back, and Frank is staring at me from the doorway. The Frank beside me gestures for me to follow him to the back. "This way, Jacob."

I look over at Armstrong and Kim, carrying on a conversation with a third person that isn't there. "This isn't hurting them, is it?"

"What? Of course not, Jacob, of course not. They think they are conversing with you, although a slightly funnier and more pleasant version of you, to be sure."

"Well, that's just great," I grumble. Frank's glamours are evidently superior to the original.

Frank's room is unchanged—same books, the same piles of paper. The double of Frank in the room walks over and merges with the Frank standing next to me. Whole again, he gestures for me to close the door behind me.

"To what do I owe the pleasure of your visit?" Frank asks grandiosely.

"We found the demon," I explain.

"Excellent!" Frank smiles. He really is very good at his semblance of mortality.

"But we don't know how to stop him."

"Well, you cannot kill a demon," Frank explains in a patronizing tone. "We are eternal. We may not be The First or The Last, but we are very close. You can kill the body we inhabit, but we will merely try to inhabit another."

"Even pigs? Like that Bible story? How did it go, exactly?" I ask. "Didn't Jesus cast out some devils, and let them go into the bodies of pigs, and the pigs went and killed themselves or something?"

Frank grimaces. "Oh, yes, that. Your summary is decidedly ignorant of the facts. But you are essentially correct. Some of my siblings will stoop to taking possession of swine or other animals. But even if you manage to destroy that body, the demon will merely wait until it finds a new host body. Or it will simply pursue you without a tangible body and hound you every second of every day for the rest of your life."

I sit down on a chair, keeping an eye on Frank. "I was hoping that wasn't the case."

His voice sounds in my ear again. "What exactly do you want from me?" I spin in my chair and see him standing behind me. My head snaps back to where he was standing a moment before; he is no longer there. I put a smile on my face as I turn back to him. OK, lesson learned. I can't keep my eye on him.

"We can't kill him. There has to be some way to . . . I don't know, banish him?"

Frank nods, sagely. "Sure. Of course. That is an excellent idea, Jacob. You could banish him. And then if a mortal knows his name he can be summoned right back. Have you found all his followers, the cult of the undead that he is working with?"

"No," I reply sourly. Clark and Abayomi were working

for the demon, but Frank is right. They may not have been the only ones working with it.

Frank's smile widens. "Then I fear banishment may not be the correct path here. If you can ensure that you have eliminated every mortal who knows his name, every book that contains it, and all knowledge of his name has been erased from humanity's memory, then perhaps banishment would work."

I think about this, try to discern if he's telling me the truth. I have to be careful about taking anything he says at face value. But I think he's right here. We don't know everyone that is working with the demon.

"So we can't kill him. Banishing him would just be a stutter and less than effective. Can we keep him out somehow?"

Frank shakes his head sadly. "Not if someone simply invites him back in."

I stew some more, thinking other angles. "Do you have any ideas?"

He shrugs, evasive. "Perhaps. Perhaps not."

I wait. Frank just smiles at me. I sigh in exasperation. He clearly wants me to think this one out myself. "We can't kill him. We can't banish him. We can't keep him out, because someone can just invite him back. What if we can, I dunno . . . We need to make it so that he can't come back. So even if he's invited, he *can't* come."

Frank nods, urging me on. "Perhaps. Continue with that thought."

"If he can't come in . . . Not because he can't get in, but because, he can't get out . . . of somewhere?"

Frank claps his hands in delight. "I think you might be on to something, Jacob."

"The Pit?" I guess.

A sad frown splits Frank's face. "Sadly, no. The Pit will not work on those like my siblings and me. It is purely a force that has power over mortality—mortality as we see it, which includes both the living and the once living."

I slap my knees in frustration. "Well if we can't trap the demon in the Pit, I don't know what we can do."

Frank smiles wickedly. "There are other methods one can use to catch a demon."

"Don't hold back! What else is there?"

"Well," Frank says, guardedly. "There are ways to build a demon trap. Such a trap can hold one of us for all eternity, or until we are let out."

"Let out?" I ask.

He nods. "You would have to take care that one of the demon's followers do not learn of its location and release the demon once again."

I breathe out a breath I didn't know I was holding. "So, we're back to where we were. If we don't know all of the demon's conspirators, one of them could simply release the demon after we've trapped it."

Frank shrugs casually, in too-poised a manner to be truly casual. "Unless the trap was located somewhere that a mortal could never reach."

I think about this for a moment, realizing what Frank is getting at. "Build a demon trap to hold the demon for all eternity, and then throw the trap in the Pit, where no mortal can ever get at it."

Frank smiles at me like a proud parent. "Yes, exactly. I do believe that would work. Well-reasoned, Jacob."

We are arriving at the conclusion he guided me to, but it seems pretty sound to me. I look at this solution from as many different angles as I can manage, and I can't see any loopholes to this plan.

"OK. Let's do that, then," I say. Frank winces like I've wounded him, and I realize what we've been building to. The hook is set. Now, he's going to try and jerk me on the line.

"Jacob Green, take a step back and think about what you are asking of me."

I glare at him suspiciously. "I'm asking you to help me stop an immortal killer."

He shakes his head sadly. "No, Jacob Green. That is not what you are asking me. You are asking me to give you instructions on how to create the one thing that could forever imprison me throughout the ages. I think that is asking a little much. Do you not agree?"

"What would entice you to tell me?" I ask, guardedly.

"Look at you, so suspicious of me. Surely, you can agree that this information would be worth nearly any price."

"What kind of price are we talking about?"

"If I give you the means to build a cage to keep a demon forever bound, then you need to build me a key to escape it."

"Key?"

Frank nods, seriously now. "Correct. You first build me a key to escape such a prison, and I will tell you how to build the cage."

It can't be that simple, I think. "How do you build one of these keys?"

Frank smiles, and that's when I know I'm right; it's not nearly so simple.

Chapter 41

Y OU WANT TO RUN THAT by me again?"

Frank smiles apologetically, but not sincerely. "Come now, Jacob Green. It is not so much to be concerned about."

"You need blood. A Seer's blood. My blood. To make this key. And it does what again?"

Frank spreads his arms wide in a gesture that attempts to put me at ease somehow. "As I told you, it will provide me with the means to escape this prison intended to hold me."

I think as quickly as I can, trying to poke holes in this plan. "Can't we just get a key that's already made? There have to be some around somewhere, right? I mean, you told me you have a recipe for one."

"Ah, Jacob. There are records of some that have been made in past millennia, but their locations are lost to me. And they are incredibly rare. It is not often a Seer willingly agrees to build a key to release those of my kind."

"There's probably a good reason for that."

"I will admit that there is ample reason for the majority of my kind. But surely, I am not as evil as all the rest. I am helping you after all."

A frown is fixed to my face, I have the nagging suspicion this was his goal all along. He meets a Seer and, hey, look at that—he just happens to know about an item I desperately need that coincidentally requires some of my blood. I don't see an alternative, but I'm suddenly very aware that I don't know enough about how things work here to recognize the pitfalls I'm about to walk into.

"How do I make this key of yours?"

He does a complicated flourish with his hands and points to a small tome covered in leather, sitting under a pile of papers.

"Open it to the bookmarked page," he encourages.

The book is old, the pages brittle. The leather is cracked, and many of the pages are water stained. Flipping the pages carefully, I reach the bookmark and look at the handwritten script. It takes a few minutes to decipher the words on the page.

"Mercury. Silver. Sulfur. Blood. Carved symbols. I don't recognize some of this other stuff. Frank, I'm not going to be able to do this. Not on my own."

Frank considers this. He mulls over his options. But I'm guessing getting this key is going to outweigh his desire for complete secrecy.

And I'm right.

"Very well. I am risking a great deal with this, Jacob Green. But you may tell one person to help you."

"It's going to have to be two."

"One! The risk is too great."

"Frank, it has to be two. If I involve anyone else, I'm going to have to explain to Ms. Greystone. And she can't be the only one I tell because she can't physically help me. It has to be her and one other."

He paces a bit, but I'm sure that is to give me the impression he's weighing the decision.

"Agreed," he says. He leans in close to me, our noses almost touching, and I can feel heat rolling off him. "You may tell this Greystone and one other. But be warned, they must not tell anyone else. If I find they have told, hinted, or even caused suspicion about me to anyone else, I will destroy the three of you and anyone else involved."

I swallow, my mouth is suddenly dry. I know Frank doesn't have a tangible form; he shouldn't be able to physically harm me. But he's not lying. I have no doubt that he is fully capable of carrying out his threat. If I agree to this, I am automatically committing my friends.

This is a bad idea. In all of the human history that I've come across in my short life, there's not a single story where someone had something good come from making a deal with a demon. I assumed those tales were metaphorical, of course, but the fact remains the same. The long-term consequences almost always overshadow the short-term gain. But what choice to do I have? There is a tangible solution in front of me, a real way to end this spree of killings and ensure that the demon can't do it again.

I nod.

Frank smiles a grin that sends shivers down my spine. "Excellent. We have a deal."

Ms. Greystone?

"Yes, Detective?"

Will you and Marsh meet me over here at Warner's? I need to discuss something with you.

"Have you gone completely insane?" Marsh bellows at me, spraying me with spittle.

I'm here with both him and Greystone in Frank's room. Frank is currently nowhere to be seen. Marsh and Greystone arrived about ten minutes ago, allowing Armstrong and Kim to return to the precinct. According to them I was warbling out some awful singing with Frank accompanying me on the piano the whole time they were there at Warner's. I ground my teeth in irritation, waved goodbye to them, and resolved to speak to Frank about the glamours he uses in the future.

And then I explained to Marsh and Ms. Greystone what was going on. The words spilled out of my mouth eagerly now that I could share them. I told all I knew about Frank, about the secret I was sharing with them, and about how it put their lives in jeopardy. I explained the trap that Frank could show us how to make, and then the price he was asking for it.

Which is what prompted Marsh's current reaction.

"I know you're as bright as a bag of hammers, Green," he leans in to hiss the words at me, "but this is beyond the pale stupid. Not only are you listening to a demon—a DE-MON!—not only are you listening to one, you're actually believing what the hell he's saying, *and* thinking it's a good idea. A dog licking its own butt shows more sense!"

Greystone clears her throat. "I'm afraid I have to agree with Detective Marsh, though not as colorfully. Surely, you don't believe this demon can be trusted?"

I shake my head. "No, of course I don't trust him. But it makes sense, him asking for a way out of the trap he's going to show us. It makes me think the thing will actually work."

"Balls!" Marsh snorts in derision. "Oh, and *then* you agree to give him some of your blood!"

I scratch my head and ask, "The blood. What does that mean? It sounds like a big deal, but I don't really know."

"Of course, it's a big deal!" Marsh yells again.

"How?" I ask sincerely.

Marsh gesticulates with his arms, his face scrunched up in confusion. "How the hell should I know, dumbass? I don't do magic. You want to know, ask the captain!"

"But we can't do that. I can't tell anyone else about this."

"Yeah, that's real convenient," Marsh huffs, turning his back on me.

"There is great power in blood, Jacob," Greystone explains. "Even normal human blood. A transfusion can provide life to another. A virus can be carried in it and cause death. Blood can fight infection, repair damage to flesh. The brain can will it to move about one's own body. It carries oxygen and sustains life. It can be removed from a body, and it replenishes.

"Then there is the blood of a Seer. Who knows what additional properties your blood contains? There must be some, or this demon wouldn't be seeking it specifically."

I mull this over. I really would like to ask Captain Radu. But there is no way I could ask him that wouldn't raise suspicion, and that would be dangerous for all of us. I'm afraid our only course of action, the only way to stop this demon is to make the key, build the trap, incarcerate the demon, and worry about any repercussions at a later time.

"I can say 'no,' obviously," I explain to my friends. "There's nothing forcing me to do this."

"Then DON'T!" Marsh yells.

I continue. "But any other solution gets us what? A brief delay? If we try to banish him, then we're just sitting around waiting for his followers to bring him back again. And then start all over? And, by that point, he'll be gunning for us, since he'll know that we know about him. But if we can build this trap, it will contain the demon forever."

"This is assuming that Frank is telling the truth," Greystone reminds us.

"Yes, assuming he's telling the truth, which I believe he is." I haven't mentioned to them that Frank can lie his way around me. My Seer gifts of truth detection don't reliably work on him, but I'm confident that on this, at least, he is telling the truth. "If we trap this demon and toss the trap into the Pit, the problem is over. Forever. And if we run into any more demon problems in the future, we'll have a way to fight them."

Marsh is silent, steaming mad but quiet. In the end, for better or for worse, I get my way.

We agree to make the key.

Marsh does most of the coordinating. It takes a couple of days to get everything put together. We find a foundry to make us a mold based on the specifications in Frank's book. Marsh mixes the ingredients together. He has to be especially careful with the silver; his skin is sensitive to it, and he bitches nonstop whenever he accidentally touches it. Silver is surprisingly hard to get a hold of here as it is poisonous to many of the city's inhabitants. And highly illegal. Marsh manages to get into the evidence room and sneak out one of the bars we found at Clark's apartment. He has less trouble with the mercury, sulfur, and the other herbs and metals.

But it wasn't the only hurdle. We have to burn certain other herbs and incense while intoning foreign words that do their best to not come out of my mouth. And I mean they actually won't come out of my mouth; it was like they were somehow fighting me to keep from saying them.

Finally, I lance my left index finger and squeeze several drops of blood into the mixture.

My blood flares first bright orange, then crimson as it mixes into the rest. Marsh pours the metal into the key mold, and we wait several hours for it to cool. Once we can handle it, I carve the necessary symbols into the key's surface. Finally, for the first time since arriving here, my background in art pays off.

In the end, I'm holding an ornate skeleton key. I don't recognize the symbols I've carved into its surface. They could be letters in some foreign language, or just gibberish, and they seem to catch the light when I see them out of the corner of my eyes. The key fits into the palm of my hand, and it feels heavier than it should. It has two whirling loops at the bow that look like angry eyes. I'm not sure how that happened as I don't remember building that into the mold. The blade of the key ends in a complex lattice of curves and ridges.

It doesn't look like it should be so important. Too fancy to put on a key ring, but not grand enough to be valuable to an eternal creature.

Greystone and Marsh accompany me back over to Warner's. The key is in my pocket, its unnatural weight making me feel unbalanced as we walk inside. Frank sees us immediately as we walk into the door, and he waves us back.

"You have it? You have the key?" he asks eagerly as we enter.

"Yes," I say, but Marsh pushes past me.

"Let's just hold up for a second. We need to get some things clear here."

Frank smiles easily. "Of course, Detective. Whatever you want."

"We've made your damned key, but I need to hear from you what we're getting for it."

"I am giving you the solution to your problem," he drawls. "All I am asking in return is a means to not be snared in my own trap. While I trust Detective Green's word to not attempt to capture and banish me, I do not extend that trust to all his friends."

Marsh nods. "Fine, smart. Very smart. Now, explain this trap."

Frank rolls his eyes, clearly exasperated that Marsh needs further explanation. "I will show you how to build a cage which can contain those of my kind for all eternity, or until such time as the cage is opened or destroyed."

"And we will actually be able to build this trap? We can

get everything we need to put it together? It's not going to do something nasty like trap us too?"

My eyes go wide, I hadn't even though of that. Frank smirks, "You are certainly a suspicious one, Detective. Yes, the materials are readily available, and the device will be perfectly safe for you to use."

Marsh ignores the jibe. "How does it work?"

"Build the cage. Open it. Put a demon inside it. Close it. Put it somewhere safe; I would recommend out of earshot. The prisoner is likely to be quite upset."

I wish we knew more about what we were dealing with or, at least, could discuss it with someone trustworthy and more knowledgeable about it than me. We're just stalling, now. I can tell Marsh is struggling to think of some other reason to delay this.

Finally, Marsh sighs and levels his gaze at Frank, "So we just hand you the key and trust that the directions you give us are the solution to all our problems?"

"Exactly that, Detective," Frank smiles. "I have a volume in this room, with the instructions to build a demon trap. You give me the key, and I give you the book. Everyone wins. You can trap demons to your hearts' content, and I will be free from that danger."

I reach into my pocket, but as soon as my fingers close around the key, I realize something. "Frank, how do I give you the key?" I ask him as Marsh beings pacing in the room. "You can't hold it."

"Are you sure about that, Detective?" he asks, and holds out his hand.

I glance at my friends. Greystone looks ill. She won't get near the demon and seems remarkably skittish even being in the same room, but she's not telling me no. Marsh is scowling fiercely, his arms folded in front of his chest. He's shaking his head, but he's not stopping me either.

I sigh, giving in. "Fine." I hand Frank the key.

I expect it to drop to the floor, but surprisingly Frank grabs the end of the key and holds it above his head. The metal flares where he is touching it, and it starts to burn like magnesium. The key is melting, dissolving into the demon's hand. He lets out a scream, half pain and half joy, and it makes my skin crawl. The scream goes on and on, making my head ring painfully, and I clap my hands over my ears to try and drown it out. The scream keeps getting louder. And then I realize I'm the one screaming, not Frank. My eyes are clenched shut, chin pressed to my chest, and I start to hear other voices in my head screaming in unison; they sound like my brother, like my mom, but they all blend together inside and echo inside my mind.

I look up to see Greystone and Marsh staring at me in concern, and I realize they aren't affected by the scream.

My heart stops in my chest, and I feel like Marsh just plowed into me. I drop to the floor, struggling to take a breath. I can see Greystone hovering above me trying to say something, but I can't hear her over my own hoarse cries.

Finally, my heart lurches back into an erratic rhythm, and my voice dies away. There are tears in my eyes and an awful ringing in my ears, but I can hear voices now.

"You bastard! What did you do to him?" Marsh is yelling from several miles away.

"Curious," Frank is saying. "That was not what I was expecting."

"*. . . tive Green? Are you OK? Can you hear me?*" Greystone asks.

Wha-?

"*Are you injured?*"

I try to think back to her, but my thoughts are groggy, and my head is swimming. I try to sit up. I'm not sure what just happened, but other than a hollow ache in my chest and

the crushing pounding in my head, I can feel myself returning back to normal. My knees are a little shaky, but finally,
I'm able to stand back up.

"Are you OK, Jacob Green?" Frank asks, the concern in
his voice is betrayed by the absolute glee on his face.

I nod, not meeting his gaze. I'm not convinced that
Frank didn't know that process would hurt me in some way.
"I'm fine. You got your key. You're free from demon traps.
Now, how do we build one?"

"Of course," he says in a conciliatory tone. "You will find
the book you require behind that small bookshelf over there."

Marsh stomps over to a waist-high bookshelf nearby.
He roughly shoves it aside with one hand, and the contents
scatter across the floor. There is a shelf in a small alcove in
the exposed wall, inside of which is a single thin volume.
The cover is bound in thick leather and wrapped in twine. I
crowd next to Marsh to look at it as he opens it up. Inside are
loose sheets of vellum, with drawings and schematics nestled
among small, elegant script in some foreign tongue.

"What the hell is this?" Marsh demands. "We can't read
this."

"It is written in a dialect unique to some forgotten order of Catalonian monks. I am sure you can find someone to
translate it." Frank tilts his head, a self-satisfied smile on his
face, "From my own reading of it, once you have the instructions, the traps should not be difficult to create."

"Dammit, Frank! You're not going anywhere until
you—"

But Frank starts fading away, a grin still spread across his
face. "I am sorry, Detective, but this whole ordeal has been
rather taxing. Be sure to let me know how it goes."

There is a bench in one of the booths on the side wall, and
it doesn't have too much debris on it. I stagger over to it and

lie down.

Marsh storms out of the room, swearing up a storm. I close my eyes and will myself to feel normal again. Even laying down, the room still feels like it is spinning.

"Is there anything I can do to help you, Detective?" Greystone asks me. She floats near the booth, looking down over me.

"How long is he going to be gone, do you think?" I ask.

"The demon?"

"No, sorry. I mean Marsh."

She frowns, puzzled. "I have no idea. Do you need me to relay a message to him?"

I shake my head. "No, nothing like that. I was just thinking, you've told me about the other members of the squad, but you haven't spoken to me about Detective Marsh yet."

"Oh, I see," she says. She mulls it over. "What can I tell you about him that you don't already know?"

"You've told me about the other detectives when they worked with Detective Olsen. What did Marsh do with him? Olsen was his partner, right?"

She is silent for a long moment. When she speaks again, it is barely louder than a whisper. "I'll tell you what I can."

Detectives Olsen and Marsh

"He was there, at the end. With Detective Olsen. Seven months ago.

"I had been interrogated extensively regarding Detective Olsen's recent actions. How much had I known? Did I have any suspicions? Being linked as we were, why hadn't I sensed anything of what he was up to?

"He had meticulously and rigidly avoided giving me any hint of his thoughts or activities during those weeks. I think he wanted to protect me. Once he was captured, Detective

Olsen didn't try and hide anything about what he had done. He freely admitted to all the crimes he had committed. He gave detailed descriptions of everyone he had thrown into the Pit, though he was less forthcoming about the reasons. His voice was defeated, passionless. All told, he had incapacitated two dozen people and thrown their remains into the Pit.

"The scope of his crimes was unprecedented. I cannot begin to describe to you the egregiousness of Detective Olsen's betrayal, not just against the police force but against the city and its citizens. As representatives of the enforcement of the laws in this city, we operate by common consent of the city's populace. If citizens of Meridian begin to feel they are in danger from the members of law enforcement, or if they think we are abusing our authority, they may attempt to flee. If they do not believe they are safe here, they will return to the mortal world and possibly endanger us all to discovery.

"Despite this, right up until the end, Detective Olsen was sure his actions were justified.

"'It was necessary,' is all he would say when asked why. Even Captain Radu couldn't get him to divulge anything more.

"I argued passionately for a reduction in his duties. I thought that stress had overcome his reason. Surely, he could remain incarcerated or under observation, but Detective Olsen asked me to stop.

"'If you let me go, I'll just continue. I won't ever stop.'

"I was speechless at that. Detective Olsen was adamant in his decision, that was clear; if he were ever released, he would pick up right where he left off. In the end, there was nothing we could do. Captain Radu ordered him thrown into the Pit, and he ordered Detective Marsh to do it.

"The last time I saw him was on that same platform where I stood with you so recently. Detectives Marsh and Olsen were there with me. Detective Olsen stood there, staring at the vortex of energy and the howling madness. And he smiled. An aura of peace settled over him, like a great weight lifted off him as he knew his journey, his responsibilities were at an end.

"'I don't understand, Olsen,' Marsh said. 'What happened to you? Just tell me. Between you and me, we can figure something out. It's not too late.'

"My esteem for Detective Marsh increased significantly that day. He tried one last time to redeem Detective Olsen.

"Detective Olsen merely turned around and looked at both of us—that sad smile on his face. The link we shared had been severed earlier, to spare me the fate of being linked to someone being tossed into the Pit. I didn't know exactly what he was thinking, but it seemed as though he was sadder for us more than for himself.

"'Someday soon, you're going to realize what I discovered. And you're going to wish you were in the Pit with me.'

"And then he stepped backward off the platform and was lost to the Pit.

"'Well, shit,' Marsh said. He and I both simply stood there on the platform, silent in the deafening roar, and stared."

I don't know what to say to her now. I replay her story in my mind.

"Ms. Greystone, do you have any idea why Olsen was disposing of people in the Pit? Was he working with the demon too?"

She shakes her head. "No. I'm certain he was not. My suspicion, though I have no evidence to back it up, my suspicion is that he stumbled onto the existence of these demons and was trying to eliminate them. The people he destroyed, I suspect many of them were innocent. He committed acts of great evil. All to serve some greater good. But he couldn't wrap his head around what he faced. He was a good man, Detective Green, but he lost his way."

Chapter 42

THE DEMON TRAP PROVED MORE difficult to build than the key. It helps to have a few geniuses working with you on the force. It turns out that obscure Catalonian dialects are part of Detective Meints' sizeable store of knowledge. He was so eager to study the book that he didn't even appear too concerned about what information it actually contained.

I admit, even after looking at the schematics in the book, I expected to be building some large contraption we would need to haul around on wheels or with a crane. Instead, it is about the size of a shoebox. When you are trying to capture something that doesn't have a body, the actual size of the trap doesn't matter too much.

It has taken us several days to gather the necessary ingredients. Some are rare, some just tedious to collect. But the hardest task has been avoiding the scrutiny of Captain Radu during this time. We've delayed informing the captain about our specific plans. The less he knows about building the trap, the less curious he may be about where we learned how to do it. And I would like him to remain in the dark about Frank's involvement in all this. It hasn't been easy. The captain has the unnerving ability to appear behind me every time I turn around.

Case in point: I turn a corner in the hall and feel the temperature drop several degrees. That's the warning I receive that the captain is nearby.

"Detective Green," the voice slithers out of the shadows in the hallway. "Your progress."

He manages to load a metric ton of weight behind those two words, asking me a question and issuing a command at the same time. I've just returned from tracking down some stupid dust of something-or-other we need. I hold a clay jar awkwardly and try not to call attention to it. I am on my way to meet with Marsh in the squad room.

"We have a lead, Captain," I stammer.

"*Oui, je sais.* I know that, Detective. You assured me of as much the last time we spoke." He glides out of the shady corner of the hall, floating effortlessly towards me, and stops just out of arm's reach—which, by the way, is still uncomfortably close for my tastes. "I would like to know what progress you have made since the last time we spoke."

I shift uncomfortably from one foot to the other. I can't think of any way to dodge his questions. "Captain, you know what we're dealing with. A demon! I think we've found a solution to capture the demon. We want to make sure when we confront this thing again, we have a way to contain him."

His arms are crossed in front of him, and he moves one hand to cup his chin in thought. His eyes never leave mine though, scanning me for subterfuge.

"Explain."

"We managed to find a book that explains how to build a trap for demons," I confess, trying not to sound too evasive. "We're building one."

He cocks his head microscopically, examining me. "*Qu'est-ce que c'est, ce livre?* You found a book? Which book?"

I shrug. "I don't know its name."

"And you believe it to be authentic?"

I nod. "Yes, sir. We're confident this is the real deal."

He frowns. "I see." He thinks silently, sliding just a little closer to me while I try not to backpedal away. Finally, he says, "I will examine this book."

I can't very well deny him, so he follows me back up to the squad room. I try to keep from running when he's looming behind me the entire length of the hallway.

"About damned time Green," Marsh bellows at me as I walk in, his back turned. He doesn't notice Radu until he starts to turn around. "You sure took your sweet-ass time . . . Eh, hello, Captain."

Marsh glances at me questioningly, but all I can do is shake my head, denying whatever it is I feel guilty of. Captain Radu continues past me over to Marsh's desk where the journal is open. The other detectives are in the room, going over what we know of Cortez and Goldman. There are maps on the chalkboard depicting the layout of the homes of both suspects. Armstrong and Kim are focusing on Goldman; Meints and Burchard are concentrating on Cortez. Marsh, Greystone, and I are working on getting this trap built. We all stop what we're doing and watch the captain.

Radu slowly scans the topmost page. He extends his hand and, with a long fingernail, flips it over to look at the next page. We all stand silently, expectantly, waiting as he leafs through all the pages and schematics.

Finally, he raises his head and looks at all of us in turn. "Who determined the authenticity of this book?"

No one responds. They're clearly waiting for Marsh or me to say something. Marsh finally clears his throat and then nods at me. "The kid found it. I thought it looked legit."

Thanks for throwing me under the bus, Marsh. I smile uneasily.

"What do you think, Captain?" I ask meekly. "Is it authentic?"

His eyes seem to be boring through my skull. His face is expressionless. "Yes. It was written by a group of monks I had the pleasure of slaughtering many centuries back. I had thought all trace of them had been removed from this earth. But I recognize their work. It is authentic, without a doubt. I'm curious why you thought it to be."

I shrug and turn to Marsh, trying to deflect the captain's curiosity. "I'm still living, old books all look legitimate to me," I answer lamely, and I don't think for a second he believes me.

Instead of waiting for him to say as much, I step around him and toward Marsh. "Excuse me, sir," I give him as wide a berth as possible and hold the jar out to Marsh. "I got your dust. I think that's the last ingredient we need."

My partner nods and takes the package from me. He goes back over to his desk where he's working on building parts of the trap. I follow him, pretending to watch what he's doing. The whole time, however, I am conscious of Radu's gaze tracking me, calculating God knows what. My skin is crawling. It's all I can concentrate on, which is why I'm shocked when I realize a couple of minutes later that Radu is no longer in the room. I was keeping track of him the whole time but never saw him leave.

I shiver and try and turn my full attention to helping Marsh.

By the end of the evening, the trap is ready. It's a bit of a letdown. As I said, I was expecting something more impressive or grandiose I guess. The final product can be held in one hand. It is made of wood with a metal frame, interwoven with wire and metallic thread. There are symbols carved into the metal, burned into the wood, and carved on the sides. The symbols are similar to what we used on the key, but somehow are nothing alike. I know that isn't helpful; I just don't know any other way to explain it. The characters look like they are from the same family but completely different. On the key, they were angry, aggressive. On the box, they are softer, stronger. I keep thinking I see pictures in the symbols, but when I look again, the picture is different or gone altogether. It makes my head hurt. None of the others seem too bothered by them.

The lid on the box has no lock. It is attached by a pair of silver hinges. I don't see how it is supposed to stay shut, but both Marsh and I agree it is built according to the specifications in the book. And, I have to admit, it looks a lot better thanks to the fact that Marsh put it together. I don't know if I could have followed some of the instructions as precisely as he did.

Marsh looks at me. "You ready, kid?"

I look over at Greystone. She nods. The other detectives in the room have paused what they are doing, looking over at us.

I nod. "Yeah. Let's see if this thing works."

We decide to hit Cortez first simply because he has a single home, whereas Goldman occupies a large warehouse. We'll try the smaller venue first. The entire squad—six detectives and Ms. Greystone—pile into a single large coach and travel nearly half an hour to Cortez's home.

It is located in one of the many offshoots of the town. We travel along a misty dirt track lined on both sides with dead and decaying trees growing up out of brackish water. The swamp extends into forest on both sides. We pass homes and shelters occasionally, but for the most part, we only see a few travelers on the way there. When we pull up, just out of view of the home, we can barely see the light from town behind us. A weak wind whistles through the trees, blowing damp dead leaves in swirling eddies. I try to convince myself that my shivering is just from a chill in the air.

We arrive at a walled villa located just off the same Black River that winds through the dock district. The river here is broad and deep out towards the center, but up near the shore, the current isn't strong. Reeds grow taller than my head along the muddy banks. The smell is rank, fetid. Swampy pools extend out from all sides of the river and stagnate in moss-covered pits. The home sits inside a few acres of willows and quaky oaks, covered with carpets of kudzu and alive with mosquitoes, moths, and large horseflies—all of which seem much more interested in me than in my dead companions. The wall is only waist high, made of river stones and mortar. I can't pinpoint the locale of the home's style. Who knows what part of the real world this was pulled out of?

Lights are on in the home, but the rest of the grounds are deserted. All I hear are insects, the rustle of blowing leaves, and the calls of night birds from the woods around the home.

"Right," Marsh says. "Greystone, normally, I'd have you scout ahead since we don't exactly know what we're dealing with here. But I don't know how much danger that will put you in. You better hang back behind us and let us know if anything tries sneaking up on us."

"Very well, Detective," Greystone replies.

Marsh continues. "Armstrong, Kim. You guys circle around back. Make sure he doesn't try running."

Kim nods; Armstrong draws his gun and waves to us as they start running around the inside of the wall to get at the back. The rest of us ready our weapons. I hold mine in one hand and the trap in the other. I don't know how accurate I'll be if I have to shoot this cannon one handed, but I'm not about to walk in without it drawn.

We're not positive we'll be running into a demon tonight, but I don't want to travel anywhere without the trap until we've caught it. If it's not here, maybe we can get Cortez to tell us where to find it. We move quickly, as quietly as possible, Marsh in the lead, heading straight at the front door.

There is a covered porch on the front of the house. A gas lantern hangs from a hook to the side of the door, casting weak light that shows us there are no surprises waiting for us.

Marsh doesn't bother with any delays or tactics. He kicks the door open, knocking it off its hinges and splitting it in half. "Police!" he yells as we all rush in, weapons forward.

The room is full of corpses. Granted, that's not all that unusual to me now. But this is different. The stench nearly knocks me over. There are bodies stacked like cordwood at the back of the room; some are propped up against the wall to our left; more still are sitting on the couch and chairs around the coffee table. Men and women. Some dressed, some not. But these are simply inanimate corpses, piled carelessly wherever there is space like discarded clothes. There must be fifty, maybe one hundred corpses in here. A narrow path winds its way between all the bodies, leading from the front door to the kitchen beyond. I can barely see the bare wooden walls, the worn carpet, or any other furniture that might be in the room as there are so many bodies stacked and stuffed throughout.

"What the hell?" Marsh mutters.

"Welcome to my home," one of the corpses says. It is Cortez. It is one of a half-dozen corpses on the couch, nearly buried under bodies. I barely register him speaking to us before Burchard's gun fires and completely disintegrates Cortez's head. The body flops over to the floor, lifeless once more. Detective Burchard keeps his gun trained on it just in case.

The voice chuckles from behind us, from one of the bodies in the throng of corpses stacked against the wall. I can see the face moving at the back of the cluster of bodies behind us.

"I thought this thing could only push someone out to inhabit their body!" Marsh growls at me like this is my fault. "It can take control of dead bodies too?"

I shrug helplessly. We're not standing in a room full of discarded husks; we're surrounded by potential hosts.

"What did you fools hope to accomplish here?" I have my gun drawn on it, but the corpse slumps back again. The eyes flare brightly before snuffing out, its face losing all life and animation.

A different body, one of the bodies leaning against the far wall, stands up straight. "Shoot me. Destroy this body. Destroy all these bodies. What good will it do you?"

"Shit," Meints mutters, keeping his gun aimed at the demon in his new body. I've got mine aimed at the corpse behind us, Burchard hasn't wavered from the one he shot. Marsh is scanning the rest of the room. We hear a commotion from the back of the house, some loud swearing from both Armstrong and Kim, and the sounds of something heavy hitting the ground.

The demon merely smiles at us.

"You think that because you have overcome death, that puts you beyond our reach. It does not."

It doesn't move; it just stands up easily in the midst of the crowd of bodies and turns its gaze to me. "And you, Seer. Do you think that seeing us protects you from us? I will enjoy defiling your body long before your spirit finally breaks free from its prison of flesh."

A dry hand caresses my face, and I spin wildly but see no sign of which body moved. Laughter travels from mouth to mouth around the room. Eyes erupt in geysers of fire in one corpse after another. "Who are you?" I ask, glancing frantically around me for signs of any other bodies coming to life.

It *tsks* at me from a new body.

"Surely, a Seer understands the importance of a name. I

will not give you my true name. You can call me Carrion. Or
Woe. Or Abandon."

One of the other bodies slowly stands up and stares at us
with malevolent eyes. I glance back at the body that was just
speaking to us. It blinks back at me, its smile growing.

"Uh, Marsh, is there supposed to be more than one?"
Burchard asks, shifting his aim to the new demon.

"You can call me Desolation. You can call me Misery,"
the second body says.

A third corpse begins to chuckle. Yeah, it's an evil chuckle; I'm not sure a demon knows any other way to do it. It
stands up behind us.

"What is the phrase again?" the third demon asks. "My
name is Legion, for we are many."

Three of them. There are three of them.

This is bad. There are three. Crap, at least three. This
whole time, we were searching for one. Did Frank know? Of
course, he knew.

I'm going to kill Frank if I survive this.

I feel Greystone nod assent in my mind, but she's too
scared to say anything. Even from outside, she can feel my
panic, sense what's going on in here. I don't know what they
can do to her; it's not like she has a body to possess. But the
fact that she fears them tells me she's vulnerable in some way.

Three corpses start shuffling toward us from different
points in the room, arms reaching to grab us. Gunfire erupts
all around me. Bodies are blown to pieces, but whenever one
falls, another rises to take its place. A hand wraps around my
ankle and starts to squeeze painfully. I look down to see an
arm reaching out from under a pile of corpses. I don't even
know which figure it is attached to. I shoot, blowing the arm
off at the elbow.

More laughter comes from the mouths of corpses
all around us. Three bodies stand up and grab Detective

Burchard, knocking his gun out of his grip and piling on top of him.

I suddenly realize I don't know exactly what to do with the trap; it's just been hanging uselessly in my hand. Since my gun seems to be less useful than I had hoped, I jam it in a pocket so that I can hold the trap with both hands. I hold it up in front of me, as far in front of me as I can reach, in the general direction of the demons. I'm holding it like a ticking bomb, turning my face from it like it will blow up at any moment. I have no idea how it is supposed to work. The instructions in the book told us how to build it, not how to use it. All three demons see it at the same time because it shuts up their laughing fast.

"What?" Abandon yells in disbelief.

"How is this possible?" Misery screams, the sound piercing painfully in the confines of the room.

"Flee!" Legion yells, but the voice sounds as if it is from a great distance.

I am holding the trap out in front of me, and while I haven't done anything to it, I can feel it start to change. The temperature begins to drop around it, growing colder by the second. The box is getting heavier, and I struggle to hold it up. It keeps gaining weight; at first, it felt like a wooden shoe-box of about ten pounds, but now it weighs at least twice that and still gaining.

The symbols on the sides of the box begin to glow. I want to say it is a dark blue, but reds and greens dance in the corners of my vision. I hear a rushing sound, like a waterfall or a jet engine taking off. The lid slowly lifts open on its own.

The windows of the house explode outward. The symbols glow blindingly bright on the sides of the trap. I hear one of the demons screaming in terror. My brain calls him Abandon though I don't really know which of the three he is. Blackness starts encroaching on the edges of my vision.

I'm struggling to breathe; it feels like there's a huge weight on my chest.

I don't know what is happening with the other demons, but Abandon is transfixed in front of me. His mouth is open as he screams, but otherwise, he is motionless. His skin is starting to flake away, floating away from him like ashes in a storm. His eyes are glowing, but the glow is starting to be pulled from the corpse's eye sockets towards my outstretched hand.

"No!" the demon shrieks. "Please, no! Not this! I will leave! You will never see me again! Please!"

Abandon's stolen body crumbles completely to dust. A blazing glow of energy streams from his formless eyes towards the trap. It gets sucked inside the box, slamming the lid shut behind it. The crash of the lid sounds like a building slamming into the earth. My ears are ringing, and I slump to the ground, dizzy and exhausted.

The trap blazes with cold. I have to peel my hands off it. The glow from the symbols dims, and my awareness of my surroundings starts to return. Greystone is hovering near me, she came into the house at some point. Marsh is crouched over me, snapping his fingers in front of my face and calling my name. Finally, I nod to him. "I'm OK."

Kim and Armstrong stagger into the room from the back. They are both battered and leaning on each other for support.

"Let me guess," Armstrong growls. "It went sideways."

Marsh taps the trap on the ground with the toe of his boot. The lid is shut, and the box looks the same as it did before, but I can tell something is different. I pick it up and feel it is buzzing with angry, restless energy. The box jolts in my hand, and I can feel something hitting against the insides. But that isn't the strangest thing.

There are no hinges on the box. In fact, as I turn it over

and around in my hands, I can't see which side used to be the lid. It is completely sealed.

In my mind, I think I can hear the demon screaming from inside. I set the box down, suddenly disgusted by touching it. The other two demons are gone. Not trapped in the box, just no longer here. The corpses that remain, both those intact or in pieces, are devoid of life.

"C'mon," Marsh says. "We've got work to do. Let's get a crew out here to clean this place up. We've got to get back to the precinct and drop this bastard into the Pit."

He smiles grimly. "And then we need to build a couple more traps."

Chapter 43

THE NEXT MORNING, I WALK through the door of Warner's with Marsh right behind me. With the other demons still on the loose once again, I can't go anywhere without an escort. I've got to figure out a way to keep myself safe without constantly requiring the protection of a babysitter. First, it was Finnegan, then that doorman Smith, now two demons. Since I remain the only one that seems to be able to recognize them, everyone on the squad has finally come to accept that it's important to keep me alive. That's a nice change from even a week ago.

A couple of guys are sitting at the bar, downing their drinks in silent, solitary companionship. Day and night don't seem to make too much of a difference to the inhabitants here. Most of them don't sleep, the days are permanently a cloud-covered gray, except when it storms, and it is even darker.

It doesn't much matter when they start their drinking. Actually, now that I think about it, I'm not sure what most of them do at all. Some have jobs, obviously. No escape from that, even after death. But whatever they do, normally there are more people here, no matter what the hour. Even though we've been trying to keep a lid on what's going on, I'm guessing that word has gotten out, and people are staying home.

Frank isn't in his room, so we just wave to Warner and head back there. He acknowledges us in that patented glowering stare he's worked on for countless years. We file into Frank's room and close the door behind us. It is empty.

"Frank?" I call out. I wait. No response. I look questioningly at Marsh. He just shrugs.

I call out again, a little louder. "Frank? You here?"

His voice sounds right behind us. "What do you want, Detectives?"

I jump nearly a foot in the air, but Marsh barely blinks; he just turns around to face Frank.

"We need to ask you a few questions."

"Of course, you do," Frank responds, frowning and leaning around Marsh to look at me. "I have already helped you a great deal, Jacob. What more do you need from me?"

"Hey, pal!" Marsh interrupts angrily. "Don't pretend you haven't made out like a king from this deal. We've got some questions. You cough up some answers!"

"Or what?" he smiles. "What will you do to me, Detective? Trap me?"

I step between them, attempting to defuse this before it escalates beyond my control. "Frank, we have a few simple questions; then we'll get out of your hair."

He nods and spreads his arms open wide. "Of course. For you, Jacob. Ask away."

"The trap worked. We captured the demon."

Frank's eyes sparkle with delight. "Truly? That is good news."

"Did you know that the demon wasn't alone?" I search his eyes for any clue of deceit.

"Oh, dear. I hope that did not cause any complications."

I don't have to put any effort into searching his expression, Frank's grin trumpets my answer. Oh, he knew.

"You don't think you could have mentioned that?" I snap.

Frank shrugs. "Why worry you with unnecessary details? Is this all you wished to know?"

Marsh is glowering, clearly wishing he had some way of getting Frank's neck in his grasp. I continue on before Marsh says something to chase Frank away.

"No, it's not. We're going to build more traps. I would like to know how many to build. Do you know how many demons we're dealing with here?"

Frank ponders for a moment. "I will admit, I do not know exactly which demons you are dealing with. I knew some had come to town. Those people you asked me about who had gone missing, some of them had started asking me questions about the existence of demons not knowing I was one. But that is what gave me a hint that some of them had arrived. And then when those people started to disappear, it became obvious to me. But I did not seek them out. I tend to keep my own company. Other demons are not much for socializing."

Marsh snorts, but Frank ignores him and continues, "Did you happen to get their names?"

"Obviously not, they are not going to use their real names," I say like I've known all along that true names are a thing. "They just said names like Abandon, Carrion, Misery."

"Oh, those assholes," Frank shakes his head in disgust. "It should not surprise me they were the ones to come up with this scheme. They have been trying to game the system for millennia."

He leans closer to me and whispers conspiratorially, "There are only three of them."

"Three? You're sure?" Marsh asks.

Frank nods. "Yes. No one else would bother spending any time with them. And they always scheme and plot and connive together. You can trust me on this one. Which did you trap, by the way?"

"The one who called himself Abandon," I answer. "I think."

"Yes!" Frank giggles in delight. "And you cast the trap into the Pit? Oh, this is excellent news. I have hated that bastard ever since Gomorrah. He is intolerable!"

He turns to me again, still chuckling. "Are those all of the questions you had for me, Jacob?"

I nod slowly. "Yeah, that's it, basically."

"Very well then," he smiles, and he is gone.

"Great," Marsh grumbles. "Fat lot of good that does us."

I shrug, trying to put a positive spin on it. "At least we know we need to build two more traps."

Marsh marches out the door, calling back over his shoulder, "If that chump is telling the truth. If we have enough stuff to build the traps."

I can't respond. I have nothing worth saying. He's right on both counts. It's going to be a long day while we get these things built.

It turns out, I was wrong on that point at least. It took us a few days last time to round up everything we needed to build one of these demon traps. After we set out to trap the first demon, Captain Radu started gathering materials to make more. It looks like we should have enough for a dozen or so with the stockpile the captain has going. Of course, he put the materials under lock and key, in some place where only he has access. Any time we need to build one, we'll have to go through him to do it.

I get volunteered to go ask him to begin the next traps. I walk confidently out of our office, but once I'm out of sight,

I slow down. I don't like seeing the captain alone. I'm never quite sure whether he feels like keeping me alive or not on any given day.

I knock hesitantly on his office door. There is no verbal response, but the door swings open on its own, tendrils of roiling black fog spilling out from the opening. I take that as an invitation.

"Captain?" I ask, searching the shadows of the room for him. The door closes behind me. I glance behind me, verify he isn't there, then turn back to see him standing two feet directly in front of me.

"I need to speak to you, Detective Green," he says, his deep voice slithering into my brain.

"Of course, Captain, but we need to build two more traps and—"

He waves my words away. His eyes glow fiercely and bore directly into me.

"I have concerns about these traps, Detective." He doesn't move and doesn't indicate I should move, but I don't want to backpedal from him. That would make it look like I'm as scared as I feel. I stay where I am, uncomfortably close to Radu.

"What kind of concerns, Captain? The first one we made worked fairly well."

"Yes." I wait for him to continue. He is staring at me, measuring me, weighing me somehow. I'm confused, not really sure what's going on this time. Finally, he appears to come to some sort of decision.

"I only want these traps built when we have a specific entity to capture. I do not want them assembled, poised to capture."

I look at him questioningly.

He whispers to me. "They call to me, Detective Green. When you built the first one, I could hear it whispering to me. It was all I could do to remain in my office and ignore its cry. I fear if we assembled several and stored them complete, ready to use, they could eventually lure me to them as well. And if they affect me, they may affect others. And as I have a body, I know not what it would do to me."

He is staring past me, his mind elsewhere. I nod, but he doesn't notice. Eventually, I mumble, "Yessir."

"Do not speak of this to anyone. I want this kept between us for now. Until we can learn more. We are not demons, Detective. I am not a demon. This I know for certain. So, it should have no power over me. That it does says there is more to them than we know. I will stay away while you build the traps you need."

He helps me gather the necessary materials. In the end, it doesn't take us long at all to build two more. By the next morning, we have them assembled.

I'm tired. I've had a disturbing lack of sleep lately. I'm sitting on my office chair, wearily sipping at what passes for coffee, staring through half-lidded eyes as Burchard and Meints put the finishing touches on the last trap. I can't stop yawning.

Marsh is going over the plan for our assault on Goldman's place with Armstrong and Kim. Captain Radu and Greystone left hours ago and have been out on surveillance, keeping an eye on the warehouse we've identified as Goldman's location. Greystone has been checking in with me hourly, giving me an account of anyone that may happen to enter or leave the building. So far, it's been pretty boring.

Right on time, I hear from her.

"Still nothing, Detective Green. It's quiet and appears empty here."

I nod, remember she can't see that, then think, OK. *Thanks, Ms. Greystone.*

"Are we sure this is where he is?" She asks.

I sip more coffee while responding, *As far as we know, yes. Just like the last dozen times you've asked.*

I can hear her sniff of disapproval.

Sighing, I apologize. *Ms. Greystone, I'm sorry. That came out rude. You know I don't—*

"Detective! Someone is attempting to leave the warehouse. Captain Radu is . . . Oh, my God."

What? Ms. Greystone, are you OK?

"The captain is preventing them from leaving. You need to hurry."

"We've got to roll!" I shout to the room. "The captain is holding them in."

Marsh swears, Meints and Burchard grab the traps while the rest of us grab guns, and we stampede out to the waiting coaches. We were still about an hour away from being ready, but we have two waiting to go. We make a mad dash for the huge black coffins on wheels, the horses straining in excitement and being held back by struggling drivers. I barely manage to get inside one of the coaches before it rolls out.

I hear the drivers shout a command in unison and I swear g-forces slam me back into the seat. The horses that pull the coaches launch out at an ungodly speed. I think I finally realize why the coaches are covered, enclosed with no windows. If they weren't, the wind shear might rip limbs off. I've never felt horses move this fast. The other detectives are nonchalant about the danger, loading their guns, sliding knives into sheaths. I'm white-knuckling an armrest, praying we don't go rolling as we round a corner at Mach 4. I hear a scream, and the coach swerves, but there isn't a bone-crunching crash, so I can assume we narrowly avoided a collision. I don't know if it would be worse to see what is happening or to just remain ignorant in my closed box.

The trip to the warehouse takes years off my life. My stomach is doing flips from the lurching and careening of the coach. I have no idea what to expect when we get there, but I bet the demons will be waiting for us. I don't know if we'll have to chase them down, or if they are spoiling for a fight. This is going to be it, one way or another. Either our traps will work, or the demons will flee. I'm sure they won't attempt to stick around if they know we can both see them and trap them. The end result might be the same for the people here. The demons would be gone. But that would only mean they would escape back to the real world. My world. And I don't want demon-possessed corpses wreaking havoc back home. Especially if they know who I am and try to track down family or friends.

Burchard slaps one of the traps into my hand. "Don't screw this up, Green."

He and Marsh are with me in the coach. I look at both of these men, looming over me in the dim confines we share, and it just seems so surreal that these two monsters, animated corpses, are my comrades. They're not exactly friends, but I know they are going to do their best to try and protect me and keep me alive. And they're relying on me to do the same for them, to protect them and to capture a creature even they are afraid of. And despite the fact that I'm marching towards what could be my death, I feel like I have value, I'm part of a team. I'm one of the good guys, dammit.

The ride ends all too quickly. The coaches come screeching to a halt right as Greystone screams into my mind, *"Quickly, Detective!"*

I hop out of the coach with the rest of the detectives in my squad, and my jaw drops at the scene before me. We're at a building covered in rusting corrugated metal. It's not huge as far as warehouses go, but it is missing most of its roof; bare steel girders are exposed to the sky. The few windows that exist are on the second story, and the glass has been broken out and boarded over. A large loading dock takes up the front of the building, and there is a concrete ramp leading down to it. Crumbling asphalt surrounds the building, piled with stacks of rotting palettes, heaps of rusting metal detritus and debris. A limp chain-link fence encircles the place about one hundred feet out on all sides, but there are so many holes and gaps that it can't possibly serve to keep anything out or in.

I take all that in with a glance because what holds my attention is the swarm of hundreds of bats, shrieking and screaming in clouds above us. Did I say hundreds? Maybe thousands of bats. None of them are large, but they are swirling in spiraling waves, swooping down to attack a couple of men trying to run out of the main doors to the loading dock. I've never seen anything like it. The sound is deafening, high-pitched squeaks from thousands of little throats, ebbing and diving in concentrated packs at the men.

The ground is littered with hundreds of bat corpses already, and a dozen or so human bodies are strewn near the doors. One of the bodies staggers up, and I recognize it as Captain Radu. He is streaked with blood, and he is swaying as he attempts to stand.

"Captain!" Marsh yells. He grips the chain link fence in front of him with both hands and, with a single motion tears the metal barrier in two, hurling sections of it to either side of him. We all draw our weapons and run in. My heart feels like it's going to burst from my chest; the captain might scare the crap out of me, but something that can take him out scares me worse. One of the two men had made it past Radu, but he skids to a stop as he sees us closing in. I recognize him from the photo; it's Goldman.

A chorus of gunshots explodes from nearby, mine joining in. The man's body is torn apart and flung in various directions. If that was one of the demons, then I know all we've done is cause him to run to another host body. We have to get close enough to use one of the traps.

A voice sounds out above the din. It is so low in pitch I feel my teeth vibrate as it rumbles out a phrase in a language I don't understand. The other man, the one who hung back as we unloaded on Goldman's body, he smiles savagely. He punches towards the sky, and a blast of force explodes upward from his upraised fist, disintegrating a swath of bats as it pierces the cloud cover above, and for the first time since I've arrived here, I see sunlight shine down in a beam.

Directly onto Captain Radu.

The captain screams in agony as he bursts into flames. Green and orange fire licks up from his head, face, and hands. The bats swirl quickly to block the hole, casting shade over the captain again, but the flames are raging all over him. Armstrong and Kim both pull their coats off and throw them on top of the captain, diving on him to smother the fire.

I'm holding one of the traps in my left hand, and suddenly it starts gaining weight. Cold radiates out from it. My gun drops from my other hand. My vision is drawn to the trap, and it's like I'm seeing it through a long tunnel. It pulls on my arm, like a strong magnet homing in on metal, and turns me to face the demon about thirty feet from me. The smile fades from the demon's face as his eyes lock onto the trap. His fist slowly drops to his side, he tries backing away from me, but his feet remain rooted in place. The runes begin to glow.

"No," he whispers. "No."

I see his eyes get closer to mine, getting pulled across the distance between us. I know he is not physically getting closer, but it feels like we are being drawn together. My sight is flickering, darkness is blurring the edge of my vision.

I hear screams, but I don't know if they're the captain's, the demon's, or my own. A bell sounds, clear and pure, and the trap slams shut. There is a sudden silence, even the bats overhead stop making noise, or maybe I simply can no longer hear them. I drop to my knees, already exhausted. Then, muffled but growing louder, I hear Marsh's voice from a mile away right next to my ear, and he hauls me to my feet. I stumble after him as we walk through the loading bay doors into the warehouse.

It takes a minute for my eyes to adjust. The interior of the building is a wreck, lit only by whatever dim light filters in through gaps in the boarded windows and the exposed sky overhead. There is a network of steel girders about fifteen feet overhead, covered with spider webs, rust, and dirt. Inside what remains of the walls are piles of bodies. Hundreds of them. Some are piled on top of each other, others casually discarded into corners like dirty laundry.

"Green, take it," Meints says irritably. I realize this isn't the first time he's said this. He hands me the remaining trap. The three detectives—Burchard, Marsh, and Meints—spread out, guns ready, moving through small lanes in the piles of corpses.

A voice sounds out from somewhere deep in a pile of bodies to my right. "Seer. Let me go. Just let me leave; you'll never see me again."

"Not going to happen," Marsh growls, kicking bodies aside as he moves towards the source of the sound.

The voice replies from the other side of the building. "You don't know what it is like, living for eternity without form. I have a body now. Don't take it from me."

"It's not your body. It belongs to someone else," I slur in response. "You're ending their lives and stealing their bodies. We're going to stop you."

The others are spreading out, looking for any signs of movement among the bodies. The same voice echoes from somewhere else. "I've seen civilizations rise and fall. I've helped them rise and fall."

The voice jumps again. "I've seen so much. You could learn so much from me. Let me teach you."

It sounds from nearby. "Do not consign me once again to the darkness. To the nothing."

I feel the trap start to gain weight in my hand again. It's starting to draw the demon in.

"Mercy," it whispers. "Please, you can have all the rest, just leave me one body. Just one. It's all I want."

The runes begin to glow on the box. The lid springs open.

The voice is closer now. I think I see one of the nearby corpses blink.

"The box in your hand, it's beautiful. Where did you find it?"

I feel the temperature dropping. It's all I can do to keep my eyes open. "Frank sends his regards," is all I can think to say.

"Frank?" one of the bodies near me starts to stand up. All the guns swivel to point in its direction. "You got it from Frank? Why would he—"

The body takes a staggering step towards me. I hear it start to laugh. "A key. A Seer. You made him a key."

The laughter grows louder. I had always thought the term maniacal laughter was an exaggeration, but I'm truly hearing it now. The demon laughs with no care, both high-pitched and a deep rumbling at the same time. My hair is standing on end as the laughter gets close enough to tickle my ears. It starts to fade away, but it seems to me that I'm getting farther from it, rather than it moving away from me. I'd try and make more sense of it, but I'm falling through a tunnel of blackness, hurtling down a long distance.

Somewhere far away, I hear the lid of the trap slam shut, and I feel the texture and taste of gravel.

Chapter 44

I'M SITTING IN MY FAVORITE spot at Warner's, far in the back-corner booth in the dim shadows where the light barely reaches. It's just warm enough to be uncomfortable; my arms stick to the faux leather seat. Sweat tickles my armpits. The familiar odor of rot wafts around me. The place is packed, but no one bothers me in my spot. I'm back to being studiously ignored. Even Maude, my waitress, seems intent on pretending I'm not there. The beer is getting dangerously low in my glass. I've tried to get her attention a couple of times but without success. I haven't bothered to get up to do anything about it.

I lean back and close my eyes, letting the sounds of bar patrons settle over me. It's been two weeks since our encounter in Goldman's warehouse. It's been nice to have some down time to let my body heal. I was barely conscious by the time we got back to the precinct. Marsh had to half carry me down to the Pit, so I could watch the traps get thrown in.

The demons were screaming in my mind the whole way down. There was some kind of connection between the trap, what was caught inside it, and myself. No one else heard anything. The fact that I keeled over when the traps were activated hints that it takes something from me or creates some sort of bond. While I held the traps with the demons inside, I could hear their whispers, their pleadings, their threats. I try not to think about that, the things they said to me. The things they said they would do to my family and friends. I want desperately to forget them. I take another large swig from my glass, finishing it off.

They went silent the second they hit the Pit. It was a huge weight off my shoulders, one I didn't even know I was carrying. All three of them are gone now, down there in emptiness. Down there with Clark, Olsen, Chuck, Calhoun, and countless others.

A shadow falls over me, blocking out the dim light I can see through my eyelids. I open my eyes to see Marsh looming over me. He's holding two mugs, one in each hand, and slams one down on the table in front of me.

"Relax, kid," he says, smiling. "I'm not staying. I just wanted to drop a few things on ya."

"If it's more beer, I approve."

He chuckles, taking a large swallow from his own glass. "Just the one. I had Warner put it on your tab." He reaches a hand into his pocket and pulls out a key on an old key ring. He tosses it onto the table next to the glasses.

"What's this?" I ask, hesitantly picking up the key. It's plain, no engravings, no indications it will break any demons out of prisons. No extra weight or pain pressing on it. It looks like just a regular key, but I'm still wary.

"It's part of the good news I'm bringing you. The captain says we're going to keep you around."

I breathe a sigh of relief. I was pretty confident they would want me to stay for a while, even after the case was solved. But you never know. And the alternative isn't very comforting. There isn't any sort of retirement plan as far as

I know.

"And," Marsh says, then pauses to take another swig of his beer. He belches and continues, pointing to the key in my hand, "And we upgraded your pad."

I look at him in surprise. "I've got a new apartment?"

He nods. "Yeah. That's a key to Clark's place. It's not like he's coming back for it any time soon. And we didn't knock too many holes in it searching."

The key fits comfortably in my pocket. This move will be pretty easy since I don't have any belongings to speak of. I can just walk over to my new apartment. It's strange, knowing how I came to inherit it. Maybe someday I will feel some guilt about taking over Clark's home, but for now, I only feel relief at being able to move out of the dive they've stuck me in for so long.

Marsh says, "Maybe it's the beer talking, but I'll say it once. You did a good job. We couldn't have done it without you."

I look at him sideways, sure he's pulling my leg. But he seems serious. "Thanks, Marsh."

"Now, we just need to train you, so you don't accidentally kill yourself or something. Because you're hopelessly incompetent. Frankly, it's amazing you haven't died already."

And just like that, Marsh is back to normal.

"Oh, and one more thing, obviously the whole squad knows about you being a Seer and all." He looks around to see if anyone is paying attention. Satisfied, he continues. "The captain has managed to contain the info to just us though. Well, and that asshole Dean. And your girlfriend. But the point is, we all know, and we're cool with it. We won't hunt you or your family down any time soon. Just don't go telling anyone, even other cops."

I nod. "Will do." I'm too tired to argue about the girlfriend comment. I assume he's talking about Jessica, not

Amber, the girl I knew a lifetime ago. Months ago.

Marsh drains the last of his drink in a large gulp, slams the glass down on my table, and nods at me. "OK, then. Take two more days to rest up, and get settled into your new digs. I'll see you at work."

He leaves, bulldozing his way through the crowd as he heads straight to the door. The mug Marsh brought me is actually cold, so I start to enjoy it. I look over to the back of the bar, to the empty room. Frank hasn't been seen since before we went after the last two demons. I'm not sure what he's been up to. But I'm hoping I can put off finding out for as long as possible.

A few minutes later, I see her approaching my table. She's reluctant; she might even turn around and leave, but she realizes I've noticed her, so she firms her resolve and walks up to me.

"Hello, Jessica," I say, smiling. "Please, sit down."

She slides onto the bench across the table from me. She's avoiding my gaze, fidgeting with her hands on top of the table.

"So," she says, but can't seem to find the words to continue. I reach across the table and place my hand on top of hers, stilling her hands. My hand rests there, softly, not forcefully. I wait until she looks up at me.

"Thanks for agreeing to come see me, Jessica. You've been avoiding me."

She shrugs. "Knowing that you can see me, I don't . . . I just haven't felt like looking you up."

"We're going to have to figure something out then because you're the best friend I have in this place. I've been through a lot, and I'm not ready to lose a friend yet. I'm hoping my friend doesn't want to lose me either."

"No, of course not," she says.

"OK, then," I wave frantically for Maude to bring

something over. I think she only agrees because someone is with me. We sit in silence until the waitress sets another glass of something down in front of Jessica.

I raise my glass. "A toast. To two friends. We've seen each other's true selves, and nothing has changed."

She raises her glass, clinking it with mine. "Two friends. With plenty more to see." And I see her dead face smile, and it's beautiful.

We talk about nothing for a while, I am able to put aside thoughts of my mother, wherever she might be; my brother, dead or undead or who knows what; and Amber, my once-girlfriend. Does she even think of me anymore, or wonder what happened to me? I push those thoughts back and simply enjoy the moment. And for the first time in weeks—surrounded by the dead, alone and trapped, far from family, far from home—I feel happy and at peace.

About the Author

Nathan Sumsion grew up in Lincoln, Nebraska on a steady diet of role-playing games, monster movies, comic books and computer games.

He turned his passion for gaming into a career and has been a video game designer since the late 90s for companies such as Disney, Crytek and KingsIsle Entertainment. For the past several years, he has worked as the lead game designer on a popular fantasy MMO.

Nathan has lived in various places including North Carolina, Utah, France and Germany. He currently lives in Round Rock, Texas with his wife and three children. Necropolis PD is his first novel.

A Word From Parvus Press

www.ParvusPress.com

THANK YOU FOR PURCHASING A Parvus book and supporting independent publishing. Double thanks if you got this copy of *Necropolis PD* from your local library. Libraries are where new readers are made!

If you loved *Necropolis PD,* your review on Goodreads or your retailer's website is the best way to support the author. Reviews are the lifeblood of the independent press.

Also, we love to hear from our readers and to know how you enjoyed our books. Reach us on our website, engage with us on Twitter (*@Parvus-Press*) or reach out directly to the publisher via email: *colin@parvuspress.com.* Yes, that's his real email. We aren't kidding when we say we're dedicated to our readers.

On our website, you can also sign up for our mailing list to win free books, get an early look at upcoming releases, and follow our growing family of authors.

Thanks for being Parvus People.

THE
RAGGED
BLADE

By: Christopher Ruz

Book One of
The Century of Sand trilogy

Richard tried to read the Kabbah's expression. Calm eyes, lips curled into a wearied smile, but his brow was furrowed like he was barely holding in his anger.

He had to treat the man carefully. No telling what would set him off. "We brought silver to trade. You've taken everything I have, so the silver's yours now. Keep it. Just let me and my daughter go."

"Seven days ago," the Kabbah said, "I sent brothers south to scout the oasis of Meile Sonyara. You know of it?"

"Take the silver and don't ask questions, Kabbah. You don't want the answers."

The Kabbah scratched his ear, where a chunk the size of a finger had been cut away and scarred over into a ropy lump. "I sent them," he said, "and yesterday a man and a girl arrive at the gates, riding my brothers' horses. A man who refuses gifts, who only speaks the Eastern tongue. Who carries daggers beneath his shirt." The Kabbah motioned for the guard to come into the light. He carried Richard's bandolier—eight slim throwing knives, elegantly weighted, molded to fit Richard's grip. "Not a scholar, then. An assassin. Did you come to kill me?"

A perceptive Meritran? That made him doubly dangerous. But the Kabbah was only half-right—an assassin needed
a patron, a master, a client. Richard had none. Not anymore.
Not since running from the Magician.

"Come to kill you?" Richard shook his head. "You don't
matter. You're nothing. You want the truth, Kabbah?" The
warlord looked on, impassive, through the bars, but Richard
couldn't keep from laughing. How many hundreds of miles
had he and Ana already crossed? How many hundreds to go?
And all of it ruined, his plans crushed, his daughter doomed,
because he'd camped at the wrong oasis and stolen the wrong
horses. "Listen. There's a man coming for us. A Magician.
The Magician, the one who killed old King Lowe and took
my country's throne. Heard of him? You should've, by now.
We've been running from him for weeks. If you want to live,
if you want anyone in this village to see tomorrow, you have
to let us go."

The Kabbah leaned in, almost touching the bars. Richard could feel the heat rising off his skin. "Maybe a scholar.
Maybe an assassin. Or even a soldier? Yes, I see it now. You
are all three. And yes, I hear the stories. Tales of a man with
fire in his hands, coming west with his army. Did he send
you? What sort of men send little girls to spy for them?"

"I told you to listen, Kabbah. My girl belonged to the
Magician, once. His experiment, his... pet. He wants her
back, and he'll crush anyone in his way."

"And you want me to simply... let you leave?"

"I'm not begging, Kabbah. I'm warning you. If we're
locked up in here when the Magician arrives, he'll crush
you and everyone you love to get to us. He has a monster
with him, a thing he built for hunting. It kills everything it...
Don't look away from me! Listen! The Magician can turn
every one of your soldiers to ash. He's broken in his head. He

doesn't know mercy. Cruelty only makes him hungry. When you stripped me, did you find the poison? It was around my neck."

The Kabbah nodded.

"It's not for me. It's for her, in case the bastard catches us. Do you understand? I'd kill my own daughter before letting him touch her again. That's the man he is."

The Kabbah leaned in until he and Richard were nose to nose, his eyes afire in the guttering light of the oil lamp. Richard was pinned. He didn't blink.

Finally, the warlord took a step back. "This is a bad place for scholars. Men who look into the darkness find themselves caught in dark places. And if this Magician is as cruel as you say... better I kill you now and send your soul cleanly along the wheel."

Richard reached into Ana's cell again, questing out until he found her ankle. She twitched against his touch. Such a small motion, but it was enough to leave his eyes burning.

He barely knew his girl. Hadn't seen her for ten years. He'd been stupid and trusting enough to pass her into the Magician's arms when she was only an infant, and now that he had her back he was about to lose her again. What sort of man was he, to drag a child out of a dungeon and haul her halfway across the mapped kingdoms, only to let her die in a different dark cell?

"She doesn't deserve this," he said.

"No. She has a warrior spirit. I saw that when we brought her down here. But you... you are a man. You wear your own decisions." The Kabbah was barely visible in the gloom, leaning against the far wall of the corridor, arms crossed, patient. "Tell me this. You run from your own lands, run from this Magician and his army. To where? This desert is no place for your kind. It eats men like you."

"There aren't many men like me, Kabbah. I've been here

before, a long time back. Walked these wastes from end to end. There's an old friend I need to see. Someone who can get the Magician off my back. Maybe even put him in the ground."

"And what friend," the Kabbah said, "would stand between you and an army?"

Richard's smile flashed in the dark.

"A demon."

ParvusPress.com/Century
Available June 4, 2019
ISBN: 978-0-9997842-9-7